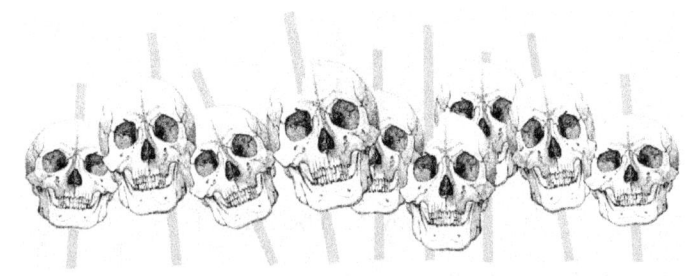

DEAD WONG

Tom Smith & W. Green

ZIPPY BOOKS®

VELOCITER · SECURUS · ERUDITIO

Dead Wong by Tom Smith and W. Green

Published by Zippy Books 623-929-206

ISBN: 978-0-9981623-8-6

—Prologue—

By 1968, the delicate sweet songs of native birds had long ago been replaced by the whine of helicopters and the screech of incoming artillery shells. Also gone were the local poetic names for geological formations. The Breath of Heaven Mountain had been rechristened by the military, solely appreciative of its elevation, as remote fire support base Hill 816. An armada of these pock-marked brown hills floated like turds in a latrine on the vast misty green plateau of Vietnam's Central Highlands. American artillery bases topped each of them.

At the bottom of Hill 816, the unseen enemy padded silently in the wilderness, tunnels, and villages. Above, only American boots walked atop the isolated muddy mound called FSB Crockett, defending their base and neighboring firebases while providing artillery support for military missions.

A young duo standing on the sandbagged perimeter watched clouds of steam rise from their tiny yellow rivers of piss flowing down the desolate hill. The breaking sun dissolved the cool restless fog, and a hidden forest of bare gnarled tree trunks below, denuded victims of the war, was exposed. As the war machine slowly awakened, the valley remained deceptively quiet until distant muffled artillery explosions from a nearby firebase announced the beginning of another day in the Vietnam War.

"Looks like 632's finished their breakfast."

The two young men, barely out of their teens, had only been in-country for a month but had already seen enough action to make them wary. One nervously scanned the valley below as he relieved himself. "Jed...I see something movin' down there."

Startled, the other soldier jumped. "Skip the bullshit, Carl. Thanks to you, I pissed my hand."

"I'm not kiddin'...something moved," he said quietly. "I did see something."

"Jesus. Relax." Jed shook his head. "We got enough heat on us already."

Soon their urine resumed its flow.

"Sorry...I'm draggin' my ass. No sleep. And too much fuckin' noise."

Mission completed, they shook off, reholstered their equipment, and stood silently.

"Nothin' like a good piss."

Jed nodded and gazed over the valley. "You know...this reminds me of home."

"How's that?"

"The Smokies in the spring. But you wouldn't know about mountains."

"Nope. This is the only mountain I care about."

"Well, we're better off up here. I wouldn't want to be street fighting in Saigon."

"No shit."

"Tet is for real. Charlie's down there. Somewhere. This is the big event. And we landed here just in time."

"Aren't we lucky? I'll tell my grandchildren. I just hope we're making his life miserable. Round after round. Hour after hour," said Carl. "At least we gotta be slowin' 'em down." He lit a cigarette and blew out the smoke. They watched it drift away, melting into the mist. "You gotta wonder if we ever hit anything. We never see the bastards." He shook his head. "Someday, the gooks might try to take this hill."

"They say they always mortar attack first. Let them try. We'll pound them into the ground. We're not the only canon cockers in the area."

"Maybe, but it only takes one lucky RPG round in the dump." Carl tossed his cigarette, crushed it with his boot, and gazed down the hill. Armless tree trunks, scattered scrub bushes, and small trees dotted the dirtball they defended. During the day, unwanted visitors would be easy to spot. But after dark, the artillery base was vulnerable. Sensors, radar, night vision observation, helicopter patrols, and trip flares at the perimeter provided early warning for the men of the firebase.

As 'Fucking New Guys,' they knew nothing except that their firebase had never been attacked. Not yet. Again something caught nervous Carl's attention. "What's that?" This time there was no doubt in his voice.

His buddy shot back. "Where?"

"Ten o'clock. Hundred fifty yards out. Just beyond the outer wire. Something's moving."

"Not seeing it. Wait...I see it. Christ. It's either a giant lizard or a goddamned sapper. Looks like he's heading our way."

"What should we do?"

"Go! Tell the Top. Now!"

With the news, the base snapped into full alert. Infantry assembled at the perimeter. An officer with binoculars focused on the intruder. "It's a man. Shorts. No shirt. Blackened body. I don't see any weapons or satchels. He's not moving. Just laying flat with arms outstretched." The officer stood silent for a moment. "Let's wait," he said. "Keep your eyes open."

They waited for fifteen minutes. Others around the base scanned past the perimeter, looking for more sappers. No other alarms had been raised.

"Zeke...we're not going out there," said the officer. "There's a tree branch right above our man. Think you can hit it?"

Sergeant Zeke grabbed the field glasses and studied the situation. Thirty seconds later, he returned the glasses. He nodded. "I think so. A couple of rounds should do it." He took the sniper rifle from one of his men, and standing in the trench, he used a perimeter sandbag as a gun rest. After making a sight adjustment and focusing on his target, he fired one shot hitting the two-inch-thick branch an inch above the crotch. The wood split, and the leafy branch swung down. Still partially attached, it struck the intruder in the head and momentarily covered the upper part of his body.

"That did it. He's moving. He's on his knees looking up at us." Fire another shot over his head. But don't hit him. He doesn't look like a sapper."

Zeke fired again.

"He's crawling toward the outer wire. Waving at us. Now he's got both hands up. He's giving us the double finger. Smiling. He's no sapper. He's a white man covered in mud." In a lowered voice, the officer faced his sergeant and said, "Send three of your best guys down there and bring him up. There's no time limit. Careful and cautious. OK?"

Thirty minutes later, the three volunteers returned from their slow, dangerous trip outside the perimeter; two guided the 'lizard man' up the hill and into the base. They let him collapse on the ground, far away from anyone and anything of value. "He's clean," said one of the soldiers.

The man's hands and knees were blackened from crawling, and open wounds covered his body. He wore cut-off shorts and beat-up *Ho Chi Minh* sandals too tiny for his feet. If it wasn't for the fact that he was a six-foot-tall white man, he might pass for an enemy sapper. He had no dog tags, tattoos, or any form of identification.

The officer cut to the chase. "What's your name, and what's your game?"

The man sat with his knees to his chest, head bowed, face streaked, sweat dripping from his forehead. He looked up. "Sergeant Michael T. Buck...S.O.G, " he replied in a voice so dry and raspy his words could hardly be understood. He tried again, but the officer stopped him.

"Save it, Buck. Welcome to Fire Support Base Crockett."

—CHAPTER ONE—

Early morning thirty-two years later, in the dark of a new moon, Mike Buck exited his car. He stood motionless and took a deep breath. Lake Michigan was bleak, black, and dead calm, animated only by the twinkling lights of ore boats gliding along the faint grey horizon. It offered little hope for the new day. A few premature sailboats, buoy bells chiming, bobbed up and down in the harbor. Across Grant Park, Soldier Field waited for the morning light to waken its famous façade as empty city buses on Lake Shore Drive snaked around the sports complex, hissing in the darkness. Cabs filled with drunks drifted away from the Loop watering holes, carrying their sleepy, vomitus loads back to the suburbs. Instinctively Buck patted his body in three places, checking his holstered weapons. Then he headed for the action.

Bright yellow sodium-vapor lighting illuminated the parking lot. About fifty people, mostly men, milled about talking loudly and laughing nervously in a scene resembling a Chicago Bear tailgate party. Buck joined them.

After a few minutes, they drifted together, marching in loose formation around the curved colonnaded front, finally squeezing through a green-copper door leading to a meeting room. Crowded together, their chatter echoed in the wedge-shaped, concrete tomb. They stood shuffling and rocking in place under the harsh light of bare fluorescent lamps, noshing on coffee and donuts. A few smoked. They all wore guns and protective vests.

Buck found Elliot, the short, stocky leader of Domestic Terrorism Squad 7, in the crowd taking charge of the troops. Elliot had handpicked Buck and the other hybrid law enforcement officers forming the Task Force. Elliot and Buck were FBI, but others were Chicago cops. The team combined street-savvy and aggressive cops with technically robust and rigidly professional Bureau agents. Although this amalgamation did not sit well with some old-school cops and elitist agents, the Task Force, protective of their own and suspicious of outsiders, remained an exceptional crime-fighting team. Secrecy and teamwork were essential elements of their job. They were good, and they knew it.

Elliot stood atop a table and spoke into the bullhorn with authority. "All right, my friends. It's time."

Buck smiled as Elliot began and quipped to the man next to him. "I see Mother Hen's not fooling around tonight. Three-fifteen on the head and a fucking bullhorn."

The cop replied, "He's gettin' into it."

"Quiet down," the bullhorn spoke, and the crowd noise disappeared. "Five weeks of planning have brought us to this point. I think you'll agree we have covered every detail *ad nauseam*."

A chorus of groans signified agreement.

"Right. Then I expect it to go down as planned. Today's raid will signal the beginning of the end of the Stateville Boyz. If we do our job right. I think we'll catch them red-handed and pants-down. And when we do, you will get them into the system correctly. I've heard some complaints about dealing with the weekend court system. But the bad guys don't care about our bureaucratic problems. Again. Do it by the book, and we'll have this thing wrapped up by lunch. Screw around, and you'll be on the phone begging the judge to skip dinner and come back downtown for arraignment." He looked around the audience for confirmation before proceeding. "We know it's going down soon. We've been eyeballing all three target locations. About three hours ago, a courier arrived at Mo's place carrying two suitcases. Probably the weapons. But it could be just a cover. Either way, the gun deal seems to be on schedule. Remember. I don't want any dumb heroes. Understood?"

He waited. "Everyone must wear a vest and a raid jacket. Understood?"

Mumbles.

"And we are a team. Do your job, and please watch out for each other." For a moment, Elliot's face betrayed a hint of his emotion. Then he returned to his talking points. "You'll have warrants that let you peek into their Jockeys. So I expect results. No shooting unless you're shot at or have to protect someone. Just arrest these guys. Secure and bring back the evidence. And read them their rights. I know in the heat of the action, you can sometimes forget. But don't."

Elliot looked around, eyeballing his troops. "These are simultaneous raids. To be successful, they must be coordinated. Maintain radio silence until five minutes before the 'go' signal. We will operate on channel C-4. That's C-4. Team leaders will report to command when in position and ready. All three teams will go at exactly 5-0-1."

"Now, in the interest of efficiency, I would like the teams to secure their warrants from the Sarge in the following order: Green Team, then Red, then Blue. We have plenty of time, so give the old Sarge room to operate, please." Elliot smiled and gave the crowd a thumbs-up. "Good luck. See you all tonight for a beer."

He dropped off the table with surprising grace, landing on his feet before Buck. "You loaded for bear?

"You can never have too much firepower, right, Mother?" said Buck. "Don't worry, I brought the whole family. My SIG. And this guy." He patted the holstered 45 on his hip. "And a snubby's riding my ass."

"Be careful, Mike. Where's your vest?"

"I'm wearing it." Buck shook his head. "Here, have a donut. You need something to calm you down."

Elliot accepted the chocolate-covered gift and bit off a chunk. "You're right. You know me. I'm always tight before a raid."

Buck heard the gravel-voiced Sarge call out, "Red Team."

7

"Gotta go. Catch you at sun up." With that, Buck walked toward the large, heavy-jowled, black man dressed in a Chicago Police uniform who sat at the table sorting a pile of large manila envelopes; the man selected three envelopes and set them out on the table.

"Here you go, Buck. Read 'em and weep."

Ten minutes later, two beat cops in a blue-and-white drove into the supermarket parking lot and pulled up next to a man standing behind the open trunk of a car. They spotted the two Remington Model 870 sawed-off shotguns, fifty rounds of buckshot, an M-16, an H & K machine gun, and a large assortment of grenades. "Hey, shithead. What's up?" said the driver, a big guy with a smiling, black-sandpaper face.

The man pulled his head out of the trunk and, holding a shotgun in one hand, turned toward the cop car. "Wake-up call for some of your buddies."

The driver pulled back his smile. "Yeah. Who dat?"

"Watch the six o'clock news." Grabbing a vest, he slammed the trunk lid, turned, and walked away from them.

"Eat me, Gleason." The cop rolled up his window and pulled away. The old Chevy bounced through the parking lot and scraped its bottom noisily as it jumped over a curb on the way out.

Gleason muttered as he walked between the parked cars toward a small group of men. "Up yours too." Three of the five men held steaming cups of coffee. All wore body armor. Guns populated their bodies. The big one, six-three, two-eighty, wore a Bulls cap and a mottled hunting shirt under his vest. Night vision glasses dangled on a strap from his neck. Sipping his coffee, he watched Gleason approach.

"What's the matter, Chuckster? Your lookin' pissed."

Headlights of another car entering the lot washed Gleason's face. He squinted. "Hey, Andre. Cops are assholes."

"That's the team spirit, Chuckster. Of course, you forget you're a cop. Or at least you were until you joined us."

"Yeah. I know. It's the same old problem. Everybody wants in on everything, but nobody wants to lay it on the line."

"Friends from the Fourteenth?"

"Yeah. What's left."

The big, muscular black man offered him a coffee.

"Don't sweat it," said Andre. "They're just jealous. That's the way it is. You ready for the big one?"

Gleason gulped down the brew.

"Couldn't sleep at all last night. I guess I'm a little bugged."

"Shit. Nobody slept last night. Except maybe Buck," said a little wiry guy in blue jeans and a grey sweatshirt who sat propped up on the blunt end of a device, which looked like a miniature Cruise missile with handles. "Don't worry. You'll do fine. After this, you'll be a Task Force veteran."

Gleason nodded. "OK, Rat. I'm with you."

Rat reached up and poked Andre in the gut with his finger. "What happened to your Bullies last night? They stunk up the stadium."

The big man looked down. "Got me. Still five over five hundred. No worries. Anyone can have an off-night."

The little man tossed his empty cup on the ground. "Fuckin' right." He recognized another car that entered the lot. "Let's go. Here comes Buck and Hansen." Rat stood and let the heavy door-buster, which had served as his chair, fall, clanging to the ground.

They gathered their weapons and Kevlar vests and headed toward the group forming around the new arrival. Buck shut off the ignition and checked his watch before opening the car door: 4:15. They were running out of time, so he would keep it brief. He got out but left the door as a prop for his right arm. The other man in the car, Hansen, greying, tall, and bony, exited the other door and joined Buck around the vehicle. Seven cops and six agents, one a woman, faced the two men.

9

"OK, Red Team. Listen up." He waited for the small talk to subside. "Glad you could make it. I'm sure you wouldn't want to miss this one. Everything looks right for this thing to go down exactly as planned. You know your assignments. Three teams of five. Hansen, Andre, and I will take the lead. Your carriage awaits..." Buck pointed to the small moving van at the edge of the lot. "That should minimize the pipeline to the brothers. Pete and I will ride together in my car. We're going to move in quietly. We want to take them all without a fight. Got it?"

He looked at each, one by one. While the clock ticked, some smoked, inhaling to the point of coughing; others, like Gleason, were beginning to hyperventilate; some just bounced on the balls of their feet. "Any questions?"

Gleason, the new man, cleared his throat first. "How many will there be?"

"Expect three or four adult males. We have warrants for Big Mo and Elvin Sanders. But figure there may be some women in there too. Just do it by the book. Take them one by one, and we'll get it done."

"How 'bout Granny. You forgot her." Rat laughed.

They all forced a laugh. Buck smiled and turned to Hansen.

"Pete...you want to do it?"

Hansen stepped forward, and everyone dropped their heads and went silent. "Heavenly Father. We pray you will watch over and protect us as we do our duty. We ask for your guidance and assistance to help us do what we have been trained to do, and we ask that you keep us from any harm. Amen."

A chorus responded. "Amen."

"All right. Let's go."

CHAPTER TWO

At Mike Buck's direction, the Task Force members headed toward the van slipping on their black and yellow raid jackets as they walked.

"Just like the Superbowl," said the rookie Gleason to Buck while adjusting the collar of his jacket.

Buck glanced back, ignoring the comment. The team gathered their equipment and loaded it. They all piled in the back except Andre, who drove, and Rat, who rode shotgun. Blue smoke filled the air as the engine started. Andre released the brake, and the purple truck claiming to be *DB Movers* motored out of the lot and advanced into the early-morning traffic. Buck and Hansen followed in the black Chevy. They headed south toward the high-rise projects, now visible as shadowed blocks, a half-mile distant beyond the Illinois Central Railroad tracks which paralleled the highway.

The lake to his left wore the faint pink glow of a coming day. He checked the luminous face of his watch. Thirty-five minutes to sunrise. Ahead, the truck rolling along the twisting, tree-lined boulevard pulled off at the first exit and headed west on the empty mean streets of Chicago's Southside. It bounced along a road littered with abandoned cars and lined on one side with ugly concrete apartment towers built for poor people but run by gangs.

"This is it," said Hansen. "Pull in."

Buck followed the van as it entered a service drive and parked behind one of the buildings. Men jumped out of the truck, grabbed weapons and equipment passed down to them, and slid into the night. Buck pulled in, and he and Hansen joined the action. Nobody spoke. They followed the plan which Buck had drilled into their heads. Two men stayed with the truck, and the

11

other thirteen dodged through a junkyard of garbage and debris to the base of the massive building. One man waited at the elevator; two others covered the stair exits at either end of the stark, rectangular structure. The rest began the climb toward their eighth-floor destination.

Buck, Hansen, and three others, including Rat, climbed the south tower stairs, a convenient toilet for kids and a shoot-up place for addicts. In the darkness, Buck, the pathfinder, wore night-vision goggles. He climbed ahead, his flashlight toggling on and off only as necessary. Stepping onto the first riser of the stairs leading to the second floor, he spoke into his walkie-talkie, "Team One to Team Two. Second Floor."

"Confirm," voiced a muffled response through his earphone.

They climbed, stopping at each floor to coordinate their location with the other team.

Buck whispered into the mike. "Dropping one off on seven."

The walkie-talkie returned, "Confirm."

Buck's goggles allowed him to spot an empty pint bottle on the next stair tread. He placed it out of the way in the corner of the stair landing and looked back. The men behind, their flashlights brightening only a few feet ahead, made the turn on the landing below. Eighty feet of climbing and fearing unknown danger had them sweating and breathing heavily. He whispered to them. "Stay cool, boys. Almost there."

"Team One to Team Two. We're at eight. Sending one to nine. Switching to C-4 to call Mother. Hold your position."

"Confirm."

Buck adjusted the radio and checked his watch: four-fifty-seven. Four minutes to go. "Red Team to Mother."

A moment later, the radio crackled. "Mother here. Are you in position?"

"Red Team secure and ready for the countdown."

The Command Post logged in the other two teams. Buck checked his watch: ten seconds.

The radio spoke. "This is your Mother. Go."

"Red Team confirm." Buck switched back to the original frequency. "Bear to Andre. Let's roll."

"Affirmative."

Buck removed his goggles, and as he pulled the steel door open, a welcome blast of fresh air rushed past him. He poked his head out of the doorway. Flickering fluorescent lamps jumbled his view of the apartment access corridor. A graffiti-laden brick wall with weather-worn steel-framed doors and windows filled one side of his vision, and opposite, a patched, floor-to-ceiling chain-link fence allowed Buck a quick look at the sparse pre-rush hour traffic snaking along the expressway below.

Buck reached into his jacket and felt for the conspiracy-to-commit murder warrant, which outlined Maurice X. Jackson's criminal exploits as a gun runner, terrorist, and hitman. He knew Big Mo, who had a reputation for knowing his way around a courtroom, would try to get off on a technicality. But he had the warrant, and that made everything legal.

Buck strained to see the other team. Just then, he caught a glimpse of a Bulls cap and the bearded cherubic face of Andre, poking out of the north stairwell doorway a couple hundred feet ahead. Three flashes of a penlight, and Buck returned the recognition signal. He looked back at his team, giving them a thumbs-up. Hansen pursed his lips and nodded. The two teams moved out of the stairwells into the corridor, approaching each other like gunfighters on a narrow street. Andre cradled the heavy door-buster and proceeded toward Buck and Hansen. Buck orchestrated Andre, Hansen, and the others into position using hand signals only.

Andre stood directly in front of the gang's apartment door. Hansen, his face taut and his back against the wall, waited to the right, holding a sawed-off shotgun close to his armored chest. Buck gripped a flash-bang grenade in his right hand and moved to the left, hugging the wall. The other two flanked them. Water dripped from a rusty crack above into a small puddle. Reflected in the pool of water, a glint of light escaped from under the bottom of the door. Buck wondered about the light.

In a quiet voice, Buck spoke. "FBI. Open the door." He nodded at Hansen. Their administrative duties were now complete.

Then the light from under the door went dark. Buck motioned to Andre. At once, the big man moved into position. He swung the doorbuster back and, in a smooth pendulum motion, drove it forward, thudding into the door and banging it open. Buck ripped the pin on the stun grenade and tossed it into the apartment. A second later, it exploded. He raised his 45, and Hansen snapped off the wall, his shotgun pointed into the dark opening.

Inside, people yelled and screamed. Buck took the lead. His flashlight lit up the living room, revealing two men still groggy from the concussion of the flash-bang. One remained on a makeshift bed holding his head. The other stumbled as a cold wind drove through a broken window, flapping the cheap-yellowed curtains and swirling dust. The stale smell of old beer and fried food mixed with the grenade's unmistakable odor. Four team members were now in the apartment, and two others stood guard outside the door. Buck signaled Andre and Rat to take the two stunned gangbangers as he and Hansen took defensive positions in the hallway leading to the bedrooms. Andre grabbed the standing man by the neck and squeezed, tossing him to the floor, then slammed his knee into the man's back and applied flexi-cuffs. The two men were also bound at the knees and ankles. The concussion grenade did its job, as neither captive offered resistance.

Less than a minute had passed since the explosion. The two unidentified men now lay face down in the center of the room guarded by Rat and his shotgun.

No human sounds could be heard other than the quiet moans of the two captives in the living room. The three law enforcement officers eased down the hallway having just enough daylight to approach without flashlights. Nearing the first door, Buck leaned against the corridor wall with the others close behind. He could hear someone inside the room.

"Comin' out, comin' out." said a deep voice.

"Hands in front. Come out. One at a time. Slowly," said Buck.

"There's just me, gentlemen. Just me."

All three hundred pounds of Big Mo appeared at the door. Arms in front of him, the fingers of both pudgy hands spread wide, he smiled at the two men holding guns to either side of his head. Andre took hold of the man while Buck checked the bedroom—empty.

"Where's Elvin, Mo?" asked Buck, using his pointed 45 for emphasis.

The illustrious ruler of the Stateville Boyz continued to smile. "I'm not in charge of bed checks, Mr. Bossman. I ain't done nothin'. Just tryin' to sleep. I want my lawyer."

Buck nodded at Andre, who waltzed Big Mo down the corridor. Hansen took the lead, with Buck following. The situation became more dangerous, with each step bringing them closer to the end of the hall. The two agents leaned against the wall separating them from the last bedroom. Hansen readied his shotgun. Buck held his 45 in one hand; his other had the 9 mm.

Big Mo was protesting in the living room. "No rough stuff now. I'm cooperating."

By now, Mo had been cuffed and laid next to his brothers. Mid-sentence, Mo stopped talking. Andre must have shoved the barrel of a shotgun into his neck.

Something caught Buck's eye. A dirty sock or a dead rat lay limp in the crusty corner of the corridor. They listened but heard nothing. Hints of daylight drifted through the open doorway like a grey mist, a peaceful dangerous illusion. Buck reacted to Hansen's nudge with a nod of his head. Then Hansen popped the grenade into the room, and the resulting teeth-rattling explosion shook the apartment's walls. Hansen leaped out, his back against the opposite corridor wall, body in a crouch with the shotgun leveled at the room. A gun fired with a flash of light. A bullet chipped the paint off the steel frame to the right of Hansen's face. He fired two quick blasts into the bedroom. A cry of pain filled the air as Hansen stood motionless, peering into the smoke-filled room. Buck reacted. He reached out, shoved Hansen to the floor, and returned to his original position. Another shot rang out. Lead slammed into the wall Buck leaned against. The slug passed through, missing him by inches, and lodged in the opposite corridor wall.

Buck let out a war whoop and spun off the wall extending his guns before him. Both were in action as soon as they cleared the jamb. He stood in the doorway, blasting the interior of the bedroom, spraying a murderous mass of projectiles. He saw the man in the corner standing on the bed for a moment, then the fusillade filled the man's chest with holes in a tight, bloody pattern. His body landed facedown on the floor. Buck, weapons still extended, swept the room, looking for another target. Finding none, he let his arms drop to his side. In the eerie silence, he felt electrified. Blood pounded inside his head, and continuous ringing overwhelmed all other sounds. Hansen touched his shaking right arm.

Buck didn't respond. He stared at the floor and the young man lying in a heap. Blood covered his back and oozed out of the open flesh, once covered by a tight-fitting, green T-shirt. Bullet holes had chewed the walls and pockmarked the window glass. The perp's weapon, a black semi-auto, lay on the floor, evidence that would remain in place for others to record. An incoming breeze blew back the sour smell of the dead man's discharged bowels.

Andre examined the two bullet holes made by the perp's gun, entered the bedroom, and approached Buck. He spoke, almost whispering, "He's dead, Mike. Relax."

Buck gathered his senses. Andre's calming words fought with the intense ringing in his head. He broke out of his trance. Slowly and carefully, he re-holstered his weapons.

"Mike, you OK?"

This time Buck heard Hansen. "Yeah. You?"

"I'm all right," Hansen replied quietly, then he raised his voice. "But what were you doing? I had control."

Buck digested his partner's words. He understood but expected more, something in the way of thanks. Hanson's ego was bruised, and he lashed out, unable to admit his mistake. Buck didn't care if the others heard him; his life was on the line too. Frustrated and straining to overcome his damaged hearing, he almost shouted. "Pete. You froze. OK? You're lucky I got you out of the way. I saved your ass."

Seconds passed, and neither man spoke. Buck's indictment hung in the air.

Hansen's face reddened. "I didn't freeze. I don't work for you, Buck. We're supposed to be partners."

Buck ignored him. They walked together down the hallway; Buck knew they were finished as partners.

Hansen continued as he walked behind Buck. "Don't go off on me because you lost your last partner. I'm not Barrett, and I didn't screw up."

Buck didn't respond.

—CHAPTER THREE—

Buck hated complaint duty, but once every year, it was his 'turn in the barrel.' By late afternoon, he was bored and tired. The office air conditioning couldn't handle the hot west sun knifing through the wall of windows behind him, and the temperature peaked at eighty degrees. Almost in a stupor, Buck struggled to document the previous complaint. An unkempt old woman, her purse stuffed with a dead cat, had claimed racist Communists poisoned her pet. She had held the bag open, and Buck viewed the fuzzy black cadaver. After looking into it, he didn't argue with her. "Commies." He nodded, his face grim. "It's OK. You can bury her now." Then with a semblance of sympathy, he dutifully acknowledged the old gal's allegations, thanked her for coming in, and quickly dismissed her. But as the nasty odors of her and her fermenting feline lingered, the unmistakable smell of stale oil and fried fish seeped into Buck's subconscious. He looked up. A skinny Asian man wearing a long-sleeved white shirt, a red tie, and shiny black pants stood before him. His leathery weathered face squinted in the bright sunlight. He waited without speaking while gripping his cap with both hands. Buck eyed him. Maybe Vietnamese. Maybe Chinese. Mid-seventies. Troubled. After glancing at his watch, Buck acknowledged the visitor. "Yes?"

"I wish to file a complaint." His soft words fought their way through the conversion to English. He lowered his head as he spoke.

"Please have a seat." Buck studied him and suspected he had a real problem. The old man's eyes betrayed his fear. Buck knew the look. As the small man arranged himself in the chair, positioning his cap on his lap, Buck asked for his name and address.

"Wong Vien Suu."

Wong spelled it out at Buck's request, and he recorded it on a notepad. He got an address in Little Vietnam on the city's north side.

"What is the nature of your complaint?"

"I get threats against my business."

"What is your business?"

"I own restaurant." The man stared into Buck's eyes. "Are you with FBI?"

"Yes. My name is Agent Buck. The threats. What form did they take?"

The man looked puzzled.

"By phone. Letter. In-person. How did you get them?"

The little man apologized before he answered. "Some came in mail, and some telephone."

"Do you have the letters with you?" Buck needed those as evidence of a Federal violation.

The man shook his head, "no."

"Were they signed?"

"No."

"Do you have any idea who sent them?"

The man looked down and did not answer.

Buck pressed. "Why were you threatened?"

The man did not answer.

"Look, I'm afraid we can't help you without some information."

"I told you before. I made a complaint. Last month I gave the letters to you," said the man.

"Told who?"

"I was here before. I signed paper. Told to wait. They would get back to me. I wait. But I have been warned again. This time they say they burn my restaurant with me in it. My niece Le An begged me to see you again. I told her. You very busy people. I am just a small person. I am here because of her."

"Did you file a complaint at this desk?"

His response required him to think. "No. I was told to go upstairs. Floor ten. They said they would help me. But I hear nothing. Now I am afraid."

Buck was perplexed. That floor housed the Foreign Counterintelligence Squad of the Bureau. "Are you sure it was the tenth floor?"

"Yes."

"Wait one moment, please." Buck checked his computer for the man's file. "Are you certain you filed a complaint with the FBI?"

The man looked at Buck and then looked around. Buck could see more fear developing in his eyes, maybe a distrust of government officials. He stood. Buck watched the computer screen for the file to appear. It didn't. The man looked toward the door.

"Wait a minute, do you want to file this complaint?" Buck stood. He towered above the Vietnamese. He laid a pen down in front of him and presented the bottom line of the complaint form for signature. The desk phone rang, and Buck answered it. A woman told of someone taking photos of her through her windows. By the time Buck hung up, Wong Vien Suu had left. Buck picked up the pen and looked at the complaint form. It was signed.

Mr. Wong ended Buck's time in the barrel. All in all, except for the cat lady, most people who visited his desk that day were legitimate, excluding the man who heard voices from outer space telling him the President would experience a death ray assassination. Even this could be said to be genuine. No matter how ridiculous, all threats against the President were handled the same way. The death ray and the little Vietnamese man provided the only real work of the day. All the others were sent away to see the local police, City Hall, a clergyman, or a doctor. Buck grabbed the file folder, locked the desk drawer, and looked about. Most of the office employees had left for the day. However, he knew his supervisor, Tom Elliot, would still be in his office.

Buck weaved through a maze of open files and cardboard boxes, clutter only outsiders would notice. Since it had accumulated slowly over many years, no one thought to make it more presentable, and the cleaning people were trained to leave everything in its place. He heard Elliot's voice and spotted him talking to Randolph Clark, a little man in the blue three-piece suit. Buck stood in the office doorway.

"Come on in," said Elliot. "The Professor and I were just exchanging old war stories." A broad smile spread across his round face. "How did your day go?"

"Give me a raid any day."

"You have my sympathy," said the Professor. "My last tour of front desk duty stole the last remaining hair on my head. The only good news about my impending retirement is that I will never again have to do that. Any basket cases today?"

"Nothing unusual. But I need your opinion on one, Tom." He held up the manila file folder.

Buck sat. The Professor offered him a lemon drop, and Buck accepted.

"An old guy came in and filed a complaint. Said he was being threatened. He runs a Vietnamese restaurant. He wasn't exactly verbose, but I would say he was telling the truth. Someone wants to burn him down."

"Why?" asked Elliot.

Buck leaned forward with one elbow on the desk and his hand to his chin. He sucked on the lemon drop. "Well, that's just it. He didn't say. He returned because we didn't help him earlier. He said he filed a complaint a month ago."

"Did he?"

"He filed it on the tenth floor."

Elliot leaned back in his chair and folded his arms across his chest. "FCI?"

"That he didn't know. He says he gave them mailed written threats. There's no file. Nothing in the computer."

Elliot looked across the desk. "What do you think, Professor? Why would Marsden and his crew be interested in this guy?"

The balding older agent looked over the top of his half-frame glasses. "It could be this old man is not as innocent as he looks. Maybe he's on the FCI list. Check who was at the front desk the first time he came in."

"If these are normal threats, it should be ours," said Elliot. "Those FCI bastards. Ever since the Communists shut down, those guys don't know what to do with themselves. You want me to handle this, Michael? It may just be inter-office politics."

Buck shook his head. "No, I'd like to take it. Let me check out his story. OK?"

"All right. Give me a copy of his current complaint. I'll check on it. Maybe someone here passed him over to FCI just to get rid of him. Or maybe he was directed to FCI by someone outside the Bureau. Anyway, you start the investigation. You know anyone you can trust in Foreign?"

Buck stood. "Yeah. I think so. I've got a friend up there."

"Well, be discrete. I don't want to make a mountain out of this right away. Just get the feel of it, and we'll talk, alright?" Buck got up.

"Mike. I forgot to mention it." Elliot, at times, liked to dangle information. Buck waited patiently at the door. "The results of the autopsy on Elvin just came back."

"Lead poisoning?" Buck smiled.

"That's right. But only yours. No pellets. Hansen never hit him. Pete's a fortunate man. But you made up for him. Eight hits. Five in the chest area with the 9. All those lodged in his vest. Didn't kill him. But you had two headshot hits with the 45. One clipped his right ear. The other went through his neck. Killing him. I think the results will close out the shooting file. Hansen owes you one."

Buck nodded. "Glad there are no surprises."

"Incidentally, Hansen's asked for a transfer to Political Corruption. Desk job. Don't worry, it wasn't you. At least, I don't think so. He says it was his wife's idea. What do you think?"

"I don't know. He said he was thinking about it. I told him to forget it."

Elliot got up and motioned to Buck. "Be back in a second, Randy." They stepped outside Clark's office. "I talked to Hansen for quite a while, Mike," Elliot spoke softly and looked directly into Buck's eyes. "I'm convinced it's a good idea for him to go over to PC. But he laid a tale of woe on me when it came to you. To put it mildly, he didn't think you were partner material. Thinks you're a loner now. Isolated. Not sociable." Elliot stopped talking and waited for a reply. Buck remained quiet. "What do you think?"

Buck cleared his throat. "I don't know. I can see his point. I'm not too keen on relationships anymore."

"Because of what happened to Barrett?"

"That's part of it. My divorce. I don't know. People are a burden. I try to keep it simple. What are you getting at?"

"Are you seeing Dr. Mathews?"

"Mathews? Not yet." He shook his head and gave Elliot a look.

"You're a funny guy, Mike. A couple of days ago, you iced a gang-banger in a gun battle. Now you're upset about shooting the breeze with a harmless shrink. Look. It's not optional. Just get through it. OK?"

Buck nodded. "It's happening."

"That's fine. Now go home. You've had a long day."

Buck made a face. "Got it. Have a good one." He checked his watch as he walked away; he would have to hustle to see his son for dinner.

—CHAPTER FOUR—

Dr. Marion Mathews liked to think he made a difference in the lives of the people he served. But when working with FBI Special Agents, it was difficult to judge. Those agents whose mental health improved tended not to want to see him again. And those who could not benefit from his efforts might be dismissed, reassigned, or transferred to another analyst. In any case, his relationship with such patients was typically short-lived.

Mathews roosted behind his desk, looking like an old barn owl. A thin band of beard connected to a widow's peak of close-cropped and thinning red hair and encircled his pale, puffy round face. He wore a pair of black-framed glasses that completed his owlish look. After a half-hour reviewing the file, he wanted to move beyond the bullet-point biography and cold medical records and meet Special Agent Michael Buck. Buck's history included a significant anomaly distinguishing him from Mathews' previous clients. Two months ago, Buck's partner, a veteran Agent in the Chicago Office, Benjamin Barrett, died of a shotgun blast. An uncommon event, over a hundred years across the nation, only thirty-five Special Agents, men and women, had been killed on duty.

Dr. Mathews was part of the process. Agents are screened extensively before and after employment. As a group, they are known for their restraint and judgment. But all field agents are experts in the killing arts: professional peace-keepers and, if necessary, professional killers, dangerous men and women who lead stress-filled and challenging lives on and off the job. Typically Dr. Mathews provided guidance and support, but occasionally he flagged problem people prone to excessive violence. These people required special handling. After reading

Buck's file, Dr. Mathews suspected his interview with the veteran agent would not be routine.

Michael Buck arrived on time for his session. He sat facing the psychiatrist, sinking deep into the green leather club chair and looking tense like a lineman awaiting the snap of the ball. As Mathews thumbed through the file, he noticed Buck watching him.

"Any chance we could sit over there?" Over his shoulder, Buck's thumb pointed at the coffee table and chairs at the other end of Mathews' office. "I feel like the bad kid in the principal's office."

"Right. Sure. I was just going to suggest that. Let's do it." Mathews smiled, grabbed his coffee, and they reset. Buck, still cautious, sat and observed. His eyes scanned the office again, a common reflex for Mathews' FBI boys. He knew they were always conscious of their surroundings, always looking for trouble, always alert. The psychiatrist put the ball in play. "It's funny. How old memories from the past hang on?"

Buck cocked his head, then offered a small smile. "Did you ever get dragged down to 'the man' back in the day?

Mathews chewed on his cold dead pipe, a bad-habit remnant from another time. Allowing a bit of give-and-take during an initial visit, he nodded and exchanged memories.

"Not me. Not my style. And you?"

Buck chuckled. "Mrs. Dobrath, my elementary school principal. I practically lived in her office."

"Troublemaker?"

"Me?" Buck turned his chair and stretched out his long legs and athletic body, appearing to relax.

Mathews nodded.

"Non-conformist," said Buck.

Matthew's smiled. "They're the best kind of trouble. They can be very creative people." The doctor scanned his notes. "I see you have a son named Richard."

Buck nodded. "Right. He's fourteen. No, fifteen." He smiled. "Good kid."

"Do you see him often?"

Buck leaned back in his chair. "Not as often as I'd like to. We're pretty close."

"Is he like you?"

Buck had a quick answer. "No. He's his own guy. A good thinker. Not an action guy like me. No problems in school. Good grades. Plays in the school band. The girls love him. So, he's doing fine."

"Good for him. Do you see him often?"

"He lives with my ex-wife, but I see him alternate weekends and every Wednesday." Buck paused. "He's growing like a weed. Five-ten already. Three more inches, and he'll be taller than his old man."

Doctor Mathews smiled and paused before asking his next question. "And why have you come to visit, Mike?"

"No offense. You know Elliot sent me here. Not my choice. Orders." Buck fidgeted. "I think he's concerned about me. I've had some shooting incidents. Three in the past two years. I lost a partner."

The doctor only nodded.

"Elliot's a mother hen. I guess he figures it's bothering me."

"Is it?" asked the doctor. He sipped his coffee.

"Yeah. But that's part of the job. Isn't it?"

Mathews waited for a few seconds, not responding to his question. "Your last partner. Agent Barrett. Were you close?"

"You get close to someone you have worked with for five years. Good guy."

"How did it happen?"

Buck's head dropped. "Barrett and I worked as a team. Two guys always in sync. But we made a mistake. Maybe we were over-confident. We assumed the flashbang would do the job. It didn't."

"Why not?"

"I don't know. Maybe the guy was ready. Maybe he was stunned and just got off a lucky shot?"

"What did the shooting team say?"

"They said we followed procedure."

"Did you?"

"Yes, but..."

Mathews waited.

"But it failed."

"Sometimes," said Mathews, "the best-laid plans fail. The protocol breaks down. It's not a perfect world. Would you have changed any actions you took? Done something differently?"

"No," he said softly, "just doing our job."

"Would you say you are a risk-taker?"

Buck didn't like that question. "I'm in the risk business. I try to manage risks. I'm not out looking to gamble with lives if that's what you're suggesting."

Mathews continued. "No. I'm not suggesting you might be out looking for trouble."

"Look, I've been in this for decades. Maybe I've been lucky, but I've only been in two gunfights over my entire career. If I'm looking for trouble, I must be blind."

"So, would you say you try to avoid dangerous situations?"

Buck chuckled. "That wouldn't be useful either. My job is dangerous. Lots of jobs are dangerous. It's like being a roofer or driving a cab. If I were a roofer, I'd watch my footing. If I drove a taxi, I'd drive carefully. But in the end, the roofer must roof, and the cab driver must reach his destination."

"Right. Do you like your job?"

"Suits me." He glanced to the left. "Yes. I do."

Mathews made some notes, then continued. "You had to shoot someone in the line of duty. Does that bother you?"

"The guy who killed Ben." His voice rose slightly, yet still controlled. "The next shell in his shotgun was intended for me."

"I understand. Self-defense." Mathews set his pipe on the table and resumed. "But how does it affect you?"

Buck tensed. "It happens. It's not a good thing. There's always some guilt no matter what."

"Does the guilt bother you?"

"I don't dwell on it."

"Have you killed many people?"

Seconds passed. "I don't know."

The doctor glanced down at his notes. "The record says you served two years in Vietnam. '67 and '68. Seems like you've seen some action." He looked up again.

Buck leaned back. "Ancient history. Who knows, Doc? Maybe hundreds. I fired thousands of rounds in Nam. We never saw much of the goddamned enemy except during Tet. Then we saw too many. We killed most of them."

"How old were you?"

"Twenty."

"Were you afraid then?"

Buck smiled. "I was a kid. Everyone was afraid except for the psychos."

"Any problem justifying those deaths?

"I don't think about it. I did what I was told. You couldn't trust anyone. A lot of the ARVN brass were corrupt. Every civilian you'd run into could fuck you. Our brilliant military brains running that war were nothing but party animals. They could give a shit. I protected my men and myself. I fired at anything that moved." Buck chuckled. "Probably killed a lot of monkeys too. We were kids. We shot up that jungle pretty good." He rubbed the back of his neck and looked up at Mathews. "You remember that war. I'm sure you watched it on television."

The doctor ignored the sarcasm. "You must have been a highly-skilled soldier. You made Staff Seargent." He looked at Buck as he pondered the question. Mathews sensed Buck editing his response.

28

"It was a game of piggy-move-up, Doc. Easy to get promoted. Hard to stay alive. All you had to do was wait for someone to die. Then step up to the plate."

"But you made it."

Buck nodded. "Yeah. It seems like I always do."

"That's a good thing. Right?"

Buck raised an eyebrow and pursed his lips. "Better than the alternative."

"You completed two tours?"

"Almost. I got into it. I was a believer. Good versus evil. You know. Black and white. I was looking for a cause. I lived on the vapors of a just war. Not like World War II. But...good enough for me. It was one big high until Tet."

"Then?"

"After Tet, it was obvious the goal wasn't about winning. We beat them. Their offensive failed, and we proved we could win a conventional war, but this was different. It was a political stalemate. A war of attrition. Un-winable. We could never win, but our politicians wouldn't quit. It didn't make sense. I got out. I had enough."

"You lost your resolve?"

"Let's just say I've got a switch inside. It's either on or off. After Tet, it was turned off. My tour of duty ended a month later, and I went home."

"What about now? Any reoccurring images of your Vietnam experiences?"

"What do you mean?" Buck tightened.

"Dreams, flashbacks, loss of memory."

Buck rubbed his chin. "No. Everything's fine. I left that world behind. My head's pretty clear."

"And you returned, went to college, graduated, and joined the Bureau. Quite an accomplishment."

Buck nodded. "When I came back, I wanted to forget Vietnam and do something good. So I dug in and made things work."

"From one dangerous job to another?"

"No comparison. I've been satisfied with my work here. And I think I've done a decent job."

Mathews sipped his coffee before dealing out another question. "Do you think the odds are against you?"

"In our business, tomorrow is always a gift, that's what Barrett used to say. I don't dwell on the odds. I just do my job." He smiled. "You're older than me. Are you worried?"

Mathews chuckled. "I'm not on the front line like you. It's pretty safe here. The most dangerous thing I face at work is this coffee."

"Nobody's invincible."

Mathews checked his clipboard notes. "You're fifty-one. Right?"

Buck nodded.

"Do you think you're burned out?"

"Hell no. I'll admit I'm a bit tired of firefights in confined spaces, but that's pretty rare. Tired of seeing good men go down. But I guess that's part of our job."

"Do you think you are a loner?"

"No." He shook his head. "We don't need loners. I'm a team leader. I'm part of the team. Sometimes I'm in command. So in a way, I'm both."

"Somebody has to lead. Somebody has to follow. Do you like to be in control?"

Buck nodded. "When I'm a leader, I'm responsible for myself and others. Things happen in a split second. People make mistakes. Part of the job of any team leader is to watch out for others."

"Do you tolerate mistakes?"

Slow to answer, Buck pursed his lips. "I guess, in a way, I don't. If you follow the rules, you stay out of trouble. If you don't, you might screw up everything."

Mathews stared at him for a moment. "Michael, everyone gets older. Reflexes slow. Bodies deteriorate. Mistakes happen. How about you? You have experience and wisdom. I could recommend to Elliot that you be reassigned to more creative work. White-collar crime. Cybercrimes. Fraud. Something that would tax your mind as well as your body. Give you more time to spend with your son. Is that something you'd like to do?

"Not really. I'm not that old. I enjoy the thrill of the hunt. I've still got my edge."

"How's your health? I've looked at your chart. All the vitals are good. Any problems sleeping?

Buck made a face. "I'm taking something from the drugstore. That helps. Sleeping all the way through the night is tough. But I work around that. Once and a while, I have nightmares. My ex-wife complained about those. I guess I get pretty active in my sleep."

"Is that why you split up?"

Buck smiled. "No, nothing like that. It's the old story. We just drifted apart. With the hours I work, I think it was inevitable. She was tired of waiting for me. Waiting for the phone to ring. She couldn't deal with it anymore."

"Did you share your job experiences with her?

"Not really. I pretty much kept that to myself." His eyes drifted downward.

"Are you dating now?"

Buck smiled. "Nothing serious. But the equipment still works. And I enjoy the company."

"What do you do for fun?"

"You mean hobbies. Stuff like that?"

Mathews raised his brow.

"A little television. Rich and I go to the movies. Sometimes bowling." He shook his head. "I'm not the kind of guy who builds coo-coo clocks for fun. My job keeps me busy."

"Is that enough for you?"

Buck pursed his lips. "It's what I have."

Mathews raised his eyebrows, made a note, and moved on. "OK. Tell me about your sleeping. Nightmares?"

"I guess."

"Same one or different?"

Buck leaned forward a little. "I've had the same one. Five or six times in the past few months." He scratched his head. "I don't like it. It gives me the creeps. I don't know why."

"What's it about?"

"It's about my dog."

"You have a dog?"

"Well, no. This was a dog I had when I was a kid. Tippy. A black and white cocker spaniel."

"What about the dream."

"Pretty simple, but strange. You know how dreams are. I'm walking around in the woods behind my house naked. Tippy is sniffing along this path. But then we run into these three kids. They come out of nowhere. Older kids. And they grab Tippy. I yell at them. But they don't seem to notice me, and I can't stop them. I'm stuck in the background without any clothes. Kind of hiding. You know how that is in a dream?"

Mathews nodded.

"Then they kill my dog. And that's it."

"You're not in control of this situation. It just happens."

"Yeah. Somehow because I was naked, I couldn't do anything. Screwy. But, yeah, it bothers me. While it's happening, I feel like I have to make them stop, but I can't. It's like I'm tied down."

"How did they kill him?"

Buck froze.

Mathews waited. "Mike?"

The words came slowly and painfully. "Yes. They cut off his head."

Something triggered. Buck swallowed hard and curled his head into his chest.

"Are you all right? Asked Mathews.

He didn't respond.

"Are you feeling OK?"

Buck inhaled and sighed. He mumbled something.

"Why don't you relax for a moment, Mike? I'll be right back."

Mathews left the room and returned with a cup of water which he handed Buck.

"Thanks."

While Buck held the paper cup to his lips and drank in small sips for a long time, Mathews wrote down a note, 'PTSD.' He tried to avoid quick diagnoses, but this one appeared likely. Buck might be experiencing Post-Traumatic Stress Disorder. More work would be necessary.

"So what about the dream?" Asked Buck.

Mathews sensed his patient had regained his composure. "I've got some ideas, Mike. But talking it out always helps. We covered enough today. You need a break. Make another appointment. Let's talk again in a week or so."

Michael Buck looked crestfallen. He's standing near the edge, thought Mathews. After Buck left the room, Mathews filled his recorder with many notes for transcription.

—CHAPTER FIVE—

In his cubicle, Buck answered the phone. He leaned back in his chair and tucked the phone under his chin. Susan Ecker sounded pleased to speak to him. Ecker was Buck's only friend in the Foreign Counterintelligence division of the Bureau. She graduated from the University of Georgia; her family had lived in Atlanta for three generations, and she was Jewish. She was accustomed to subtle discrimination. As a member of the FCI, she was tolerated but not welcomed by the population of spooks, primarily male, macho, pseudo-sophisticated Ivy League birds hatched in the 'old boy' Establishment. Initially, for a minority like her, growth opportunities within FCI appeared excellent. Still, she became aware of the 'glass ceiling,' which kept some birds from flying to the top of the cage. She was pragmatic. It was in her best interest to maintain friendly relations with the Domestic division of the FBI, where minorities and women could advance.

"Mike, I can't find anything in the file on your man. But that's because I can't get into that file. Classified 'Secret.' I just don't have access, and the last few volumes of the Vietnamese files are checked out to Marsden. You're going to have to talk to him."

"Great. Make my day." Buck droned sarcastically.

"Don't worry; I arranged a meeting this morning at eleven. Can you make it?"

"Yeah. I can. You coming?"

"Sure, Mike. Would I miss this great opportunity to snuggle up to the boss?"

Twenty minutes later, they met in Marsden's office. He disposed of Susan Ecker in seconds. "Thank you, Agent Ecker. That will be all. I'm sure Agent Buck and I can take it from here."

His elbows resting on his heavy oak desk, he steepled his long fingers, maintaining eye contact with Susan long enough to ensure her departure from the room. Then he turned to face Buck. "Have a seat."

Buck squared himself in front of the fifty-ish father figure, Assistant Special Agent in charge of Foreign Counterintelligence. To him, Marsden's grease-ball, swept-back, jet-black hair symbolized everything there was to know about the man. Marsden was 'all show and no go' with his Armani suit, stainless steel desk set, and black leather diplomatic pouch briefcase. Buck didn't like him. However, he wasn't in here to befriend this snake. His only purpose was to secure information. But Marsden was a master at controlling people and information. "Thanks for taking the time to see me on short notice."

"Anything I can do to improve inter-departmental relations." Marsden smiled a tight smile. "How may we assist you?"

"We have a complainant, a Vietnamese-American who owns a restaurant in Little Saigon named Wong Vien Suu, who indicated he received mail and phone threats against his life and property. Yesterday he filed a complaint downstairs, but..." Buck pushed up on the arms of his chair, "he also says he filed the same complaint on this floor about a month ago. Of course, I checked our computer files, and I asked Ecker to review yours, but there is no record of any complaint filed."

Marsden leaned back in his high-back leather chair and gazed out the wall of windows. Without looking at Buck, he said, "Yes..."

"Well, is it possible such a complaint was filed? Can you check your files? Ecker doesn't have clearance on SRV material."

Marsden turned back to Buck, viewing him coldly. "What makes you think this man filed a complaint?"

He responded somewhat defensively. "I interviewed him. I think he was telling the truth."

35

Marsden smiled. "Ah. The old gut reaction. Interesting. But if Ecker found nothing in the files. Then no complaint was filed. Maybe the man may have stopped by this office, but it is just as possible we sent him on his way to make a report with Chicago PD. You realize that most of the crime in that part of Chicago is not the concern of this office."

Buck ignored the rhetoric. "Mind checking your Socialist Republic of Vietnam files? Just to put this issue to bed."

Marsden looked at his Rolex and then up at Buck. In silence, they stared at each other. Buck was determined to win this little mind game. Finally, Marsden spoke, "Well, if you insist, Agent Buck, I'll check out your Mister..."

Buck smiled, "Wong."

Marsden turned in his chair to face the computer terminal to his right. Quickly he tapped the keys, and as he did, Buck edged his chair closer to get a better look at the screen. Marsden glanced at him and gave Buck a mocking look of disappointment. In an officious tone, he droned, "Please, Buck, you know you're not cleared for this file." He twisted the monitor away from Buck's view. He tapped the keys in sequences, uttering a soft "no" between each. After four such apparent searches, he turned his chair to face Buck. "Sorry. No record. As I said before, most likely, we sent him to the local police." He stood, from his point of view ending the meeting.

Buck found himself standing also. "What district?"

"Just a supposition, Buck, not a fact. Who knows? We've all got better things to do than worry about this matter. You've got this on file now. I'm sure you can handle it." He nodded a fatherly nod.

"I'm sure we can." Buck gritted his teeth as he grabbed his file from the desk and shook hands with Marsden. "Thanks for your help."

Marsden smiled. "As I said, anytime."

Buck turned to leave and then turned halfway back. "One more thing. Do your records indicate any recent violence in the Vietnamese community?"

Marsden looked pissed. "In Chicago?"

"Anywhere."

"Well, there is a record of several deaths on the West Coast, which could be a matter of internal political strife within the Vietnamese community."

"West Coast...Seattle?"

"No." Marsden looked at his watch again.

"LA?"

"San Francisco," Marsden released the words grudgingly. "All right? Now, if you'll excuse me." He turned his back to Buck and picked up the phone, looking over his shoulder to ensure Buck was on his way out. Buck left the office wearing a small smile—tie-game with the chief asshole—not bad.

—CHAPTER SIX—

Vince Gorski squinted and smiled, exposing a mouth full of yellowed teeth. Gold fillings glinted in the mid-day sun.

"Well, where's your man, Buck? This is the corner of Bullshit and Main."

"Give me a minute. Buck almost mumbled. "We're looking for a needle in a needle factory. All of these joints look the same to me." He shrugged.

"What's his name?"

Buck reached in his breast pocket to retrieve a small notepad, which he flipped open and surveyed. "Wong Vien Suu."

"A boy named Suu, right. I'll bet he's pissed with that name. What's the number?

"1417."

Vince surveyed the address numbers. "Shit, Mike, why did you park so far away?"

"You could use the exercise. Might wear down last night's pizza."

Vince hiked up his pants. "You pretty-boy Feds are all the same. Always working out. Eating right. Dressed like a fucking model. Still trying to look good for Mr. Hoover? I got news for you. Your lover is dead."

"Eat me."

As they reached the corner and waited for the light to change, the two men stood hands on hips and surveyed the city street lined with small shops. Many years ago, the neighborhood was filled with delicatessens, butchers, and cigar and clothing stores owned by Jewish merchants. One by one, as the customers departed for the safety of the suburbs, the once-thriving shops closed. Sons and daughters of the original merchants carried the tradition away from the old neighborhood replanting it in the new strip shopping centers to the north and west of the city. Between the departing merchants and the next wave of enterprising immigrants, the Vietnamese, the buildings only provided shelter for rats and roaches. The once bright awnings, now faded and tattered, flapped in the wind. Ghost letters of the names of forgotten retail wet-dreams gone dry hid beneath layers of paint on store signs. Vince and Buck negotiated the narrow, uneven concrete sidewalk glancing through the storefronts into another world. Vietnamese merchants lifted their heads quickly to view the two white men. Their heads swung in a single rotary motion, beginning and ending with the task before them without causing them to lose a stitch or break the steam-hissing rhythm of the pressing machine.

Vince pointed to a poster in the window, which announced a new city program to provide free legal services to recent immigrants. "The Mayor's boy Pham Van Tien is workin' his home turf, huh? Buckin' for an alderman post, I'll bet. I hear he's real grease, but his people love him. I guess everyone's entitled. Right?"

Yeah," said Buck, "everyone has a right to their own crooked politician. It's a tradition in this town."

Vince laughed. "Twenty-two aldermen convicted in the last twenty years. They got seven in Silver Shovel alone. Shit. That must be the current record for municipal misconduct. Twenty-one aldermen and one alderlady. I forgot Laverne Tuppie. Remember her? She sold driveway permits. High-profit business."

"Yeah, while it lasted. But Tien's not going anywhere. He's a Vietnamese war hero who's still fighting the war. Some people like that kind of talk. Go back and blow out the Commies."

"Like that would ever happen. Shit, Vietnam's gonna be a cruise boat destination pretty soon. Nobody gives a shit about the Commies anymore."

"You're wrong, Vince. The Commies are still serious business in this part of town. Look at the White Tiger."

"Street punks."

"Maybe to you. But they have connections."

"Tien?"

"So I hear."

Vince grunted as he led the way, walking ahead to accommodate the two big men on the sidewalk. Buck studied Vince as he ambled along. Never one for a GQ ad, the burly Chicago cop, now in his eighth year on the Task Force, stretched the seams of his burgundy sport coat. The brown pants glistened with wear, but the black department-issue shoes were impeccable. The boys joked that he was a 'cross-dresser,' a cross between bad taste and expediency. Vince could be 'made' as quickly as an old brown Chevy 4 door with drip guards on the windows. But the fact that everyone in Little Saigon knew that two plainclothes cops were casing their turf didn't concern Buck. He had nothing to fear from the Asian ghetto dwellers. He knew them well enough to know they feared him. Gorski slowed in front of the narrow storefront of an isolated one-story retail building. Wong's place sat between two vacant stores.

"This could be it. Looks like someone took a hit." The board-up installation looked recent, but freshly-sprayed gang graffiti covered the plywood panels. A small neon sign flickered in the remaining window of Wong's place.

"Let's go in, and try not to eat anything, Vince."

The big man laughed. "I don't eat fish head soup or monkey brains, so you won't be offended."

A little bell jangled above the door as they entered the empty restaurant. The smell of fishy, burned palm oil clung to every surface. For a moment, Buck's head rippled with uneasy memories of the loud, odorous Saigon restaurants he frequented in Nam. Gorski moved up the left aisle. Buck took the right side. Booths lined one side, and a continuous counter ran along the other. Gorski saw the busboy glance at them and then disappear into the darkness of the back room. As he walked, Buck tapped his fingers along the counter. The old man smiled at the two, eyeing each as they approached from different directions. Buck stood across from the restaurant owner.

"Hello, Mr. Wong. I'm Agent Buck with the FBI. We met downtown." Buck extended his hand, but the man didn't bite. "This is Detective Gorski." Gorski didn't bother.

"It is good of you to come. Please, I have some tea. We sit."

"Not right now, Mr. Wong. We'll just take a few minutes of your time with a couple of questions."

The old man smiled and nodded.

"You filed a complaint with our office, and we're here to investigate. You said you had been threatened. Is that part of the threat?" Buck looked at the boarded-up window.

The man did not respond.

"What about it, Wong? When did that happen?" Vince moved closer to the counter and stared at Wong.

The old man's eyes dropped. "I do not know how the window was broken. I am sorry. Maybe a child with a stone. I am not wanting to complain now."

Buck notched up the volume. "What do you mean?"

Wong brought another polite smile to his weary face. "I am sorry to have bothered you." He stepped back, joined his hands in front, and bowed gently.

"Have you been threatened again? How about the White Tiger? Have they ever contacted you?"

"No, I do not know them. Children did it. That is all."

Vince looked at him like a can opener eyeing a can.

"Please. I have no complaint. It was a mistake. I must close my shop now. Good day, Mr. Buck." He bowed. "Mr. Gorski."

"Are you certain, Mr. Wong?"

His weary eyes focused on Buck. "I am."

41

The two men looked at each other, shrugged, and turned toward the door.

"Call me if you change your mind," said Buck as he left his business card on the counter. The old man stared vacantly at the card, not lifting his head to watch them go. They both donned sunglasses as the bright sunlight hit their faces.

Vince uncurled his gravelly voice. "What d'ya make of that, Mike? Change of heart."

"I'd say so. He might be scared. Or crazy. He might not like you. Who can tell? He did light up when we mentioned the White Tiger."

"The little prick's hiding something. Him with that shit-eatin' grin."

"Easy, Rambo. Just another citizen with a complaint. Or without one."

Deciding to get a better feel of the neighborhood, they left Wong's place, walked up the street, and carefully surveyed the various establishments of the Vietnamese community. Vince made written notes about different locations: *'possible bookie, gang markings, and rough-looking bar.'* Years of street work taught him to catalog his hunches, and he maintained them in a neat three-ring binder, a cop's journal. As they walked, Buck questioned the value of his chronic note-making. In response, Vince suggested they run a test in a month to see who could remember the most about their little walk. Buck agreed the veteran cop had a point. After about twenty minutes, they found themselves across the street from Wong's place in front of a drugstore.

Buck looked at Wong's restaurant and noticed the dead neon sign and the shade covering the front door glass was down. "Banker's hours."

"What?"

"Our friend closed early."

Vince looked back. "Yeah, like his mouth. Come on. Let's get a coffee. Maybe someone in the ring-side seats knows who broke the window."

The drug store looked like a place to get a headache and cure it all in one sitting. Gorski and Buck recoiled at the buildup of cigarette smoke and loud Vietnamese chatter rising from the mouths of eight or ten men seated at the half-dozen tables which paralleled the lunch counter. They took seats at the counter. The noise level dropped. Vince eyeballed the crowd while the counterman, a young skinny kid of about twenty, drew the two coffees.

"We're a big hit. They just don't know how to show it."

"Tough to make friends down here."

"One black. One Boston." The kid delivered the coffee.

"Still nursing that ulcer?"

"Yeah. Butterfat helps."

"Now, they say they're caused by a virus."

"Huh?"

"You know. Not stress-related."

"Virus. Schimirus. The fat helps." Vince looked up at the counterman, obviously hanging around, listening. Vince gave him a look, and he turned away.

"One second." Buck caught his eye, flashed his credentials, and quickly returned them to his suit pocket. The kid's eyes darted about the room. "Who broke that window?" Buck pointed toward Wong's restaurant across the street.

The counterman remained quiet, and several men at the tables rose to leave. Gorski glared at the men.

"Do you understand the question?"

The man looked at Buck and spoke quietly. "It was the wind. Only the wind."

"Not the Tiger?"

The man pulled back, shaking his head side-to-side in quick movements. Others waited at the register demanding service in

43

Vietnamese. The kid shuffled backward away from Gorski and Buck to assist his customers.

Vince sipped his coffee. "Mike. You're talkin' to yourself."

"You're right." Buck gazed at Vince over the top of his cup. "How are your girls?"

Vince's face brightened. "Sharon's doing great. Just completed beautician school. I got her a spot at my sister's girlfriend's shop on Belmont Avenue. Starts next week."

"And the little one..."

Vince rotated his stool back toward the counter. "She's a tough case. I don't like her friends. Things are different today. Kids don't listen to their old man anymore. Tough without Mary, and I don't make much of a mother.

"Is she getting into trouble?"

"Nothing serious. Drinking. Late nights. That kind of stuff."

"Drugs?"

Vince made a face. "Shit, I don't know. I hope not."

"Well..." Buck never finished his sentence. A flash of orange and blue flame flared out of the front of the Viet Valley restaurant, followed by a muffled explosion. Shards of glass and chunks of wood struck the drugstore glazing. Everyone ducked. Buck looked up at Wong's burning building. The two cops raced out of the drugstore and crossed the street but were stopped short by the fire's intense heat. They ran to the back alley, and Buck grabbed the doorknob of the rear service door. The red-hot knob burned his hand. The door had a rusty hasp and a bright new padlock. Deep inside the building, someone shouted and cried out. Buck removed his jacket and used it to protect his hands as he pulled on the door, but the lock held. He found a rock and smashed it against the padlock without result. Finally, intending to use his pistol to shoot into the padlock, he shouted at Gorski to move back. But at that moment, the small transom window above exploded out, and the hot breath of the fire struck them again. They backed away from the inferno. They heard cans of food popping and compressed gas tanks exploding, but no more human sounds.

"Forget it, Mike. We can't help. Call it in."

Buck made the call from his mobile. As a formality, he also requested an ambulance.

—CHAPTER SEVEN—

Three days later, Buck and Gorski had a sit-down with their boss. "Gentlemen. Meet Do Tron." After the men exchanged handshakes, Elliot, Gorski, and Buck sat at the conference table. The new man, Tron, stood rigid.

Bucks studied him. He had the look of an ARVN officer. He stood at attention, a skinny five and a half feet tall, his black hair slicked back, and his smile nervous. After Elliot pointed to the remaining chair, he sat.

"Do Tron is on loan to us from CPD. I asked Commander Wilson for assistance in the Wong matter. He is permanently assigned to Squad 7, and his first job will be to work with the two of you. I think he can help us communicate with the citizens of the Vietnamese community. Maybe break through their natural reluctance to talk to cops." Elliot looked at Buck and Gorski. He pushed on. "Do Tron, do you speak Vietnamese?"

"Yes, sir."

"Go ahead."

Do Tron waited dumbly.

"Well, say something in Vietnamese."

Tron nodded, then spoke for about twenty seconds. Then he smiled.

"Thank you," said Elliot.

Buck broke the ice. "I didn't catch that."

Do Tron spoke slowly in clear English, "I told a joke."

Buck waited.

Tron rolled his dark eyes. "I asked if you heard about the blind man who walked into the fish store and said, "Good morning, ladies."

Vince Gorski laughed aloud. Tron leaned back in his chair, more relaxed now.

Elliot wore a look of dismay. "A good demonstration, Tron. But we have to limit those around here. Some of our female agents might not find it so amusing." Tron looked down. "Anyway, you can see how helpful it will be to have Do Tron with you for an interview."

"A regular Shecky Greene," said Vince.

Ignoring the comment, Elliot continued, "As you know, there are several possibilities for Wong's death. Accident or negligence. Arson-turned-murder. Murder. At this point, we don't have an autopsy file or a lab report. I've asked the Professor to take a look. Checking for patterns. Chicago and elsewhere. Tron, I'm sure you agree. Investigations in the Vietnamese community are difficult to conduct."

Tron nodded.

"But the computer files can look objectively at the facts. Wong wasn't the first Vietnamese to be killed. There have been many unexplained killings across the country. Vietnamese victims. Some street crime. Some may be hits. Some are driven by greed. Some motivated by patriotism."

"You mean right-wingers?" asked Vince.

"Possible. There are enough of them around. Check out Wong. Maybe he was a suspected Commie or compromised. Once they're given that tag, true or not, word spreads fast. People have been killed for less. I want all three of you to re-read the special report on Vietnamese violence that San Francisco provided us. You'll find plenty of cases of politically motivated violence. Buck, why don't you and Tron work the streets? Get some background on Wong. Vince, follow up on the autopsy of the old man. I want to eliminate any ambiguity about the cause of death. OK?"

Vince, Buck, and Tron walked single file out of Elliot's office. Vince returned to his desk while Buck and Tron rode the elevator to the parking lot.

—CHAPTER EIGHT—

Buck weaseled through late afternoon traffic and headed north on Lake Shore Drive. The sun, interrupted by a wall of high-rise apartment buildings, cast long, dark shadows on the roadway as the two drove north toward the site of Wong's death. To their right, the silent fury of the lake attacked the rocky shoreline. Tron sat quiet and reserved. Buck opened him up with questions about his role with the Chicago Police. Buck had some idea of this background. Tron got a commendation for saving the life of a three-year-old girl who had been held hostage by an armed and deranged uncle. He had directed the CPD hostage team and talked the man into releasing the child in four hours of negotiation. Later the man stated he released the girl because he found a friend in Do Tron. Buck turned down the radio chatter.

"Do you go by Do Tron...Tron...Do?"

He smiled, "Tron is fine. It is easy to remember and understand. Like Mike."

"OK, Tron. Let's talk about Wong. Did you know him?"

"No, but I read the file. I think I have a good understanding of the man."

"And..."

"An elderly, local businessman. Quiet. Polite. Ran a clean restaurant. Never in trouble. Minded his own business. Sociable and never aggressive. Honest and hard-working, Modest income. Religious and respectful of tradition. A man with few friends except for his family. A man who wished to maintain an unspectacular, peaceful life. Then he filed a complaint with the FBI and died.

"That's pretty good for never having met him."

Tron smiled. "Except for his death and the FBI part, I could have been describing most Vietnamese people over 50 years old in this town. You see, we are a tight little group. Very close. Very similar in our likes and dislikes. Old country ways remain. And except for the young people, we have excluded much of the new. The young are disenchanted nihilists. They reject traditional values. They have taken on the values of the underclass of this country. Cool, fast, loud, and violent. And most of all, they like the gang family. It fits better than a real family. It's as American as apple pie or Al Capone."

"Elliot says you worked in a gang crime unit. You must know the local boys?"

"I know them, and they know me."

"Pretty hard to get undercover, I guess."

"Impossible."

"And dangerous."

"Yes, the Vietnamese community suffers. The gangs feed off them. My people are suspicious of banks. They often keep large sums of money in their houses. They're attractive targets."

Buck took the off-ramp and turned west. "I've heard the gangs drive a thousand miles round-trip to make a weekend hit on a house in Ohio."

Tron nodded. "Sometimes they'll pick up twenty or twenty-five thousand. Usually, nobody reports the crime. The Vietnamese don't trust the police."

Buck wheeled the car to a stop in front of Wong's burned-out restaurant. "Well, that's why we need you, Tron. This is it."

A persistent nippy wind cut into the two men as they strolled around the boarded, blackened masonry structure surrounded by vacant lots. The smell of water-soaked timbers and rotten food belched out of the building. Stopping at the rear of the building, Tron bent over to examine the service door. It hung half-open; the hasp had been ripped off the frame, and the lock dangling from

49

the door. Yellow police tape spanned the opening. "This was locked? Looks new."

"Yep. CPD found an old beat-up lock on the ground. Someone tossed the old one and replaced it with a new one."

"Front locked?"

"Yep."

"Someone locked him in, intentionally or accidentally."

Tron stepped under the tape and pushed the door as a test. "Can we get in?"

"What for? The tech people gave it a good review. It's a real mess in there."

"You never know. We might as well while we're here."

Buck looked down at his polished shoes. "OK." He handed Tron a small flashlight, and they entered.

"Watch your step. There's oil everywhere. It's slippery." The foul air made breathing difficult. Broken glass, rice, and liquid foodstuffs covered the stock room floor. They tiptoed through what had been the storeroom.

They moved further into the interior. Firefighters had hacked a jagged hole in the roof to relieve smoke. The dim, waning daylight illuminated the pyric tomb. Water, dripping from a faucet, pulsed onto the bottom of a stainless steel sink drumming into the quiet of the dead room. Tron and Buck rummaged for a few minutes, avoiding touching the charred surfaces. Moving to the kitchen, Tron commented, "This looks like the hot spot. Did the fire start here?"

"That's what the boys downtown think. Quite a few natural accelerants here. Cooking oil and alcohol-fueled the fire. You read the report. They couldn't say if it was a grease fire gone wild or deliberately started. The grease in the exhaust duct had been burning, but the fire started in the kitchen, not the duct."

Dodging debris, Tron and Buck scanned the kitchen. "What's this?" Tron flashed his beam into a small room off the kitchen which showed minor fire damage.

"It was Wong's bedroom. His apartment. He lived and died here."

"It's in good shape. I guess this door was closed." Tron examined the heavy door still on its hinges."

"Yep. Amazing isn't it?" said Buck. "The old man's world survived the fire, but he didn't."

"Is this where he died?" asked Tron.

"Yes. Wong was found lying here."

"Was he burned?"

"Not badly."

"Smoke?"

"Don't know yet. That's what Gorski is after. He's going to the Medical Examiner's Office today. Maybe he'll get some answers."

Buck looked at a framed photo of a young Vietnamese girl on a dresser.

"Pretty girl," said Tron, "a daughter?"

Buck shook his head. "Wong had no children as far as we know." He pondered the photo, pulled it out of the frame, and placed it in his breast pocket. He looked about the room at the chipping blue paint, worn asphalt tiles, tired furniture, and a beat-up bathroom. So little was left in a man's life. A bed, a desk, some tattered books, a small closet half-filled with grayed clothing, and the photo. In its gold-toned frame, it was the only bright thing in the room. He wondered about the young lady who occupied a special place in the old man's otherwise dull existence.

Tron ran his delicate fingers across a line of books having Vietnamese titles. "Religion, tradition, cooking, and birds. Nice little library." Tron picked up the books one by one and leafed through them. A business card dropped to the floor. He bent over to retrieve it and read it aloud in a low voice. "Nguyen Dang Duc, *Thay Phap*."

"What's that?

Tron handed Buck the card. He read it. "*Thay Phap*. What does that mean?"

"Voodoo. A *Thay Phap* is a performer, a medium, a confidant who practices voodoo."

"A witch doctor?"

Tron smiled. "Vietnamese voodoo is quite different than the Caribbean version. It descended from Taoism. Very old. Very subtle. No dolls, no masks, no dances. *Bua* is the voodoo. A blessing or a curse."

"Do people still believe in it?"

"Some do, some don't. It still has quite a following, particularly among the older generation."

"Like Wong."

"Maybe."

"This *Thay Phap* could be a confidant. We should visit the witch doctor. He may know something about Wong's troubles. What about it?"

Tron brushed the card across his chin and wore an impish look. "I think that's a good idea. But now, I'd like to get a feel for Wong's neighbors. Let's start with that joint across the street."

Conversations died as they entered the drug store, and dirty looks abounded. Tron proceeded to a magazine rack. He thumbed through several Vietnamese newsprint magazines while Buck surveyed the store.

Tron tapped Buck on the arm. "Take a look at this." He opened the magazine to two pages containing Vietnamese writing and the bordered names of businesses. The title read "The National Freedom Union." Buck scanned the business names of dry cleaners, restaurants, take-out places, and a funeral home."

"What is it? A Viet yellow pages?" asked Buck.

"It's an editorial put out by the NFU. Right-wing pronouncements about government injustice in not helping the boat people." Tron read from the paper. "According to this, some 45,000 former citizens of South Vietnam will be sent back to

Vietnam to face persecution if they do not get refugee status. It's a typical NFU editorial ad. I've seen them before. Lots of stories about Communist atrocities and the coming fall of the Communist government in Vietnam. They're dedicated to the proposition that their old enemy will be ousted from their homeland. The business names are lists of supporters. Probably pay to have their ad run."

Buck looked over Tron's shoulder to scan the individual names on the list. "Anyone we know?"

Tron looked back. "It's a long list."

"Is that this place?"

"Appears that way." Tron ran his finger beyond the drugstore listing, stopping at another ad. "Viet Valley Restaurant. Looks like Wong was a supporter too." Tron folded the magazine and replaced it in the rack. "We should talk with the owner. He's in the back. Please let me do the talking."

Buck followed Tron. The balding, bespectacled pharmacist and owner eyed their approach; the two Vietnamese exchanged smiles and greetings. Tron told the man who they were but showed no credentials. He explained they were investigating the fire across the street. "Could they talk?"

"Yes." The soft-spoken man nodded with a smile. "That would be possible." He invited them to join him in the back room. The owner opened a gate and stepped down from the platform area. He looked up at the taller man and passed a quick smile motioning them to follow him through a doorway of hanging beads. The man slid through the colorful portal, as did Tron, while Buck dragged the beads with him as he entered a small, neat office. The pharmacist offered tea from a small kettle on a hot plate. Buck at first declined, but a nudge from Tron changed his mind. They sat about a small wooden desk, clearing papers for cups and saucers and wearing grins. Tron thanked the man for his hospitality, and they talked about the neighborhood and the old country for at least fifteen minutes. The pharmacist spoke of his children and the difficulties of raising them in today's world, the old country and old ways, and the weather. Tron covered everything but the fire. Buck fidgeted. He declined offers of more tea and gave Tron a look that begged him to move on.

Tron ignored his pain. After about a half-hour, the two men laughed at each other's jokes and talked in English and Vietnamese. Buck hoped Tron would finally begin the interrogation.

"Can you tell me about Wong Suu?"

The pharmacist looked into space as if he could see the empty, burned-out restaurant across the street. "Wong was a fine man. Terrible thing."

"Did he have any family?"

"I do not know. Once or twice I saw a young woman. She may have been family." He removed his glasses, wiped them with his tie, then replaced them, hooking the wires around his tiny ears and carefully adjusting the bridge. He continued, "I did not know him that well."

"The restaurant storefront was boarded up before the fire occurred. Do you know how it was broken?"

The man looked at Tron and dropped his eyes. "I have been told it was young boys."

"Like the White Tiger?"

The man recoiled internally. "Some of the young men in our neighborhood do not respect the property of others."

"Members of the White Tiger?"

"Some Tiger. Some others. There are several gangs. You know."

"Are you afraid of them?"

The man seemed to think before answering. "Not fear. I left my fear in the old country. I am aware of them like I am aware of the weather. If you know it will rain, you can become prepared."

"So you buy an umbrella?" Tron smiled at the man as he tossed the question.

The man nodded. "It is good business."

54

"Where do you buy an umbrella? From the NFU newspaper?"

The pharmacist leaned back in his chair. His smile tightened. "I am sorry. I must now attend to my customers. If you do not mind." The three men stood.

"No. Thank you so much for your time and the tea. May we come back again to talk?"

"Yes," said the man with an edge of relief, "yes."

Before exiting the beaded doorway, Tron stopped and turned to face the store owner. "You know Wong bought an umbrella, and it still rained on him."

The man dropped his head. "These things happen. Goodbye, gentlemen."

They made their way to the front of the store. The patrons ignored Buck and Tron's departure. Outside, twilight lingered. Buck looked around and then at his watch. "That didn't amount to much. Want to call it a day, Tron?"

"I would say we learned something. You may not see it, but our new friend just went out on a limb for us. He may become a good asset. And we found out that the White Tiger gang broke Wong's window. The pharmacist pays protection money to someone, maybe the NFU. And maybe Wong was also paying. And maybe he stopped paying, resulting in the broken window warning. And then a fire." Tron smiled at Buck. "Also, I would prefer to talk to the *Thay Phap* rather than end my day."

"Is he near?"

"Not far."

"OK. A little Voodoo, then we head home. Hell, maybe I can get my fortune read."

—CHAPTER NINE—

The two men walked along a tight street lined with frame bungalows. Tron spotted a small sign tacked to the building corner that read *Nguyen Dang Duc, Thay Phap* and showed a tiny arrow pointing down the passageway leading back to a coach house.

"This must be the place. Think our friend will be pissed? We don't have an appointment," said Buck.

Tron smiled. "If he is any good, he will know we are here."

They walked single file along the cracked concrete path through the dark, narrow passage between buildings and emerged in the courtyard of a modest coach house. A few wooden steps led to a small porch. As they climbed the stairs, the door opened. A tall, thin, smiling Vietnamese man appeared wearing a black suit with a broad red silk belt. From his Vietnam days, Buck knew of this symbol of distinction. The *Thay Phap*'s shiny nails were perfectly manicured, his face tanned, and grey streaks coursed through his thick black hair. Buck could not guess his age. He could be fifty or maybe sixty.

"Come in, gentlemen. Please." He spoke in a soft voice using tightly formed, precise words. "I have been expecting you."

Buck and Tron displayed their credentials. Nguyen Dang Duc simply nodded and invited them in. His front room served as an office, sanctuary, and living room. Light incense floated in the air. Jade figurines, candles in brass bases, and colored wall hangings set the tone. The three men sat on simple wooden furniture. A few small logs burned in the fireplace.

For a moment, no one spoke. The man seemed to be drifting. Suddenly, he laughed loudly. It startled both Buck and Tron.

"I am sorry, gentlemen. Sometimes I amuse myself." He straightened his belt. "You seek an answer in *Bua*?"

Tron leaned in to speak. "Please pardon our unannounced arrival. We would like to ask you a few questions."

"I am always available to assist the police. Now, how may I be of help? A blessing. A curse. Of course, you know who I am." The *Thay Phap* looked directly into Tron's eyes.

"Yes. We would like to ask you about one of your clients."

A look of concern replaced his smile. "My clients are important to me. I have helped many people. I can sense you are a spiritual man. You are aware of the trust placed upon me by those that I serve."

Tron cleared his throat quietly and waited for a moment before he spoke. "I am aware of your position. We are investigating the death of Mr. Wong Vien Suu. One of your clients?"

"It would be disrespectful to those I serve for me to speak of them without their knowledge."

"And bad business," added Buck.

Duc looked at Buck with mild disdain and stared at the agent's holstered gun, exposed between the folds of his coat.

Tron looked over to Buck and rolled his eyes. Then he returned to Duc. "Are you suggesting some kind of confidential relationship exists between you and your patrons, which keeps you from answering our questions? If so, I can assure you that no such situation is recognized by the law."

"Please, Agent Tron, let us not speak of the law. Not the laws of man. God is the master. We are but his servants."

"Yes, this is true." Tron squared himself. "But, sir. Did you know Wong?"

Duc leaned back in his chair, then eased toward Tron, placing his face inches from the detective's face. He spoke very softly. "Of course, I knew him. He was a fine man."

Tron looked him in the eye. "Was he troubled?"

Duc pushed back, placing his hands delicately together beneath his chin. "Who is not troubled in these troubled times? A songbird whose tree is also home to a viper can still sing a beautiful song. Wong was a fine man."

"Did he come to you for help?"

"I can tell you he was a very spiritual man who believed in the *Bua*. We often shared a common bowl of rice and a pot of tea. I enjoyed the hospitality of his restaurant from time to time. Sometimes he came to my home. It is sad. He has passed from this world. I will miss him."

Tron took his right hand and brushed back his hair. In doing so, he got a look at Buck, who appeared to be biting his tongue and whose eyes appeared to say, "Let's get out of here." Tron fidgeted. "Do you know any reason why someone would wish to harm Wong?"

Duc's eyes looked to the ceiling as he spoke. "I make every effort to provide cures, not curses. I am looking for the positive in every situation. I know Mr. Wong was a hard-working, quiet person. Such good people should not have to fight the vipers of this world, but God made both vipers and birds. I cannot say why this is such."

"Who are the vipers?"

Duc smiled. "You, Agent Tron, are the policeman. It is your job to find the vipers. But if I were you, I would look under the rocks with caution." Duc laughed loudly and stood. "Now, I must ask you to leave. I must pray. Please come again. You also, Agent Buck. The next time you may come alone. I could help you with your problem."

Buck looked down at the man. "What problem?"

"We each have problems. I was speaking of the one which fills your eyes so sadly. I may be able to help."

Tron looked at the two men quizzically. "All right. Goodnight, sir. Again thank you for your time."

As Duc held the door open, he said, "Go with care, gentlemen." He looked out toward the street. His face tightened, possibly in fear. He held that look as they marched down the steps.

When they entered the gangway, Buck finally released his opinion. "Not exactly a high-powered interrogation. That guy's a nut-case."

Tron frowned. "Things move more slowly with these people. You must be patient. Duc has his eccentricities, but don't discredit him and his voodoo. Tron looked quizzically at Buck. "He seemed to see something in you. Maybe you should see him for advice."

"Thanks, but I'll stick with my *Ouija* board." Buck continued walking his back to Tron.

"I'm serious."

"Forget it."

Buck walked past the corner of the house. A street light started its night cycle, providing a flickering light. "Shit," Buck muttered.

Two young men sat on the Bureau car's fenders while the other six milled about watching. Buck pressed his elbow against his side, feeling his weapon's familiar bulk. Tron noticed. "Easy, Mike," he whispered under his breath.

The biggest of these not-so-big, late-teen trouble-makers struck up a conversation as he leaned against the driver's side door. Buck approached the talker, a man of about twenty wearing a bowl haircut and two earrings. Tron made his way to the other side as Buck studied the man.

"Evening, boys." Buck gave him a 'shit-eater' and edged closer. After taking a long and dramatic drag on his cigarette, one of the two fender-boys jumped off and crushed it on the car's hood.

"It's not an ashtray, *đụ má*."

The boy's face tensed, and he moved toward Buck, but he stopped short after a disapproving look from their leader. Tron watched intently as he opened the other door. He hung onto the roof edge with his left hand, which opened his coat for easy access to his gun. "Hey, Tommy," Tron spoke to one of the two who grazed behind the car.

A boyish-looking man of about eighteen lifted his head and acknowledged the greeting, "Hey."

"We'd like to go," said Tron, "OK?"

The leader looked at Tommy, who nodded. We'll let you go, brother"; he smiled as he spoke. "But don't hurry back. You too, bossman." He pointed with his thumb to the car.

Buck reentered, Tron followed, and the boys stepped to either side of the car. As Buck started the engine, they spat upon the side windows and windshield. Buck looked at Tron. "Go, Mike," Tron's voice had a bit of a plea. Buck took one last look at his smiling tormentors.

"Little gook pricks."

Tron blurted out. "What?"

Buck's face flushed. He hit the gas, and they flew along the side street, ignoring stop signs.

Tron spoke in quick breaths. "We're lucky those guys didn't rip us a couple of new assholes. This is their turf, Mike. They can do what they want in this part of town."

Buck didn't talk.

"Tommy's OK. These gangs just suck these kids in. Even decent kids."

Buck nodded.

"He saved our butt."

"Right," replied Buck in a sarcastic tone. He gripped the wheel and focused on the road ahead.

—CHAPTER TEN—

At the office the following day, Tron avoided Buck. He saw him briefly, but they didn't talk. Vince Gorski asked for his help today. Tron found the veteran cop in a small, back-area conference room. A burly man sat across from him. "Tron. Meet Pat Roche. Gang Crime. CPD. A former partner of mine." The two men shook hands. Roche held a cardboard box in his lap, his two bear-paw-like hands resting atop. Tron half-sat on the corner of the table.

"So..." said Vince, looking at the box.

Quickly Roche set it on the desk. "Here's the tapes you wanted, Vince. Untranslated. Vietnamese." His voice was scratchy and tinged with an Irish brogue. He looked toward Tron, then back at Gorski.

"What's the source," asked Tron.

"White Tiger clubhouse. Wiretap. Calls in and out. Local and long-distance. The tapes cover about three months. A couple of years ago. We got the tap after talking to the Lima, Ohio PD Home invasion. Rich Vietnamese family. Somebody saw a vanload of Viets leaving after they beat up the family and stole the family jewels. The victims didn't talk much though. But the local boys put together enough to figure our own White Tigers were the perps."

Vince lit a cigarette. Tron gave him a look. "It's OK. No one bothers me here. The big wigs are smokin' in their offices all the time." He continued talking, the smoke still bubbling from his mouth. "You didn't need the tapes?"

"No. We busted one of their houses, found most of the loot, and arrested three Tigers. Played one against the other and plea-bargained two of them into Joliet. Case closed."

"You ever heard of that, Tron?" asked Vince.

"Sure. I remember it. These gangs pick out-of-town targets. Hit-and-run style. Tough to detect. As I told Buck, the Vietnamese community doesn't trust the police. Usually, such crimes never make it to a written report."

"That's for sure," said Roche. "We got no help from anyone. We were just plain lucky to find the house with the loot. A beat cop traffic-stopped one of them and found a trunk-load of shit. Otherwise, we had nothing. Watched 'em for weeks and got nothing. Then the trunk opened, and we had 'em. Bing-bang-boom."

"Hey, sometimes it's better to be lucky than good?"

"You're not shittin'" said Roche with a smile.

"Has Gang Crime ever run into any gang-related arson in Little Saigon?"

Roche pushed his chair around to face Tron. "Three or four suspicious fires in the Uptown area. Gangs may have something to do with 'em. But we got no proof. Anyway, some shit came down on us to dance around those fires."

"What do you mean?" asked Tron. He frowned.

Roche turned away and mumbled, "You know what I mean. Word gets out to spend our time on something else. So we do."

Tron looked across the desk at Vince for help.

"Hey, you can't fight City Hall. We don't make the rules, right, Pat?"

Like an Irish priest untangling the Latin Mass, Roche stretched out a distorted response. "*Is fada an bóthar nach mbíonn casadh ann.*"

Vince nodded and smiled as if he understood.

Tron ignored their banter. "What about violent crime?"

"Don't know...been one death and a couple of severe beatings. Armed robberies. The dead guy probably resisted. Sometimes we see gang warfare, but not much. Somebody might end up in an emergency room cut up a bit. But they don't fight for turf like other gangs. No dealers. We don't get those Westside drive-bys with these guys. And nobody talks. Argyle Boyz, White Tiger, Yellow Peril, Uptown Rats. They all hate cops. They stick together like glue. Just one big happy family. Gangbangers, victims, and everybody else. You know what I mean. Right, Tron?"

Tron nodded. "So, nothing like Wong's demise?"

"Huh?"

"No possible arson-murders."

Roche drowned his cigarette in a half-empty paper cup and blew smoke across the desk, causing Tron to lean back. "No. Nothin' like that. You think this guy Wong was taken out?"

Vince answered, "We don't know. For now, it looks like an accident. No real evidence. Bomb-arson found flammable trails across the floor, but there was a lot of juice in that restaurant. Cooking wines. Oils. Something could have popped in a fire. And we don't have an autopsy yet, so we don't know how he died."

"Who's tracin' the autopsy?" asked Roche with a smile.

"Me," said Vince.

Roche reproached his old partner. "You still on bad paper with the stiff-slitters?"

Vince winced and sank back into his chair. "We get along."

"Let's get on with the tapes," said Tron.

"OK."

Tron removed one of the tapes from the box of about ten and placed it on a reel-to-reel recorder. Spinning it to trim the slack, he pronounced it ready for action. The tape began in mid-conversation. Scratchy Vietnamese voices sputtered out of the machine.

Roche slowly extracted his body from the chair and stood. "Well, good luck, boys. I'm outta here. I can't stick around for ten hours and listen to this crap." Roche looked at Tron. "No offense intended."

"None taken," said Tron as he tried to listen to the recorded voices.

"Hey, Pat," Vince demanded. "Kiss my ass goodbye."

"You wish. You faggot. See ya."

"Thanks for the warning."

Tron nodded and weakly smiled at Roche, acknowledging his departure. He moved over to the vacated chair, and they both listened. Tron made notes on a yellow pad. Minutes passed. Vince smoked.

"What d'ya have?"

Tron clicked off the machine. "I have two guys talking about their girlfriends. One complaining he's not getting enough sex, and the other bragging he's getting too much. Vince, I don't see any reason for you to waste time listening. You can't understand a word, can you?"

"Nope. But I'll stick around. I gotta learn. Maybe I can get a feel for these folks. You know, voice inflection. Tone. Something. Anyway, you stop when you've got something, and we'll talk it out. OK?" The big man leaned over and placed his meaty forearms on the table.

Tron smiled. "OK." He flipped the lever, and the voices came to life.

Hours passed. Tron and Vince listened to reel after reel between coffee breaks and pit stops. Most of the conversations were personal, and parts were inaudible. Tron guessed they were gang members using a phone in a shared house. Almost all the calls were short and ambiguous. Tron translated: "Indiana. Let's get it on tonight. Same boys. Same place. Eight o'clock." The other side of the conversation quickly acknowledged the proposal with a quiet "OK." Then the conversation clicked to an end.

"Somethin' goin' on there."

"Maybe a burglary or robbery."

Two more uninteresting calls followed. Then another call mentioned the "Wilton building." Although somewhat garbled, the words "it's time" could be understood. Tron felt the caller's voice was older and authoritarian. The person in the house only listened while the outside caller spoke and then hung up. Vince and Tron were intrigued.

"Wilton. Wilton Street. That's in the middle of things, right?"

"Right," Tron replied. "Strange. This is the first mention of "building" in three hours of tapes.

"'Building.' You're right; that's different. These guys talk about people, cars, money, sex, video games, weapons, broads. But no buildings. And this guy sounds like he's in charge. Am I right?"

Tron nodded and replied, "Yes. He didn't even wait for a response. He just spoke and hung up. His tone was imperious."

"Keep listening. Maybe we'll catch somethin' else on this Wilton building."

They spent another forty-five minutes at their task with no further utterance of the word "building" and nothing else of interest. Vince checked his watch and stood. "That's enough for me. I'm outta here. I gotta lunch with a friend. You going to pack it in for lunch?"

Tron looked at the remaining tapes and then back at Vince. "I'll grab something. I'll listen a bit more. This time with headphones. I have to go over these again to pick up some of the inaudibles. You know it is challenging to understand when they all talk at once."

The phone rang. Vince grabbed it on the first ring. After a half-minute banter, Gorski pressed the person on the other end. "What's the story, Ralph?" Tron listened to one side of the conversation. "So, was he dead before he died or not?" Gorski's face screwed up with impatience. "Not good enough. What about tissue samples?" The voice answered. Vince walked back and forth behind his desk. "Go for it," said Vince, "sooner, the better.

Thanks, Doc. Get back to me as soon as you hear somethin'" He hung up."

"Medical Examiner's Office?"

"Yeah. Washburn."

Tron waited for Vince to sit down.

"If he had to put money on it, he'd go with a heart attack. Wong's lungs were clean. No clenched fists. No burns. No other evidence of violence except a small bump on the back of his head that didn't kill him. Nothing unusual in the stomach. They're going to do tissue samples. Maybe somethin' will show up."

Tron scratched behind his ear as he spoke. "So we have a fire which could be accidental and a death which could be natural. And some prior threats. You still think this is a case?"

Gorski glanced at his watch, then stood and reached over to fetch his trench coat. "Let's keep at it," said Gorski. "There's somethin' here. You work on the tapes. You're the only one who can make somethin' out of them. See you after lunch." Over the top of a file cabinet, Vince surveyed the entire office, including Buck's desk about thirty feet away. The conversation between Buck and his guest seemed animated and loud. "Check it out, Tron."

Tron pushed his chair back and looked out into the office. A beautiful Asian woman sat in Buck's guest chair while Tron watched and listened.

"I have my rights, Agent Buck. I would like to see the autopsy results."

"I agree," said Buck, "but the autopsy report has not been released, and we have no control over that part of the investigation. We will both have to wait."

She took a moment to compose herself. "How long will that be?"

Buck gave her a half-smile, "Maybe a week."

"Too long," Agent Buck said. "Mr. Wong was a dear friend. For me, he was like a favorite uncle. We have to know."

"Who's 'we'?" asked Buck.

"Me. My father. We are like family. Do you understand?"

"I understand completely. There's nothing I can do to speed up the work of the medical examiner, but maybe you can help the investigation."

The dark-haired woman readjusted her position. She took a deep breath. "Of course, I will help."

Before she could speak again, Buck reached into his top desk drawer and retrieved the small photo of the young woman he had found in Wong's residence. He handed it to her. She held it between two fingers, staring at it for a moment. "I found this in Wong's bedroom. Is that a photo of you?"

"Yes," she said, wiping back a tear, "may I keep this?"

Buck nodded. "It was the only bright spot in that room." He smiled.

She thanked him and placed the photo in her purse. They both stood. She grabbed her jacket. "I'm sorry I raised my voice. I will wait to hear from you. Please call me when you get the results."

"I realize this is a difficult time for you. I'll call you if I have new information to be shared." With that, she turned and exited. Tron noticed Buck studying her as she walked away. Gorski also looked. She was a pleasant sight dressed in a leather jacket, somewhat short skirt, and heels. Buck looked back at a smiling Gorski.

"Caught ya."

Buck shrugged his shoulders. "Hey, I'm not dead, Gorski. What about you?"

Vince smiled. "Nope. Still above the grass. Eyes wide open. Ready for action."

—CHAPTER ELEVEN—

Not seeing the sign in front, a passerby might think it was a warehouse. True, but the modest dull grey one-story building tucked into the medical research neighborhood of the Near West Side was filled with bodies. A refrigerated room fifty feet wide by a hundred feet long accommodated rows of continuous shelving sixteen feet high, stacked shelf above shelf they lay. Light-blue dead people, some eyes open, others closed, some with one of each, some clad in clear plastic wrappers, all wearing the symbolic toe-tag of the typical morgue resident. New arrivals lay on gurneys, wrinkled, tattered, bullet-holed and battered, sliced, diced, and broken, waiting for their last visit to the doctor. On the other side of the wall, the body-viewing waiting room was filled with nervous activity. Small children labored over coloring books while their parents thumbed through magazines. Vince made his way into the room. He smiled lightly at a little girl who looked at him with fearful and sad eyes. She held onto her red-eyed mother's dress, not returning the smile and burrowing her head into the woman's leg. He continued to the main desk.

"Hey Vince, how's it hanging?" The fortyish bottle-blonde receptionist greeted the big cop with genuine affection.

"Sweetheart."

She lifted her potato sack body out of the swivel chair with surprising grace and slid around the edge of her desk to greet him properly. Against regulations, they hugged, and then she quickly retired to her spot behind the counter, looking about to see if anyone was watching. Vince leaned in with both elbows on the counter.

"You big lug. What's happening? I hear Sharon's coming to work for Betty. That's great. I'll give her a shot at my hair."

Fluffing the hair on both sides of her head, "Can't hurt this mop," she lamented.

"Thanks, Jean. Appreciate it. I'm real happy she's got the job."

"And how's Cindy?"

Gorski couldn't conceal his disappointment with a lie. "She's good too. Thanks."

The receptionist accepted the lie with a smile.

"You know we've got a brunch at St. Al's this Sunday. You comin'?"

Vince stepped back quickly in mock surprise. "What about Harry? He might gag if I took you to the ball."

"Don't worry about him. Got him on a leash and a muzzle. He won't bother us. Anyway, I got a girlfriend you might want to meet. She's coming. Very pretty."

Vince smiled and shrugged his shoulders. "Sorry, Jean. Not ready yet."

"I got ya. Well, how 'bout my potato salad. That will be there too."

"That might convince me. Maybe I will. We'll see." Vince straightened up and tucked in his shirt. "Anyway, I'm here to see a stiff."

"Stiffs we got. Name?"

"Wong's the last or the first. I never get that straight." He pulled a little leather-bound notepad from his jacket pocket and flipped through the pages. He spelled the words: W O N G V I E N S U U."

"Ah. So. Mr. Wong. Let me check." She consulted her computer. "He's in the warehouse. Dr. Washburn. Know how to get there?"

"Yep. Thanks." He waved goodbye.

"Don't forget. Sunday. Eleven o'clock. Bring an appetite."

"I'll try." Vince did a pirouette and headed down the hall.

69

Dr. Ralph Washburn sat at his desk facing a wall. Vince peered at him through the small square of glass in the door. Washburn hummed and tapped his right foot to his music while his long, bony fingers danced across the computer keys. Vince knew those fingers could glide down a guitar neck just as nimbly. The forensic pathologist sometimes moon-lighted as a studio musician and regularly played with a small ensemble. Vince didn't know much about jazz, but he had heard that Doctor Ralph was pretty damn good. Washburn had the manual dexterity, concentration, leadership, and knowledge to be a great surgeon but disliked cutting live patients. However, his skills were not wasted, as his comprehensive examinations of victims often helped solve many murders. Vince pushed open the door.

Dr. Washburn stood, stretching out his large, lanky frame. "Brother Vince. What a pleasant surprise."

"Hey, Ralph. You're lookin' happy."

"You're right in time. The king of happiness. And you?"

Vince flipped his tie in his hands, "I'm a party fool, Doc. You know that."

"Good for you. Life's too short. Look around this place. Last big party on earth, and nobody's laughing but me."

They talked for about ten minutes before Vince explained his mission. Dr. Washburn knew all about Wong, including that Wong's niece was coming to make an identification. Vince asked to see the cadaver. Washburn escorted him to a viewing room as an attendant wheeled in Wong's body. The naked man, a skeleton draped in wrinkled sheets of old skin, appeared at peace. His arms and feet showed minor burns, his body mole-marked and rumpled, but his face was placid. "Not too much damage."

"No. He came out of the fire looking pretty good."

"Did the fire kill him?" asked Vince.

"Damned if I know. Seen enough? I'll get started on him soon."

"Right. Page me when she arrives. I'll be in the lunchroom. OK?"

Washburn nodded.

Vince left Washburn and walked to the small lunchroom to grab a coffee and watch the people. The place buzzed with conversation and laughter. It amazed him that the Medical Examiner employees would choose to work in this house of death. Even on a cop's beat or in a hospital, somebody comes out alive, but not in the morgue. The morgue workers were surrounded by the dead every day. They were inured to the environment, but the friends and relatives of the victims were not. They had to be handled. For decades, Vince had skillfully patrolled the border between the living and the dead. Today his work continued.

She was exiting when Vince arrived at the closed-circuit television viewing room door. She held Washburn's arm for support. Her pretty face was flat and pale. Vince approached cautiously, easing his big body next to the couple like a ship to a dock. She didn't notice him.

"Vince, this is Miss Le An," said the doctor as he slipped away. "And this is Vince Gorski of the Federal Bureau of Investigation."

She looked up. Vince was stunned by her eyes, large, dark, and beautiful against her tanned complexion. He reached, and his big mitt surrounded her delicate hand. She returned the greeting slowly.

"My condolences," said Vince. He held her hand as he spoke, slowly releasing it. "I know this is a difficult time, but I would like to talk to you for a moment...if I may."

"Yes, I understand." She studied him and appeared to gather strength. Her body language evolved from a wounded sparrow to a more aggressive jay. "I have some questions for you also."

Vince brightened in response to her transformation. "OK. Please wait here. Just give me a moment with the good doctor. You and I can grab a coffee."

She nodded. Vince stepped away and walked down the corridor with Washburn toward the double doors of the autopsy room. He whispered to his friend, "Ralph, I want a good one."

"Hey, they're all good, my man. We don't do shoddy autopsies here."

"I know that. I mean, I want the deluxe car wash with the hot wax and the tire shine. I want old man Wong detailed and looking sharp. Spend some quality time on it. OK?"

"Vince, I got a lot of work here. Look, new clients as we speak." Washburn pointed at the view window in the door. Several bodies were parked neatly in a corner, and a young orderly wheeled in another. Further in the process, others were being dissected by deans who cut flesh, sawed bones, and removed organs for doctor evaluation.

"I see them. They can wait, Ralph. I can't. Work with me this time. I want all the tests and a complete inspection. I want certainty. I want to know what killed him and how. No gall stone unturned, Doc."

"You're into this one, Vince. What's driving you?"

Vince scratched his head. His eyes wandered to the woman, then he returned his gaze to Washburn. "The guy died on my watch. He's my business. He asked us for help, and he's going to get it. Alive or dead."

"OK, brother. I get it. But you'll owe me." Washburn smiled at Vince and gently waved off Wong's niece before entering the room. Vince puckered his big lips and nodded. He knew a bottle of single malt scotch would complete the bargain.

Vince escorted the woman from the morgue and took her to a nearby cop joint. The place bubbled with the voices of the living. She appeared to relax. He drank coffee, chewed politely on a glazed donut, and questioned Le An even more politely. "U of C. That's a good school. How long have you been teaching there?"

"About a year and a half. I was an assistant while working on my doctorate."

"What was it about?"

She smiled. "It was about the effect of the evolution of the Pacific Rim market on U.S.—Vietnamese relations."

"Very interesting. Things are always changing, aren't they?"

"A lot has happened since the end of the Vietnam War," she said. "From the standpoint of geopolitical economics, everything is different."

Vince smiled. "People adapt. Life goes on." He nipped on the donut, followed by a sip of coffee, then cleared his throat. "Were you close to your uncle?"

She lowered her head and then looked up. "Yes. Very close. He was a kind man. He was not my uncle. But, he was an old and close friend of my father who took an interest in me. Like an uncle."

"Do you think Wong acted troubled toward the end?"

She looked up at the ceiling for a moment. "Yes. Preoccupied. But he hid it well. He was always indulgent toward me. Every time we met, he would give me a gift. Nothing big. He was not a rich man. But always something sweet. He gave me this the last time." She grasped the lapel of her jacket and fingered a little gold bird with jeweled green eyes.

"Nice. He must have loved you very much."

She gazed into his eyes for the first time and said, "Yes, he did. I was like his little girl."

"Did he have relatives here?"

"No, he escaped the old country as one of the 'boat people.' He left everything and everyone behind."

"Except your father."

"No. My father and Wong Suu became friends in this country. They were both immigrants. They had much in common except for their stations in life. When they first arrived in America, they were poor people with untested skills and language difficulties.

But, they overcame problems together and, in doing so, built their friendship."

Vince leaned forward. "What's your take on the fire?"

She slid to the back of her chair. "What do you mean?"

"I mean, do you think it was an accident?"

Her head snapped back. "I think that it is your job to determine that. However, my uncle was an old man. They become forgetful and often lose their concentration or their sensibilities. Maybe he made a mistake. He smoked those rope cigars, and he worked around cooking equipment. He could have fallen asleep and accidentally started the fire. I don't know. What do you know?"

"Not much yet. The fire boys have yet to report, and Dr. Washburn will do his autopsy."

She nodded. "But if the FBI is involved, something must be suspected. The government wouldn't get into my uncle's death if this was simply a terrible accident, would they?"

Vince popped the last bit of donut in his mouth and swallowed. "You're right. We're not interested in accidents. The Bureau is responding to your uncle's complaint."

"Complaint?"

Vince fidgeted in his chair. "Your uncle reported threats. We suspect he was being harassed."

"By whom?"

"Maybe gangs. We don't know yet. We're just startin' our investigation."

Her dark eyes caught fire. "I am very interested in finding out the truth, Detective Gorski."

Call me Vince." He waited for her to nod. "Do you know anything about these threats? Did your uncle mention them?"

"No, he would never burden me with his problems," she said lightly. "I'm sorry I can't help you. But please, I would like to be apprised of any developments. When will we hear something on the autopsy?"

"I don't know exactly." Vince backed up his chair and stood. "I'll need your number."

"Certainly." She reached into her purse, retrieved a business card, and handed it to him. "Please keep me informed."

"I will."

—CHAPTER TWELVE—

Buck squinted over the top of his coffee mug as he gazed to his left, catching a view of Grant Park and the lake, then returned to the man seated at the desk before him. The Professor focused on statistical descriptions of criminals. He cataloged their modes of operations, arrest records, known associates, geographical locations, and opportunities for committing crimes. His analysis could determine their attributes and tendencies and estimate their probabilities as suspects. Only information that could be grouped, categorized, analyzed, and tested was interesting to him. He headed the Chicago Office Department of Artificial Intelligence aided by his protégé, Nelson O. Watson.

Buck respected the fifty-six-year-old veteran, whose real name, Randolph Clark, was almost lost in normal office conversation. Never a street cop, he had been in the Chicago office since joining the Bureau. Methodical and brilliant in his casework analysis, he pioneered computer technology for crime-solving. For three decades, the activities of mobsters, Klansmen, Weathermen, con men, and drug runners that crossed his path were cataloged and analyzed initially on punchcards and mainframe computers tied to mechanical sorters and massive printouts. In the Sixties and Seventies, J. Edgar Hoover used a massive public relations campaign to make people think the FBI files were a vast and well-organized knowledge web. However, Hoover's files, while extensive and detailed, were unmanageable. But, working on his own, experimenting with every new advancement in hardware and software, the Professor created one of the best stand-alone databases in the Bureau. He used any system or equipment he could find, including the often newer and better equipment owned and shared by private industry. Over time, Randy Clark became a leading expert in the country on the forensic use of computers. His local-office computer organization expertise was a legend within the Bureau, and he lectured at Bureau offices nationwide.

Ending his phone conversation, the Professor cradled the receiver and looked up at Buck with a smile. "Marilyn. She's making travel plans."

"Where to?"

He shook his head. "Everywhere. According to her, we're going to see everything we haven't seen. The Eiffel Tower, the pyramids, Mount Fuji, and maybe the moon. Who knows?"

Buck laughed. "Well, you still have a couple months left. Can you help me?"

"Yes, sir, Agent Buck. Let's get on with it." Buck handed him a file. The older agent adjusted his glasses and read the report for a few minutes, stopping now and then to make tiny notes on a legal pad. Then he closed the file, handed it back to Buck, and picked up his notes, referring to them as he spoke. "So not long after Wong comes to us complaining about threats, he is found dead in his burned-out restaurant. There is some potential for gang activity related to him. His adopted niece, whose father is a mover and shaker in the Vietnamese community, seems very concerned about this possibility. Like many other businessmen, he had advertised in the local right-wing Vietnamese propaganda journal. He had a relationship with the neighborhood shaman. And last but not least, he doesn't have an FCI record, according to Mr. Marsden. Is that about it?"

Buck nodded. "Except for the autopsy and the fact that Marsden mentioned some Vietnamese-Americans had been killed on the West Coast, possibly related to Viet politics."

The Professor removed his glasses and placed them carefully in the top desk drawer. He pushed his chair back and turned sideways, swinging one leg atop the other. "What do you think?"

Buck tapped his fingertips together while regrouping. "It could be an accident. In which case, we're out of it. It could be an arson with a related death. If we can tie it back to a mail threat, we've got some jurisdiction. Of course, according to Wong, he handed over all the letter threats to Marsden's boys, and they say they never heard of him."

"Mardsen playing dumb?"

Buck shook his head and smiled, resuming his line of reasoning, "Could be a murder, a rough-up, or a botched robbery attempt with an arson cover-up.

"Did Wong appear to be a man of means with a till full of cash?"

"No. That place was no McDonald's. But folks kill each other nowadays battling over the TV remote."

"In the Vietnamese community?"

"You're right. Crime is less random in that part of town. So maybe no robbery. It's a stretch to see an arson-cover for a store robbery anyway. Or, for that matter, if some gangbanger was just pushing him around for an 'insurance premium' and went too far, would they bother to cover up?"

The Professor put his hand to his chin as if to think and then, with a smile, said, "They lean on the old man for money. Grab him. Threaten him. Shake him up. He's terrified. He has a heart attack and dies. Then they decide to torch the place? Why bother? To cover the bruises?"

Buck shrugged his shoulders, "No bruises. Vince says the old man looked very nice in the morgue. No burns. No bruises."

"And murder with arson for dessert?"

"That's a tough one. Motive?"

"Unknown."

"Means?"

"Unknown. Need the autopsy."

"Suspects."

"Unknown. Need a motive."

The Professor cradled his coffee and leaned back in his chair. "Well. You've given me something to do. I'll look for a motive. It may be a waste of time, but you never know. You and Vince saw him about a half-hour before the fire. He closed his store. He locked his security grille in the front, and the back door was also locked outside. Then the fire starts, and he's presumably trapped and dies. If you ignore the threats, it seems like an accident's a good possibility. Or maybe a reasonably sophisticated killer. Anyway, we'll run it through the machine to find any patterns. It would be useful to get our hands on those letters, though."

Buck smiled. "If they exist, I don't think Marsden's going to hand them over to us."

"You're right, but if the head of FCI is working on this Wong matter also, and I would guess he is. This suggests there may be a motive out there. And I love looking for motives."

Buck stood up and stretched out his frame, and the Professor did the same, bending his torso intentionally.

"Sitting or, for that matter, just about anything is less pleasant as you get older." The Professor looked into Buck's eyes and smiled.

"Tell me about it." Buck turned to leave and stopped at the door. "Couple of days?"

"Two days work for sure."

—CHAPTER THIRTEEN—

The Squad 7 car entered the parking garage. The old Hilton Hotel on South Michigan Avenue had been the site of one of the most violent anti-Vietnam war protests.

Buck chuckled.

"What's the joke, Mike?" asked Tron.

"Just thinking how strange things are. What goes around comes around."

"How's that?"

"Back in '68. The big battle against the war was fought across the street in Grant Park. The real war, my war, ended six years later. But tonight, our old allies, the South Vietnamese, are still in the fight decades later. Like it never ended."

Tron nodded while Buck reached out the window to claim the parking gate ticket. "You're right, but tonight's different."

Buck wheeled the car up the spiraling ramp. "What?"

"Our uniforms. These rented tuxedos. No hippies. No love beads. No meat wagons. No cops with billy clubs."

Buck smiled. "Guess that's progress, but I'd rather be at home watching the Bulls."

"Elliot loves goodwill gestures."

"As long as he doesn't have to attend."

"For the price of a couple of tickets, the Bureau will impress the Mayor's Special Assistant. And maybe we can make some useful contacts in the community."

"We'll see." He shook his head.

The ornate hotel lobby buzzed with a high-pitched conversation from the gathering of Vietnamese Americans. For Buck, it was his first day in Saigon for a moment. Traffic-filled streets choked with multicolored buses, sputtering motorcycles, diesel fumes, three-wheeled cyclo-pedicabs, police whistles, blaring ambulances, and thousands of Vietnamese civilians milling about blending with an almost equal number of ARVN and American troops.

"This must be it, Mike."

It took a moment for Buck to return. They found their seating cards and entered the cavernous gilded ballroom. Hors d'oeuvres and drinks were being served. On duty, they passed up the wine server but accepted a few tooth-picked chicken skewers from a pretty waitress. Tron spotted an elderly couple he knew, and they exchanged greetings. "Friends of my mother's. Haven't seen them for years. "See anyone you know?"

"Actually, I did. The Mayor's boy, Pham Van Tien. He's standing over there."

Tron looked toward the on-stage band and spotted the fifty-year-old, native-born Vietnamese. As the Mayor's Special Assistant for Minority Affairs, he was among the most politically powerful and popular Vietnamese. His black hair was peppered with only a hint of grey, giving him the look of a diplomat. He wore his characteristic broad smile like a kabuki mask, and worked the crowd in the proud tradition of an old-time Chicago politician armed with a two-handed shake and a reverent bow. Tron said he wanted to be the first Vietnamese alderman in the City, but his hard-line political positions worked against him.

"Glad handing as usual. Have you ever met him?"

"No."

"Well, maybe we'll get our chance tonight."

"You know these folks," said Buck. "Who else is a player? Who's the brass?" Buck nodded toward a square-headed, grey-haired man wearing a full uniform of the Army of South Vietnam, including stars and battle ribbons, engaged in a conversation with three women.

Tron smiled. "General Le Dinh. Never goes anywhere in civilian clothes. He's a man with lots of money but no job. Ready to go to war any moment."

"Is he for real?" asked Buck.

Tron sipped on his cola before answering. "Absolutely. A general officer in the ARVN. Obviously, he didn't go down with the ship. It's rumored he not only got himself out safely but also managed to take a fortune in gold with him."

"And the well-preserved lady in the gold dress?"

Tron's eyebrows raised. "Madame Vu Tai Hong. She's the chairperson of the group that's running this show. Very big in Vietnamese society. Not to tell stories, but it has been said that she was a very successful business person in Saigon."

Buck waited for more from his partner. "How's that?"

"Well, again, it is only a rumor, but I have heard she ran a string of whore houses."

Buck chuckled.

"Only a rumor. The Madame's a player on the charity circuit."

"A real Mother Theresa. Well, that's nice. Anyone else?"

Tron scanned the room and noted a tiny man dressed in an immaculate dark blue-vested suit accented with a red pocket handkerchief. As the man studied the crowd peering through gold wire glasses, he smoked a cigarette with a holder, and with an air of dignity, he blew his smoke toward the ceiling. "Mai Van Ba. Attorney. Very successful."

"What's his specialty?" asked Buck.

Tron twisted his head and shrugged his shoulders. "I'd say he's a generalist. There are only a few Vietnamese attorneys in town. They cover a lot of ground. If he has a specialty, it may be wealthy widows. On the other hand, he's even represented some of the White Tigers."

"How?"

"Someone claimed they stole some electronic equipment from a warehouse, but Mai got them off. He's no fool."

"Is he into the cause?"

"You mean to return to Viet Nam? "I don't know. He's doing pretty well here. Why would he want to leave?"

"For the cause. Is he in the National Freedom Union?"

"Sure. And so is the good General and Madame Vu."

"How about Tien?"

"Not officially, but for all practical purposes, he is."

At that moment, three bells rang lightly. The house lights dimmed and brightened again, signaling the end of the preliminaries and the beginning of the dinner. Slowly the guests changed their focus, disengaged themselves from conversations, and quickly found their seats at assigned tables. Buck and Tron looked about for their table. Tron spotted it. "We're moving up, Agent Buck."

"What do you mean?"

"I mean. We're sitting with Dr. Luy Van Le and his daughter. Follow me."

Eight people were already seated. The two remaining chairs were adjacent to a distinguished-looking middle-aged man, and someone Buck recognized, Mr. Wong's niece, Le An. "Welcome, gentlemen." Dr. Le stood and introduced himself and the others seated at the table. "And, of course, you have met my daughter Le An." She smiled demurely at both men. Tron sat next to Dr. Le and Buck next to Le An.

She looked at Buck. "I didn't know you had such an interest in educational matters." Her voice was soft but crisp, her dark eyes welcoming; Buck focused on her eyes, but briefly, his view drifted down to admire her scoop-neck black sequined dress. Without the tailored jacket, it would have been provocative. What remained to be seen was still enjoyable. She noticed and smiled.

"The Bureau purchased the tickets. I'm pretty familiar with the 'rubber chicken' circuit."

He fumbled with his napkin across his lap and adjusted his position to permit two waiters to fill his water and wine. She adjusted, too, leaning into Buck just enough for her elbow to touch. He sensed the warmth of her body. A delicate perfume floated in the air.

"Well, whatever the reason, it's nice to have you here tonight." Her eyes lingered on Buck for a second too long. They didn't speak. Salads appeared. Le An looked around the table, eyeing the others individually, offering each a courteous smile. Dinner began.

The voices around him swelled into a background din. "Vince Gorski tells me you teach at the U of C." His statement floated as she nodded. "What do you teach?"

She rested her silverware and dabbed her napkin gently on her lips. "Economics, with a special focus on the Asian economy."

"How's Vietnam doing?"

She pondered it while he sipped on his wine. "I think the economy of Vietnam is not unlike the economies of other countries transitioning from a centralized controlled State to a hybrid mix of communism and capitalism. Like Russia and the Iron Curtain countries. It's in transition."

"But moving in a positive direction?"

"Yes, as a matter of survival, the current government has opened the doors to foreign trade, and the U.S. government has lifted the embargo. This is encouraging trade. For the moment, mostly with local partners. Taiwan, Hong Kong, Singapore, and Korea. But there are problems."

Buck waited.

"Vietnam remains a communist country with vast entrenched bureaucracies unwilling to relinquish their control. They want *Doi Moi*, but they can't achieve that while maintaining a police state which continues to spy and pry into the lives of every citizen."

"*Doi Moi*?"

"It's the official name given to economic renewal in Vietnam."

"Is that going to work?"

"It could. The economic potential of Vietnam is immense. But people are human. The Party managers want to control the economy in their interest. Too much corruption and ignorance. It would be best if the current political system was changed completely. You can't mix the two systems. In today's global economy, countries must choose one or the other."

"So you are in favor of the liberation of Vietnam?"

"A trick question, Agent Buck." She reached for a glass of water, took a sip, and answered, "I am a teacher of economics, not politics."

"But the two are entwined. Right?"

"Yes, like tea and the teapot, but I study the tea. The leaves, the mix, the spices, the taste, the best weather for growth, and the packaging, but not the pot's design. I leave that to others."

"I guess my Uncle Sam hired me to redesign the teapot."

She contemplated his ambiguous statement. "That was a long time ago. The war is over."

"Even for the National Freedom Union?" Buck watched for a reaction. Father and daughter made eye contact, and Dr. Le gave her a look. Before she could answer, the main course arrived. Buck liked her spirit, but he didn't like the look on her father's face. He wouldn't push for an answer. Tron said something to Dr. Le. He ignored him and leaned in, directing his attention to Buck.

"Agent Buck, I understand from your partner that you spent some time in Vietnam."

"Two years."

Dr. Le's eyebrows raised. "Two tours. Very commendable. What years?"

"67 and 68," said Buck.

A stiff white collar corralled Le's neck. He was a fit man for his age. But it seemed to Buck that his tan and taut skin was almost too smooth. His dark and black eyes revealed little. Le straightened in his chair and nodded. "Those were tough years for everyone. I was there."

Buck didn't respond. His lips pursed.

Dr. Le smiled. "For the sake of your privacy, I will not ask everyone here to join me, but Le An and Do Tron, please offer a toast to Agent Buck for his service to our country."

Buck, obviously not pleased, looked at Tron, who gave him the 'go along with the program' look, and the three lifted their wine glasses to Dr. Le's toast, "To our heroes and friends from the past, we offer our thanks."

Buck mumbled a few words.

Dr. Le continued, "I couldn't help overhearing some of your conversation with Le An." He put his elbow on the table and leaned in. "The National Freedom Union is a fine organization with many functions. It is structured to assist our countrymen in creating a peaceful adaptation into the fabric of American society. Also, to ensure that all our sacrifices are not forgotten. We represent the people of Vietnam in their continuing struggle for freedom." His daughter gave him a look of disapproval. He leaned back. "Perhaps I should not fill the evening air with my pet causes. Tonight we are here for the education of children. God bless them."

Plates were cleared, and the drone of speakers began. All table conversations declined as people focused on the speaker's platform. Eventually, the 'Man of the Year" award was given to a man Tron later described as very rich but with no other redeeming qualities. Then the band played. Couples moved to the center of the floor to dance. Le An asked her father if he would like to dance.

"No, thank you, dear. I have some business to attend to. But you have two fine choices here." He wished them well, excused himself, and headed toward the speaker's table.

She looked back to Buck, her eyes animated. "Mr. Buck?"

"Michael."

"Well, is the prospect too daunting?"

He smiled, and they stood.

Carefully she placed her jacket on the back of the chair, leaving her purse with Tron to guard.

"Have fun," said Tron.

Buck and Le An walked to the dance floor arm in arm. She was almost a head shorter than Buck, but her high heels compensated. They danced well together. For a moment, Buck was back in Saigon with another woman, long dead. Quickly, he let that memory go. He looked at Le An and smiled.

"What is funny, Michael?" she said, looking into his eyes.

"Oh. I guess guys never grow up. I feel like I'm at a high school dance."

She threw her head back. "Well, I hope you're not disappointed. You're here because of me."

"What?"

"I requested the seating arrangements."

"Glad you did."

She paused, and he couldn't tell if she took offense.

"I was bothered by my behavior in your office. Sorry I pressed you so hard about my uncle."

"That's OK. It's part of my job."

"Maybe, but I was a bit obnoxious."

"Well..." he smiled.

"Enough, Agent Buck."

"Michael."

She looked down and said "Michael" softly. They danced the remainder without speaking again and returned to the table. Doctor Le had moved to Le An's chair. She sat next to her father.

"I see you're enjoying yourself." She blushed, and Buck rescued her.

"Well, Dr. Le would you mind commenting about Mr. Wong?" asked Buck. Before he could answer, Le An retrieved her purse from Tron, excused herself, and left the table.

"Not at all. But there is not much to say except that it was regrettable," answered the doctor. "Very sad, but for the fact that he was old and had lived a full life. It is too bad he could not have died in peace."

"You were good friends?"

"I was his friend. There were not many. As I said, he was old. We shared a cause common to many gathered here tonight. We came to this country with nothing and created a new life. To that end, most of us have been successful. Wong ran a nice little restaurant."

"Did you see him often?"

Dr. Le looked upward. "Not over the past few years. I have been busy. Time has flown. However, years ago, we saw each other quite often. I enjoyed his company."

"Did you know he had received threats?"

"Le An mentioned this, and I was shocked. He was not a troublemaker. He kept to himself. I am sure he was a man of modest wealth."

"What about the insurance proceeds on the fire?"

Le's face adjusted to show a hint of displeasure. "I know he was a renter. I doubt his estate will benefit."

Buck glanced at Tron, and his look told Buck to back off. Buck reacted. "Sorry to bother you tonight with such questions. It is not the right time."

Dr. Le nodded without comment. Instead, he excused himself to talk with Pham Van Tien and others.

"I'm glad you stopped the interrogation. I don't think this is the place," said Tron.

"You're right. But he knew about the fire insurance. That's not public knowledge."

Tron corrected him. "He didn't know. He only said he knew Wong was a renter. He's guessing about the proceeds."

Buck nodded. They changed the subject and talked for a moment about other office matters. Then Le An and her father returned. They had a short conversation several feet from the table. Ending it, they approached, and Buck and Tron stood to face them.

"I have to ask you a favor, gentlemen. I have some matters to attend to here. Le An needs a ride home. Could you..."

Le An interrupted. "Father, I can simply take a cab. I'm only going to River North." She seemed annoyed with his suggestion.

Her father continued, "I know, but I feel responsible since I brought you here. I would feel better if you had an escort."

"We would be pleased to help," responded Tron.

"Fine, you have my appreciation. You know how fathers are." He helped his daughter with her jacket. She still looked unhappy, but she said nothing. She kissed her father and the three left.

—CHAPTER FOURTEEN—

Tron's townhouse, about six blocks west of the Hilton, was a short ride, and Buck dropped him off first. Then he drove north across the Loop on Wacker Drive and over the Franklin Street bridge to her place adjacent to the Merchandise Mart.

"I am sorry I've been so quiet," she said, but sometimes my father's protective nature gets to me."

"I'm the same way with my son. I know the mindset."

"How old is he?"

"Fifteen."

"Well, I'm older than that. Anyway, I do appreciate the ride. Is your wife overly protective?"

"I don't think so. We're divorced, and I only get one side of the story. My son's side. I think he's looking for a little more attention. He's asked to live with me."

"Could that happen?"

"Maybe. He's a determined young man. We'll see."

"Is this it?" asked Buck.

"You can just drop me in front."

"I take my responsibilities seriously, Le An. I'd rather see you in. It's a dad thing."

She smiled. "OK. Park in that lot." She pointed to an attended parking lot adjacent to her building. An elevated train rumbled overhead. They parked and entered the former printing company structure, now converted to residential use. His guardianship extended to her apartment door. "I guess we made it safe and sound," she said, somewhat mockingly.

"Hey, don't be too hard on me. I'm only doing my job."

She retracted her keys from her purse and glanced at her watch. "It's still early. Would you like to come in and have a drink?"

"Sure. I'd like to see your place." He smiled.

They entered a spacious, well-appointed loft. Tall windows at the corner faced the river looking east to the lake and north. Buck gazed out into the night. Towering office buildings lined both sides of the river. A lattice of illuminated ornate bascule drawbridges marked the streets between the Wolf Point confluence below and Michigan Avenue in the distance. "Looks like the river is still green from St. Patrick's Day."

From the kitchen, she answered. "It's like that until June. It takes a long time for the Mayor's emerald dye to flush downstream." She held up a bottle. "Red?"

"Fine." He walked toward the open counter, which separated the kitchen space from the combined living-dining area. "Great place."

She handed him a glass, and he followed her. He removed his jacket and laid it over the back of a stool. Carefully he placed the gun and shoulder holster on the counter. The two sat on a leather sofa facing the corner windows. "I'll tune down the lighting so you can appreciate the view," she said. The room took on a dim glow, and the view became a twinkling mural. She held up her wine glass. "To St. Patrick."

"To one of Chicago's finest excuses to drink and be merry," said Buck as they toasted the legendary bishop. She kicked off her shoes and tucked one leg under the other to face Buck. Her black dress flowed over the curves of her body. It wasn't short, but the position she had assumed pulled it above her knees, exposing the softer flesh of her thighs. The wine relaxed him. He eased into the soft leather folds, leaning his head back and stretching his frame.

Le An smiled. "You look more comfortable now. FBI men never relax. Do they?"

"A little uptight?"

"I guess that goes with the job. Always ready for action." She slid over to close the space between them.

Buck curled over, facing her. Their eyes met for only a moment. They sat quietly, enjoying the view and appreciating the closeness of their bodies. Nervous small talk, knowing smiles, and mildly provocative innuendo passed between them. Buck knew the direction of the evening. He eased into the moment without hesitation, subconsciously absolving himself of any possible impropriety.

She drank her wine, downing the last of the glass, and leaned over Buck to place it on the end table. Her softness touched him as she slid across his chest. "You know my father entrusted my care to you tonight. That's very unusual." With one hand, she loosened his tie as she spoke. Her long painted fingernails gently brushed the top of his chest to either side of the dangling tie. He set his glass on the table. She continued, "Vietnamese fathers are very protective of their daughters. My father must trust you implicitly."

Buck smiled, "And you?" She reached out and pulled him toward her gently. Her body moved up his chest.

"Yes," she said quietly, eyes half-closed. Their lips met and lingered. Finally, they pulled apart. "I'd like you to stay if you would like to."

He could think of a few good reasons to leave. Conflict of interest, for one. Or the obvious—a beautiful, too-young woman. However, in the heat of the moment, these speculations quickly evaporated.

About three hours later, Buck, still sleeping, sat straight up and shouted, "No! No!"

Le An awakened. She looked over to Buck, saying nothing, stroking his back. His reaction was fierce. He twisted his torso and flailed his arms, shouting again in garbled speech. She fell back against her pillow to avoid being hit. "Michael. Wake up!"

He appeared to be breaking out of his dream. "Michael. It's Le An. You're all right."

His normal voice returned. "Sorry," he mumbled, "did I hurt you?"

"No, but not for want of trying. Are you OK?"

He shook his head. "Yes."

"What was it?"

"Just a dream."

"About what..."

His lips trembled. "About the war." She looked at him with understanding. He turned his head. "I'm sorry. I've got to go." He got up, picked up, dressed, and kissed her. She didn't seem disturbed by the abrupt departure, only concerned. He squeezed her hand as he went. "I'll be all right. Thanks."

He walked to retrieve his car. Glancing across the street, he spotted a man at the wheel of a grey sedan. The car was not running, and he appeared to adjust his radio as Buck passed. Buck gave no indication that he spotted the man. When questioned by Buck, the parking lot attendant said he had not noticed the man in the car. Buck made a mental note of the car's license plate. Before starting the car, he wrote the number on his notepad, marking the location and time. The car didn't move. He eyed the rearview mirror several times on the way to his apartment. There was little traffic at this early morning hour, and he saw nothing to make him believe he was being followed.

But the feeling in his gut at that moment would stick with him. His paranoia and the aftereffects of his nightmare kept him tossing all night. Over the years, he had had many dreams about his Vietnam experiences. He never talked to his ex-wife or anyone else about what happened in Nam. Feelings of frustration, fear, guilt, and pain had been exposed, digested, and ultimately deleted from his subconscious or pushed into a corner of his mind. Occasionally, after a few too many drinks and sometimes out of nowhere, terrible memories would flash into his consciousness, forcing him to deal with them. He could control his personal hell. Over time, the flames and heat of those incidents diminished. But tonight's nightmare revealed something suppressed for over thirty years and lay before him like a dormant unexploded psychic bomb. Now it was visible and disturbing. As he lay in bed, eyes open, waiting for morning's first light, he wrestled with his conscience until he gave up, got out of bed, drank a stiff cup of coffee, and started his day.

—CHAPTER FIFTEEN—

"I appreciate that, and I thank you for your cooperation," said Buck. He never met the woman on the other end of the line, but every time they talked, he needed something. So he always gave her special treatment.

"Anything for you, Agent Buck," crooned the DMV lady.

He hung up, grabbed his coffee, and walked through the office, which buzzed with morning energy. He found the Professor at his desk, who greeted Buck. "Sit down, Mike. Watson's on his way up. I had him searching files."

"Did he find anything?"

"I'll let him tell you."

Buck turned and smiled at the tall, lanky agent. Nelson O. Watson, Squad 7's resident computer geek, looked younger than his thirty-four years with his sandy-brown, somewhat tasseled hair, wire-rim glasses, and lumberjack shirt. "How are things in the Backroom?" asked Buck. He referred to the Squad 7 semi-secret locally-based computer center located in a DePaul area storefront, a workaround of the Bureau's antiquated centralized, inaccessible, inefficient computer system, which relied on Hoover's infamous but hopelessly outdated, 3 x 5 file card technology. The Backroom was a Sensitive Compartmented Information Facility or SCIF, a physical and electronically secure anti-terrorism facility. Watson's top-of-the-line system connected to similar stand-alone FBI operations nationwide and the internet, providing the squad a formidable crime-fighting tool. He sat next to Buck and opened the manila file he had been carrying. He handed copies of his twelve-page report to both men.

Buck thumbed through the document. "So. What do you have?"

"There is a fair amount of activity and some interesting connections. The Professor and I created a plan of attack to analyze newspaper accounts and other FBI and local PD offices. Look at page two." They both flipped over a page.

Buck read the report. Seven pages listed one hundred and fourteen individual acts of violence or threats of violence over the past fifteen years committed in Vietnamese communities—death threats, arson, assaults, attempted murder, and murders. "You've been busy."

Watson smiled. "Yeah. We may not have them all, but we're close. We've got eight arson-firebombs and one murder-arson in addition to everything else."

The Professor took off his glasses and laid them on his desk. "How much of this is street crime versus organized activity?"

"I'd say a good eighty percent is street crime. The remainder could be more organized. Some of the death threats have been traced to anti-Communist Vietnamese groups. Also, a couple of the deaths, including a newspaper publisher in Virginia, can be tied to Vietnamese politics. But no arrests or convictions."

"Who are these anti-Communists?" asked Buck.

"The biggest is the National Freedom Union. Others are not as big, but maybe more dangerous. Like the group, Vietnamese for the Death of Communists," said the Professor.

"Very subtle," said Buck.

"These groups may only be one with different purposes and target audiences. We don't know. What we do know is that wounds will not heal very quickly. This battle's been going on since World War Two. It bubbled over into America starting at the war's end in 1975, resulting in an influx of Vietnamese refugees. Feelings in the Vietnamese community were intense. Some felt guilty for leaving others behind. Others who were in power in Vietnam sought to return to their positions. And others were Vietnamese patriots. They brought the war with them, and they're fighting it in this country." The Professor leaned back in his chair.

"Difficult to get a handle on. We're dealing with frightened, isolated people with a village mentality. Anti-Communists promote fear in the community and a call to arms. They collect money and purport to use it for men and equipment to fight a war on homeland soil."

"Think that will ever happen?" asked Buck.

The Professor considered his answer. "I think they've had their day. Too much time has passed. However, passions can be aroused easily. Not too long ago that things erupted in Orange County, California. They have a huge concentration of Vietnamese Americans. Maybe 200,000. A video store owner put a poster image of Ho Chi Minh in his shop window. He wasn't even a Commie-sympathizer. The communists had killed his brother. He said he was trying to open the dialogue about Vietnam. The local community was outraged. A judge ruled in the storeowner's favor. But a protest followed. It turned violent, and the guy was severely beaten. Most of these relocated Vietnamese see our current administration as soft on communism."

"And are they controllable by the radicals?"

"Possibly. But even if the general populace moderates its position, there will always be hardcore Commie-haters."

"Let's get back to Wong. Was he involved with any of these groups?" asked Buck.

Watson responded. "We can't tie him to any anti-Communist activity. He purchased some advertisements in their house organs. Nothing new there. Up to now, his name never appears in any file. Except one."

"Did you get into the FCI files?" Buck looked at Watson with a smile.

"Don't I wish? No, I looked at INS.

"Everyone goes through immigration and gets a file. That's important."

"Right." said the Professor. "Here's the kicker. There are a total of fifteen deaths on this list. Sixteen with Mr. Wong. And of those, eight entered the United States on the same day. Including Mr. Wong."

Watson and the Professor smiled like a husband and wife showing baby photos. "That's something," said Buck. "Eight on the same day, and all of them are dead. Any thoughts?"

"I think it's too early for speculation, Mike, but I agree. It's a good start. And it makes the possibility of foul play in Wong's death seem more likely."

"How did the eight die?"

Watson picked up the report and related the data. "Wong, you know about. Others." He flipped the page. "Two throats slit. One bullet to the temple. One auto accident. One jumped off a bridge. One Karate chop to the throat. One clubbed to death."

"Street crime?"

The Professor shook his head. "Some of these look like executions. Or they were made to look like street crime."

"Where did these occur?"

"Four up and down the coast in California. One was in Houston. One in Boston and the last in Virginia."

"That's it?"

"Yes, I think so?"

"Righto, Professor. I think we covered it."

Buck stood. "Great. Everything in here?"

"Everything we have so far," answered Watson.

"Tell me if anything else comes up. Thanks."

Buck returned to his desk and quickly reviewed the files. The Vietnamese names and the descriptions of their deaths made him uneasy. Vietnam still churned in the back of his head, including last night's dream. Abruptly he picked up the phone and connected to Dr. Mathews's office. He scheduled an appointment for that afternoon. He felt better.

He processed paperwork, wrote memos, and made telephone calls for the next half-hour. Then Do Tron appeared. He had not yet been assigned a regular workplace and temporarily shared a desk with Buck. He looked at Buck and smiled as he inquired about what had happened after dropping him off last night. Buck didn't bite and instead brought him up to date on the findings of the Professor and Watson.

"This is getting interesting," said Tron. "I've got something for you." Tron handed Buck a file report to Buck. "I found this by reading back copies of the National Freedom Union monthly magazine. My translation. It's an op-ed by our new friend, Dr. Luy Van Le."

"Le An's father."

"Right. I translated it. Give it a read. It appears to be in response to an earlier editorial put out by General Le Dinh."

"I remember him. We saw him at the ball. They called him the General Patton of Vietnam. Quite a character." Buck read the document.

"My dear General, I agree with your premise that the criminals running our country are the last of a dying breed joined in their final pained breaths by the Communists in North Korea, China, Cuba, and Albania. However, we have no reason to celebrate. The rape of the culture of our homeland will accelerate with the homogenization of politics and economics in Vietnam. The criminal communist leaders of today will become the progressive criminal leaders of the future democracy. I use that word with some sarcasm.

Will we see a multi-party system after the inevitable political window-dressing? Will we see a genuine acknowledgment of human rights, social justice, and the establishment of an actual market economy? I think not. So long as the current players control our country, the roots of their immorality will entwine and choke the true patriots waiting for direction and guidance. We must give those patriots hope and assistance, or else we will end up with the same mobster-controlled democratic anarchy that drives the former Soviet Union today. No, it is not enough to be pleased with the apparent demise of the old system. We must ensure the future of Vietnam includes the traditions of the past, the beliefs, the philosophy, the heart and soul of Vietnam must be preserved.

We have transported our culture to America, carefully maintaining its light like a flickering candle in the wind. We must rekindle that flame in Vietnam. Now is the time."

"Quite eloquent. Obviously. A true believer. Dyed in the wool anti-communist."

"Maybe it runs in the family."

"What are you saying?"

Tron cocked his head. "Daughter like father."

Buck made a face and then answered the phone. A minute later, he hung up.

"Bad news? asked Tron.

Buck rolled his eyes. "You've probably figured out I spent some time at Le An's apartment. When I left about three this morning, I thought I spotted someone doing surveillance on me. A guy in a car. I got the plate number."

"And."

"That was DMV. The plate is not registered with the State. It's a Bureau car. Squad 8. FCI."

"One of Marsden's boys?"

"Those bastards. Marsden's got them tailing me. That son of a bitch."

Tron reflected for a moment. "Maybe not you. Maybe they're tailing Le An."

"Maybe. The FCI can do what they want. I think they're wasting their time, but I don't know what's driving them. They've got something on the old man Wong. If we knew what's driving them, we could avoid getting sucked into a turf war."

"Marsden's not going to tell you, right?"

Buck shook his head. "We need someone inside who has access to those files. We just need a peek. Just to see what's motivating them."

Tron looked out into the air. "You know Rat's on very good paper with Susan Ecker."

"I've heard the scuttlebutt. But she's locked out. Marsden treats her like a doorstop."

"Rat thinks she could be helpful. He thinks she might want to jump ship from FCI to our little boat."

Buck pursed his lips. "Might be worth a try. I'll talk to Rat today." He checked his watch. "I've got to go. You keep working on those tapes. We need to understand what the White Tigers are doing. I don't know if they had anything to do with Wong's death, but we both know they're trouble."

CHAPTER SIXTEEN

Mathews walked in and sat across from Buck. "Agent Buck."
Buck fidgeted in his chair.

"How are things going?" Mathews waited.

"Another dream," Buck spoke slowly. For a moment, his mind drifted.

"Go on," said Mathews. Buck didn't respond. "The dog dream again?"

"No. A new one. About Vietnam." He rubbed the back of his neck. "It was a weird night. I was staying at this woman's place. Vietnamese American. She's involved with a case I'm working on." Buck looked at Mathews for a reaction but found none. "She's only peripherally involved. Not a witness or a suspect. I don't know. Maybe spending time with her set me off. My partner and I attended a dinner for Vietnamese Americans. It brought back memories. Anyway. That night, at her place, I had another dream. Very nasty. I didn't stay the night."

"What about the dream?"

"It made me remember things. Things I'd rather forget."

Buck looked at Mathews and debated getting up and taking off, but he trusted the man and needed to talk to someone. "It was a dream about Nam."

"Go ahead."

Buck hesitated. "You know I wasn't entirely honest with you the last time we met. My Nam experience has been an issue. I told you I left all that behind."

"And you haven't?"

He shrugged his shoulders, wondering if he should open up. Buck was afraid to talk about Nam. Once, after a few drinks with friends, he made the mistake of talking too much about the war.

A simple conversation had unexpectantly devolved into gushing, uncontrollable emotions. Something he couldn't handle. He hated losing control. He looked into the psychiatrist's eyes and willed himself to remain grounded. He moved ahead with the caution of a soldier padding along a jungle trail in enemy territory. "It doesn't go away. It's better now. But I had trouble sleeping. I still do, but not as bad. I kept dwelling on the past. I don't know if you'd call them 'flash-backs,' but whatever, they were there.

"Mike. Use this opportunity to get it out. This is a safe zone. It has to come out sometime."

Buck looked up and pursed his lips. "People got killed."

"It was war."

"But sometimes the wrong people," he raised his voice. Perspiration dotted his forehead. "I saw a lot of shit."

Mathews waited.

Buck shook his head. "Lots of collateral damage. Messy. Guys were wound-up, junked-up, fucked-up. You couldn't tell the players without a scorecard. And there was no scorecard. Just Charlie, the soldier with a thousand faces. So we killed. Sometimes, in the darkness, anything that moved. Anything that threatened us. Anything that made noise. Made us jumpy." Buck stopped. He sat silent, hands folded in his lap.

Mathews questioned quietly, "And you?"

Buck raised his gaze enough to engage the man's eyes again. "Yeah. Me too," he said slowly.

"Go on."

Buck put his hand to his forehead. "A boy." He felt hot. Perspiration dripped from his armpits. "We entered the village on a footbridge crossing a small river. I had the point. Everything was quiet. People milled about on the other side, but they seemed to ignore us. We moved ahead cautiously. Two days before, I had lost two men on a village recon. We were tight. I was tight. Then out of a clump of mostly women, someone came running toward us on the bridge. He was screaming something. The bridge bounced up and down. He had a black bag over his shoulder. I never looked at his face. He kept screaming. The women on the other side were screaming too. My guys behind were shouting. I saw the bag coming at us. I moved my muzzle up slightly. Hardly moved it at all. I don't remember pulling the trigger. My weapon fired and hit the kid with the bag. Almost cut him in half. He went down. Then it was quiet again. No screaming. No shouting. No guns. He twitched and moaned like a dying animal. His mother ran to him and cradled his head in her arms. One of my guys moved ahead and pushed her aside. He grabbed the bag from the dead boy and emptied it onto the bridge. Books. Fuckin' books. I killed the little bastard for books."

"How old was he?"

Buck stared at Mathews and tapped his toes on the floor nervously. "Eight. Nine. He was a kid. Just a kid."

"Any inquiry?"

Buck puffed some air. "No. Just another dead VC. No big deal."

"It is, though. Isn't it?" asked Mathews.

"Yeah."

Mathews rested his elbow on the arm of his chair and set his chin in the clenched fist of his right hand. "Are you looking for absolution?"

"I'd like an answer."

Mathews leaned forward and stared into Buck's eyes. "Think about this. It's today or yesterday, or tomorrow. You're in an alley, on duty. Chasing a suspect. A man with a gun. It's night. You just ran two blocks, and the man has disappeared. Gun drawn, senses screaming, you hear a noise in a backyard. Four or five young punks stand in the yard taunting you. Calling you names. You have no backup. You're focused on them. You move backward slowly until you bump into a fence. And then, a person leaps over the fence and lands in front of you. You're frightened.

Adrenaline flows. You raise your gun. You see something in his hand. Do you fire?"

Buck leaned back. "I don't know. Does it look like a gun in his hand? Is it the same guy I was chasing? Is he breathing as hard as I am? What's behind him? Can I duck out of the line of fire? What are those other punks doing? I don't know."

Mathews smiled. "I don't know either. I wasn't there, and I wasn't in your shoes in Vietnam. Don't be too hard on yourself, Michael. You're not a murderer any more than you would be in that alley. You had to make a decision. You did. Now you have to live with it. Only you can judge whether it made sense at that moment. You're the only one who can forgive yourself. The world will forgive you, Michael. That's done. We forgive you and the others for all our sins."

Buck turned his head, crying quietly.

Mathews got up and walked around his office. Minutes later, when he returned, he stood next to Buck and almost whispered his name.

Buck wiped his eyes and looked up at the doctor.

"Was that the dream?"

"No." Buck drew in a deep breath.

"Tell me about the dream. The nightmare that awakened you at your friend's place."

"I don't know."

"Just go slowly. Relax. Lean back. Close your eyes. Pretend you're in bed dreaming. What image do you have?"

Buck sat quietly, attempting to remember that forgotten. Finally, he spoke. "I'm in the bushes."

"Where?"

"I'm in the bushes alone. They got my dog."

"Who?"

"VC. I can hear their voices. Vietnamese. My dog is yelping. But I can't move. The brush is like a maze. But I don't even try to get through it. I'm frozen. Afraid."

"Afraid of being hurt?"

"No. Afraid that they're hurting him."

"Who. Your dog?"

"Yes. Terrible sounds. VC laughing."

"What else?"

A few seconds pass. "I can see something. A hand with a knife over bare flesh."

"Whose flesh? Your dog?"

Buck sputtered, "No, a man. The knife cuts open his gut. Blood. Screams."

"What are you doing now?"

"I'm stuck where I am. I can't move, but I want to move."

"What about the knife?"

"It's gone," Buck answered, breathing heavily. "A hand reaches into the gut and pulls something out." Buck stopped and looked at Mathews. He put his hands to his face and emitted jagged gasps. He moaned as he curled into a ball and sobbed.

Fifteen minutes passed. Buck, quiet now, spent, didn't move. The doctor offered him a glass of water, and Buck wiped his face and thanked him. He sipped the drink while he regained his composure.

Mathews cleared his throat before speaking. "Are you OK?"

"Yes," said Buck quietly.

"Good. Who was the man? Do you know?"

"I know now. Yes."

"Tell me."

After a long pause, Buck recalled the story. "Just before Tet, we were sent out on a special mission. Long-range recon. Our guys suspected the VC were sending a large group of spies south. We were inserted just...." He caught himself and held back the location. "At twilight, the Huey dropped us behind the lines. A five-man squad. Anyway, the next morning, we found Charlie. Everywhere. I should say he found us. We were pinned down in a firefight. I lost three guys. Real quick." Buck swallowed. The words wouldn't come.

Mathews waited. "Continue."

Buck nodded. "Only my Vietnamese guide and I were left. A guy named Van Chuong. We held out, but not long. We were captured. There were too many of them. Blindfolded and hands tied behind us with bayonets in our backs, we stumbled through the jungle. They tied me to a tree. I figured I would be shot. I think I said something not so nice about their mothers, and somebody hit me in the face with something hard. I went out."

Buck put his hand to his chin and turned his head. He showed Mathews the long scar that ran across his jawline. He ran his hand over it as if to draw out the memory of that moment. "When I came to, it was late in the day. I was lying half-naked at the base of the tree. Alone. But I heard something. The blindfold had loosened. Out of the corner of my eye, I saw Charlie. One guy. Sleeping and snoring. Maybe ten feet away. I figured this was a one-time chance. I fought with the ropes until I broke free. I didn't wake him. I grabbed his sandals. Then I got out of there."

"What about your guide?"

Buck looked dazed. "He was gone. I searched the area. I had no weapon. Then I heard voices. Screams. As I got closer, I saw my guide tied to a tree in a clearing. I lay hidden in the tall grass. Maybe twenty yards from him. His face was all beat up." Buck took a deep breath. "I was useless. I couldn't do anything. They would make him talk. Probably VC Intelligence. Three guys worked on Chuong while two others stood guard. I couldn't catch it all. But Chuong kept his mouth shut. I couldn't see any of their faces. Two VC had hold of him.

The leader had a knife. Chuong's blood dripped from the blade. Before finishing his job, the guy with the knife took off his shirt and handed it to one of the guards to hold. He didn't rush. He taunted Chuong and sliced into both shoulders one by one. Not too deep. Provoking him. Torturing him. I'll never forget the weird nasty hook scar on that guy's chest. It looked like he had been branded with a hot iron. That was all I could see."

"My guide gave them nothing. The man continued to cut into him. First, his chest. Then under his arms. Then finally, his gut. This went on forever. He screamed. I watched him die as they pulled out his guts. Then slit his throat. They didn't have to kill him that way. I wanted him to confess. Something to save his life. But he wouldn't. Stubborn man. I was glad when he died." Seconds passed. Buck shook his head. "But I killed him too."

"What could you have done?"

Buck's eyes drifted toward the ceiling. "Nothing. I was stuck." He paused. "At first, I couldn't watch. I covered my ears. When I knew he was dead. I got out of there. No one ever found him or any of the others on that mission. Only I survived."

"Did you ever talk to anyone about this?"

"After I escaped, I covered a lot of ground. Many miles over rough territory. Navigating by feel. Eventually, I heard some of our big guns firing and crawled toward them. I was lucky. After four days, I made it back to one of our firebases. But by that time, we had Tet. My recon mission was no longer important. Everyone knew where the enemy was. Charlie was right in our faces and all across the country."

"How do you feel now?"

"Sad. Very sad."

Mathews appeared to choose his words carefully. "For now, when you can, I'd like you to think about this incident in light of your partners Barrett and Hansen. This dream and what happened in Viet Nam have great meaning in your life. Can you see that?"

Buck reflected. "I see where you're going, Doc. I might be a little hyper."

"Your words, Agent Buck." He smiled. "But for certain, the past can frame the future. People try to avoid reliving the painful parts of their past. This applies to everyone. Many veterans have to deal with it. Once you see how these past events impact your current decisions, you will better understand your actions, feelings, and relationships with others."

Buck contemplated Mathews' words. "PTSD?"

"Yes. But don't let a name bother you. Once a problem is recognized, you've opened the door to remedy the problem."

Buck cocked his head and looked up at Mathews. "And my job. The FBI. This isn't going to be an issue. Is it?"

"I don't believe it will. That's not something you should worry about. You are still in control of your work and your life. It's really up to you, Agent Buck. I am only a guide." They talked for a few more minutes before Mathews called an end to the session.

CHAPTER SEVENTEEN

The Professor stepped out of his office and waved Buck in. Still recovering from his visit with Mathews, Buck reacted slowly. "Mike. I need to see you for a few minutes."

"Sorry. My mind was elsewhere."

"Come on in." They stood facing each other. "I want you to be careful with this, Mike, or it could blow up in your face."

"OK."

"Our friend, the Mayor's Special Assistant, Mr. Pham Van Tien, is a part-owner of a real estate firm with his two brothers. They own a few multi-family residential projects in the neighborhood. Tron tells me 'street talk' has it some of the fires over the past year may be insurance-related arson. This doesn't square with police reports. The last confirmed arson was sixteen months ago."

"Like Wong's place. Inconclusive."

"Right. Lots of inconclusives. Anyway, I looked up the ownership of Wong's building. Land trust. I got a court order and sent Tron over to LaSalle Street to talk turkey with the Trustee. He got the lowdown on the owner. Guess who?"

"Tien?"

"That's correct. I've asked Tron to correlate the other neighborhood fires over the past two years to check for an ownership pattern. This will take time, though. He has to find the fire reports. Check building addresses against real estate tax numbers. And if in trust, we need more court orders. I wonder if Tien's company owns some of these other burnouts?"

"How long will it take Tron?"

"Most likely by the end of the day tomorrow. Tron should be able to clear them all by then. Nine fires were investigated."

"What about the one arson?" asked Buck.

"Not Tien's. That building was owned by Morris and Edwards. Downtown boys. The owner of a failing body shop who rented it from them decided to burn the place down for the contents insurance proceeds. He's coming up for retrial again next month. They threw out the first conviction. Illegal confession. The arresting officers forgot to offer an interpreter to the firebug. In any event, that one has nothing to do with Tien."

"I'll see Tron tomorrow evening at the Zig Zag. You coming?"

The Professor cleared his throat before answering. "Mike, you know I'm not much for the nightlife. Marilyn and I will be at home tomorrow night, as always. We're planning our trip to San Francisco. The financial retirement symposium. She's very excited about it. Loves that stuff. I guess I'm lucky. Without her, I'd be just another retired cop with a gold watch and empty pockets."

"Lucky man." Buck turned and drifted toward the door. He looked back and spoke quietly. "Don't mention the Zig Zag to Elliot. He's not fond of official business being conducted at a bar."

"Got it," he responded with a wink.

—CHAPTER EIGHTEEN—

Indochine, located on the lake in Uptown adjacent to the area populated by Vietnamese Chicagoans, maintained an authentic colonial Vietnamese menu. Le An and Buck were seated at an intimate table. White table cloths, rattan armchairs, palm plants, ceiling fans, painted scenes of Vietnam during the French colonial period, and soft, rich colors replicated an enduring theme capturing the pleasant paternalism of possibly the late Twenties or early Thirties. They shared some *try goi cuon,* spring rolls stuffed with a delicate combination of shrimp, vegetables, rice noodles, and mint. Buck called them egg rolls, which according to Le An only reflected his epicurean ignorance, a fact that he did not deny. However, he recovered and ordered a perfect white wine, the second glass of which took them beyond such critical commentary and into a more exciting and sensuous phase affirmed by a hand-holding communion: a quiet time they spent gazing into each other's eyes. To an outsider, they may have appeared as lovers. Their silent spell was only interrupted by the arrival of dinner: *bo cuon la lot* for him and ginger-spiced trout for her. They ate, laughed, and drank their way through the better part of a bottle, tackling conversational subjects without depth or import. The joy of the moment written on their soft faces and in their placid eyes went unsaid but known. The stuff of love songs and poetry was too much for either to handle early in a relationship. It ended when she spoke first.

"Why did you leave that night? What was the dream?"

Buck looked at the beautiful woman and hesitated. Then, much to his surprise, the entire dream unfolded, revealing his secrets. Somehow with her, it came easy, but he did not disclose details of the torture of his guide. She listened patiently. She did not interrupt. Only at the end of his monologue did she comment. "Now I understand. You have carried this weight for a long time, Michael. Maybe somehow, I helped to bring this nightmare into the light. You will be a better person because of it. I forgive you for leaving me." She reached forward and took his hand. Her dark eyes connected with his. "But never again. OK?" She smiled. He smiled.

"You know I am lucky to have you here. So many died. Your guide was tortured for one reason. To get information. You were soldiers. You're still a soldier."

"But…" Buck shook his head. "I came out alive."

She touched his hand. "The Vietnamese say: 'Sometimes the smartest action is inaction.' But being right is only a part of life." A few seconds of silence passed.

"Enough. Tell me something about you. I've dumped on you, but you've been inscrutable."

She smiled. "That is our way. What are they thinking? We're like house cats." She quipped. "All right. I'll open up. That's fair. What do you want to know?"

"Tell me how you got to this table. You were born in Nam, right?"

"Yes, I am a child of the war, although I was too young to understand it. In Viet Nam, I believed the entire world was based on movement and uncertainty. My family struggled. We fought the French and our own people. Grandfather was a freedom fighter with the Viet Minh. He lived in Saigon but was killed by the Nationalists after the French were defeated at Dien Bien Phu."

"Why?"

"Somehow, he was perceived as a Communist, although this was not true."

"Because Ho Chi Minh was the leader of the Viet Minh?"

She sipped on the last of her wine before responding. "If everyone who fought with the Viet Minh were Communists, there would have been no Viet Nam War. My grandfather was a poor

113

merchant who was caught in the crosswinds. They killed my grandmother also."

"These were your father's people?"

"Yes." She leaned back in her chair. "I know nothing of my mother's people. My father does not speak of her. It is too difficult for him."

"And your father."

She smiled. "My father, against all odds, was befriended by a rich acquaintance of my grandparents. A government person adopted my father when he was in his teens. I don't know why. Although I suspect he may have had something to do with my grandparents' deaths, my father has never explained. Maybe it was out of a sense of guilt. Anyway, this man had enough power to keep my father out of the fighting. Otherwise, he would have been in the war just like you. But he was sent to school. Eventually, medical school. I think my father met my mother then. She was killed by 'friendly fire'". She stopped.

"Americans?" asked Buck.

"I don't know. I don't even know if this is true. It is something I understand from listening to my father. His tone. Sometimes when he has had an extra drink or two."

"OK. How about you? How did you get here?"

"Almost there. When the Americans left Vietnam, my father only had his black bag, and I. It was rough. The Communists treated their new southern citizens harshly. They found out about the man who had adopted him. He was killed by the Communists. I don't know why they did not kill the two of us. But we were treated like dirt. Father cleaned bedpans and bathed patients at the hospital. He had no money or connections. Finally, he decided to leave. We became boat people, eventually arriving in the States. I was just a little kid. First, I lived with another family, but he sent for me in time. By then, he had the money to make it happen. I arrived in Chicago and began a new life. Then, you and I met at the dinner, and here I am."

"You forgot the part about acclimating to a new country. Schooling. Achievement. You're too modest. Anyway, glad you made it. He reached around her shoulders and leaned over, and kissed her on the cheek. She smiled like a little girl, and with that, her eyes quickly searched the room to see if others were watching.

After dinner, they walked the neighborhood west of the restaurant. Hand in hand, her shoes clicking on the sidewalk, they drifted along.

"Great dinner."

"I'm glad you liked it. You know Vietnamese cuisine is considered one the finest in the world. We took the best of the French and best of the Chinese."

Buck looked at her face as they continued to walk. "You know you have a bit of French in your face. Is that possible?"

She laughed lightly, seeming almost embarrassed at the question. "Michael. I told you my personal history. If you see French, then I am French. If you see Chinese, then I am Chinese. If you see Japanese, you are seeing things." She smiled.

He pulled her closer as several teenage boys bobbed along the walk, passing them wearing toothy smiles as gifts to the pretty lady. "You're a big hit tonight, Le An."

"Given a choice between you or me, I get the smiles from the boys. The women are all yours, Michael." She smiled at him. They stopped and kissed again, but she pulled back. "You know we should not do this."

"What?"

"Public displays of affection are frowned upon in this neighborhood."

"Oh. So sorry." He kissed her again.

"Michael," she shook her head in exasperation.

Dark now, they walked and admired the delicate glass figurines in the glow of show window lighting. Buck broke the magic of the moment. Propped up against one corner of the showcase, a cardboard advertisement for the National Freedom Union beckoned. "Your father's group. Always promoting."

She pursed her lips as she looked at him. "Dedicated to the cause. They are a serious political force in this country. My father works with them on behalf of freedom for Vietnamese." She pulled back from him. "You know, it's funny Americans applaud the Germans, Hungarians, and Poles for shedding the Communist yoke, but if the Vietnamese work for the same cause, they are criticized."

In defense, he put his hands up in front of him. "Hey, take it easy. I'm not the enemy. I put in two tours, remember?"

She grabbed his arm with two hands and nuzzled her head into his shoulder. "Sorry." Her muffled plea was answered when he pulled her closer.

"Le An, you may be right, but I see your Union friends running with some bad people."

"Like who?"

"Like the White Tigers. Why is a nice clean democratic group cozying up to a gang like the Tigers?"

"Why did Hoover cozy up to the Mob in World War Two?"

He smiled. "*Touché!*"

"One last question."

"Yes, Agent Buck."

"What about Pham Van Tien? Did you know he owned the building your Uncle Wong Suu died in?"

She looked down as she walked. "No."

"Did you know he owns quite a few buildings that have burned to the ground?"

She stopped walking. "Michael, Special Assistant Tien is a good friend of my father. He was also a close friend of my uncle. I am certain he had nothing to do with his death if that's what you are suggesting."

"I wasn't suggesting anything. I just wondered what you had heard. What about this Tommy guy?"

She grimaced. "Tommy Mac is just a kid. Not too much older than your boy. He just needs some positive direction. I'm on his side. My father and I try to help him."

"Tron said about the same thing."

"Tron's right. He's a young man who's trying to move away from the gangs. He's not much older than your son. Maybe seventeen. His father is dead, and his mother and three sisters live in a three-room apartment. I think he's up to here with women. The gang is one alternative the community offers. My father gives him odd jobs to help him make ends meet.

"Well, be careful. You can take the boy out of the ghetto, but you can't take the ghetto out of the boy."

"Michael. You're showing your prejudice."

He shrugged his shoulders. "Hey, I'm an FBI agent. Not a counselor."

She let his hand fall away, and she stopped walking. "Are we done with this? You know you have a way." She looked hurt. "I thought we were on a date. Am I wrong? When do you go off duty?"

Buck feigned surprise. "Ah. A date. Now I remember. Have I told you 'You look beautiful?'"

She tilted her head and brushed back her hair. "No, not enough."

"You look," he held her delicate face in his large hands, "very, very beautiful."

They kissed. She pulled away.

"You know. You're a difficult man to understand. In that way, you are like my father."

The comparison was not lost on Buck. He didn't need a reminder.

—CHAPTER NINETEEN—

From time to time, Rat and Susan Ecker cooperated. They lunched together with some regularity, Rat had a belly full of real-life street-cop stories, and Ecker loved to hear them. Her career with FCI was routine and unexciting. Her bosses didn't share and didn't care. She was perceived as a well-educated office assistant. But at a gut level, she wanted to work the streets with Squad 7. Helping Rat learn more about the Wong incident might move her career in another direction.

She usually blended into the office background like everyone else. But today was different. To the FCI co-workers who greeted her that morning, she may have appeared unusually sexy. As she walked through the office, she noticed their interest. Her techniques for distinguishing herself were subtle. She had carefully created her new image. Even without her moving, the simple tan leather pumps had just enough heel to flex her calves delicately, stretching taut the sheer of her nylons. Her tight wool skirt reached her knees but squeezed the flesh as she walked. The smooth white silk blouse invited the eye to watch for the movement of her substantial breasts, well-shaped and, with her careful bra selection, not restrained. A simple gold band adorned her wrist while a small gold bird pin crusted with tiny jewels clung to the silk below her left shoulder. Her hair was up and stylish, and a light dash of perfume completed the magic of the plan she and Rat had evolved, that of an alluring spy. The cloak and dagger work excited her, and the fact that they compromised her boss's files only increased the excitement.

She fingered the bird pin, which roosted below. It contained an electronic lens, which peered out from a clear round eye about the size of a mustard seed. She wore a 'wire,' a microchip embedded in the bird that acted as an electronic retina. Wires were taped above her left breast, ran loose under her armpit, taped down at her waist, and terminated in a transmitter in the small of her back. The flounce of her blouse effectively concealed the presence of the small flat box which connected her by radio wave to her Squad 7 comrades. She remembered Rat's admonition not to cloud the lens and quickly removed her fingers from their grasp on the bird's tail. Earlier, in the washroom, she had waved to the camera in the mirror. She hoped Watson enjoyed his voyeur viewing. By now, he would have adjusted the device and activated the videotape. Last night, with Watson and Rat coaching her, she had practiced with the camera, learning to avoid sudden movements and aim it directly at a target. After about two hours of this effort, Rat proclaimed she was the "Best Breast in the West." He advised her to simply point her nipple toward the target and shoot. She knew what had to be done once in Marsden's office.

She spotted Marsden carrying an empty coffee mug and moving quickly out of his office down the aisle. She knew his routine. A cup of coffee, a trip to the washroom, then back to the kitchen to reload. When he arrived, he found her waiting.

"Ah. Good morning Agent Ecker," Marsden slid the phony greeting through a fake smile. She returned the smile. He moved toward the coffee maker but then looked back at her. Standing erect, holding a manila file folder in her hands, her body in profile, she pretended to look at a bulletin board announcement. At that moment, she knew Marsden's routine was broken. He looked at Ecker as if he had never seen her before, gazing upon her body. She looked back at him, almost catching his eyes lingering.

"I was just thinking," she said almost as if she were talking to herself, "I could use your help if you have a few minutes."

Marsden poured his coffee and moved closer to her. Maybe her scent came into play. "How's that?" he asked.

"I'm working on that Russian report, and I'm having a bit of trouble understanding the chain of command. You're an expert on the Russian underworld, right?". She smiled.

Marsden shuffled his feet. "I've been watching these guys for ten years now. What's your question?"

Susan moved into his personal space, and he didn't back away. "The computer mentions a guy named Yaroslavovich who has been seen in New York. He owns a manufacturing firm in Queens. Yaroslavovich is suspected of being involved with money laundering for the organization. He could be a bagman for someone in White Plains named Breshkovsky. According to the computer, he works for Vinodoff, the big guy. But I can't figure out where he fits in the organization. The computer seems to have nothing on him." She moved back a little, and he did the same.

"I've heard of them, but I don't keep a file of every two-bit Russian mobster in my head. Have you checked the international database?"

"Yes. Nothing there either. But maybe I'm not tracking it right. I'm getting automatically spun back into the main file every time I access it. Is there another way?"

"Have you tried accessing the New York office's computer?"

She shook her head. "No. I can't get into New York with my clearance."

Marsden nodded. "Right."

There was a pause. Susan took a deep breath as if somewhat frustrated. Her breasts heaved beneath the silk blouse, and their movement did not go unnoticed by her boss. She waited. "Maybe I can help. Come in my office, and I'll pull it up on my machine." She smiled, and he followed her to his office. She waited for him to take his seat at his computer terminal. "Have a seat," he nodded to the chair.

"Thanks. If you don't mind, I'll stand. Sitting all morning." She needed to be standing to capture a view of his fingers upon the keys. Marsden had carefully positioned his monitor to prevent visitors from seeing it. However, he didn't consider the need to curtail any view of the keyboard. He could not suspect he was about to be violated by his attractive if not loyal, servant. She positioned herself almost behind his monitor, which maintained a view of the keyboard. As his fingers worked, Ecker aimed her nipple exactly as Rat had suggested. In a moment, the deed was done. Marsden keyed in his password and entered the computer of the New York Bureau office. Her view had copied the sequence on videotape. With computer enhancement, Watson could easily decipher Marsden's password. With that information, he could enter any file, including the Wong file, and electronically copy it in seconds. After cleaning the house, he would leave behind a confusing trail that would not alert Marsden that his files had been compromised.

With a few more keystrokes, Marsden finished his search. Her mission complete, Agent Ecker sat down in the chair before him, releasing a sigh. He looked at her. She smiled brightly. "Any luck?"

Misinterpreting her breathing patterns, he responded, "Don't worry. I'll get it." Five more seconds, then he read from his screen. 'Semen Breshkovsky.' Nice name. Employed by New American Trucking', a local cartage firm owned in part by Vinodoff,". Marsden hit the print button, and the file began to spit out of a printer. "It's all there. I'll make it easy for you Agent Ecker. I'll make a copy. OK?"

"Great. I really appreciate this."

He lifted the three sheets from the printer, handed them to her, rose from his chair, and looked into her eyes. "Susan, anytime I can be of help, I would be happy to see you." He smiled his best smile, which Susan would later describe as positively reptilian.

"Thank you, sir. I'll keep that in mind." She turned quickly. She knew he would be watching. Her movements were more provocative than would be expected or permitted by a Bureau Agent. She left wearing a tiny smile: mission accomplished.

—CHAPTER TWENTY—

The Zig Zag, a cop bar located in the noisy netherworld of Lower Wacker Drive, was a safe venue for a team meeting. Its private back room offered a place to play cards, swap stories, and, for Squad 7, a place to plan their attack tonight. "Shut that door, Vince," ordered Buck.

The veteran cop closed the door, which eliminated the raucous sounds of the adjacent bar area. Still, the meeting room's beat-up wood paneling and patched ceramic floor tile accentuated the din. Noisy disjointed conversations ping-ponged about. A large ceiling fan barely rotated, relieving the heat as it blended a malodorous cocktail of stale air, second-hand smoke, and sweat. The members of Squad 7 waited below in a loose circle of chairs and small tables, second drinks in hand.

Like a rumpled ringmaster, Buck, his jacket removed, the armpits of his white shirt dampened, and his tie dangling loose, stood amid his assembled troops. Sensing the meeting could quickly devolve into a rumpus, he took control. "Sit, Andre. Please. And cut the chatter, everyone. Time to start the proceedings," barked Buck wearing a half-smile, the other half all-business.

"But, Mike. We were just discussing the possibilities of Ecker's porno film career. Those nipple-camera shots of hers in the ladies' were spectacular." Rat looked over to Susan Ecker, who sat across the table.

"Anything for the team." Ecker enjoyed the attention.

"Great work, Susan. Let's move on," said Buck. He looked around the room. "First, let's welcome Pete Hansen back to the action." Sitting next to Buck on his right, Hansen smiled and took a mock bow to his friends' cheers and scattered applause.

"Thanks. Good to be back. Thanks, Mike, for inviting me." Hansen gave Buck a knowing nod and smile, signaling that he and his ex-partner were still blood brothers.

"We're going to need some help from your Political Corruption Squad, Pete." Buck got back to business. In detail, he covered Wong's several visits to the Bureau, his death, the FCI denials of any relationship to Wong, their surveillance of Buck, Susan Ecker's video odyssey, the history of the National Freedom Union and its Chicago representatives, the dangerous nature of the White Tiger gang, its probable relationships to the National Freedom Union and its crime patterns in the community. Setting down the last note card, he looked around the table. "Vince. What about the autopsy. Anything new?"

One of two new team members in the room, Jena Ward, sat beside her mentor Vince. She moved her chair to make room. Vince stood and removed his jacket. "Fuckin' hot in here," he said as he set his massive, hairy forearms on a tabletop and leaned in for emphasis, looking more like a Chicago politician than a cop. "I spoke with the M.E.'s office today. They got the tissue sample results. No trace of poison. But they did find a chemical they couldn't identify. I asked Dr. Washburn to do an inch-by-inch on Wong's body. He found a tiny puncture wound in the palm of Wong's right hand." He leaned back. "That's it."

"So?" asked Buck.

"So. Washburn doesn't know. The unknown chemical could be anything. From some kind of cleaning agent to prescription medicine. He said it would be very tough to I.D. it, and the pinhole could have been caused by a needle or some other sharp instrument."

"Hypo?" asked Andre.

"Don't know. Wong could have slammed his hand into something during the fire. A nail or a kitchen tool. A very tiny hole about a quarter-inch deep. The M.E. officially declared the cause of death as heart failure. Not killed by the smoke or flames directly. That's all we're going to get out of them. Doesn't say yes or no to murder. We don't know how the fire started, but we do know Wong was trapped. Mike and I saw the padlocked back door. Bad luck or intentional?"

"I looked into that," said Chuckie Gleason, the rookie. "I checked with the restaurant delivery truckers. I talked to three of them. They all said Wong kept the back door padlocked. They brought deliveries in through the front door. Only grease and garbage went out the back. Probably once a day. They all wanted Wong to use the rear door for deliveries, but he wouldn't. Concerned about security. I spoke with the Health Department also." He flipped through the pages of a small notebook. "Inspector Raceck has that area. He didn't remember if the door was padlocked, but he gave the place reasonably high marks for being clean and bug-free. That's about it." He flipped the notebook closed. "Oh, and the fire department never looked at the place before the fire. So far as I know. But the padlocked back door was a code violation. The place needed two exits." Gleason leaned back in his chair.

"Thanks." Buck's eyes shifted to his Vietnamese partner. "Tron's been reviewing tapes of a White Tiger phone tap and also tracking burnouts in the area. Got an update?"

Looking relaxed and calm, Do Tron, dressed in a dark blue suit, white shirt, and tie, popped up. Holding his hands together in front of him, he appeared prepared to speak. "My review of the real estate records shows that Pham Van Tien's group owned the building Wong died in. One of Tien's brothers is an insurance agent and co-owner. They filed a claim on that fire which is still pending." He nodded. "However, other buildings owned by the Tien group have burned. Five in total. All these fires were ruled accidental by Bomb and Arson. All resulted in fire insurance claims and awards to Mr. Tien and his brother. Lastly, one building was located on Wilton Avenue. Wilton Avenue is mentioned on the White Tiger pool room tapes at a time just before that fire."

"I remember that one," Vince chimed in, "sounded like a go-ahead from some big guy, right?"

"Right," said Tron.

"Pham Van…the Man…Tien?" suggested Rat.

"Can't say that. Yet," said Tron, "the dates of the tape do mesh with the fire in Tien's Wilton Avenue building."

"What about voiceprints?" Asked Susan Ecker.

"You mean did we compare the voice on the Tiger tapes to Pham Van Tien's voice?" asked Buck.

She nodded. Buck looked around. Rat shook his head, wearing a goofy smile and beaming it to Andre. Buck flung him a grimace before getting back to Susan Ecker. "Excellent idea. Any tapes of the Mayor's boy exist?" No one answered. "Professor?"

The older man sucked on a dead pipe, pulling it out just enough to talk. "I'm sure we have something in the archives. I'd be pleased to research it myself. But I'm leaving for San Francisco tomorrow. Why don't you provide that Wilton Avenue tape to Watson? He'll find prior tape on Tien in the files and compare them. But…" He tapped the contents of his pipe into an ashtray.

"But what?" Buck asked.

"But we may be moving into uncharted and hazardous waters, Mike. Tron says Pat Roche was informed that investigations into anything related to Pham Van Tien should be dropped. That came from someone in the Mayor's Office."

"Are you saying we lay down on a possible murder-arson because we might disturb Hizzoner?"

The Professor continued to toy with his pipe. He looked out into space. "It's your case, Mike. I'm just pointing out a tilt in the playing field."

Pete Hansen cleared his throat in the silence that followed that comment. "I can verify the Special Assistant's clout. It's real."

Buck changed his approach. "You're right, Professor. I appreciate your advice. We have to cover all the bases with discretion." Buck leaned against a wall and smiled. "Tell us about your vacation plans."

The Professor relaxed in his chair. "Well, Marilyn is going to learn all about triple-A bonds or something, and I'm going to check out those eight Vietnamese boat people who entered through Frisco immigration on the same day." He looked around. "For those of you who don't know. Those eight are all dead now. All violent deaths. Like Wong. He's one of eight. Interesting, eh?"

"A toast to the Professor. The man never quits," shouted Rat, lifting his beer glass above his head.

The toast drowned any tension in the air. Chit-chat erupted. Buck tapped his beer bottle on the table with no effect. Then placing two fingers into his mouth, he created a piercing and attention-getting whistle. "Thank you," he said with a smirk. "Since we seem to be taking a break of sorts, I'd like to formally introduce the new guy." He focused on the man at the end of the table who, until now, had said nothing. "Eusebio. A quick bio, please."

The new guy, early thirties, handsome, dark-skinned, shaved head, wearing black slacks, a black silk shirt, and a smart gold chain, smiled. "I am Eusebio Martinez. Been with the CPD since I was nineteen. Detective. This is my first week on the Squad. I guess I'm the new kid on the block." He smiled. "Any slack you can cut will be appreciated."

"Slack. My ass," offered Rat with typical diplomatic flair.

Andre shook his head at Rat. "Don't mind, Mr. Rodent, Eusebio. He failed charm school. Welcome aboard." Andre's deep voice resonated with confidence and certainty and was reflected in the new man's look of relief.

Buck brought them back to attention. "OK. Moving on. Thanks to Ms. Ecker's efforts, Watson could dig out the FCI files on Wong. They show that FCI tried to open him up as an asset."

He checked his notes, "There's an undetermined source named CHICAGO 16 G1279 who says Wong was a fringe member of the National Freedom Union but is suspected as a possible Communist because he was a boat person. Wong's name has been associated with Dr. Le, a prominent physician. As you know, I have been followed by FCI when I spent time with Le's daughter."

The men all rolled their eyes and smiled. Someone cleared his throat. Even Susan Ecker adjusted her position.

Buck ignored them. "According to the files, several FCI high assets have been reporting on my activities, so I must be doing something right."

"We hope so," said Rat.

They laughed. Buck waited, then resumed. "The Wong files are minimal. Maybe it's a setup. There may be deeper files. We don't know. All we know is that Marsden's boys are very protective of this case for some reason. But I say," he paused and held back the epitaph, "that's too bad. We've got a legitimate case, and as far as we know, it's ours, not theirs." He looked around, looking for a dissenter. There was none.

The meeting proceeded in a relatively orderly fashion. Some guessed the identity of the FCI unknown source, and others suggested opinions about the Wong fire. Buck was good with the banter. It kept everyone focused on the problem. However, after Rat went on another raucous rant about Susan Ecker's candid camera, Buck decided to put a cap on the bottle. "OK. OK." He settled them down. "Before we call it an evening. Let's recap. Professor's going on a busman's holiday to San Francisco to check out immigration records on our eight bogies. Pete, you're going to check out Tien's invisible clout shield. Vince, why don't you talk to Watson about a match on those Tien tapes." Buck looked at Tron. "I think we should also keep an eye on that White Tiger poolroom. The one CPD bugged."

"I've been thinking on that, Mike. Thinking a lot. I suggest we put a close watch on it. We know they're dirty, but they're also smart. We've been monitoring them with one car intermittently. Very ineffective." Tron lowered his eyes and then looked back at Buck. "We need four cars to make this work. There are too many people coming in and out. Can we get that many?"

"I'll talk to the boss. How many days?"

"Five minimum," Tron answered without hesitation.

"Four cars. Five days," said Buck. "Nights only?"

"Yes, that's fine."

"When?"

"Now."

"Right."

"We will have to be very good, or the Tigers will make us," said Tron.

Rat set his beer bottle on the table, holding it with two hands in front of him. "Squad 7 is always outstanding, right?" He looked around. The team members nodded and grunted. "Right," said Rat with conviction. "Damn right."

—CHAPTER TWENTY-ONE—

Buck wheeled his car up the Lower Wacker Drive off-ramp. His cell phone rang as it cleared air space above the concrete superstructure. He had a feeling about the caller.

"Where have you been?" asked the familiar voice of Elliot. "I've been trying to get you for two hours."

"A good evening to you too, Thomas."

"Don't give me that 'good evening' shit. Do you want to be removed from the Wong case?"

Buck's mind raced. Elliot was pissed. "Sorry, boss. We had a team meeting tonight at the Zig Zag. I forgot to invite you."

"Forgot bullshit. But that's not the problem. The problem is one Mr. Pham Van Tien. I got a call from the Mayor's Special Assistant himself not two hours ago. He says our investigation of his real estate holdings is slandering his name in his community, not to mention on the Fifth Floor of City Hall."

Buck swallowed. How the hell did Tien get wind of their investigation? Tom, there is no investigation. Or hardly any. We got wind of some heat. I've got Hansen checking it out discreetly with the PC unit. No one has been slandering the man."

"Tien says you," with emphasis, Elliot repeated the word "you," then continued, "have been slandering him. That you have stated that he burned his real estate to the ground for profit."

Buck remembered last night's conversation with Le An. His words somehow made it to Tien. Things were slipping away. "I mentioned the possibility of arson to one of my assets. She must have passed it on."

On the other end, Elliot could be heard almost muttering to himself. "Well, you better pick your assets and your words more carefully. Who are we talking about?"

"Le An," answered Buck with resignation.

"Dr. Le's daughter?"

"Right."

"Buck, there's talk about you and her. I suggest you watch where you are going. We've got a job to do, you know?"

"Right," Buck replied flatly. "Lecture over?"

"Just doing *my* job, Agent Buck. You do yours."

"I'm trying. I'll watch my step with Tien. But if I step in dog shit, I hope you don't mind the smell."

"Don't worry about that," Elliot replied in a quieter and more positive tone. "Just be a little smarter. I'll get back to Tien and massage him."

"Good. Now we want to lay a net on the White Tiger clubhouse. We need a four-car team for five days. Can we get that?"

The airwaves went dead for a moment of Elliot's thinking. "OK, four cars, five days. Who's running the show?"

"Tron."

"All right. But keep me in the loop, Mike. Understand?"

Buck knew one more fuck-up, and Elliot would pull him off the case. "Not to worry. I'm your guy, boss."

"Good." Elliot's exhaled his final word in relief.

Buck also was relieved. No more permissions would be required for the next five days. He had a free hand.

—CHAPTER TWENTY-TWO—

The living room of the vacant second-floor apartment offered a clear view of the front entrance to the White Tiger clubhouse one block distant. Tron gazed out the window. It looked like a scene from an early 90s video game, a simple but unreal reality simulation. Within this urban trough, oversized cars silently slid along Broadway, a black and grey asphalt path framed by two-story red brick buildings illuminated in the garish yellow light of sodium vapor streetlights. Tron knew the area and had selected the 'perch.' As a Chicago cop, this was his beat.

Years ago, the gang's building was a corner grocery store serving a local population of middle-class city dwellers. In the 60s, it was converted to a country-western bar, a waterhole for the heavy-drinking, heavy-smoking, bar-fighting redneck painters, drywallers, and handymen who had wandered north to Chicago and occupied the deteriorating Uptown neighborhood housing. The late 70s brought a massive surge of Asian migrants who doubled up in the large apartment buildings, blowing out most previous residents. On the night that John Lennon was shot, a knife fight broke out in the bar, the Jackson Hole as it was then called, resulting in the death of two good old boys and a padlock on the door courtesy of the Chicago Police. It stood vacant for about five years, then the White Tiger moved in and made it a home away from home for nearly thirty Vietnamese boys and men. It was a base of operation for the exciting world of semi-organized crime practiced by the largest Vietnamese gang in Chicago. Tron knew that for most of the youthful members, in addition to the fast money and status among peers, the Tigers offered an exciting and Westernized alternative to boring traditional Vietnamese family life. But for many of the sons of immigrants, it was also the first step leading to prison.

The 6 p.m. to 4 a.m. watch continued the third night of the surveillance mission. Tron checked his watch: 11:22. The dim blue light from the video monitor set the tone for their work. A microwave signal beamed from a camera mounted on the building parapet across from the White Tiger clubhouse, providing the feed to the monitor. The two Squad 7 men worked surveillance. Tron and Chuckie Gleason took turns watching. Initially, Gleason had been enthusiastic about the operation. He wanted to connect the Tiger gang to the Mayor's man, Pham Van Tien. But twenty hours of watching the black and white video screen dampened his zest. The usual comings and goings of young bangers toting pool cue cases or six-packs of beer were tedious. Occasionally loud, sometimes even boisterous, the supposed Viet bad boys looked like non-threatening and typical American teenagers. They hung out, wasted time, and did nothing that would interest any lawman. This fact had not slipped by the rookie. He gazed at the monitor and then at Tron, who sat in an aluminum lawn chair reading a book illuminated by a clip light at the top of the page.

"We're running out of time. This is day three of a five-day gig."

Tron looked up. "Patience, grasshopper." His bright eyes offered wisdom and hope. "The tiger will enter the trap sooner or later. Watch the screen, please. We don't want to miss anyone." Then he returned to the book.

"Right," said Gleason. He sipped his cola, set down the drink, stretched his arms out, and yawned. Then he caught a movement in the circle of a streetlight that illuminated the area in front of the old Jackson Hole building. "Hey. Got something. Look." Tron set the book on the floor and scurried to the monitor. The camera viewed down and slightly to the left of the building entrance.

"Zoom in a little," demanded Tron. Gleason pushed the lever of the remote control. The black and white figures of a bent-over man, about forty and one of the gang members, appeared larger. "I've seen that one before. The young ugly looking guy. That's Ky."

"Who's he?"

"I think he's a handyman for one of Tien's buildings. That big one on Sheridan Road." On-screen, the man turned toward the camera as if on cue. "Yes, that's him." The older man had a package under his arm, which he handed over. Ky grabbed it and nodded. Then turning his back on the man, he quickly reentered the clubhouse. The other man drifted out of the camera view.

"A drop?" asked Gleason.

"Yes. Maybe a drop," responded Tron as he grabbed his walkie-talkie. Static cleared as he depressed the button and quietly spoke. "Eagle to Buck. Come in."

"Buck here."

"See that? What happened to 'package man'?"

"He left in an old maroon Buick. No time for a tracker. But we got the plate."

"Good. Anything else happening?"

"No. Still quiet."

Tron and Gleason listened for a few minutes more. Another voice broke in quickly. "Rat here. We've got movement out the back. Four guys. Quick departure. Something's going down. Stay clear." Moments passed. "They're in a green Olds. Heading north on Kenmore. Should we follow?"

Tron answered quickly. "Affirmative. Move out. But give them room."

"Copy that. Rat is now tracking the cat."

"Eagle to Buck."

"Buck here."

"You on this? Take the west parallel."

"West parallel, copy that. Heading north on Broadway."

"Eagle to Crow."

"Crow here," answered Vince.

"Take the east parallel."

"Got it. We're moving out now. Heading north on Sheridan," Vince's distinctive voice vibrated from Tron's transmitter.

Tron smiled at the rookie. "Your patience is rewarded, Chuckie. Just like the movies. Buck and Eusebio on the west. Vince and Jena on the east. And Rat and Andre have the chase car."

Tron's receiver came alive. "Rat here, we're dropping out. They may have spotted us. Crow, you pick them up," said Andre.

Seconds passed. "Got it," Jena's soft voice crossed the airwaves.

"Back on the east parallel," said Andre.

"Crow here. Got 'em. They're turning west on Lawrence. Watch for 'em, Buck. Can you take 'em?" asked Vince.

"Right. They just passed us. We're back on them," said Buck. "Crow, you go north to the next major. We'll take them for a while. Rat, where are you?"

The tiny speaker scratched out words. Andre answered. "We're heading for Wilson. South parallel".

Minutes passed. Tron grabbed the walkie-talkie. "Talk it up, guys."

"Rat here. On Wilson. Twenty-one. Twenty-two hundred heading west."

"Crow here. We're heading west on Foster. North parallel."

"Buck here. We still have them in front of us. Crossing Western Avenue. Maintain positions." A few minutes later, Buck's voice jumped out. "Turning north on California. We still have them. They're slowing down. They made a right turn on Agatha and parked just beyond the next alley east. Got eyes on them. Suspect car is now parked mid-block between California and the next street east. It's not moving."

Tron checked his map. "That next street is Holland. Crow, move into position on Arnold. That's one block north of Agatha. Hold the intersection of Holland and Arnold. But don't expose your position."

"Copy that," said Jena.

"Rat. Take Washtenaw north. Wait at the intersection of Agatha and Washtenaw. Let's see what they're up to."

"Copy that," said Andre.

Buck spoke. "Four men, all dressed in black, exiting the car. Heading north in the alley. One is carrying a duffle. Possible weapons bag. I say again. They may be armed." Five seconds passed. "Buck here. We're taking a position on Agatha behind the suspect's car. Sending one on foot to check on them."

CHAPTER TWENTY-THREE

Eusebio came back to the car, out of breath and sweating. He flopped into the passenger seat. "All four are standing in the backyard near the alley. Six houses in. Whatever they're up to is happening on the next street over."

Buck checked his map. "Suspects have entered the backyard of a house on the west side of Holland. Six houses north of Agatha. Crow, park on Holland facing south. Stay well short of the middle of the block."

"Copy that. We're two minutes away."

"Rat, head west on Agatha. Hold short of the intersection of Holland and Agatha. It's one way against you, so watch yourself."

"What's goin' down?" asked Eusebio.

Buck looked at him. Beads of sweat glistened on his forehead. His chest heaved. "Settle down, my friend. Take a deep breath."

"What?"

"Relax. Take a deep breath."

The other agent obeyed.

"Another."

Again he breathed deeply. He looked over to Buck. "Thanks," he said quietly.

Buck saw Rat's car approach with headlights out. It parked just short of the intersection. Buck flashed his headlights, and Rat returned the signal. Buck drove ahead. As they passed the suspects' car, he glanced in—empty. Eusebio looked at Buck. He said nothing. Buck caught his glance. "Just hold on. Unhook your seat belt." Sheepishly, Eusebio released the mechanism. Pausing the car, Buck tapped his fingers on the steering wheel. He looked left across the fenced backyards between him and the sixth house.

"See anything?"

"I can't see anything. Too damn dark."

Buck drove ahead, made a left on Holland Avenue, and parked.

"Suspects' car is empty," said Buck. "Rat, send one up the street on foot in front of the house. Then roll west and block in the suspects' car. You take a safe position at the north end of the alley."

"Copy that."

"Eagle to Buck," Tron interrupted. "Where are they now? In the house?"

"Unknown," said Buck.

"There's Andre," said Eusebio.

Buck looked to his left and saw Andre running along the sidewalk on the other side of the street. In the rearview mirror, he saw Rat's car cross the intersection.

"Andre, we'll join you in front on foot. Hold your position. Rat, take a position in the alley. Vince, take the back with Rat. Jena, stay with the car at the intersection."

"Andre copy."

"Vince copy."

"Jena copy."

"Rat copy. I'm in the alley now." Seconds later, he came back on. "I think they're in that house. Shades are being drawn."

"Eagle here." Tron's voice tensed. "You may have a home invasion. Are you sure about the house?"

Rat came back, "No."

"Wait, we'll check name-address." They waited about a minute and a half until Tron broke in again. "The sixth house is owned by Nguyen Manh Duc. He's a banker. I've met him. That's the one. This is a hostage-rescue. Get into the house. Now. Get a plan. Blow cover. You're plain clothes. Whatever. If you wait, someone may die. Copy Buck?"

"Copy. We copy. Stay clear." Andre waved to them from a position partially concealed by the bushes of the neighboring

137

house. The two agents exited their car and trotted across the street. While the other three huddled and talked in hushed tones. Buck looked up at the first-floor window of the neighbor's house. A little blond-haired girl watched them. He waved at her, and she smiled. Buck offered his impromptu plan to the two others. "Diversion at the rear. Bust down the front. Old but simple," said Buck. He radioed the scheme to Vince and Rat, waiting in the backyard. They agreed to move at the count of 'three.'

"Well, you stick with a winner," said Andre.

Eusebio's brow furrowed. "That's it?"

"That's it. We're going in. Now."

"I'm not wearing a vest, Mike," said the youngest agent opening his palms in a gesture of apparent helplessness. "They're in the trunk. Should I get them?"

"No time. We're all going bareback tonight. Andre, you're going to have to pop that lock quick."

Andre held up the wrecking bar he had pulled from the back seat of his car. Standing at the base of the concrete stairs, he looked at the front entry door of the brick bungalow. "No deadbolt. Just a latch. It should pop. I hope." He smiled.

"Andre and I will enter. You stay in this position. If one of those guys tries to leave, he's yours. Most likely, these fellows are well-armed. So don't take chances. Got it?"

Eusebio's brow glistened. "Yes, sir."

"Fuck the 'sir' shit. Just don't shoot us. We may be back sooner than you think," said Buck.

"Right." The rookie nodded and extracted his weapon from its holster. Andre and Buck did the same. Just then, a woman's scream came from inside the house.

Buck spoke softly and quickly into the transceiver, "Back door. That's our cue. We're ready. Let's go. One. Two. Three. Moving now." It took Vince and Rat about ten seconds to reach the back door. The men in the back made all kinds of noise. Later Rat said he broke at least twenty small panes of glass in the back porch while Vince muscled through the two-bit hardware securing the half-glass wood door.

Buck heard shots fired. A semi-automatic weapon. He ran up the steps and held open the screen door while Andre shoved the crowbar between the door jam and the doorknob. In one quick, steady motion, the knob flew off and bounced across the concrete front porch and down the steps. That noise, compared to the din in the back, went unheard. The diversion worked.

Without hesitation, Buck inserted the blade of his knife in the hole where the knob had been. A short turn and the latch opened. He pushed the door wide open. Screams and sobbing could be heard somewhere. Vietnamese voices mixed in. Buck entered.

"Buck here. We're in." He moved quickly, taking a position in the living room near the fireplace. He crouched low, invisible in the semi-darkness. The space had been ransacked. Desk and table drawers, loose papers, and all the little junk from the drawers were strewn over the Oriental rug. Lights blazed in the rear of the house. An open door leading to the basement blasted a shaft of light down the hall ahead. Andre stayed in the vestibule concealed behind a wall.

In the back, more shots were fired. A gruff voice, maybe Vince's, commanded something. "Vince here. Perp on the run coming your way." Someone approached fast. A man, breathing heavily and wearing black pants, a black tee-shirt, and a ski mask, ran past Buck without seeing him. Buck watched him stop short at the open door, frozen for a second.

Andre rammed the barrel of his 44 into the man's left temple. He offered no resistance as the big agent shoved him against the wall and removed his mask. "On your stomach. Now." The man dropped down. Andre searched him with dispatch finding no weapons. In the dim light of the vestibule, the man's outstretched arms exposed crudely constructed gang sign tattoos on both biceps and similar hieroglyphics on each finger of his left hand.

Eusebio reacted quickly, cuffing the young gangbanger, and then led him outside, forcing him to lie flat on the lawn. He read him his rights.

—CHAPTER TWENTY-FOUR—

Tron arrived with Chuck Gleason. They pulled in ahead of Buck's car. Tron ordered Gleason to take care of their capture. He followed Gleason as he dragged the man across the street. Tron spoke in Vietnamese. The man did not reply. He said the same thing three times. Then, crouching before him, Tron leaned over and delivered another message, his mouth inches from his right ear. Words slowly oozed from the man's mouth. Another question from Tron yielded another answer. One last question and answer: Tron patted his captive's head lightly and arose. Tron rushed toward the house while Gleason maintained his watch. Approaching Eusebio, Tron quietly questioned him. "Who's inside?"

"Buck and Andre. Buck to the left. Andre in the vestibule."

"The others?"

"Plan says they're out back making noise. Shots were fired. Nobody reported hit."

"Civilians?"

"Don't know. We heard a scream. A woman."

"OK. Stay here. Radio this into CPD. I don't want those boys guessing who's who. Tell them this is an FBI Task Force operation. Tell them we interrupted an attempted robbery, which resulted in a hostage situation. Have them work with Jena to set a perimeter and evacuate the neighbors," he said as he moved up the steps with cat-like movements. Eusebio nodded, moved back to his area of concealment, and contacted Jena directing her per Tron's instructions.

Tron met Andre in the vestibule. Buck acknowledged Tron's presence with a lift of his chin. Only the muffled sounds of women sobbing could be heard. Tron radioed. "Eagle to Crow."

"Crow here. All's quiet. We're in the backyard. No shooting for a while. We got one guy who tried to run. Rat's sitting on his head. We're OK."

"We have one of them cuffed in front," said Tron. "That leaves two in the house. Maintain your position. We may flush them out."

"Copy that," said Vince.

Tron called Buck back with a wave of his hand. The three huddled in the small vestibule. "What's up? asked Buck."

"The guy out front told me Ky and one other guy are holding a family of four in the basement. Mother, father, and two young daughters. Hostage situation. I know the man that owns this house. I've met his wife and children. I will try to get them to give up some of the family. They've already cut off the father's finger. They needed a combination for a safe. Andre, you hold this position. Radio Rat. See if he can quietly break into a basement window to get inside. I'm going to talk to them. Buck back me up."

"Wait a minute," said Buck before Tron could turn away. "Don't take any chances. You know the book. Give them some time."

"No time. Ky has a nasty reputation. I'm sure he performed the surgery on Manh Duc's hand. He's a trapped rat now. We've got to release some pressure on him. Give him some room."

"Maybe we should give him a lot of room. He's a two-time loser. He may not care about living. Think about it."

"I am," said Tron. He stripped off his jacket and folded it carefully, placing it on the arm of a dining room chair. Retrieving his holstered gun, he handed it to Buck. "This one's my call, Mike. I understand these people," he said to end the discussion. Then he walked toward the opened basement door. He stopped about eight feet from the doorway and spoke loudly in Vietnamese. He gave them his full name and professional identification. A voice responded from the basement. Tron told him they were surrounded and it was futile to continue; the entire neighborhood was ringed with police. "Release the family now. Give up."

The men below did not answer, but their low voices revealed a discussion, maybe between the two gang members. Then sounds of furniture being pushed around were heard. The woman screamed again. The girls could be heard crying. The unmistakable sound of flesh being swatted and the victim moaning followed. Tron listened intently and then looked back to Andre. "What about Rat?"

"He's in. Backroom," Andre whispered.

Tron edged closer to the door. "We are waiting," he said, "and we can wait forever. Release the woman and children, Ky. Their crying is making it difficult to think. You are a man. Leave this to the men." After a few moments, Tron heard Vietnamese filled with expletives.

Ky spoke in Vietnamese. "We're sending the bitch up. She's all yours." Soon the sobbing victim, a middle-aged, slightly built woman bleeding from the corner of her mouth, still wearing pieces of the grey-colored duct-tape handcuffs, appeared at the top of the stairs hysterically, gesturing and speaking rapidly in her mother tongue. Tron grabbed her, calming her in Vietnamese with a soft voice. Then he quickly passed her off to be handled by Buck and Andre.

"That's good, Ky," said Tron. "We're making progress. You are fortunate. No one has been hurt. It is a good time to end this matter. What do you say?"

Again, murmurs of discussion could be heard from the basement.

"Now, how about the two girls. You don't want them to get hurt. No good can come from involving them. Imagine if they were your sisters. Hurting them can only reflect poorly on you, Ky. What do you think?" Tron waited for a reply. "Ky?"

"I hear you, Mr. Policeman. All right. I'll send them up, but you come down. Just you. No guns. We can talk face to face. Any funny stuff and the girls will be playing piano with stumps for fingers. What do you say? A fair exchange, no?"

Buck made his dislike of this option clear. "Forget it, Tron."

Utterly calm, Tron looked at Buck directly and held his gaze for seconds. "This must be done. I've got back up. I'll make sure Rat knows what's up. Be prepared to fall back if I ask you to. Keep everyone but you and Andre out of the building. Wish me luck," he said as he turned toward the stair. He spoke more loudly than before in a voice sure to be heard by Rat. "Send the girls up, and I will come down."

Hoarse laughter bounced up the stairs. "Right. That won't work." A few seconds later, Ky spoke again, "I'll give you one. Then you come down, and we'll send the other up. OK.?"

Tron answered. "Good. Send her up."

Girl's voices cut the air of tension. Tron heard them complain about leaving their father. Good daughters, but not the time for such loyalty. "Come up now, young lady, now," demanded Tron. Footsteps on the carpeted steps signaled the girl's arrival. She poked her head out the doorway like a wary prairie dog leaving its burrow. Her dark wet eyes met Tron's. He beckoned her toward him, and she ran to him. He held her briefly, then looked at her face. "Are you all right?"

"I'm fine, but my father..."

"We're waiting, Mr. Policeman. You better get down here, or maybe I'll change my mind," the voice boomed from the bottom of the stairs.

Buck gently grabbed the girl and pulled her away while Tron moved to the top of the stair. He presented himself knowing he was a perfect sitting duck. His eyes searched, and he saw Ky, heavyset and sweating, aiming an automatic weapon at his midsection. Ky could cut him in half in two seconds. He reacted and eased his hands up as a show. "May I come?" he said in a clear, steady voice.

"Come. Come, my friend. But don't fuck with me. You better not be armed."

Tron did not hesitate. "I am not."

"Come."

Tron tiptoed the descent. He got to the third stair from the bottom before the leader spoke. "Stop. Turn around." He caught a quick glimpse of the agonized face of the pale, diminutive owner of the house. The other gangbanger buried the barrel of his pistol into the head of the seated man. The banker's daughter sat against the far wall whimpering. She looked at Tron with terror in her eyes. Tron turned to face the stairs. "Bend over and touch the stairs." Tron did as ordered and bent over, grasping the carpeted tread with both hands. It was clear that Tron was weaponless, but Ky grabbed both of Tron's ankles and released them.

"I told you. No gun."

"Come down slow. Backward." Tron gracefully descended the stairs, heels first, until he felt the gun barrel in his back. He recoiled slightly, then recovered. "Keep coming. Put your hands on your head."

Very deliberately, Tron interlocked his hands behind his head and looked about as he eased off the last stair. He looked around. The remodeled wood-paneled basement had been turned inside out. The green felt of the pool table was littered with overturned boxes hurriedly dumped in the quest for valuables. Someone had kicked a hole in the television, and a wall panel had been ripped off its hinges, exposing an unopened safe. No sign of Rat, but a door at the rear of the large recreation room could conceal his presence.

"Move next to your friend, and sit."

Tron sat about three feet from the homeowner. He looked at the man's hands. The good one tightly held the other in a bloody attempt to arrest the pain and disguise the reality of the evil deed. Tron nodded at the man, offering comfort with his eyes. "So I am here now, Ky. It is time for the girl to leave. That was the deal."

145

Ky's cold, black, non-blinking eyes fixed on Tron. A badly-healed scar ran from his right ear connecting to a corner of his mouth. When he smiled, it only made his face more hideous.

Tron cleared his throat and straightened his posture. "It would be best if the young lady was sent upstairs. I will tell my men she is coming."

"Keep your mouth shut, Mr. Policeman. I am in charge here." Turning to the girl and wearing an imperious look, he raised his chin in the direction of the stair. With this single gesture, he motivated the young girl into movement, painfully slow, then faster, as she realized she was almost free. Her eyes hung on her father's face as she moved toward the stairs, and then, released by some look in his eyes, she raced up, climbing with feet and hands spider-like to the top.

As she made her way up, Ky ordered her to close the door. Someone closed it. The latch clicked shut.

"Very good, and if the gentleman could be permitted medical attention, maybe his finger could be reunited with his hand."

"And what do we get for Christmas, Mr. Policeman?" said Ky. His buddy nervously chuckled.

"Do Tron."

Ky's face shed his crooked smile like a snake leaving its skin. "We want out of here. We don't want your bullshit. The old man has his fucking finger. We gave it back to him. We want out."

"Would you like something to drink? Some coffee, tea, maybe a sandwich?"

"No. Fuck the coffee. What about it? We don't have all night." Ky raised the barrel of the AR-15 pistol nestled in his arm.

"Look, Ky. You know who I am. I'm a Chicago cop."

"An FBI dick now moving up the dick ladder, so I hear." Again Ky's buddy chuckled. "Shut up, Skate." The young man buttoned up in mid-chuckle.

146

"I'm on loan," Tron talked, almost to himself, maybe for a brief moment aware of his place in the universal scheme. He recovered. "What's next, Ky?"

The corner of Ky's small lips turned upward. "That's better. One thing at a time. First, we're moving upstairs. Tell your dick buddies to move out. I don't want anyone up there. Tell them to get out and close the door behind them. Now." He moved next to the homeowner and ripped apart his hands. The finger dropped to the floor. "Fuck, there it is." He picked it up and flipped it to Tron. The little red trophy bounced off his chest into his lap. Ky pulled out a knife and held the man's good hand.

In Vietnamese, the man yelled out, crying, "No! No!"

Ky looked at Tron. "Go ahead. Tell them." He held the blade on the thumb of the trembling hand. He cocked his head sideways. "No fuck-ups, or I'll take another."

Tron yelled loudly, directing Buck and Andre above. Soon footfalls were heard, and the door slammed.

"Skate." The younger man jumped at the mention of his name. "Take a look upstairs."

Somewhat reluctantly, Ky's boy made his way up the stairs. In thirty seconds, he returned. Breathing heavily, he spoke. "They're gone. There's no one up there."

"Good. Take our banker buddy up. Stay low in the living room. I'll follow with Mr. Policeman."

Skate pulled the banker off the floor, smashed him into the stairs, grabbed him by the back of his collar, and lifted him enough to get his legs moving. The banker clasped his hands together again in pain and shock and climbed up, followed by Skate. Tron watched them disappear into the darkness above.

"Stand up and turn around."

Ky faced him, with the gun pointed in Tron's direction. "Don't worry, I'm just going to cuff you. That way, we eliminate problems. All right. Cuff your one wrist."

Tron reached behind to retrieve his cuffs and placed one section on his left wrist.

"Both hands behind your back."

Tron turned and moved his hands behind him. He felt a strong hand grab his wrists and clamp the remaining cuff shut. Then seconds of nothing. The hair on his back raised in a primitive reaction to the sound of the blade of Ky's knife snapping open. Tron swung around in a pirouette. In one clean motion, Ky drove the knife at Tron's middle. His hands, useless and cuffed behind his back, nevertheless strained the shackles in an attempted defense. Still, his exposed middle lay bare like the waiting gut of a pig to be slaughtered. He knew he was dead.

Then the room exploded with gunfire. Two quick shots created a deafening noise in the confined space. One missed and ripped into the wood paneling to the right of Tron. The other sliced through the left side of Ky's neck, blowing out pieces of pink flesh. Ky wore a look of pain mixed with surprise, but his knife had momentum and continued along its arc toward Tron's belly. Then a third shot caught his head dead-center. Ky's skull exploded with a chunky, watermelon-like mist spraying into the air at supersonic speed. Wide-eyed and open-mouthed, frame by frame, Tron captured every detail etched in his mind, with eternal knowledge, without fear, knowing that Rat had saved his life. He knew he had made a terrible mistake. The warm, wet, disgusting flesh and blood splattered on his face was his violent baptism into the faith of his calling, the religion of his brotherhood, and the belief of the living. Something rolled about in his mouth. He spat out a chunk of Ky's brain.

He heard Rat bark into his transceiver. "Rat here. Go! Go!" In seconds, window glass broke upstairs. Teargas canisters bounced about on the floor above. The world remained in slow motion for Tron but not for Rat, who flipped the light switch, dropping the room into blackness. Soft echoes of light sliding under the door above outlined him as he crawled up the stairs.

Tron was stunned. Intense ringing filled his head, but he heard distant sounds from above. Muffled coughs, men shouting orders, police sirens, a door busted open, Rat's voice, Buck's voice, Andre's voice, a body hitting the floor. Tron had not moved an inch. He was plastered against the wood paneling throughout the entire movie. Now he quivered and sank into a motionless lump. In the dark, his mind went blank.

The door above opened, and the room filled with light. Smoke swirled hypnotically. Rat pulled off his mask, smiled, then coughed as he descended the stair, still gripping the 357 that had saved Tron's life and ended Ky's. Tron stared at the gun, Rat, and Ky's headless body.

Rat shook his head. "What a mess. Turn around, Tron. You don't want the boys seeing you like this," said the little man. He holstered his gun.

Tron rolled over and turned his back to Rat, who keyed the cuffs open in seconds. He shook his wrists in freedom.

Rat sniffed and chuckled. "Forgot to duck, eh? You look like a Jackson Pollack."

Tron blinked. "What?"

"Forget it, brother," said Rat. He handed him a handkerchief. "Here. Fix your face. You look like shit."

CHAPTER TWENTY-FIVE

Tron brushed himself clean, and they climbed out of the basement. Upstairs, he recovered his composure and walked quickly to the door. A sobering gust of cool night air hit his face. Jena, Vince, and Buck stood at the bottom of the concrete steps. An ambulance arrived, and one attendant treated the banker's hand. The other had gone down to the basement to retrieve the finger. His family huddled and cried. The two cuffed prisoners lay on the grass guarded by Eusebio. "Bring one of them here, please," said Tron to Buck. Buck retrieved the man he and Andre had captured and held him to face Tron. He grabbed the boy's arms and examined the tattoos with disdain. "Who gives you orders?" The boy did not speak. Tron's face became contorted. He ran the palm of his outstretched hand down his soggy chest like a lint brush collecting a coating of blood and bits and pieces of Ky's flesh. He shoved his hand into the boy's face. "This is all that's left of Ky. Do you understand?" The boy nodded, his lips quivering. "Now. Who gives you orders?" demanded Tron.

The boy looked at Tron's hand. "He did."

"And what was in the package that was delivered tonight?"

"Magazines."

Tron looked quizzical. Then Jena spoke. She held a black and white magazine, "VNFU, the Vietnamese National Freedom Union magazine. We found about fifty in the trunk of their car. We also found these. She held out a blue-paper letter-size page of Vietnamese printing."

Tron grabbed it and read. "An advertising agreement for the magazine," he said slowly. He looked at the gangbanger. "So you're an ad man. How much?"

"They pay us two hundred an issue. We keep fifty for selling them."

"You mean extorting them," corrected Tron, not expecting an answer. "Who gets the money?"

The boy didn't answer.

"Who?" Tron said, his voice rising.

"Ky collected it."

"For whom?"

"Fuck if I know. I just sold them."

"What about tonight?"

The boy almost smiled. "Supposed to be an easy deal. You know."

Tron nodded. "Right. Easy money."

Vince broke off to talk to two uniformed Chicago cops who had arrived on the scene. "You done with him, Tron?" asked Vince. Tron nodded, and Vince rolled his eyes toward the perp. The two beefy men in blue surrounded the boy and half-lifted him across the ground, tossing him into the back of the meat wagon. Eusebio brought the other man over, and he joined his comrade. One cop slammed the door of the wagon shut and shouted to Vince. "See you in church, Gorski."

Vince laughed. "Take care of our catch, Teddy boy." He watched the wagon roll down the street, now blocked off by uniformed Chicago squad cars at both ends. Vince turned to face his task force buddies as they chattered together: Buck, Tron, Jena, Andre, Eusebio, and Rat. Someone had provided a round of coffee and some donuts. The cops kept reporters from the action, and the Squad members could relax and enjoy the break. Vince's booming bass cut through the chatter. "Hey, Tron. You, OK, Buddy?"

Tron smiled and shook his head. "Thanks to my friend Rat, yes."

"Well, let me tell you. You're not the first cop to get involved in a showdown. Remember that Westside standoff, Rat? The domestic."

151

Rat chuckled. "How could I forget it. You tell this story every time we bend our elbows."

"Hey, these kids haven't heard it," said Vince referring to Jena and Eusebio, "maybe they'll learn something."

Jena smiled.

"So..." said Eusebio.

Vince had captured an audience. He took a swig of black coffee and lit a cigarette before speaking. "Two beat cops. One older guy and one new guy..."

"Who can remain nameless..." interjected Rat.

Vince waved Rat off. "Right... anyway, they responded to a domestic. One of those hot, sweaty August nights on the west side. Maybe two...three in the morning. Action's just beginning. Anyway. These two take a 'man with a gun' report. It turns out it was some guy holdin' a gun on his mother. God knows why. Money. Dope. Don't remember. By the time the two cops get there, this guy's standing at the top of the stairs. His piece up against the mom's head. They've got their guns out too..."

"So they get the guy to waltz his mother down the stairs holding the gun on her..." interjected Rat.

Vince rolled his eyes. "Hey. Who's telling this story? Me or you?"

"OK, OK."

Vince continued. "So now everybody's in the lobby of some shithole apartment building. It's hotter than hell, and they got their guns on him, and he's got the old woman. Now the one cop, he's a nice young fella with some college. Maybe took a psych course. I don't know. Anyway. He sweet-talks sonny-boy into letting his mother go. She cuts out, and now it's the three of them. It's a Mexican standoff. Sonny-boy has his gun pointed at them. They got theirs pointed at him." Vince sucked on his cigarette and talked out the smoke. "Now, these boys are in close quarters. So you know somebody's goin' to get hurt. They order him to drop his weapon. He ain't droppin' nothin'. A minute passes. Then two. Everyone is sweating bullets. Bystanders are shouting at the perp to shoot."

Finally, the young cop gets inspired. He says to the perp, real-calm like, 'Look. We all want to go home tonight in one piece. Right?' And the perp thinks about it and nods his head. But he keeps his weapon pointed at them. So the kid continues. 'On the count of three, let's lower our weapons and set them on the floor. OK.?'

Meanwhile, his partner is givin' him the look. Never mind, the perp looks like he might be fallin' for this, how should I say, unorthodox approach. The kid starts lowering his revolver just a little while he's talkin' to this guy. 'Now, I'm going to begin counting to three,' says the college boy.

'Are you ready?' The perp doesn't say nothin', and neither does his partner, who by this point is goin' nuts. Finally, this goofy kid starts countin': 'ONE,' he says." Vince chuckled to himself. "And right then, the old cop fires whatever cannon he's holdin' and blows a hole in perp's chest. The guy goes down out of commission. And the old cop looks over to the kid and laughs, and laughs, and laughs."

"The kid. He's all shook-up now and a little embarrassed. He's lookin' at the crowd, who, by the way, are really pissed now. Shoutin' and spittin'. And then the young cop looks at the perp, shrugs his shoulders, and says, 'You know. I thought I could talk him down.' The old cop stops laughin' long enough to tell him he should have been an air traffic controller. Not a cop. Then they both start laughin'."

"Did the guy die?" asked Jena.

"Na. He made it," replied Vince with a wave of his hand. "The kid's a good cop now too. I know his old man. Kids. They think too much." The veteran cop then looked over to Do Tron, "So Tron. Don't worry. There's a helluva lot better shooting stories out there than yours."

Tron smiled. "I hope so. I'm just happy to be able to listen to your B.S., Vince."

They all laughed because Tron was lightening up. After the violence he had faced that evening, it was a good indication that he would handle it well. Half an hour later, the evidence team arrived, weapons were collected, the house was sealed, its occupants were transferred to safer ground, and the Squad members returned to complete their reports late into the night.

—CHAPTER TWENTY-SIX—

The next day all those who participated in the home invasion raid straggled in late. The excitement of the previous evening ignited conversations. Coffee cup chatter bubbled over into storytelling and retelling. The rookies, Jena and Eusebio, were verbose. They were full-fledged team members now. Buck noticed that Elliot stayed in his office, but intermittently, he would look up and listen in. Buck knew he was enjoying the success of their mission and that he was relieved not one of his people was hurt. He let them blow off steam after a very long, stress-filled week. Buck got into the office at about 11 o'clock. He had slept well but suspected Do Tron had a rough night. Buck had called him twice this morning without an answer. He left messages. Noon arrived. He decided to relieve his concern. After a quick trip from the office to Tron's townhouse, he approached the door, somewhat ill at ease. Typically he avoided the families of his coworkers. He preferred to maintain a distance, having convinced himself that it was more professional not to get involved with the domestic details of their lives. One exception to that rule was his late partner Barrett. He and Barrett's family had been on close terms with Buck before and after his partner's death, and he paid an emotional price for this closeness.

Tron's wife answered the door, a nice-looking tiny woman with big tired eyes. It was apparent she had been crying. After he introduced himself, she welcomed him into the house. She explained that Tron was still in bed. She checked on him about half an hour earlier, but he sent her away.

"I'm so glad you are here, Agent Buck. I'm worried about him."

"Did he tell you what happened last night?"

She frowned and shook her head. "Something bad. I know. This morning I found all of his clothes in the garbage. I took a quick look. Blood. And this morning, when I looked in on him, he was sleeping, but I found a spot on our bed. His blood. I asked him about it, but he just rolled over. I looked at his belly. There was a cut. Not too deep. And the blood was dried. Something scratched him." Her face demanded an answer. "What happened last night?"

Buck related the events of the entire evening, leaving out the details of Ky's death. He explained Tron had been close to a criminal who was shot. Tron would be responsible for presenting the facts of the previous night to his wife. "Can I see him? Our work can be pretty traumatic. You know that, and he knows that. But he has to move on. Less time in bed and more time back in the saddle. If you know what I mean. He has to move along."

"I understand. Please go up there. Please, Agent Buck."

He sensed that Tron was in a bad place. He knew the feeling. He wanted to help.

Buck knocked lightly and entered the room slowly with two cups of coffee on a small tray.

Tron wasn't sleeping and was dressed for work, including shoes. He swung around and faced Buck while sitting at the end of the bed. "Mike. What are you doing here?"

Buck smiled. He grabbed a chair and sat a few feet from Tron. "Not feeling up to it today?"

Tron made a face. "Feel like crap. I'm a mess. Last night tossed a monkey wrench into my brain."

"No surprise there."

Tron sipped his coffee, holding his response. "You know." He stopped and swallowed before he choked up. "I fucked up last night."

Buck paused before responding. He understood, and he decided to lie. "Not a fuck up, Tron. All's well that ends well.

You've handled hostage situations before. You were in charge. All the hostages survived."

"Sure. But I made a big mistake with those cuffs."

"That's why we work as a team. Rat solved the problem. You knew you had backup. You knew he was there, and you relied on him. You put yourself in an awful position, but you saved those people. Who knows what would have happened if you decided to battle Ky?"

"That's second-guessing," said Tron. "I didn't plan on Rat saving my ass. He did. But that didn't enter my mind at that moment. Ky had the drop on me. I rushed the whole deal. I should have listened to you."

"Every one of us eventually gets trapped in one of these 'damned if you do and damned if you don't situations. At that point, you make a decision. Your decision last night turned out to be the right decision for everyone but Ky. I've been there, Tron. I'm still trying to make things right for decisions I made decades ago."

Tron ran his fingers through his hair. "The whole thing was...too brutal. I almost swallowed a part of Ky's brain." He shivered. "Too close."

Buck cocked his head and smiled. "Almost," he said. "We live in an 'almost' world of split-second decisions. It's not a bad idea to go over what happened last night. You'll end up doing that formally anyway. But the bottom line won't change the fact that it was your decision based on your assessment of the situation. No one can second-guess you. And our buddy Rat. He's home free. He shot a bad guy about to stab an FBI agent in the gut. By the way, your wife told me you got a battle scar last night. Anything to worry about?"

Tron shook his head. "She doesn't miss a thing. No. It's nothing. I put some peroxide and a bandage on it. Good as new."

"Great. Let's finish our coffee and head down to work. OK?"

Tron nodded. "Thanks, Mike."

"Partners," said Buck as he slugged down the last of his coffee. "One for all and all for one."

—CHAPTER TWENTY-SEVEN—

Standing at the end of the conference table, Elliot took command of the meeting. "People." He waited. "People." The background talk subsided. "Thank you." The conference room was jammed with everyone working on Wong's death. Today they worked out of an old CPD building in a large room cluttered with cardboard boxes and piles of disjointed, obsolete computer parts left by parties unknown. The beat-up table, threadbare chairs, spotted carpet, and the scuffed paint on the walls reflected the Bureau's tendency to save its budget for Bureau buildings. Fighting off the heat, his face red and dripping sweat Elliiot loosened his tie.

"I called us here for two reasons. I wanted a session to review and set the direction for this case. And two, I want you to know that as incredible as it may sound, I am still running this little party." Laughter bubbled up and just as quickly was extinguished by Elliot. "OK. Let's go. Professor, you lead the way. I know you can always be trusted to provide an exemplary report." Eliott eased himself into his chair.

The Professor set his empty pipe on the table, arranged his notes, and stood. In three and a half minutes, he summarized the results of his trip to San Francisco. This was news for most of the table, and they listened intently. But Rat had a question. He interrupted the Professor, much to Elliot's dismay. "Wait a minute. We had a file with eight thoroughly dead Vietnamese guys who all arrived in the U.S. on the same day. Now you say they're all from the same ship, and they're all survivors of some kind of wild-ass pirate attack. No offense Professor, but this sounds like improbable bullshit."

The Professor pulled off his glasses. "I find it astounding also. But something has to tie these men to each other, from late-seventies Vietnam to today. These eight men and several other boat people were picked up by a Japanese freighter, having been attacked by pirates. For many days, the crippled boat floundered, filled with dead and wounded refugees, and shot up by the pirates. Remember, the first death was over twenty years ago, and the last was Mr. Wong. Without a connection, the odds against all these men coming off the same ship and all dying separate violent deaths are more than improbable. They're astronomical. Nothing in the records provides us with the answer. But we may find that connection.

For one thing, I had a bit of luck. While the captain of the Kobe Maru, the ship carrying the eight, is also dead, one of his crew is alive and well and living in New Orleans. I tried to talk to this man on the phone, but he only spoke Japanese. He's there, though. I talked to his daughter. Tom, I think sending someone to New Orleans to meet with him would be worthwhile. We need to get a handle on the eight men. This guy snatched them from the sea and dropped them off in San Francisco. What do you think?"

Elliot nodded and gazed into the air. "I think we should send our best linguist." He waited. "Vince...how about it?" He smiled at Vince Gorski.

"You just want me to go because I'm too old to party."

"Well, maturity has its virtue. But I think New Orleans is your kind of town too."

"Yeah. Hot and dirty. Like Chicago used to be. That's OK with me, boss. Maybe I'll like it so much I'll move down there."

"No Maxwell Street Polish sausage there, Vince. You'll starve," Rat quipped.

"I've been around a bit, Rat. I think I might enjoy a little alligator bisque."

Rat pursed his lips, turned his head, and shrugged his shoulders, mocking his friend. "Mr. Bisque goes on a vacation." Then he turned to Tom Elliot. Can I join him?"

"No," said Elliot. "We're fighting a budget as it is. This is a one-man job, and Vince is our man." Vince tossed a gloating look at Rat. Elliot looked at his yellow pad for direction. "Mike. What do your 'interdepartmental' sources have to say." Everyone knew this was code for the Susan Ecker connection.

Buck answered quickly. "Watson has had an opportunity to get 'abreast' of things, so to speak." At Buck's punned reference to Susan Ecker's secret camera spying, polite chuckles bubbled up.

Wearing unconventional horn-rim glasses and his traditional lumberjack shirt, Nelson O. Watson looked like he might be a visiting, geeky teenage son of one of the senior agents at the table. He continued to slouch in his chair, even under the limelight. He cleared his throat before speaking. "Right, Mike. I've been cyber-surfing. I guess everyone knows there was some interest in Mr. Wong before his death. And considerable interest after his death by our brother-agents upstairs. I have confirmed the existence of another department file on him. Something else. However, that file is locked, at least to me."

"Also, assets abound in the files. They're all local to Chicago. As usual, they are numbered with no cross-reference. The only thing new I have found is a somewhat dated file on the Freedom Union, which reports the possibility of a Communist intelligence officer operating in the organization. This information came from an asset in Houston in 1992 who provided background for prosecutors in a murder trial. The murder was allegedly committed by one Union member on another. The asset suggested a motive...to kill a suspected Communist agent. But he didn't believe the murdered man was a Commie-agent. In his opinion, the man was killed by mistake. The legal defense fund for the suspected murderer was funded by Union members across the county, including the Chicago branch. There is nothing illegal about that, but it shows nationwide cooperation and concern about Communist infiltrators."

He scratched the back of his head. "Other than that...and I'm reading between the lines here, everything suggests the boys on ten know as little as we do about the NFU. I'll build a complete dossier on the Union from the public information system and keep you posted." Finished with his report, the sandy-haired man adjusted his lithe frame to an even more comfortable laid-back position.

"What about the voiceprints?" asked Andre, seated next to Buck at the opposite end of the table from Elliot.

Watson leaned over the table to face Andre. "No good."

Andre shrugged his shoulders for an explanation.

"I had the tape analyzed. Tron spotted for me, but we're talking crummy eavesdrop-quality. Telephone to telephone with a lot of static. We had it compared with a TV tape of a Tien press conference. The Technical Section couldn't make a case. Some matches. Some not. Inconclusive. A good idea, though."

Elliot interjected. "What are we talking about?"

"We suspected one of the voices on a White Tiger tap might have been Pham Van Tien. So, Watson had it checked out."

"Oh. OK." Elliot looked at Pete Hansen, sitting at Vince Gorski's right. "Pete, I can tell your new assignment is wearing well. You don't carry that permanent look of pain that everyone else at this table does. Anyway, what can you tell us about Political Corruption and Mr. Tien?"

Appearing somewhat ill at ease, Hansen stroked his salt-and-pepper mustache with the fingers of his right hand. He leaned forward, his head swiveling right to left to survey the entire group. "My wife says the same thing. I admit the PC pace is less hectic. But let me say, it's nice to visit with old Squad 7 on official business."

"Our pleasure, Pete. What's up?"

162

"Well, the CPD Organized Crime unit does have a wiretap on Tien. They're looking for a connection to Viet crime bosses. Hints of bribes and payoffs. And our unit may open a file on Tien concerning his real estate holdings. But the fact is my new group is spread pretty thin. Not enough manpower. Too much corruption. It's a question of asset allocation. I think I've got my new boss convinced that doing an initial investigation would be worthwhile. For now, Tien is like most of our Aldermen. He looks kinky. But he's very well respected by the Mayor. He's a member of his cabinet. Tien is very sensitive to criticism, as Elliot will attest. I'm hoping we can investigate his dealings. If I see something that ties to Wong's case, I'll follow it through and report it to you."

"Appreciate the cooperation," said Elliot. Hansen simply nodded. "What else?"

Tron raised his hand and spoke. "One of my assets is a fringe member of the White Tiger. I spent some time with him to make him more comfortable with our relationship. He may know something about Wong's death. He told me that the White Tiger was not involved. He says the Tiger never pressured Mr. Wong. I asked him why Wong didn't get the same treatment that all businessmen in Little Saigon got? I couldn't get a straight answer, but he said he believed Wong might have had clout. Enough to keep the gang off his case."

"Tron," Buck interjected. "Old man Wong came to me before he died and said he had been receiving threats. Somebody was putting pressure on him. Another gang?"

"No. The Tigers control that area. I'm inclined to believe my asset. If Wong was threatened, it was someone outside the gang."

"Who?" asked Buck with a smile.

"Ah, yes, who? Maybe there was no threat. Maybe Wong wanted to create a straw man. So he could give his restaurant a dose of 'Greek lightning'".

"That's good, except he had no fire insurance. However, his landlord, Pham Van Tien, did."

"But if we're right about Tien, he would have taken the Tiger by the tail and accidentally cooked Mr. Wong's goose," said Rat."

"Somebody else then?" asked Vince. "Someone with influence. Enough to keep the Tiger at bay."

"That could be someone in the Union," said Tron. "We don't have any real connection between Wong and the Union."

"Except Dr. Le," said Vince Gorski. "Le's daughter said that he and Wong were old friends. Maybe the good doctor kept the Tiger heat off him. Hey, I don't know. Just thinkin' we've been hot for this Tiger-Tien connection. Burn and earn. But, maybe, it's not that simple."

Elliot interjected. "Buck, you're tight with the Le's. What do you think?"

Buck answered slowly. "Don't know. Le An and her father were very close to Wong. Maybe Le could have taken the Tiger pressure off Wong based on their friendship. I'll find out."

"Do that," said Elliot. "OK., that's it. Rat and Andre keep watch on Union activities. Hansen, get back with anything on Tien. Buck, check out the Le family. And Gorski, get a ticket to 'Nawlins'".

Elliot stood and took a deep breath. "We've got to get moving on this case. We're spending a lot of the taxpayer's money. Hell, we still don't even know if Wong was murdered. Another couple of weeks. If we don't get a better direction by then, we may have to shut it down. Show's over, folks."

—CHAPTER TWENTY-EIGHT—

The lights from the interior of the Hungry Hornet restaurant across Milwaukee Avenue cast a cold fluorescent glow on the web of bleak rapid transit ironwork that engulfed the modest eatery. The L trains rumbled overhead, interrupting the two men's conversations. Inside, tee-shirted, hard-working locals ate the best in Polish cuisine alongside foppish, adventuresome gentry seeking a taste of authentic city dining. A bald man sat at a booth facing the window in the back of the shotgun space. Because of the reflections, he couldn't see out, but Hansen and fellow agent Lasic could see him. He drank two glasses of beer and smoked three cigarettes in twenty minutes. The waitress appeared again, standing before him, seeking an order. He shook her off.

"Maybe it's time, Pete. We don't want to spook him."

"I think you're right. He's ready now. Let's open him up and see what kind of dirt he has on Pham Van Tien."

The two men, Lasic, a small dark-haired, dark-skinned man about forty, thin and wearing an ill-fitting and rumpled black suit, and the other, the tall and rather stylishly dressed Pete Hansen, shuttled across the broad street. They entered the Hornet, filled with cigarette and cooking smoke, smelling both bad and good; patrons talking loudly, the jukebox up high bellowing a big band sound and the help, screaming orders to the cooks, and the cooks bantering back almost chorus-like. Lasic caught the little man's eye. "Let me massage him a bit first. Then we'll work him. OK?" Hansen nodded as they turned toward the back of the restaurant.

It was a suitably noisy area for a private discussion. As they squeezed into the booth, the man whined, "About time, Sid. You guys are twenty minutes late." Lasic sat next to the man, Hansen across.

"Sorry, Chester. We got here as fast as we could. This is Pete Hansen from downtown. Pete, Chester Pechocki." Hansen gave and got a nod from the man.

"You guy's better not have any fuckin' wires."

"Take it easy, Chet. We're just here to talk about your problems. How about dinner?"

"Fine. I'm fuckin' starved. Busted my ass today, as usual. I could eat a horse." The man's many chins rippled as he spoke.

Sid flagged the waitress, and they placed their orders: Polish sausage and potato pancakes for the two and a meatloaf dinner for Hansen with beers around. The middle-aged, bleached-blond, pretty-in-over-stuffed-pink waitress scribbled in her book and shouted to the nearby kitchen. She returned with the beer.

"Cheers," toasted Lasic. They tossed them back. Sid set the glass down and folded his hands in front of him on the table. "How was work today?"

The man ran his hands over his baldness. "You know how it is, Sid. Every jerk wants what he wants faster than the next jerk. What am I? A slave? Twenty fuckin' years. I ain't rushin' for no asshole. I pace myself. Ya know what I mean?"

Sid nodded with respect, and the two men carried on about the difficulty of maintaining a fresh outlook within the daily grind of City Hall bureaucracy. Sid, a lawyer in his pre-Bureau life, recounted his time in the City's Law Department. They reminisced about working together on Zoning Department projects. Five minutes of boastful B.S. mixed with the beer seemed to lighten Chester's load. He even exchanged some pleasant words with Hansen. The food arrived, and the men crossed into the Hungry Hornet world of chew, nod, grunt, swallow, talk and wipe. After ordering another beer, they got down to business halfway through dinner.

Hansen set down his silverware and ran a paper napkin across his lips before speaking. "Sid tells me you process zoning matters."

"Every day. Twenty years."

"Long time."

"Right." He nodded. "I'm good at it too. I run those changes through the City Council like goose shit through a tin horn."

Hansen smiled.

Chester took a bite and studied Hansen's face while chewing. He didn't wait to finish swallowing before speaking again. "You think it's funny. It's not easy." He looked at Lasic. "You know, Sid. You've been there."

Lasic jumped in quickly. "Absolutely. It takes some skill to package rather complicated legalities into a form that the average alderman can understand."

"Idiots."

"Aldermen?"

"Right. More jerks. It wasn't so bad when I started. Mostly drunken Irish. Now you got every fuckin' fringe fucker in the world. Blacks, women, fruits, gooks. You name it. All aldermen. I had a shot when I started with the City. Once in a while, they'd move a Polack who knew what he was doing up through the ranks. You know we're a big voting block. Doesn't hurt to spread the wealth. But forget it now."

"The Poles out of favor now?" asked Hansen.

The man laughed loudly. "Out of favor? They don't exist. Everyone else is cutting up the pie, and we get the knife. I gotta' get out of this bullshit. You know what I mean, Sid. Like you. You figured it out. Jews are out too. Been out since before you went to the FBI. You were smart, Sid. Smart." Chester gulped his beer and attacked the remaining Polish sausage, killing it topped off with the last bite of potato pancake.

Sid nodded. "Yeah. I'm happy with my move. What about the Mayor's boy. Is he a chosen one?"

The man looked at him and rolled the empty beer glass between his hands. Sid ordered another round. The busboy cleaned the table, and the waitress returned with two more drinks. Pechocki lit a cigarette and took a deep drag. With a look of suspicion, Chester eyed Hansen nursing his beer. He blew out the smoke. "What's the matter, big guy? Don't like the beer here?"

Hansen smiled. "Makes me pee too much."

Pechocki laughed. "Your partner's a blast, Sid. He's OK. Where were you? Oh yeah, Pham Van Tien. Busy man. Gettin' rich off the city."

"How's that?" asked Sid.

"Real estate."

"He's in the business."

"That's right. Fuckin' real estate tycoon workin' in the Hall. Nothin' wrong with that. 'Cept he's feeding the cow on one end and gettin' bottled milk on the other."

Hansen leaned in. "You mean he's getting paid off?"

Pechocki frowned. "Nothing so crude. What I see is old Tien assembling land. He buys everthing cheap, or so I hear. Check the tax stamps. And somehow, he always knows exactly where the most capital improvements are going. You know. New streets, sewers, parks. So he's puttin' together sites. Had one come through the other day. Half-block. C-zoned. He's makin' a shoppin' center. All very legal. He's not even asking for a variance or nothin'".

"So, what's the rub?"

"The rub..." Pechocki stuffed his cigarette in the green glass ashtray now filled with butts. "That's the bottled milk. The shoppin' center."

"What's going in that cow's mouth?" asked Sid.

Chester smiled and held back, demanding a stage. He gulped the beer again before answering. "No-bids."

"No-bid contracts?"

"Right, baby. The old no-bid bullshit. Tien lobbies the Hall for all the minority contractors in town. He gets 'em work. High profit. No-bid."

"And what do they do for him?"

"They buy up property and sell to Tien at bargain rates. Of course, everything is done through third parties and land trusts. Tien just looks like a fuckin' Vietnamese Donald Trump instead of the crook he is."

"What about fires?" asked Hansen.

"Greek lightning? Well, that's not my turf. I heard rumors that he's a very lucky man. Owns well-insured bullshit buildings that burn. Wouldn't doubt it, but that's only office scuttlebutt."

"The other. More scuttlebutt?"

Chester looked offended. "No. Not scuttlebutt. I've tracked one of his deals. I've got a paper trail. Start to finish. All the way from the South Side paving contractor to Tien's business. That's for real."

Sid leaned in on the man. "Will you work with us? We'd like to nail this guy."

Chester sighed. "What's in it for me?"

"Nothing. Except you get to fuck the system." Sid's eyes twinkled as he enticed the man.

Chester nodded, smiling. "I could use a good fuck. But I ain't gonna' lose my job for that bag of shit."

"Don't worry," said Sid. "Get it together. I'll meet you again for a drink. You hand it over. And we'll do the rest. That's what we get paid for."

"OK," said Pechocki with determination. "I can do that. I know what you need. Take me a week or so. But I'll get you started on the right foot." He paused. "Nothin' for me, though?"

Sid looked at Hansen for an answer. He responded, "We'll get you something for your trouble, Chet. Say five hundred to cover your expenses?"

His red face glowed. "That'll be fine. Something, so I can tell my old lady. You know what I mean?"

"Keep it to yourself, Chet," directed Hansen. "Buy her some flowers. You know what I mean?"

The city worker scrunched his face and nodded. "Gotcha, boss. Thanks for the meal. See ya' later. I gotta' get home to see the Mrs."

The meeting was over, and Sid slid out to release Chester from the confines of the booth. They watched him waddle away. Hansen knocked down the last of his beer. He looked at Sid. "This guy's a short-timer. He'll shoot his mouth off."

"Maybe so, Pete, but we need him. This is a one-time deal, but maybe it will pay off."

"You're right, Sid. I shouldn't look a gift horse in the mouth. If he comes through just this once, it will be worth the five hundred. If we had more time, we could develop him slowly." Hansen shrugged his shoulders, and the two men rose. As was his habit, Hansen left an oversize tip for the waitress. It was good business. With an incredible awareness, seemingly out of nowhere, the waitress quickly bounced back to wish them a special 'goodnight.' Money, money, and money, from greasy-spoon waitresses, to greasy-palm politicians, was Chicago's lifeblood. Maybe someplace else, it played second fiddle, but not here. In Chicago, no money, no city. It was as simple as that.

—CHAPTER TWENTY-NINE—

As Vince Gorski ambled along Decatur Street through the French Quarter of New Orleans, images of Chicago and earlier times filled his head, an almost comforting nostalgic reminiscence of South State Street in the Fifties. Jazz horns, laughter, and random alcohol-based cries and shouts blasted out of the doors of watering holes as he passed. Clouds of used cigarette smoke hung below the canopies, sliding up to the free air above, steam-like. But even at this peaceful time of the day, a few minutes before six in the evening, Vince sensed the corruption, deception, and wildness of the Crescent City. Too early for the hawkers, whores, pigeons, and drunks, the Quarter looked like a bored matron awaiting her suitor. A young woman about twenty-five approached him on the walk and, in passing, smiled. He smiled back, realizing New Orleans was not Chicago. The South is a friendlier place.

He ordered a hot dog from a wagon vendor and popped it down in a few bites. The hot dog man agreed with Vince's navigation, pointing beyond Jackson Square to his destination. In the background, barge whistles echoed across the river, and the bells of the tourist-filled streetcars nearby reminded him of his youth in Chicago. Every Sunday, the big red machines on Milwaukee Avenue carried him and his mother from Division Street to the end of the streetcar line to attend to his father's grave and leave flowers. The tracks were paved over now, but every Sunday, Vince traced the path of his childhood to visit his mother, father, and beloved Mary. All dead, but all remembered. A stiff breeze caused him to lean into the wind as he turned left and headed toward Dauphine Street. Maybe because of the wind, his eyes squinted tears. He wiped them dry, dragging a fleshy paw across his broad, reddened face. Four blocks later, breathing heavily, he arrived at the doorstep of Yoshino's building, three stories high with apartments on the top floors and a local eatery and watering hole on the ground level. It was a neighborhood of washed-out and tattered old structures.

Vince looked up at the building, attempting to make sense of the place. Pea-green moss oozed out of and stained the edges of cracks in the plaster facade. Taped to the inside of one of the dirty, second-floor windowpanes above, a faded and torn rising sun paper flag caught his eye. He re-checked the address against his notebook and returned it to his vest pocket as he climbed the worn wooden stairs to the second floor. His footsteps echoed against the plaster walls. At the top of the stairs, he removed the bottle from the deep pocket of his trench coat. He doubled back to the front of the building and worked his way to the end of a short, dark corridor blackened by the burned-out bare bulb. A skinny yellow tabby spat at him, then leaped off a sill onto Vince's foot to freedom. Never forgetting his training, Vince stood to one side and rapped on the door marked 276.

"Hello," came a small female voice from the other side of the door.

"Hello. Vince Gorski. I'm here to see Mr. Yoshino."

"Yes, yes," the voice came again, and he could hear the opening of the lock. The door opened in a few seconds, and Vince faced a small, dignified Japanese woman about fifty years old. She wore a simple, bright blue dress with a green silk scarf. "Come in, please. Mr. Gorski. I am Tomika," she said, bowing slightly. He entered a small corridor. "Let me take your coat. If you please, place your shoes on the mat."

Vince first handed her the bottle of sake, then his coat. She looked at the bottle somewhat suspiciously but accepted it. He slid out of his shoes and placed them carefully as directed. He saw she had hung his coat from a hook on the wall next to a well-worn naval cap. He heard a growl from the next room, a bear speaking Japanese.

"He wishes to see you. Please." She smiled and beckoned him to follow.

Gorski entered the modest living room of the old sailor's two-room bachelor apartment. The dim light revealed worn furniture, gray walls, chipped paint, a tired carpet, and little decoration. An old man sat in a chair near the window. He was large. Vince speculated he had been at least five feet ten and well over two hundred fifty pounds in his former life. Now worn down and weakened by age, he rose, straightened with some effort, and faced Gorski. Shiny black hair still topped his head. Wire glasses stretched around his broad face, a tawny bronze casting complete with a web of lines and creases worn in by decades of wind, sun, and spray. Two large hands met and shook. He laughed and said something.

"Two meat hooks united," she translated.

Vince smiled. He nodded to the woman who held the bottle in her hand. She reacted and offered the sake to her uncle. He gave thanks and asked his niece to open the bottle and pour two glasses, which she did with expert efficiency. Vince sat on the small sofa against the windowed wall. The old man pulled his chair over to face Vince and then sat. Each took a glass from Tomika. She sat next to her uncle, waiting. The two men toasted Vince in Polish, then Yoshino in Japanese. He drank heartily, gasping for breath afterward, wiping his mouth with the back of his hand and nodding in affirmation. Grabbing the bottle, he poured again for each.

Yoshino's niece commented to her uncle. Vince got the impression it was something about the sake. The man's face turned sour, and his response was terse. She dropped her head and nodded. When he spoke next, she translated. "We had a Polish cook on my last ship. Good cook but a big gambler too. Stayed with us for three or four years. One time in Marseilles, he went ashore and never came back. Maybe he was killed or got married. Either way, what is the difference?" She made a face while saying the words. He laughed. "So, it is honor to have an official of the FBI visit me on my last watch."

"The honor is mine," said Vince. "I was a sailor too. Many years ago. U.S. Navy. 'Tin cans.' You know. Destroyers."

The old man nodded and smiled at the translation. "A good sailor?"

Vince laughed. "Better boxer than a sailor. But I loved the sea. It gets in your blood."

She paused in her translation, finding a fit for the expression. But Yoshino got it.

"*Ahso,*" he said, pursing his lips and nodding. Then a musical-sounding phrase eased out. His niece paused again before speaking. "It is a saying…treasure every encounter, for it happens only once."

Vince took a deep breath contemplating the man's words. "Right."

They both sipped their drinks. Then Vince went to work. "This old sailor could use your help, my friend. We need information regarding an incident on your ship, the Kobe Maru."

"Captain Ariga's ship. I was a fitter on that ship for six years. Worked engine room. A container ship. 15,000 ton."

"I'm interested in September 12, 1977. The Kobe Maru was docked in San Francisco. We need to know about the boat people you picked up."

The man sipped his sake and snorted. "Boat people. Captain Ariga lived by the code of the sea. An honorable man. He hauled in boat people like tuna. Too many. Slowed us down. Too much trouble. Me...I would keep going. You know what I mean?"

"Yeah. But do you remember the time?"

The man swirled his sake around and around in the glass, appearing self-hypnotized, the glass eventually freezing motionless in his hand.

"Mr. Yoshino..."

The old sailor awakened and took another drink before speaking. "Sorry. Many years. Things tend to go together. I can't say I remember that date or where we were."

"We know your ship was there. Maybe this will help. I was told that the boat people who boarded your ship that day were victims of pirates. Do you remember pirates?"

Vince looked to the woman for help.

"Uncle. You told me about the pirates in the China Sea. You said they killed many boat people."

The old man's eyes flickered. "Pirates. Oh. Yes. We heard of pirates." He leaned back and looked into space. "One time. Only one. Many dead. Killed by pirates. We had to sink the damn boat filled with rotting corpses. It was a..." she paused to rephrase the epithet, "a pile of human manure. We should never have stopped. But Ariga had to get them."

"Were the people from this boat taken to San Francisco?"

The old man smiled. "Yes. We carried them to America. Maybe '77. Could be. We made the voyage from Singapore to San Francisco several times."

"Tell me about the boat people. Where did you find them?"

He laughed. "We did not find them. They found us. North end of the Balanac Straight in the South China Sea. Early morning we spot a flare. Captain Ariga orders the helmsman to bring the ship about. It looked like a distress signal. We had a junk in our searchlight. We could see it was in trouble. Listing badly. One man clung to a mast, waving a torch. Others not moving. Ariga moved ahead with caution. I give him that. Not stupid. He knew the dangers of these waters. Vietnamese Navy, pirates. Crazy boat people. Trouble came in buckets in the South China. We were about to pick up some crazies one time. They had guns. And fired on us. I don't know why. But Ariga rammed them, and we said goodbye." He laughed again, looking to his niece for accompaniment. She didn't oblige.

175

"What about the junk?" The old man grabbed the bottle and filled Vince's glass. He wasn't about to be rushed. He thanked his host with a toast and a sip. Vince looked at Yoshino. His face appeared visibly younger, more animated, and alive.

"The junk was not problem. Nobody moved on that boat except the man on the mast. He just waved back and forth like a clock. Captain Ariga ordered us to board the junk. We pulled alongside and looked down. People on the deck looked up at us but didn't move. Much blood everywhere. It smelled bad. They had been at sea for weeks. Drifting. People smell." Yoshino nodded, making the declaration complete. "And most of them were dead. Dead people smell. A week of hot summer sun. We weren't about to board that boat. The mate told Captain. He agreed. We tossed them a ladder, and one of them came aboard. The man on the mast.Vietnamese. Not armed. A boat person. Others on the junk were stirring, so we pulled up the ladder. A man was covered in blood and vomit. He smelled like an old fish. We took him to the Captain."

"How old was he?" asked Vince.

The sailor screwed up his face. "Twenty-five. Maybe."

"Go ahead, please."

The old man continued. "The Captain saw him, and he came down from the bridge. I don't think he wanted to be with the smell." He chuckled. "The Vietnamese said their boat had been attacked by pirates a week earlier. Then we heard shouting. My mates were afraid the junk was sinking. People panicked. Ariga ordered the ladder be lowered. We went down to get the survivors. Maybe fifteen of them. Some wounded."

"Men or women?"

"Both. Younger men. Two women. A child. Little girl. Three of them died on our ship. We poked through the rest of the bodies."

"Where were they located?"

He rolled his eyes. "All below deck. Not good to see...smell. They were all wounded. Many bullet holes. Very bloody. There were maybe twenty. Thirty. Men. Women. Children. The stench was bad. We gave up and climbed out. Everyone looked dead." Yoshino removed his glasses and rubbed his eyes with one hand. The memories were more vivid now. He slugged down the bottom of his sake glass and then continued. "Captain Ariga ordered us. Get identification. There was not much. Then we reboarded our ship. Our ship moved away. The junk didn't sink. The Captain said it wasn't going down by itself. He wanted those people to have a proper burial. Already many had their eyes picked out by birds. He sent us to scuttle it. We hacked at the hull with axes and got out of there. Down like a stone."

"A couple of things," said Vince. "You said they sent up a distress signal."

"Yes"

"Is that normal for these boat people to have that kind of equipment?"

"No. Junks are for local waters. Very simple. No equipment. Just an engine."

"The ship was listing before you sunk it, right?"

The old man nodded.

"But it wasn't taking water."

"No," he scratched the top of his head. "All the bodies on one side. That made it list."

"The bodies. All on one side." Vince made his notation. "And who died on board the Kobe Maru?"

"The women. Two of them. And an old man. Captain interrogated the survivors. Later he told us the junk had been attacked by pirates. They grabbed anything of value from the boat people. Raped the women. Pulled gold teeth out. Beat people. Stripped them naked. They wanted gold and jewels, and the boat people had them."

"The people who were killed. Were they all shot?"

177

"No. I saw maybe knife wounds. Some had no wounds. But all dead. Old ones. Maybe heart attack."

Vince made notes in his book. "The survivors. Were they wounded?"

"Some. Two women died soon. A man died a couple of days later. Our pharmacist mate couldn't help them. Sea burial."

"Were they kept in the same room?"

He paused. "I don't know. Yes. I guess so. The three died. The last man was moved to Mate's cabin."

At that moment, Yoshino's niece excused herself to go to the bathroom. Vince and the old seaman sat facing each other in silence. The pink neon of the restaurant sign hanging outside the window flickered, reflecting off the cracked plaster of the dingy apartment. Music from a distant jukebox slid through the rusted window screen. Occasional puffs of the damp night air drifted in. They waited. Then, in Japanese, he spoke. Vince just smiled. He tried some English. "More. Mr. Vince." He held up the bottle, grinning. "Tomika no like drink." Vince smiled and held up his glass. Yoshino refilled them both before his niece returned.

She sat down and looked at the old man, then at Vince. "You know he's going to kill himself with that stuff."

"I'm sorry. I didn't know," said Vince.

"It's fine," she said. "Maybe it doesn't make any difference. He seems happy. Do you have more questions, Mr. Gorski?"

Vince nodded. "I'd like to know more about the people on his ship. The people who went to America. Were they wounded? How old? What did they look like?"

She asked the questions of her uncle.

He replied, his words slurring now. "I like you, Mr. Vince. I tell you. They were in good shape. All young men. Some knife wounds. Not bad. Except for the three that died and the one man. Shot up bad. We transferred him to a Dutch cruise ship. They took him to a hospital in Hawaii."

Vince continued to fill his book with notes.

"Did he live?"

The old sailor made a face.

"Did he get to the mainland?"

The man shrugged his shoulders.

"The rest?"

"They went to San Francisco."

"And the little girl?"

The sailor smiled. "Pretty. Covered with blood when we pulled her up. It was probably her mother's. We found her hugging a dead woman. She didn't have a scratch on her."

"How old was she?"

"Three. Four. Maybe."

"Where did the survivors stay on your ship?"

"The little girl stayed with the cook. The others not wounded stayed in a storeroom at night. On deck during the day. Little girl played games with the others on deck."

"Did the man explain why some people lived and some people died? Why didn't the pirates kill them all?"

Yoshino paused. "I think the pirates just machine-gunned the junk when they left. Some lived. Some died. Bodies acted as shields for some. Those that lived looked pretty good to me. Mostly seasick. Sunburned. Exposure. You know."

"You said there was blood on the deck?"

"Yes."

"How about below?"

The old man tugged off his glasses, wiped them with his shirt, and then held them loosely in his lap. He was thinking. "Not much blood below. Except for the ceiling. It dripped down." He stumbled on a word, and his niece helped him. "And congealed."

"Why wasn't the junk taking water from the bullet holes?"

"Bullet holes?" The old man looked perplexed.

"You said it had been machine-gunned."

"Yes. No bullet holes through the hull. Bullet holes in the deck above. Blood above. "I see, Mr. Vince." He smiled and nodded.

179

"You are detective. I don't know. They must have been killed on deck. Maybe survivors couldn't stand the sight of them and took them below?"

Vince shrugged his shoulders. "Maybe. Did you get any names of survivors?"

Yoshino just laughed and drank the rest of his sake.

"I didn't think so," said Vince. The sake was getting to him now. His interrogation skills were dwindling. He folded his notebook and placed it in his pocket. "I'm done, Mr. Yoshino. Thank you."

She translated.

He wore a sad face. He got up and hobbled to the wooden desk in the corner and retrieved something from the top drawer. Returning, he held the old photo, his hand shaking, before Vince. It was a freighter, another ship. "Last ship," he said in English. "Ten years. I was chief."

Vince took the photo from him and stood. He looked at the dog-eared, yellowed, black-and-white image. A freighter was cutting through the waves of some unknown body of water, looking new and fit. "Very nice. Very large. Impressive."

The woman translated, and the old man beamed. Vince returned the photo. Yoshino looked at Vince; tears filled his eyes, oozing out and down his cheeks. Vince nodded, achieving some kind of agreement between the two men. They shook hands for a long time. Vince cleared his throat and thanked the old sailor. He gave him his business card. The old man nodded and placed the card in his shirt pocket; Yoshino moved away and sat near the window. Head down, he stared at the photo. Tomika escorted Vince to the door. "Thank you for coming, Mr. Gorski. My uncle enjoyed the evening very much. He doesn't get many visitors."

Vince pulled out his wallet, removed a hundred-dollar bill, and handed it to her. "Do me a favor. Buy your uncle a Hawaiian shirt or somethin'."

She smiled and nodded. Vince gave her a wave and made a move for the door. "Mr. Gorski..." She pointed at his feet. Sheepishly he retrieved his shoes, slipped them on, and bid her good evening.

—CHAPTER THIRTY—

Buck had arranged for a meeting with Dr. Le at his office. The successful doctor in the Vietnamese community agreed to meet Buck on his paperwork day when he would not be seeing patients. Buck waited in the reception area under the watchful eye of Le's office manager. This middle-aged Vietnamese woman looked at Buck as if he was from outer space, a feeling Buck shared with her. Alone in the Vietnamese community, he felt the old edginess, Nam edgy. Buck tried to shake it, but it gripped him like a hangover; no real pain, just an incredible raw nerve, skin-tingling sensitivity. Anxious, he read Dr. Le's framed documents on the walls. Two of them appeared to be issued in Vietnam, maybe a medical school, an internship at Los Angeles County General, an Illinois license, and a couple of awards from the Vietnamese community.

"Agent Buck." A voice from behind startled Buck. He turned to face a smiling Dr. Le. What's new? Round-the-clock smiling, a cultural phenomenon that Buck found annoying. Nevertheless, he returned the smile. "Hello. I was just reading your certificates. I didn't know you were originally from LA."

"Originally from Vietnam. But I spent some time in California before coming here. I miss the climate."

"Why did you leave?"

"I liked the climate. I didn't like the culture. Not a good place for a single parent to raise a child. Better to do it surrounded by mid-western values, if you know what I mean."

"I understand. Raising children is a challenge."

"Yes. Come into my office. Please." Le extended his hand toward the open door. Buck entered, and before Dr. Le closed the door, he asked the office manager to hold any calls. They sat across from each other at the mahogany desk. A large fish tank was positioned in front of the only window in the room, and a single brilliant red fish wearing long trailing fins about three inches long claimed residency.

"Nice fish."

"Thank you. It is a Betta."

"No friends, though."

"He is a fighting fish. He never had any friends. If I provide him company, he immediately kills the new fish. He is very competitive. Put your finger up to the side of the tank."

Buck touched his index finger to the glass. The fish swam directly to it in a moment and attacked the visitor through the glass. "Tough little guy."

"Very. He is the king of the tank now, but he is so vicious no other fish can join him."

"A sad victory."

"Maybe, but he is still alive. In nature, survival is the bottom line. Isn't it?"

"I suppose if you're a fish. Anyway, I'm sorry to bother you. But we could use your help with our investigation."

Dr. Le's smile disappeared. The muscles in his neck tightened. "Anything. How can I help?"

"I'm interested in Mr. Wong's relationship with the Freedom Union. We noticed he was an advertiser in the magazine."

Le smiled again. This time his face twitched subtly. "He was, and he wasn't."

"What do you mean?" asked Buck. "I've seen his ads in the magazine."

Le appeared to think before speaking. "I'm sure you have. He did advertise, but I paid for his ads."

Buck looked at him, his face seeking an explanation.

"He supported our cause, of course, but he couldn't afford the ads. Old friends. I bought the ads. I get a discount. I hoped it would help his business."

"By keeping the White Tiger away?"

Le leaned back. "I am disappointed, Agent Buck. Le An has spoken highly of you. But I fear I do not follow your logic."

It was Buck's turn. "And I am somewhat disappointed also. Le An has told me you are very influential in the Freedom Union. I find it hard to believe you are not aware that the White Tiger markets the ads in the Union magazine on a buy-or-else basis."

Le rubbed the back of his neck. "There have been incidents Agent Buck. The advertisements are sold on commission, sometimes by people you might categorize as undesirable, and sometimes their sales techniques are extreme. However, the Union does not condone such behavior. And when we discovered such things happening, we acted quickly to remove the people involved. We do not need to coerce advertisers. The circulation is quite substantial, and advertising in the local edition is a sensible option for many businesses."

Buck didn't see the point of arguing. "We think Wong's death was not an accident. Do you have any idea who might have wanted him out of the way?"

"No. I think you are wrong. I think it was just a fire with tragic consequences."

Buck pushed. "What if Wong wasn't loyal enough or, worse, had Communist tendencies? Do you think someone might want to eliminate him?"

"This is America, Agent Buck. Not Vietnam. If Wong wasn't behind the movement to return Vietnam to its former greatness, the community would shun him. Not kill him. But the point is moot. He was a true supporter, if not financially, then in spirit."

"What then? Arson for profit? Robbery?"

"I told you what I think. But if you want me to speculate. Think street crime. This county, unfortunately, has too much of it. If you discount accident, then the next most logical thought. Money."

"Robbery?" asked Buck.

"It happens every day. Tens of times a day in Chicago. Compare that with a crime based on politics. As to arson for profit, Wong was not a rich man. I doubt he had insurance. Fire insurance, or any insurance, is a commodity not well known by the Vietnamese community."

"Without thinking about Elliot's concerns, Buck responded, "What about Mr. Pham Van Tien? His buildings are insured."

"I wouldn't know. It's not the kind of question I would ask a friend."

"You mean you haven't talked to him about the fires in his buildings?"

"No. I have no interest in such things."

"Didn't your daughter mention my interest?"

Le shifted in his chair. "Maybe she did. I don't know. It would mean nothing to me."

Buck knew he was lying. He suspected Le An had told her father about the Tien arson for profit possibility. It had to be her father who had spread the word to Tien. "Well, it's unimportant. Mr. Tien is, of course, not a suspect."

"Of course not. He is a distinguished person in the community."

For an annoying ten seconds, Buck focused on Le's face. Something bothered him.

Le broke the silence. "What makes you think Mr. Wong's death was not accidental?"

"Death threats, Dr. Le. Plain and simple. People who get death threats and then die soon after are often murder victims. Someone threatened Mr. Wong, and someone killed him."

Dr. Le swallowed hard. "I hope you are wrong."

"Why?"

"I abhor violence, Agent Buck. I was brought up in Vietnam. I experienced enough violence in my life. Mr. Wong was a friend. If he was a victim of violence here in America after struggling so hard to get here...to get away from that kind of life. To America. An island of freedom. I would be sad."

Buck listened to his answer and decided to end the meeting. As he was leaving, Dr. Le suggested that Buck have dinner at his home tonight with Le An. "We should get together. Le An has grown quite fond of you. And," he smiled, "a father must get to know his only daughter's suitors. Do you agree?"

Slightly unnerved by Dr. Le's old-school attitude, he knew the man was playing him. He agreed to dinner for three, but only after quickly weighing the issues. Although he wasn't comfortable walking the fine line between his personal and professional lives, he knew he would have to endure the discomfort.

"Tonight. Seven o'clock. Le An can give you directions."

"That's fine, Doctor."

Outside Dr. Le's office, he sorted. Things were getting tangled. They always did in relationships. While waiting for the elevator, Buck scratched an irritating mental itch. In his interview with Le, he studied facial expressions and reactions carefully. But something else also popped into his mind. Dr. Le's looked like he'd had a facelift. His face was too tight and pinched to be expected for a man his age. He wondered if Le had it done for vanity or to cover facial damage. He thought it strange. He would ask Le An about it, maybe tonight.

—CHAPTER THIRTY-ONE—

Buck returned to the office for a team meeting on the Wong case. Afterward, he followed Elliot into his office, and a productive meeting followed, but it ended ambiguously. Gorski's report on the old sailor in New Orleans convinced everyone at the meeting, except Elliot, that someone, probably Tron, because of his ability to speak Vietnamese, should go to Hawaii to meet with the wounded survivor of the boat person pirate attack. With the help of a cop friend in Honolulu he had met at a National Academy training class at Quantico, Gorski had tracked the man, now in his seventies, to a nursing home on the big island of Hawaii. Elliot seemed to agree an interview might be productive. Still, he was even more certain the Task Force budget could not accommodate such an expenditure. The others could argue the point, but Elliot controlled the purse strings. Buck caught up with his boss and closed the office door behind him. Elliot faced Buck. "Something on your mind, Mike?"

"Tom. You have to rethink this one. This old guy in Hawaii could be our big break."

"Could be he's a vegetable too, an expensive one at that. Forget it. The Bureau doesn't have the resources to have our little team track down leads worldwide. You're getting off on a tangent. We've got other work. Domestic terrorism, for one. We can't spend all our time and money on one murder case. We've got an office there. Maybe we can get one of their agents to interview him."

"You think they have an agent who speaks Vietnamese?"

Elliot shrugged his shoulders. "We can check. You never know. I'll have Watson run it down. Anyway, there's plenty to do.

We have to be careful. You heard the Rat's report. Marsden's men are also watching the Union leaders."

"Watching or being watched. Using or being used?"

"Hey, who knows? Those Vietnamese may have Marsden's number. That's his problem. If the Union is plotting to finance a counter-insurgency or manipulate Vietnamese politics, his people have jurisdiction. These are delicate matters. People in Washington are making nice-nice with the incumbents in Ho Chi Minh City. Nobody wants to rock the boat. Mike, this isn't me talking. It's from up above. Marsden's tattled on us. Now, we're taking some heat. That's another good reason for avoiding world travel. We're not a bunch of globe-trotting spooks."

"Hey, I don't give a rat's ass about the politics. I want to find Wong's killer."

"If there was one."

"You think it's a coincidence that all those former boat people are dead? I don't. There's something here. Wong was the last of a long line of targets."

"You may be right, Mike, but we spent a fair amount of time and money on this one. Rat's surveillance team didn't pick up much. Except for that high-powered radio signal from the Union's safe house. Half a dozen words in Vietnamese. Same words every fifteen minutes for two hours. Words that mean nothing, according to Tron."

"A code," suggested Buck.

"Maybe, who knows? Any of them could have sent them. Phan, Dr. Le, and the attorney..."

"Mai Van Ba."

Elliot nodded. "Or the General. It's a long list. I gave Watson the tape, the times, and the frequency reading. Maybe he can make something of it. In the meantime, Hansen's PC team is sniffing up Tien's butt. Maybe they'll tie him to the Wong case. But forget about Hawaii."

"Right." Buck looked at his watch and moved to the door opening it. "Sorry, I have to run."

Elliot sat up in his chair. "I forgot to ask. How are you doing with Dr. Mathews?"

"He's a good guy. We both agreed that I had completed the course. At least for now. It was a good idea to see him. Thanks."

"OK," said Elliot. "OK. Glad to hear that."

Buck returned to his desk, confident that the Wong case was coming together. He had a scheme in mind to keep the ball rolling.

—CHAPTER THIRTY-TWO—

As Buck drove home from work, Le An called. She seemed excited. "I'm glad you decided to have dinner with us tonight. It is most auspicious."

"Is that a bad thing?"

She laughed. "No. It's terrific."

Buck wondered. For all his pleasant feelings for Le An, it seemed he was reliving his high school years filled with prom dates, corsages, and meeting the parents. Everything about Le An was fresh and bright, but he felt old and dim. She gave him the address and time. He had a few hours to go home, clean up, and adopt a different attitude.

He called his son and made arrangements to move him into his apartment. Richard had decided he would rather live with Buck than with his mother. It was his choice, and Buck could hardly blame him. Buck knew his ex-wife drank more and enjoyed life even less than when they shared a bed. And Richard, approaching sixteen, made it quite clear that he was unhappy with the current arrangement. The boy-man resented her constant mothering. And he didn't want to be her caretaker or surrogate friend. He knew greater independence was possible if he lived with a father who was always too busy with his job. As Buck showered and cleaned up for the evening, he thought about Richard. Le An, Richard, and he had gone out to dinner recently. It went well. He was pleased that the two seemed to be becoming friends. He hoped this would ease his transition into full-time fatherhood.

Later, as Buck journeyed up Lake Shore Drive to meet with Le An and her father, his mind bounced from work to personal issues and back. As the sun set, the towering high-rise residences cast long, deep shadows across his path. He thought about Le An and his son. He thought about Wong dying in the fire. He had a vision of Tron handcuffed in the basement with the bloody headless gangbanger Ky at his feet. He wondered about the sole survivor of the pirate attack in the South China Sea. Finally, he shook it off. For several soothing seconds, he looked out across Lake Michigan's vast, endless churning waters. His mind quieted, and he took a deep breath and focused on his destination.

He swung his car north into a quiet neighborhood on a fashionable Uptown street lined with large, almost mansion-like, older homes that dead-ended into the lake. Unlike other gentrified sections of the northside, the area was not part of an upscale neighborhood but stood as an island of wealth in a sea of lower-middle-class housing. Arching hundred-year-old oaks on both sides of the street capped by the blueness of Lake Michigan at its terminus. It had the feel of the North Shore without the commute. These homes were owned by a newly urbanized gentry who eschewed the suburbs, the Mag Mile, and even Lincoln Park in favor of in-town mansion living. Le's location permitted him to blend in and stand out simultaneously. And it was geographically close enough to his mostly Vietnamese-American clientele to allow him to claim a commonality of neighborhood.

Finding the address on the brick piers at the gated driveway entrance, Buck wheeled his car into Le's estate. He spotted a familiar figure, Tommy, the Tiger gang member, Tron informant, and handyman for the Le's, not ten feet up the drive. Tommy leaned on his shovel and looked up at the approaching car; his bleached yellow buzz-cut hair glowed in the setting sun's light, and his face grew stormy as Buck stopped the car a few feet away. Buck exited, slammed the car door, and returned the young man's stare. Neither exchanged words.

"Mike," her lyrical voice carried across the gap between Buck and Tommy. Le An approached and stood between the two. "You remember each other. Michael Buck. Tommy Mac." Her smile

191

helped relieve some of the tension. The young man wiped his hand on his jeans before offering a handshake.

Buck accepted the gesture and inquired, "Doing some planting for Dr. Le?"

Before speaking, Tommy cocked his head to the side in a manner Buck interpreted as hostile. "Right, I've been planting *Bac Le's* bushes." As a show, he flexed his youthful arm muscles as he gripped the shovel.

Buck sensed hostility.

Le An frowned and then spoke. "Tommy's just been hired by my dad to work around the house. Dad's putting him up in his basement flat."

"Nice. Hope it works out for you."

"Mike," interrupted Le An. "We should go in. My father's expecting us."

Le An led Buck through the living room to a study off the dining room. The house had a Prairie School look with an open plan, ribbon windows, geometric glazing, and hardwood trim. Through a pair of open doors in the study, they saw Dr. Le. He arose from his desk and removed his reading glasses. "Michael. Nice to see you again. Twice in one day. Thank you for visiting my humble abode.

"Hardly humble, Doctor."

Le looked about with evident pride. "The rewards of hard work in a great country. However, it has been less special since Le An moved out. I do miss her."

Le An chuckled. "Father, it's been three years."

"Nevertheless. You know how it is to have children, Agent Buck. You never appreciate them completely until they leave the nest."

"Mine's just flown back to the nest."

Dr. Le nodded.

"He's chosen to live with me for a while."

"How nice. A time for bonding between men."

"Right." Buck put one hand on his hip. "Le An says you've asked Tommy to stay here. That should help the emptiness."

Dr. Le nodded. "It's a big house. I'm hoping Tommy will take care of the upkeep here and provide a little life to the place."

"You don't have any concerns?" Buck's bluntness was reflected in Le An's face, which grew colder.

"Concerns?" Le wore a vacant look. "Oh. You mean Tommy's gang connections. I don't think that will be a problem. He never really was in the gang. Maybe we can straighten him out by giving him an opportunity here."

An image of the banker's missing finger came to mind. "I hope so. But please be careful."

"I forget. You are a policeman, Agent Buck. I appreciate your concern. Le An is in good hands."

A housekeeper-cook older woman stood at the study door and announced that dinner would be served shortly. As they followed her out of the room, Dr. Le held Buck back for a second. "One more thing. A last bit of business before dinner. I have talked to some of my friends in the community regarding you and your efforts to resolve the issues related to Mr. Wong's death. They would be most interested in meeting with you to discuss how we can help you. Would you be willing to meet with us?" Le smiled, awaiting an answer.

Buck looked at Le An and then back to Dr. Le. Pluses and minuses flashed across his brain, but Le An's look ultimately drove him to answer affirmatively, "Why not?"

"Very good. I'll get back to you. Now, it is time for dinner." He smiled.

CHAPTER THIRTY-THREE

The breeze blasting through the open convertible top of the rental car mussed Tron's hair. He swept it back with his right hand. Although an added expense, the convertible gave him the less conspicuous look of a tourist enjoying the spectacular ocean view while motoring along the resort-laden South Kohala section of the Kona Coast on the Big Island of Hawaii. Distant whitecaps, stirred by tradewinds, bristled on the water's surface below, which changed color, mixing green and blue to almost black when it reached the volcanic lava edge, all but concealed by the lush green golf courses linking the highway with the ocean. In contrast, the topography rose to his right and inland with black, frozen lava fields like a barren moonscape.

Tron owned his current pleasant travel assignment to a combination of events. He spoke Vietnamese. And his wife worked as a ticket agent for an airline, allowing him alone to secure a deep-discounted ticket from Chicago to Hawaii. This was a pre-requisite given Tom Elliot's opposition to using Bureau funds. At Buck's recommendation, the team's individual members each kicked in a cash donation to finance the ground package costs of the trip. All of this was necessary to complete the puzzle. Tron wanted to know what happened in the South China Sea in 1977. He was about to interview an old man who might hold the key to Wong's death.

Rat gave Tron fifty dollars but stipulated that Tron had to bring back a pineapple. Tron suggested macadamia nuts would be more appropriate for Rat. They compromised on a can of Kona coffee for the office. Elliot was not advised of the trip. For the record, Tron planned a three-day vacation set up by his wife through a local travel agency. And although she was displeased that she would be left behind, Tron convinced her that a subsequent Hawaiian vacation for two was coming. On the way back from today's interview, he would stop in each luxury hotel that graced the shoreline winding north ahead of him and gather brochures, thus providing his wife tangible evidence of his commitment to the idea. He speculated that these brochures and some island jewelry would be enough to smooth things with her upon his return.

He turned right, heading towards the old Parker Ranch. The shore terrain fell away behind him as he followed the road leading to the plateau area of the island. Another thirty minutes of easy driving led Tron to his destination. He turned into the unpaved drive at a crisp white sign adorned with a small pediment that read in dark green script letters, *Sunny Meadows Retirement Home.* Tron's convertible bounced toward the distant building complex, kicking up a dust cloud. A red clay-tiled roof capped the low, undulating whitewashed building, glistening in the afternoon sun. Tron guided the car into the modest parking lot in front of this building. Once inside, sunglasses now in hand, he looked about. The male nurse, a dark-skinned, dark-haired man, studied his identification.

"We've been expecting you, Detective Tron."

Tron smiled. "And Mr. Nguyen Kim Nhi."

"Yes, he is ready. Please have a seat. I will be back shortly." The white-coated man motioned to the seating area, turned his back, and walked away.

Tron checked his watch, looked outside, and sat near the window. Low clouds were rolling in off the sea, offering rain. Inside, many of the residents had taken notice of him. A slow parade of wheelchairs, walkers, and canes aided them as they checked out the never-before-seen visitor. Maybe in her early eighties, a woman dressed in a colorful yellow and red muumuu smiled at him and mouthed the word 'hello.' Tron smiled back. Lunch was a big event at Sunny Meadows, and the residents all moved toward a large room behind the reception desk, taking their places at the tables. Tron's mind wandered. He thought of his aging parents and their future. Then the Filipino man returned.

"He will see you, Detective Tron. However, as you can see, it is almost lunchtime here, and Mr. Nhi does not want to interrupt his schedule. He will meet you at the meadow terrace at twelve-thirty."

"The terrace?"

"Out this set of doors and to the right. You'll see a grove of large trees at the top of a rise."

"Thank you. Twelve-thirty. I'll wait."

Tron went out and sat in his car. Ten minutes later, with the temperature rising, the possibility of rain gone, and the sky cloudless, he moved on. After securing his gun and jacket in the trunk of his car, he walked the meandering path to the terrace, sat on a bench, and waited. Twenty minutes later, a small vehicle rolled down the ramp of the administration building below. It headed his way, a battery-powered scooter with an elderly man aboard, possibly Mr. Nhi. The device rambled up the path, its electric motor whirring, the aged operator seemingly struggling to keep it within the hard-surface boundaries. Nearing the top of the little hill, it slowed to almost a crawl. Mr. Nhi, his bald head clad in a scruffy, crushed pork-pie hat, wearing cock-eyed, smudged wire-rimmed glasses, his skin wrinkled and yellowed, his bones protruding like golf clubs in the bottom of an old leather bag, smiled a toothy grin at Tron as he crossed the finish line.

"Bet you thought I wouldn't make it," he spoke in a low voice with a stiff accent, which might have offered a challenge to some but not Tron.

"Let me help you," he said as he pulled the scooter's handlebars, guiding the man to flat ground.

"Thanks. Needs charge, I think." The old man removed his hat, revealing his polished, liver-spotted scalp with a nasty crease above his right temple. "Whew. Hot. Hot. Hot. Take seat. Please, Detective Tron. Sorry to make you wait, but we have a routine. Cannot change. Too many questions will be asked. We will be alone up here. I need to see your badge, please." The man smiled. Tron returned the smile and pulled out his badge. The old man brought it close to his dulled eyes, studied it, then held it in his hand as if to weigh it. "Looks official. You are a policeman."

"Yes, sir, that I am."

"Are there many Vietnamese policemen in Chicago?"

Tron chuckled. "We have more Vietnamese on the force than the Saigon police have Americans."

"Ho Chi Minh City," the man corrected.

"Ah, yes. I forget my revisionist geography."

"You must get used to change. Always change."

"Right."

"Where are your ancestors from?"

"Hue. My father was a teacher there."

"The Imperial City. Very beautiful. Much history."

"And you?"

"Nha Trang. I owned a little shop. Wood carvings. Brass things. For the tourists. On the beach."

"Sounds nice."

The old man reflected. "Yes, very nice. Long time ago." He looked pained, then returned a smile. "OK, you tell me why you come to visit me from Chicago. I have no one in Chicago. "

"It is a serious matter which brings me here. We are investigating the death of an older Vietnamese gentleman who died in a fire in his restaurant in Chicago. Our investigation has led to you. We are most interested in your sea journey here to Hawaii in 1977."

The old man's face dropped, possibly eroded by fear. Tron backtracked. "You seem upset, Mr. Nhi."

"I expected this. I knew someday, someone would find me."

"What do you mean?"

197

"Many years ago, I arrived. I said then that I was lucky. I was alive. But I knew it was only luck. Luck would run out. I needed to disappear. I did. Twenty years. But now you find me. Others can find me. How did you find me? Social security? Medicare?"

"Yes, the Honolulu police found your name in the government records."

"I knew. I knew this would happen. But I had no choice. Too old to work. Legs don't work. I was a gardener. I lived on this island on a ranch for my keep and spent a few dollars. Everyone called me *Bac Joe*. No other name. I never went anywhere. I never saw anyone new. Until I got old. Then I had to come here."

"Why, sir, did you wish to remain hidden?"

The man appeared perplexed. "You don't know?"

"No."

Nhi asked for assistance to move from the scooter to the bench next to Tron. Tron gently held him while he carefully shuffled the three-foot distance. The task appeared exhausting for him, and his recovery was slow. Finally, he spontaneously spilled out his untold tale without prodding from Tron, even before Tron opened his notebook. Nhi told the most remarkable story of his life, about the days after the Vietnam War. While he had been a simple shopkeeper his entire adult life in Vietnam, he and his family were somehow perceived as a threat to his new comrades or, at the very least, a nuisance. He knew his family was possibly in danger and did not have a future.

As time passed, the pain increased, and escaping became an obsession. Finally, he found someone who would buy his business, and he assembled the modest fortunes of his family. He convinced his daughter and son-in-law to join him, and they all departed in a small ancient junk at the cost of half their collective wealth. The risks were considerable but appeared reasonable to him and the many other boat people who also threw in their lot with five rogue sailors of fortune who had agreed to sail the junk to freedom. Three days at sea had made him and most others doubt their choice. Storm-driven, gale-force rains had tossed them about the choppy waters of the South China Sea for thirty-six straight hours. Some begged the junk's captain to return them to land. Others, too seasick to care, moaned and vomited below deck. On the fourth day, the winds subsided, and late in the day, the sun returned. The boat people lay about the deck now enjoying the trip as if it were a cruise ship excursion until they noticed the crew's behavior reacting to a speck of darkness on the horizon.

Under full sail, the little ship danced across the waves, first to escape detection and then to escape destruction. Both efforts failed. The Thai pirate ship bore down on them like a black knife cutting the waters. People huddled together in fear while the sailors worked desperately to escape. Soon their efforts were terminated. The pirate ship overtook them. Sharpshooters killed all the sailors. The boat people, still huddling, screamed and wept. Nguyen Kim Nhi knew then that he had made a terrible mistake.

Nhi's voice cracked, and he coughed a dry, spasmodic cough for at least a minute. The man asked him to retrieve a bottle of water from the scooter, and almost in desperation, he grabbed the bottle from Tron's hand, quickly watering his throat. The cough subsided, and he appeared calmer. "Thank you, Detective. I'm always dry now. Old and dry. Like a prune."

"Please continue if you can."

"I am OK now. Yes. Many pirates from Thailand. Fishermen or farmers. They are pirates for the money. Much easier to steal from seasick people than to catch fish or grow rice. Sometimes boat people attacked more than once. Same boat. Different pirates. All very bad people."

"And after they killed the crew. They boarded your boat?"

"Yes. Boarded. Lined people up. Made them take off clothes. Ripped through them. Looking for gold, silver, jewels. They found everything. Even in mouths. Even in other places. They took the young women below. They took my daughter." He

199

stopped and looked up and across the landscape, trying to contain the painful memory. His lip quivered. He said nothing for a moment, then he spoke softly. "She is dead. Her husband is dead. They were killed that day. Shot to death. But not by pirates."

"Who?"

"Another boat came. It fired a cannon. Then again. The shells burst next to the pirate boat. Pirates shouted. They ran to the rail and jumped onto their boat. They left. They got about to that tree," he said, pointing to a palm about fifty yards from them, "and the cannons fired again. Two hits. Pirate boat exploded like bomb. My people cheered. Then boat came closer. Then we see it was North Vietnamese. Sailors. They had machine guns. They shot at the pirates in the water. Killed them. Then guns pointed at us. People stopped cheering. They fired machine guns. Hit in the leg. Here." He put his hand on his right thigh. "People screamed. They kept firing. People ran to get below. I ran. But leg would not work. I stumbled. They knocked me down. More bullets. People fell on me. Then I must have been hit here." He pointed to the indentation above his right temple. "Then I was out."

"The North Vietnamese killed the pirates and the boat people?"

"Yes. They killed my daughter."

"I am sorry," said Tron. The old man sensed his genuine concern.

"You are very kind. It still hurts here," he said, pointing to his gut.

"What happened after that, Mr. Nhi?

The man leaned back on the bench, exhaling audibly as if he expelling the past. He smiled. "Then I float for days on end. In and out. Awake and asleep. Until I get to the hospital in Hawaii."

"You don't remember anything after the attack?"

The man grimaced. "Bits and pieces. I remember the ship. The engine. I felt it. A freighter picked us up."

"Wait…back to the junk. Let's go back there first. How long were you on the junk before it was rescued?"

The old man pondered the question. Time was not a friend to his memory. "Three, four, maybe, five days."

"Where were you?"

"Below deck. I know that. At times I would wake. Boat rocking. I was like a baby, in and out of sleep. Bodies were on top of me. Dead people."

"How did you get there?"

"I must have been carried there."

"Did you see anyone? Any living people?"

"No. The boat just drifted. I drifted. Very peaceful."

"What else?"

"After two or three days, I heard voices above. Men walking. Then hear motor in distance. And feel the sea. Our boat is towed."

"How long?"

"I can't say."

"Go ahead."

"Then boat is drifting again. Voices above. Footsteps. Then hours, days, I do not know. I feel hands on me. The Japanese taking me to their ship. Sunlight blinded me."

"Did you see any of the other men on the junk? Sailors. Anyone?"

"No."

"Did you see any men from the junk on the freighter?"

The old man took his time before answering. "I remember on the freighter. Seeing two other people. Vietnamese women. In beds. They died. I saw them killed."

"Killed? On the ship?"

"Yes. Someone smothered them. I think."

"Who?"

"A man. I don't know. It was like a dream. Someone said, 'just let him die' in Vietnamese."

"Do you remember being moved to a different cabin?"

"No. I was very ill, Detective Tron."

"Yes, I know. They transferred you to a ship heading for Hawaii. Did you know that?"

The man nodded. "I was told so by a nurse."

"Did you tell anyone the story about the North Vietnamese?"

"No. No one until now."

"Because of the two women?"

"Because I knew I was supposed to be dead. Only luck made me live."

"Do you know who the North Vietnamese men were? Why did they kill everyone?"

"I don't know. But it was not mistake. Everyone killed except me, and I know something I should not. But I do not know. Yet I am still afraid."

"Afraid of whom?"

The man did not hesitate. "Communists." Nhi looked down at the buildings below. "I must get back. Help me please to my machine." Tron assisted him onto the vehicle. "Detective Tron. Please do not call on me again. Please, I have told you all. Please."

Tron offered his hand to shake. The man's hand trembled in his. "Don't worry. I will not return. I thank you very much for your help."

"May I go?"

Tron nodded and smiled. "*Tam biet, Ong Nhi. Tam biet.*"

"*Tam biet,*" said the old man faintly. He guided the scooter down the hill with the same lack of skill exhibited in the upward journey, ending at one of the small private patios. Tron watched him park the red scooter and make his painfully slow passage to the sliding door and into the building. Through the open door, he looked back at Tron. Tron waved, but Nhi did not return the wave. The glass door slid shut. Assessing his work was almost done, Tron sat on the bench to review his notes. After making a few clarifications, he closed the book, took a deep breath, and relaxed while gentle warm breezes drifted past.

Nhi was probably watching him, nervously awaiting his departure. The man was old and frightened, worried about a decades-old event. Tron silently wished him well as he strode to his car. If he was correct in supposition, the men who arrived on the Japanese freighter on the same day in 1977 were all North Vietnamese. They may have been spies sent forth as part of a well-executed and brutal plan to make them appear as boat people to the admitting authorities in the United States. But they were not typical boat people. They were sympathetic victims of piracy, without papers or anything except for cover stories. It was a perfect way to plant them on American soil.

As he wheeled his car onto the long, dusty drive leading to the main road, he passed a yellow and green cab approaching. Strange, clear air on the road ahead. No dust trail from the cab. He looked in the rear mirror, and dust billowed like smoke from a lighted fuse. But his mind focused on the North Vietnamese scheme. He had heard rumors of such spies within the Vietnamese community, but he had dismissed these as the paranoid fantasies of war-torn immigrants. Now those rumors were fact.

He turned onto the main road and headed to his hotel. With a soft hand, the dipping sun blanketed the green meadows to either side, making them glow as if illuminated from below. For a moment, he relaxed and enjoyed the scenery. His mission was successful; he found the connection between the eight dead men. But he was uneasy. He sensed something was wrong. The hair on the back of his neck tingled. He shivered. "Damn," he said as he pulled the car to the side of the road, jammed on the brakes, and spun the car around.

He pounded the accelerator down, and the convertible shot ahead into the sun. His mind raced as he replayed his fleeting glimpse of the cab driver. He had seen his face for only a second. He was Japanese, but he was not. He was Vietnamese. It was the same man he had seen at his hotel that morning. The same man was at the airport the night before. "Damn...damn," he said under his breath. A few minutes from Sunny Meadows, he looked ahead and saw the sign visible in the distance, a white dot across a sea of green. He slowed abruptly to make the turn, sliding across the stones almost into the ditch at the far side. His car fish-tailed and careened down the road. Ahead the whitewashed building reflected a red sun. Tron saw the empty cab in the parking lot. After sliding to a stop in front of the entrance and flinging the door open, he exited and ran to the building, crashing through the glass doors, banging them against the wall, and snapping the white-uniformed Filipino to attention.

"Nhi's room. Where?" Tron shouted.

The man pointed toward the hallway entrance.

"He may be in danger. Show me. Now."

The nurse didn't hesitate. He stepped out from behind the counter. "Follow me." They walked rapidly through the pair of doors down the carpeted corridor. Startled residents hanging onto side rails gaped at them as they moved past, almost running. Near the end of the hall, the nurse stopped and pointed at a door. Tron tried the handle. It was locked.

"Key."

The nurse handed him a small ring of keys.

"The brass one."

Tron cautioned the man to stand away from the door as he unlocked it and swung it open. A steady breeze blew through the half-open sliding door that led to the patio. Mr. Nhi sat in a rocking chair with his head cocked at an unusual angle facing away from Tron. Tron surveyed the room carefully before approaching Nhi. A glance at the empty bathroom completed the survey. No one was in the studio apartment, but he and Mr. Nhi. Tron had the sickening feeling that Nhi was no longer with the living. He tiptoed around the chair to face him. The man's wire-rimmed glasses lay on the floor at his feet. Nhi could have been sleeping, except one eye remained open, and his head was twisted on his shoulder like it was about to fall onto the floor.

One look told Tron Nhi's neck was broken. Over his shoulder, Tron glanced out the window. He saw the cab in the parking lot and the man who killed Nguyen Kim Nhi walking rapidly toward it. Tron raced past the frightened nurse and down the hall-dodging people, shouting to clear them to the side. His hip caught one old man spinning him around and almost dropping him to the floor. Tron shot through the front doors looking for the cab. It was moving now. He fumbled for his car key in his pants pocket. With his right hand still in his pocket, he hip-hopped the last few steps to the back of his car. He found his keys, popped the lid on the trunk, and grabbed his gun. As he flipped the trunk lid and looked out, he heard the cab spinning its wheels on the gravel. Its driver forced his vehicle ahead on the loose stone at full throttle. The car made a lazy arc like a water skier spitting pebbles instead of water and then gained momentum. Almost out of control, it veered toward Tron on a collision course. Tron stood mannequin-like, watching three thousand rolling pounds of menacing metal rushing toward him. With no hope of escape, he raised his automatic and aimed it at the driver's side of the windshield.

Squeezing the trigger for the first shot, then clicking off the other fourteen shots with less discipline, he emptied the clip in less than three seconds, demolishing the windshield. The driver's face stared at Tron, a bloody death mask. Sometime between the first shot and the last, the cab turned, almost imperceptibly at first and then full cut to the left, causing the car to move forward and sideways in one movement, nearly tipping it over on top of Tron. Its rear end slid into the detective as he maintained his shooter's stance. The glancing blow knocked him to the ground, and his gun flew out of his hand. Like a jack-in-the-box, he was down and then up. Half-crouching, he watched the car drive off the parking surface onto the long grass, traveling maybe another hundred feet before stopping. Tron straightened up, ran, and reached the car in seconds. He ripped the door open.

The man keeled over and out onto the ground, a dead sardine from a crumpled can. Blood oozed from an exit wound behind the man's ear and another wound in the back of his neck. He pushed the body with his foot. Flesh flopped over. Face lacerated by flying glass, and bullet holes in his forehead and neck, the man appeared dead enough to permit Tron to unwind. He slumped into the tall grass, sucking in air, the fingers of his interlocked trembling hands as if praying. Slowly, others gathered around him, not talking, only staring, the way people do the first time they see such mayhem. He looked at them without focusing and then returned his gaze to the dead man. After taking a minute, he stood and took charge.

—CHAPTER THIRTY-FOUR—

Buck's phone rang, almost unheard amid the noisy activity of the Squad 7 office pool. Buck interrupted his conversation with Andre to answer it.

"Agent Buck."

"Mike. I'd like to see you in my office now."

Buck didn't like the tone of Elliot's voice. Elliot had been out for the last three days at a conference. Buck suspected his boss had gotten wind of Tron's trip. "What's up?" Elliot didn't answer. "I'll be right in."

He looked into Elliot's office through the glass partition as he walked. Marsden sat on the edge of Elliot's desk. "Shit," he mumbled. He stood in the doorway and faced the two men. Seeing Buck, Marsden stood and squared himself, his twelve hundred dollar suit falling into place as designed. Elliot waved Buck into the office.

"Gentlemen." Marsden lifted his chin as a greeting.

"Mike. Marsden has asked me some questions I can't answer. Maybe you can help?"

This sounded like Elliot was hanging him out to dry. He must be pissed. "Maybe I can. What's the question?"

"Well..."

Marsden interrupted Elliot. "We want to know why your man Do Tron has been traveling overseas, doing investigative work, and interfering with ongoing FCI investigations?" His voice was well-modulated and carried that edge that Buck hated.

"You mean Tron's visit to Hawaii? I wouldn't call that 'overseas.' After all, Hawaii is our fiftieth state, not some foreign country." Buck's smile was wasted on the two men.

207

"Don't jerk me around, Buck. From the first day you got involved with this Wong case, you've been pushing into areas you don't belong."

"Well, you would know. Your boys have been tailing me from day one. I suppose that's all part of your quest to improve interdepartmental relations?"

"Apparently, we had good reason to keep an eye on you," Marsden's voice grew louder.

Buck moved closer to the FCI supervisor. Although only a couple of inches taller, Buck seemed to tower over him. He stared at him coldly. "Keeping an eye on me?"

Elliot moved around his desk. "OK, gentlemen. Relax."

"Relax? This man's interfering with our work."

"Which is?" asked Elliot.

Marsden looked over to Buck's boss. "You know the FCI concerns as well as anyone. We're watching The Union as a possible threat to national security. This is a right-wing organization. Its leaders have publicly expressed their intent to re-establish themselves in Vietnam. In case you weren't watching, the war is over, Buck. We're not interested in having another Bay of Pigs, and our agents have this matter well taken care of, thank you very much. We don't need your help."

"I'm familiar with the war, and from what I can see, it never ended. There are still people dying, including Mr. Wong. You had to know most of those murders weren't ordinary street crimes. They tie together. If you had leveled with us, we could have cooperated. I'm sure you dug up the same dirt we did."

Marsden ignored this line of thinking. "Elliot, did you know that Detective Tron is currently in the custody of the Hilo police?"

Elliot's face reddened. He glared at Buck. Then, after a moment, the blood subsided. "As I mentioned, I've been out of the office at a conference for the past three days. I haven't had time to confer with my staff regarding Tron's investigation. However, this is something Agent Buck and I will cover next."

"Did you authorize this Hawaiian investigation?"

Elliot looked at Buck. Buck waited, wondering. "Yeah. Of course. We're following up on some issues related to this Wong death. Nothing wrong with that." He smiled.

"And the police..."

"Let's leave that for later after I am briefed. All right, Marsden?"

Buck realized he had made a big mistake by keeping Elliot out of the loop. But the old man was doing a great job of covering.

Marsden wasn't about to back down. "Another thing. I think Agent Buck has compromised the security of my office. He may have someone spying on us. We have verified that unknown parties have accessed our computer files. You know. I could bring you up to the Office of Professional Review."

Elliot moved back around his desk and looked at Buck. "Mike. Do you know how anybody could get into FCI files?"

Buck smiled. "I'd watch out for those hackers, Marsden. They're very industrious. Maybe you need to look into your security. Things getting a bit lax over there?"

Marsden's reddened neck bristled over his starched white shirt collar.

"Were you able to track these hacks into your computers?" Elliot looked at Marsden for an answer.

"No. Damn it. The gateways were from many different places."

"Not here?"

"No. But that doesn't mean somebody's smart computer jock couldn't have arranged everything. You know, two can play those games, Buck."

"I have my doubts."

"What?"

Buck shook his head. "I don't think you people are competent enough to play in the real world. You're in bed with some strange people, Marsden. Corrupt city officials. Old Viet generals. I think they're pulling your chain. I don't want you screwing up my investigation. If you do, I'll expose every one of your assets."

Marsden looked at Elliot like he was the owner of a rabid dog on a long leash. "Agent Buck has been venturing into areas of National Security. FCI jurisdiction. If he continues, I'll have him busted. I'll ignore his threats and his bad manners for the moment. I suggest you talk with him."

"Thanks for your advice," Elliot's voice dripped with sarcasm. "In consideration of the nature of our concurrent investigations, I think we should take this matter to the Assistant Special Agent in Charge for direction if you agree."

"I'll think about that. Good morning." With that, Marsden slid out of the office.

Watching him walk down the hall, Buck wondered whether he could find his way back to his office. Buck tried to constrain his delight that Marsden was upset.

Elliot must have seen the twinkle in his eyes. "I'm not as happy about this as you are. I told you we couldn't cover a trip to Hawaii. Now I find out Tron's gone there. Worse yet, I find out from Marsden."

"Tom..."

"Wait. I'm not finished. Bad enough that he's there. But held by the Hilo PD. What the hell is going on?"

"Settle down. Tron took vacation days. He paid for the trip. No Bureau funds. I admit he didn't ask you if he could take the time. But you were out."

"More like I left, and he took off."

Buck smiled. "Come on, Tom. Tron's on to something big."

"What?"

Buck's smile disappeared. "We don't know all of it, but it looks like our eight dead guys could be North Viet spies."

"Spies," Elliot mumbled the word to himself. "And what the hell is Tron doing with the Hilo police?"

Buck waited, trying to formulate the words to reduce their impact, but they came out, "He killed someone."

Elliot dropped back down into his chair. "Great. That's just great. I go away for three fucking days, and one of my guys flies to Hawaii and kills someone. I hope it was justified."

"It was. He was being run down intentionally. The car as a weapon. Hilo has no problem. Tron will be back here tomorrow. I'm sorry this happened. I know this is going to mean extra paperwork."

"Paperwork. What do you think I am? A secretary. I'm supposed to be in charge here. You're making it very difficult for me. Why the hell are you going around me?"

"I'm sorry. You're right. I was wrong. I apologize. We really weren't going around you. It just worked out that way. You left..."

"And the mice began to play."

Buck sensed he was relaxing. "I'm not nuts, Tom. We had a window. Tron's wife had access to a ticket. The timing was critical. We moved on it. Anyway, would you have given the OK? If we had told you?"

Elliot didn't hesitate, "No. But you left me hanging. You should have brought me up to date this morning. First thing. That's not just a slam on me, but you almost made us all look like idiots. Do you get that?"

Undaunted, Buck pushed on, "Well, I was going to bring you up to date this morning, but Marsden got here first."

Elliot made a face and shook his head. "How did that bastard find out about it?"

Buck sat on the edge of the desk and looked out Elliot's window toward the Squad room, then back at his boss. "This whole case has more leaks than a Vietnamese junk. Somebody knew Tron was going to Hawaii. Somebody tipped off an assassin. He knew when Tron was arriving. He must have followed him. He killed Tron's contact, and he almost killed Tron. I hope FCI's not queering our case."

"More likely, they're getting news back from their informants. Who knows? Our agents in Hilo had to know about this. Once it gets in the system, it's fair game. Who knew about Tron's trip?"

"Nobody. Our guys. Tron's wife."

"Forget them. Did she make the arrangements?"

"She...his wife?"

"Right."

"I don't know."

"Well, I can tell you right now if his wife booked this trip through a local travel agent, it was probably Vietnamese. She might as well have printed it on the front page of the VNFU magazine. Check it out, Mike. You, of all people, and Tron. For Christ's sake. You guys should know how tight that community is."

"Hey Tom, we don't know." Buck sounded doubtful, but in the pit of his stomach, he knew Elliot might be right.

"Tell me the rest," said Elliot, moving back into his chair.

For the next fifteen minutes, Buck related the story of Tron's trip to Hawaii. Elliot listened intently, not interrupting. Buck proclaimed, "So, you've got to agree this is the biggest case we've got right now."

Elliot didn't bite. "I'll give you one thing. This is our case. Not Marsden's. Yet. He's not the only one who can conduct a complicated high-level investigation. We'll keep on it, but we'll probably have to turn it over to FCI if we find out they were spies. Until then, it's ours. Elliot looked into Buck's eyes. "Mike, you're a good agent. But don't get ahead of yourself. This is not a private detective agency. You understand me?"

Buck nodded.

"If not, you may need to take a break. Get off this Wong thing. Maybe take a vacation. I thought you said you and the Medicine Man were making progress."

"I think I am Tom. We have."

"OK," he waved his hand. "Go. Get back when you know something."

Buck headed for the door and turned back, "Thanks."

Elliot tightened his jaw. "Don't thank me. I'm pulling half your people off this case today. We've got other business too. And I want a full written report on Tron's Hawaii adventure."

"Right."

"Work it out. Get it done." He shook his head. "But don't take chances. Don't trust anyone in the Vietnamese community, and no more Lone Ranger."

Elliot returned to his paperwork, and Buck slid out of his office, knowing he had dodged a bullet.

—CHAPTER THIRTY-FIVE—

Buck drove uptown. His mind drifted to time spent with Le An. As much as the Wong case, she was on his mind. And she was a more pleasant obsession. He had never been so taken by a woman. It wasn't like him, and he wasn't sure where it led. But since his sessions with Dr. Mathews, he surprised himself. He was more open to having a real relationship, something he had never permitted himself to have. He and his ex-wife hadn't qualified. The closest he got to a real relationship was with his Nam buddies, and those ended abruptly, painfully, and permanently. He sensed an opportunity to create something new with Le An. Despite their age differences, they seemed to have much in common. They laughed at the same things. They were always at ease. And other than the Wong case, which was out-of-bounds, they could talk about anything at length, like old friends. It all seemed to work. Also, their intimacy worked perfectly, naturally, and from what he could judge, to their mutual satisfaction. He smiled to himself, and then the car hit another pothole.

Le An bounced out of his head, replaced by thoughts of her father. Something had caused Dr. Le to ask him to meet with some influential Union members of the Vietnamese community. Dr. Le only hinted to Buck about the purpose of the meeting. Buck made some guesses as to the reasons behind the call. Buck's team investigating Wong's death could interfere with the Union's operations. Or maybe Hansen's Political Corruption team breathing down Tien's neck had brought Tien over to their side. Possibly Buck and his group of investigators were making progress. Maybe the string of deaths was linked to fanatics in their organization systematically wiping out Communist spies. Buck wrestled with ideas on his way to the dinner. This time, taking no chances, he had brought Elliot on board. Buck pulled into a spot on the street three doors from the modest storefront restaurant. A green neon sign glowing behind the large pane of glass identified the *May Ngan Phuong Restaurant*.

Outsiders rarely entered its smoky environment; it was not a place one might find in a city guidebook of ethnic experiences. The owner immediately made Buck as he walked in. He bowed, smiled, and beckoned Buck to follow. Burning peanut oil fumes blended with cigarette smoke, forming a blue haze in the over-heated interior. The male diners' unfettered, alcohol-altered Vietnamese voices chopped through the thick air and bounced off the tin ceiling. The atmosphere unnerved Buck. He followed the little man out of the main space to a separate room in the back. The five men at the table stopped their discussion and stood as if called to attention. Dr. Lee walked up to Buck, shook his hand, and escorted him to the head of the table.

"Agent Buck. May I introduce General Le Dinh? A true patriot and soldier. Mr. Mai Van Ba, our attorney. Mr. Tran Trong Do, noted publisher. And Mr. Pham Van Tien, a distinguished cabinet member of the Mayor's Office. One by one, the men came forward, shook Buck's hand, then returned to stand at their chairs. In an uncomfortable moment, they waited for Buck to sit. He smiled at them and sat, and they joined him.

Dinner and wine were served. Buck ate some of everything offered, which seemed to please his hosts. The initial small talk, almost unbearable in its banality, appeared to be ending. The General asked him if he missed the cuisine.

Buck responded, "Never had any. We ate army-issue at basecamp or C-rations in the field. Back then, we didn't want to get too comfortable. We didn't even take R and R. We left the fancy food to the brass, with all due respect."

The General smiled like a Cheshire cat, puffing his pudgy cheeks around his flat black eyes. "You're right. General Staff did eat well, especially when we dealt with the politicians, but we all started as foot soldiers like you. I had many days in the field eating out of tin cans in the pouring rain. Of course, that was a long time ago. I was a little bit thinner then." He laughed.

Buck smiled a polite smile, as did the others. "Yes. For me, the war is over. How about you?"

The General's smile disappeared into his fleshy face. "Our war is over too, Agent Buck. It ended on April 29, 1975. But love for our homeland has not ended. Our people are scattered across the globe. Tossed about. We seek to unite them. Yet, our former enemies are being courted as trading partners. As if economics had replaced higher truths. Now, the U.S. government is forcing political refugees from our country to go back to live with the Communists. Supposedly to be resettled later. But our people are trapped. In refugee camps or as powerless victims under Communist control in Vietnam."

Sipping his plum wine, Buck listened carefully, deciding to check the room temperature by playing 'devil's advocate.' "Well, that aside, General, isn't it true that the current government is making some economic progress. I admit they're just getting a grip on capitalism over there, but '*doi moi*' is working, isn't it? It takes a bit of time to take a war-torn, rural country into the twenty-first century, doesn't it? Isn't it just a matter of time before your people assimilate into Vietnam?" Buck looked about the table to open up this topic for discussion.

Pham Van Tien looked like he would pop out of his reddening skin. "Maybe you don't understand, Agent Buck. Your government. I mean, the U.S. government has made deals with the Communist leaders in Vietnam. The purpose is to increase free trade with Vietnam. The politicians have paid lip service to the plight of expatriates. The boat people, refugees, and those who stayed behind unable to escape the tyranny. They have given into the Communists. Those people would self-destruct without the help of the government. Whatever the Commies promised, they lied. They promised to help people freely emigrate. This hasn't happened. Over 18,000 boat people were returned to Vietnam and promised resettlement. But you know who decides whether they can leave?"

"The Communists?" Buck guessed.

"Exactly. They made a good show of it for a while to influence Congress. Then once the die was cast. Nobody gets out. As if that were not enough. No former political prisoners can get out. No one with relatives who are American citizens. 15,000 former U.S. government employees who will never get out. The whole resettlement program in Vietnam is run by corrupt bureaucrats."

"Five thousand dollars for an exit permit. If you can get one," offered Mai Van Ba. "The U.S. sold out Vietnam. We agreed to finance the Communists, and they agreed to nothing."

"That is right," added Tran Trong Do. "Our people are not granted the same respect that others have been. Cuban-Americans retained their love for their homeland and loyalty to the United States. And the U.S. government does not recognize Communist Castro. The U.S. government is quite willing to intervene in the internal affairs of Iraq. And to be demanding with the Russians in the interest of democracy. But not so with the Vietnamese Communists. They get away with murder. For what did we fight the war?"

"But, gentlemen," Buck said quietly, "as we agreed, the war is over."

"For you, maybe," said the General in a jarring tone. Almost as soon as the words came out, he backtracked quietly, "Forgive me, Agent Buck. I am an old soldier. You know we never die. We just fade away. Maybe you did not experience the methods of the Communists. The torture. The cruelty."

Buck looked him in the eye. "I've seen my share of cruelty."

"Gentlemen," interjected Dr. Le, "let's not forget Agent Buck is our guest and that he is no stranger to our cause. He is a distinguished veteran."

"You're right. Forgive my passion for the homeland."

"No need," said Buck calmly. These were true believers.

"Yes, maybe foreign politics is not Agent Buck's interest. In any event, that is not the purpose of our meeting tonight. We would..."

"Wait a minute," said Dr. Le as a waiter and busboy entered. Le nodded to them to complete their work. They cleared the table and poured coffee. Speaking in his native tongue, he appeared to send them away for the evening. The restaurant owner bowed to all on his way out the door. Buck noticed a back exit directly from the room. He suspected the men at the table came and went through that door, avoiding the ordinary people out front. "Mr. Ba, please go on."

"As I was saying," Ba sipped on his cigarette holder, exhaling with a puff, "we asked you here tonight because we are concerned about your investigation. We know your group has been watching some of us. We presume it relates to the death of Mr. Wong. We also know that certain people here have a special relationship with factions within your organization. You are familiar with Agent Marsden." He paused, waiting for a reaction from Buck. None forthcoming, he proceeded. "And as you can perceive, even from our discussion tonight, strong sentiment exists for our homeland, and strong political viewpoints are maintained. Lastly, all of us have our own business and personal affairs, which we hope remain ours alone." He looked around the table, then focused on Buck's face. Another drag on his cigarette completed the attorney's well-timed pause. "Putting all of this aside, we do share a common goal, Agent Buck. We all desire to get to the truth related to Mr. Wong's death. We have no idea whether he was killed intentionally or accidentally, but we would like to put his matter to rest. For the sake of the community and to permit everyone to resume their normal lives. Therefore, we are asking that you accept our cooperation."

"What do you mean?"

218

"Mr. Tien..." Ba passed the verbal ball to the veteran politician and real estate mogul.

"Mr. Buck. Our chapter of the National Freedom Union will, with your permission, offer a $10,000 reward for information leading to the arrest and conviction of the person or persons, if any, involved in Mr. Wong's death. Again, with your permission, I shall make this announcement at the next City Council meeting. We are making this offer to demonstrate our concern for the welfare of our community and to assure you that the National Freedom Union had no part in this matter. What do you say, Agent Buck?"

Buck straightened in his chair before speaking. "Gentlemen, I am not authorized to speak for the Bureau, but personally, I see no reason why you should move in this direction. I would stress that Wong's death is only under investigation and that no determination of foul play has been made. However, I am impressed by your concern. If you were to make such a reward public, the public might assist our investigation, but I would only recommend it to my people if all leads were processed through my task force. On the other hand...please do not take this the wrong way...the Bureau would most likely find the possibility of such an alliance, necessity, and good intentions aside, not within the policy of our organization."

"What are you saying?" asked Mai Van Ba.

"I guess I'm saying that practically speaking, you may wish to make such a reward public, but the Bureau can't become involved. If, as a result of this, you get some useful information. We must evaluate it."

"Makes sense," commented the General. "That approach will be fine, Agent Buck." The aging warrior looked around the table for dissenters. There were none. "All right, that's settled. What else?"

Buck waited quietly for others to speak. They said nothing. He decided to go for broke. "Gentlemen. There is one other item."

The General fixed his gaze on Buck.

"Our investigation within the Vietnamese community has been difficult. As you know, the people here mistrust the police, and while not overtly offering resistance to our efforts, they have been less than cooperative. There could be many reasons for this, but my question to you is, can you create a more positive atmosphere for us?"

They all smiled, and Dr. Le responded, "While we are honored by your opinion that our little group can influence the will of the people of our community. I am afraid to disappoint you. The Vietnamese people are who they are. We cannot change that. They will always mistrust the police. Always on alert, always careful, and always very private. The nature of your work is opposed to the nature of the people. That we cannot change. However, maybe you have something specific for which we can assist. Is there something?" Dr. Le looked at Buck expectantly.

Buck did not want to reveal anything about the investigation to these men. But one piece of the puzzle was missing. So thoroughly missing that even Do Tron, who generally had a delicate finger on the pulse of the Vietnamese community, had come up empty. Finally, he answered, "Wong's busboy. We know he existed. I saw him. But he's missing or hiding. In any event, we can't find him. He was in Wong's place moments before the fire. He may know something. Do you know where he is, or can you find him? We don't even know his name."

Mai Van Ba looked around the table, checking the faces of each of his fellow Union members before answering. "We will try to help you. It is possible. You will be notified if we find him."

"Very good. There is one more thing." Buck paused. "Wong had been threatened. He came to us for help. Maybe he was afraid of the White Tiger. Maybe they broke his windows. Maybe they threatened him. Some say the Tiger is influenced by your organization. Is that true?"

Tien spoke. "Mr. Wong was a devoted supporter of the Freedom Union. If we had influenced the White Tiger, we would have asked them to stay away from Mr. Wong. I'm sure you can see the logic of that, Agent Buck."

"Yes, that makes sense...if Mr. Wong was one of your flock, but what if we found evidence connecting him to your enemies?"

"Do you have such evidence?" asked Ba.

Buck shook his head. "I only said 'what if.' Because if that were true, then the threats make sense."

"Your logic is too simple. We threaten no one. The community has, in the past, ostracized those suspected of Communist sympathies. While we understand such positions, we need not be concerned, for the community is self-policing in this regard. In any event, there is no need to blacken Mr. Wong's name with such speculation. Is there?"

"I suppose you are right. It is only speculation. But the terrorist tactics of the White Tiger are not. You know about the latest home invasion."

"Yes, but we do not support such activities, and we thank you for helping to eliminate this danger from our community," said Tien, sounding like a politician.

"You can't deny involvement with the Tiger. They do help your magazine's advertising campaigns, don't they?"

"Young men, some of whom may have connections with the White Tiger, help us present the truth by distributing our magazine," said Tran Trong Do. "They get a real job selling the paper or the ads for a part of the income, and we get the distribution of our views and a circulation base. It is a fair deal for both parties. We offer an alternative to gang activity. A small door to honest work and self-respect for the young men in our community. This is the national policy of our organization and a very successful one, I might add. If this was an African-American magazine offering employment to their community, would you even be asking such questions? I think not."

Buck sensed he was pushing up a rope. "What if we find that someone in the National Freedom Union was involved with Wong's death?"

The General answered. "If that is the case, but it is not, the law will decide, Agent Buck. Always you will have our cooperation."

"Appreciate that." He paused. "And what do you want?"

Buck waited. It was the General who took up the challenge. "We want your group to accept our relationship with the Bureau. We are not the enemy. We were your comrades in arms, Agent Buck. We remain that way. Details aside, let me say we have an understanding with some members of the Bureau. One that has been very satisfactory to all sides. Now with the unfortunate death of Mr. Wong," the General raised an eyebrow, "our arrangement is less certain."

"General, I'm not involved with foreign affairs. We're strictly domestic. Domestic terrorism. Threats by mail. That's our charge. We're pretty good at staying on our side of the playground. That can be easily confirmed."

"Thank you, Agent Buck. You have expressed your position very well. And I hope we have so clearly expressed ours. Please allow us to be helpful to you," said Pham Van Tien, "cooperation can bring all of us down from our mountain tops into the valley of understanding."

With that line of bullshit, this man should be an alderman. Buck left that conclusion, and many others, unexpressed. Tired of dancing with five guys who wanted to lead, the party was over. He hoped they could help him find the busboy. Perhaps something else would come up. But he doubted it.

On the other hand, maybe the Union just looked like it was at the bottom of every nasty thing in the Vietnamese community. Maybe these guys were just old patriots blowing off steam who had nothing to do with Wong's death and the others...and maybe pigs can fly. "Good night, gentlemen. Thank you."

222

—CHAPTER THIRTY-SIX—

"I have reduced the Team members working on the Wong case to the people at this table." Elliot looked at Do Tron, Vince, Buck, the Professor, Rat, and Andre. "I think we can close out the Wong matter." He turned to Randolph Clark, "Professor. You're up."

Clark stood and moved into position behind the projector. "Rat. Please kill the lights."

"Bang, bang," Rat waited for the groans before throwing the light switch.

"Thank you," said the Professor ignoring Rat's antics.

"Today, I have some photos of the boat people who arrived in San Francisco with Mr. Wong. I thought it would be good for us to have a mental picture of the puzzle pieces. Unfortunately, they were all camera-shy up until their untimely deaths. These are morgue shots, which I received from various places around the country. I am presenting them chronologically by date-of-death. Here's the first." The screen filled with a black and white photo of a burned face, blackened skin, and features almost destroyed. "Our first man, or what's left of him. Trung Xuan Truc. He was burned to death in an auto accident in California in late 1979. The medical examiner ruled this an accidental death. Truc drove a stolen car over an embankment. His car burned with him in it. He worked as a waiter after arriving in the country. He had entered the country with the others less than a year before his death."

He clicked to the next slide. The image showed a Vietnamese man who looked to be sleeping except for what appeared to be a bruised right temple. "This is Duong Trong Phu. He looks pretty good, but that's a bullet hole in his head. Found dead in his home in a suburb of Los Angeles about three years ago. He was a freelance writer and appears to have been rather outspoken about the need to normalize relations with the current government of Vietnam."

Rat interrupted. "Suicide, or did somebody help him?"

"Sorry. The M.E. said he could not have killed himself. Some of his fingers were cut off. Local police reported it as a burglary gone bad. No suspects or arrests."

"Maybe a writer without fingers provides the message," suggested Buck.

"I was thinking the same. Here's the next one. About four months later, in Houston. Name, Nguyen Ngoc Mo. He died by a razor across his throat. Incidentally, we don't know their ages. But we can assume other than the first, Truc, who was maybe in his late twenties, they were all in their forties. Anyway, this fellow, Mr. Mo, was an auto mechanic. He was also a card-carrying member of the National Freedom Union. To the Houston cops, it was street crime. His empty wallet was found a few blocks from the crime scene. Two suspects were arrested and later released. No one charged."

Clark clicked to a blank screen. "No photo for next guy. Hai Rau. He was a big one. Weighed in at 276 pounds. Clubbed to death about two years ago. I'm glad we don't have his photo. I imagine he was a mess. Found him upside down in a dumpster in the alley behind his restaurant in San Francisco. He may have been a member of the Union. His death remains unsolved.

Here's an interesting one," the Professor flipped to the next image and adjusted his glasses to see his notes. "This guy was a newspaperman." The photo of a bloated floater popped up. "He had a regular column in a local San Diego paper. His body washed in from the ocean. They suspect he jumped or was pushed off a bridge. No determination was made. Before he drowned, he wrote about Vietnamese issues. Some of his columns suggested moderation toward the Communist regime. I talked to some of his co-workers. He was well-liked. And they don't think he killed himself. They said he was a good family man. However, they didn't want to speculate who killed him."

"Did they seem afraid? asked Vince.

"That could be. I would guess if they talked too much, they might get the urge to jump off a bridge."

"Here's number six. Another slasher throat job. A bit messier than the first." The color image presented evidence of a problematic kill. Several minor cuts high on the man's neck were visible above the severe slash across his Adam's apple. "This fellow Vu Van Ha tried to fight off his assailant." Clark clicked on a second image of the same man. "You can see the cuts on his hands and arms. Defensive wounds. But he lost the battle. He owned a noodle shop in the wharf area. As far as the Boston police were concerned, he had no political ax to grind. Just a regular businessman.

"And our finalist, Mr. Dang Hung Duc. This photo was taken in Fairfax, Virginia, about six months ago. But he was a resident of Miami. The police could find no reason for him to be in Fairfax. He was karate-chopped coming out of a motel bathroom." The photo showed a well-tanned man with slicked-back black hair and good musculature. "In Miami, he owned a very successful martial arts school. He had a large following of students. Miami PD says he was as much a preacher as a teacher. Very pro-conservative. We know he was in the Union, and he was killed by one of his students, the young man he was traveling with. Duc was drying off after a shower. He flipped his head back, and his student crushed his windpipe with a single blow. Obviously, Duc was a good teacher. That's the last of them."

"What about the kid? The student?" asked Elliot.

"He's dead too. Suicide in jail. He left a note apologizing to the Duc family...said he had made a mistake. No other explanation." He switched off the projector, and Rat flipped the light switch.

"I must say, Professor, if you don't watch out, your slide shows are going cable for Halloween," said Elliot. "That was a lot of carnage over a short period. Put together any theories?"

"Have I connected the deaths? Only in one way. Each of these men arrived on the Kobe Maru on September 12, 1977."

Tron cleared his throat before speaking. "Well, we know one thing the local police didn't. We know these men were special boat people. Handpicked to play the role. North Vietnamese. Killers. And probably spies. That is the second connection."

Rat jumped in. "And all violent deaths. Some look like murders. But all pretty rough." He scratched the top of his crew-cut head. "A lot of common elements."

"Yes, but how are they different?" asked Buck.

"Different times," said Vince. He loosened his tie, freeing a couple of his chins. "One right after he entered the country. Accidental death. All the others within the last three years. And all different locations."

"Some Commie-sympathetic. Some pure Union guys," said Elliot. "Seems like a mixed bag."

"Don't forget the eighth man, Mr. Wong," said Buck. "Possibly a murder, but maybe not."

Clark killed the projector fan, and suddenly the room fell quiet. It stayed quiet until Elliot spoke, "Let's go from the supposition that all these guys were planted here by the Communists. What did they intend to accomplish?"

Andre spoke. "Disrupt or discredit former South Vietnamese leaders. I would guess that was their main goal. They might manipulate opinion by identifying Union people with Communist relatives in Vietnam. Communist spies could identify these people easily. Then compromise them and turn them."

"What else?" asked Elliot.

"Change public opinion," said Rat. "I don't know if a handful of spies could do that?"

"If they were writers. Newspaper guys. They could. Right? Like that fellow in San Diego," said Buck.

The Professor interjected. "We've got a couple of dead writers and four Union members. If you count Mr. Wong. One guy who died too soon to become much of anything, and one who wasn't into politics. I'd say some of them could have influenced community or Union opinion. But they also could have just been reporting. In effect, 'doubles.' Attending Union meetings, identifying leaders, and reporting back to headquarters."

"What about cleanin' house?" asked Vince. "Couldn't their job be to kill off Union people?"

"Possible. But risky. I don't think the Communists would waste these infiltrators as killers. They might hire somebody, though."

"How 'bout that martial arts guru? He could probably get his students lining up to try out their skills," suggested Rat.

"I don't know," replied Clark, chewing on an empty pipe. "Most of the cases I've researched look the other way around. Guys killed who protested against the Union or appeared to promote the Communist line. There have been quite a few writers and publishers taken out."

"Unless the spy killed some Commie-Symp just to prove his loyalty. Might help his cover," suggested Vince.

"Fellows." Do Tron cleared his throat, "You forget one thing. These Vietnamese communities are very tight. Everybody knows everybody. I doubt a spy would want to be subject to the scrutiny of the conservative Vietnamese, which he would certainly be if he was involved in intimidation or killings. Most likely, he would stay low-key in the background. Observing and reporting. Maybe waiting for a final order. If the Communists needed it done, they could use the spies to kill the South Vietnamese leadership here in America as a last desperate act. However, I doubt it. It's more likely they would use subtle influence to create an environment of acceptance of the new government of Vietnam. All they would need to do is to undermine the old South Vietnamese leaders. To make them appear out of touch. Extremists. With or without the help of spies, that is what happened over the past decades. A quiet revolution of words. An acquiescence. And passing the dimming torch of South Vietnamese patriotism to a generation more interested in the stock market's status than who controls the old country. Let's face it, except for Cuba and a few hard-liners in Russia, Communism is dead. The world is one big market economy. I think the spies probably ran out of real work."

"Maybe, Tron. But that wouldn't stop the conservatives from icing them if they found out who they were," said Rat.

Elliot looked puzzled. "How would they find out? You know how these spies would have been organized. Typical cell-structure. Their initial set of instructions would come from only one person. A control. A minimum number of links in the chain. That way, if one person is caught, he only has limited knowledge. An individual spy may not even know his control. With well-planned drops, they need never meet to exchange information. And these men were spread all over the country." Elliot paused, thinking, "The more outspoken the writers and publishers, maybe even the martial arts guy, could have slipped up. Become too obvious. They could have been eliminated by right-wingers because of their public positions. But the others. A couple of restaurant owners, if you include Wong. An auto mechanic. A noodle shop owner. Those aren't provocative occupations. A good spy would maintain a low profile. Possibly one of these guys spilled his guts about the September 12th group, and somehow whoever is killing tracked them down just like we did."

"Except," said the Professor, "we made them because they were dead. Until they died, they would just blend in." He looked across the table. "Tron. If someone had the names of the eight men, could they track them down across the county?"

Tron smiled. "A good Vietnamese skip-tracer could find these men if they maintained the same names they entered with. I think most Americans are confused by Vietnamese names. In some way, they all look the same. But the fact is Vietnamese people can be tracked like anyone else. If they had the names, smart people could find them and kill them. The second man, Mr. Phu, I believe. The fellow had his fingers removed before taking a bullet to the head. Maybe he was tortured, or maybe he talked and opened the door to the whole gang of spies. These people play rough. Once they had the ship's name or the entry date, they could determine the names of the others. Maybe all eight weren't spies. But maybe they killed everyone on the list. Maybe they dug further, like we did, identifying the man in Hawaii. They took no chances and tracked me to Hawaii and killed Mr. Nhi even though he knew nothing about spying. Professor, do you have a detailed medical examiner report on Mr. Phu? I wonder if there was any evidence of other torture. Beating bruises, cuts, whatever."

"We don't have detailed reports, but we can get them. We should also check if anyone else made inquiries about the eight men at Immigration. Phu was killed only about three years ago. That trail could be pretty fresh."

"Sounds good. Are you taking that one, Professor?" asked Elliot.

The Professor nodded.

"Vince, what about the busboy?" asked Elliot. "You and Buck saw him in Wong's restaurant on the day of the fire. What about him? What does he have to say?"

Vince shrugged his shoulders. "Don't know. Can't find him. Got a name, but that's it. He's disappeared. Tron's on this one."

"If he saw something, he might be fearing for his life," said Tron. "I think he's gone underground. I've spoken to his cousin. She hasn't seen him since the fire. Nobody else has either."

"Find him," said Elliot with authority. "If he's got answers, we want him."

229

Do Tron smiled at his boss. "If he's gone underground, it will be tough to find him. He may be out of the city by now. Someplace else. A safer location. Remember, a busboy is not exactly a company president. He doesn't have much to lose by leaving Chicago. He may have a lot to gain. Like his life."

"You're right," said Elliot. "But keep at it, Tron." Elliot looked around the table, about to close the meeting. "OK, what else? Mike, you've been kind of quiet. What are you thinking?"

Buck looked up. "I guess I'm thinking about the first guy. Mr. Auto Accident. The waiter. He certainly had bad luck. Everyone else enters and succeeds in building businesses, becoming columnists and martial arts school owners, but this poor bastard dies in an auto accident."

"Accidents happen, Mike," said Rat.

Buck shrugged his shoulders and nodded. "Yeah. I know. But it just seems sloppy. These guys must have been well-trained to be trusted with such an assignment. My gut says well-trained people avoid mistakes of all kinds. Tron's theory may well be true. Maybe the right-wingers got lucky. With a little torture, they blew the ring's cover. That still doesn't explain the early death of Mr. Auto Accident. I think we should check him out. He's an oddity. Let's find out exactly how he died. Let's make sure it was him. Hell, all we saw was a burned body. Was he properly identified? If so, how? We're dealing with North Vietnamese intelligence officers. I know these people. They're sharp. That first guy could have shoved a bum into a burning car and tossed his wallet on the ground. The cops find the ID and bingo. Spy number one dead, at least as far as the world is concerned."

Elliot seemed unconvinced. "Who knows? Anyone want it?" Nobody responded.

Buck looked around. "OK. I'll take it," said Buck. "I've got the bug." He smiled.

"Good," said Elliot. "Forget about the rest of these guys. What about Tien? I spoke with Hansen. He says he got a judge to issue a Traveling Title 3. Rat, are you working with him?"

Rat nodded. "Yep. Andre and I are going on a fishing expedition. Tien's phones."

"You better take Tron along," said Elliot.

Rat gave Tron a look. "Ready for a little fishing, Tron?"

"Why not?" said Tron wearing a smile. "We might hook a big one."

The meeting ended with Tron informing them that the $10,000 reward offered by the Union was causing quite a stir in the Vietnamese community. But he also assessed that some people might view the Union's unusual largess as a way of exposing witnesses, and nobody wanted to be an exposed witness.

In closing the meeting, Elliot warned them that time was running out. If something didn't pop soon, the Wong case would go on the back burner, manned part-time by Buck alone.

CHAPTER THIRTY-SEVEN

"Hello, Mrs. Hang. This is Special Agent Clark in Chicago. I visited with you regarding the boat people."

"Oh yes, the Professor," said the soft female voice on the other end. "How good to hear from you."

"I'm not interrupting anything. I hope." Clark looked at his watch. It was about 10:30 PM, two hours earlier, in San Francisco.

She chuckled. "It's not past my bedtime. If you were concerned."

"Thanks. I hope you can help us again."

The old woman was quiet. He could hear her breathing.

"One of those men who entered on the freighter Kobe Maru. He died soon after entering the country. Auto crash. Burned to death. But we need some way to positively identify him. One way would be dental records. According to the coroner's office, the man we've identified had a pretty distinctive set of teeth. Nice bridgework and caps."

"Well, Agent Clark, I'm thinking, but I can't remember any boat person arriving with their dental records. But I would guess dental work was fairly uncommon for the boat people."

"Yes. I thought so too. But what about their teeth? Do you know anyone who took care of their teeth, or maybe a doctor? Someone who would recommend a dentist."

"Let me think..." she said, sounding as if she had turned her head away from the receiver.

Clark waited. He sucked on his pipe, blowing the smoke toward the beamed ceiling of his home study.

"Most often, the new arrivals would be interviewed by a health officer. They would look for infectious diseases. I'm certain there were no records of their teeth. And a person would have to have needed emergency work to get a referral from INS."

"What about after INS?"

"They would be on their own. They could use any dentist in town. But most likely, the dentist would be Vietnamese."

"Do you have any names, Mrs. Hang?"

"Well, it's been over twenty years..." she hesitated. I have one person I can check with. Let me do that and call you back. All right?"

"That would be fine. I appreciate it."

"Did you spend any time in my files?"

Clark was taken aback. He had almost forgotten the newspaper files on the Union that Mrs. Hang had loaned to him. "No. Not yet."

"Oh. I hoped they might have been of some use."

Clark cleared his throat. "To tell you the truth, I put them on the back burner. But thanks for reminding me."

"All right. I'll call you back as soon as I can."

"Mrs. Hang, thank you very much. I'm asking a lot."

She tittered. "Please, Professor. What does an old woman have to do? This is wonderful. I'm happy to assist you."

He gave her all his numbers, thanked her again, and hung up, sucking on his pipe for inspiration. He spent the rest of the evening going over Mrs. Hang's information. The accordion file had sat on the corner of his desk since he and Marilyn had returned from San Francisco. He began to thumb through the material. Most of the articles were from the *San Francisco Examiner*, but some were from other cities in California. Others written in Vietnamese appeared to be local to the San Francisco area. The articles highlighted the words 'National Freedom Union' as a means of identity. Meetings, rallies, and protests seemed to be constant. Ten minutes of random review convinced him the pieces were irrelevant to his concerns. He focused on 1977 and 1978, looking for anything related to the spy who died in the auto crash.

The crash occurred north of Los Angeles, so he focused on an advertisement from 1978 for a Vietnamese restaurant in that area. He remembered the police report said he was a waiter. Still, he couldn't remember if it mentioned the restaurant that employed him. He shuffled the papers on his desk, and finding the police report, he determined the dead man, Trung Xuan Truc, had worked at a *Maison Vietnam* restaurant. He returned to the Los Angeles papers to find a restaurant section in one. In the review section, he located *Maison Vietnam*. From what he could determine, it was a fine restaurant with elegant cuisine, probably a place those with money and success would frequent. A good place for a spy to work. It would have attracted the movers and shakers in the Los Angeles Vietnamese community.

For the hell of it, he dialed the number of the restaurant. A man answered, eager to take his reservation. Clark identified himself and asked if he could speak to the manager. Quickly he was connected to Mr. Renard. The Professor identified himself as FBI and provided bare-bones reasons for his inquiry. He asked the man if anyone at the restaurant had worked there in 1977 or '78.

"No," the man answered quickly, his voice somewhat breathless and wearing a slight French accent, which Clark adjudged to be affected, "there is no one here from those days. The restaurant opened in 1977, and we have made many improvements since then. Many years have passed. We don't even have records from then."

"Nothing?"

"No." He paused. "I think," he said. "Maybe. There is someone who, I think, worked here in the '80s. Hold the phone." A minute passed. Renard returned. "Hello?"

"Yes."

"I spoke to one of the cooks. He remembers this fellow as a waiter for the first few years. A man named Bao. Worked here from the start. The cook says he resigned to open his own place in Santa Barbara."

"Do you have the name of the restaurant in Santa Barbara?" asked Clark.

The phone was silent but for the sound of canned music in the background. "No."

"Please. It's essential."

"Hold, please." Clark heard the man lower the phone and shout to someone. Another person could be heard. They spoke in Vietnamese for at least a minute, then Renard returned online. "Cook remembered. The Green Bamboo Cafe. *C'est bon?*"

"*Tres bon. Merci beaucoup.* Green Bamboo. Santa Barbara. Mr. Bao."

"Correct. But just 'Bao,' not Mister. Like Liberace or Cher. He just goes by 'Bao.'"

"Bao. Got it. Thanks, Mr. Renard. Have a pleasant evening." Clark hung up. He immediately dialed information for the Santa Barbara restaurant. He called and got a recorded message. The restaurant was closed but would reopen tomorrow. As he hung up again, his wife called to him. It was time for their favorite British television mystery show, something they had never missed. He tucked in his files and shut down his computer for the evening, joining Marilyn in front of the rec room TV for a bowl of popcorn and someone else's mystery.

—CHAPTER THIRTY-EIGHT—

Judge Thomas Bannen, a Federal Judge in the Northern District, wasn't always a friend of the Bureau. But this time, Pete had convinced him to authorize the wiretap on Pham Van Tien based on the evidence presented by the Political Corruption Squad. To save time, the PC Squad had submitted and expedited a written affidavit requesting the wiretap through the U.S. Attorney General's local offices, claiming a possible life-and-death situation. The document was approved in Washington, D.C., and returned to the judge. Hansen and his partner Sid Lasic had followed up on the leads provided by their new asset, Pechocki. Solid evidence of real estate transfer from the South Side paving contractor to a third party and, ultimately, to a trust controlled by Tien was presented. The decision-makers had also looked at evidence tying Tien to insurance proceeds on fire-ravaged buildings. Wiretaps would be permitted on all of Tien's phones.

Under the law, the FBI could monitor them. They could eavesdrop when Tien was on the phone. This meant his home phone was fair game since he had a separate line for his City Hall phone that could be monitored whenever he was in the building. Hard-wired phones were simple to tap, requiring only the cooperation of the phone company, but cellular phones required proximity to the user and special equipment to intercept the signal.

Andre and Rat sat secreted in the back of the van, concealed by a black curtain behind the split seat. Rat adjusted the bulky black earphones wrapped over his ever-present Bulls cap, his attention focused on the scanner screen. The dim dial lights of the equipment cast a reddish glow on his unshaven, beard-stubbled face. Sitting with his back to Rat, Andre watched a small monitor connected to a concealed camera focused on the suspect's home. A constant cold rain beat on the van's roof. They had parked across the street from Tien's three-story townhouse on a corner of the DePaul neighborhood. They were in the third hour of their shift, having relieved Vince Gorski and Buck at about four that afternoon.

The mayor's man, Tien, had arrived home at about five o'clock, parking his municipal car in a garage. Tien, dodging raindrops and in a hurry, seemed not to notice the van disguised as a contractor vehicle. If a suspicious someone called the suburban phone number on the truck logo, they would get an answering machine connected to a phone line registered to the mythical flooring company. Such calls were also monitored to identify the caller. Tien hadn't called that number, but he had made three calls, one to his dentist and the others to a phone registered to someone named Dung Vu at a Chicago Uptown address. The Mayor's Special Assistant had allowed the phone to ring eight times. No one answered. Immediately, he placed the same call again, rang six times, and hung up.

Rat looked at his Mickey Mouse watch. "Been about twenty-five minutes. I gotta' hunch something's goin' down."

"Hope so. I'm cramping." Andre adjusted his large frame, half-standing, to stretch his muscles. In doing so, he accidentally pushed Rat halfway off his chair as Rat's equipment beeped twice, and an icon popped up on the flat-screen of the scanner device set to intercept Tien's cell phone calls.

"Jesus H. Christ, start the tape Andre," directed Rat. Andre activated the tape recorder while Rat scrambled to regain his position. He held the headphones tight to his ears to cut out all other noises but for the sounds coming from Tien's phone. After it ended, he spoke. "Jeez, that was quick. That was him. All Vietnamese. Did you get it?"

"I think so. Hold on," said Andre as he reversed the tape and replayed it as both men listened on headphones. Tien's voice answered with one word. The other side responded in kind, one word. Then Tien uttered a few more words before terminating the call—about ten seconds of conversation.

"Get Tron." Rat made the call to his home.

A familiar voice answered.

"Tron, Rat here. Listen. Can you translate this?" He played the Vietnamese conversation.

Tron came back at him quickly. "This is it. First-person says 'Water.' Second-person says 'Mountain.' Is this number fourteen?" First-person says 'No.' Second person says, 'Sorry.' And that's it."

"That's it?" asked Rat loudly in disbelief.

"Is that Tien?"

"Right."

"Did you get the number?"

"Andre's checking that now. Just wait."

"I'm eating dinner."

"Sorry."

"Payphone. Uptown. On Leland."

"Do you think this is it?" asked Tron quietly.

"Shit. I don't know. What do you think? You dig the lingo. I don't." There was no response. "Tron?"

"Yes..." Seconds passed. "This might be something. Put CPD on alert. Agreed?"

"Copy that. We'll be monitoring. Talk later." The phone clicked without waiting for a reply from the Vietnamese cop. Rat fingered the list looking for the Town Hall District Commander's number. Earlier, the task force had transmitted a list of twelve properties known to be owned or managed by Tien's real estate company. Nine of these were occupied. Three were vacant, two apartment buildings and one store. This list was in the hands of the local area Chicago Police beat cops. He made the call and spoke with the Watch Commander securing the alert.

Thirty minutes later, the two Squad 7 agents were outside one of Pham Van Tien's buildings. It faced the main thoroughfare in the middle of an otherwise vacant, rubble-filled block north of Little Saigon. From a real estate standpoint, this area offered the possibility of gentrification. The beat cops had radioed a description of two men acting suspiciously. The men entered the building from the rear, observed by the cops carrying cardboard boxes and appearing to strain under the load. Andre and Rat had the cops park their car near the front of the building, ready to catch anyone attempting to flee in that direction. Rat requested additional CPD undercover backup via walkie-talkie, and he and Andre decided to enter now. They wanted to catch the two men in the act of arson if that indeed was their intent.

"Quiet," said Andre. Rat nodded. They proceeded with caution. The rain had subsided into a misty, wind-driven drizzle, which reduced night vision and foot traction. Low rumbles of thunder stumbled across the sky, and intermittent cloud lightning flashed above like soft, giant light bulbs. Approaching from the alley, they looked at the old, empty, three-story, three-flat brick structure. Rat radioed to the cops in front that they were entering the building from the rear.

"I'm thinking first floor," Rat whispered to the big man.

"Why not the basement?"

"Look." Rat pointed to the basement door. Its weather-beaten and plywood board-up job appeared defiant. The first-floor deck was located about four feet above the ground. It seemed like a stair had been purposely removed to make entry into the building more difficult. "Give me a boost, and then I'll pull you up." Andre shook his head but complied with the diminutive man's request. Standing in front of an area of broken railing, Rat held his hands out, elbows cocked, allowing Andre to grip him beneath his elbows. Rat kept his arms stiff to his sides. Then in one smooth movement, Andre effortlessly lifted him, depositing his butt on the porch. Quickly Rat scrambled to his feet and leaned down to

239

help Andre up. For a moment, the two stood chest-to-chest, breathing heavily. They smelled the gasoline fumes.

"Jesus. Quick." Rat spun away and slid his pistol from his shoulder holster. Carefully, he opened a beat-up screen door. The rusted hinges announced the penetration. Noticing evidence of a forced entry, he pushed the door open. Andre followed. In the cold darkness, Rat shivered. Deep inside the building, they heard the bang of an empty can bouncing along the floor and voices speaking Vietnamese.

"Rat," whispered Andre. "Let's wait for them to come out." The little man looked at him almost as if he hadn't heard. Andre tried again. "They've got to come this way. That's their truck out back." Rat nodded in agreement. Slowly Andre stepped out, holding the door for his partner. Rat had one foot out the door when something scrambled across the dirty ceramic tiles of the kitchen floor and then onto his foot on its way out. A two-pound rat dug its claws into the leather top of his shoe before making a frenzied exit.

"Shit!" shouted Rat in a voice loud enough for anyone in the building to hear. He backed out of the opening, and the door slammed before Andre could catch it. Voices inside erupted. Another rat outran the gasoline spill and exited.

"Rat, this thing's going. Let's get out!" shouted Andre. They scrambled off the deck, landing in the mud below, and quickly took positions about thirty feet from the porch.

The night, black with heavy clouds, stole the edges of the old hulk of a building, meshing it into the mist. They waited. A couple of minutes passed. The wind died down—silence—then the night erupted into a war zone. A brilliant white flash illuminated every brick and joint of the building, every puddle and stone in the backyard, and every drop of mist in the air with searchlight intensity. Lightning had struck and exploded the pole-mounted ComEd transformer in the alley. A blue-white electric snake rippled above the service line and traveled into the basement down the rear wall conduit. A half-second later, the entire first floor exploded, raining down shards of glass. Andre and Rat flattened out, covered their heads, and then looked up to see the flames withdrawing into the building like serpent's tongues. Eerie, animalistic sounds pierced the night. A horde of rats appeared, fighting to get out, screaming and sliding on the kitchen floor, then shooting through the screen door, their coats aflame. Moving as one, they swelled as a burning waterfall of fur over the edge onto the ground, scurrying past the two stunned agents into the darkness, then dying in a mass grave as strangely festive, smoldering, smelly smudge pots.

A figure appeared at the door. A man in flames. He stumbled through the opening onto the porch and stood Christ-like against the night, arms raised to the sky. He screamed for help and then fell headfirst off the porch. Andre and Rat rushed to his aid. Rat pulled off his jacket and threw it over the man's flaming head and shoulders, extinguishing them. Andre rolled him over in the mud. The arsonist had become an ugly whimpering mound of steamy mud-covered flesh.

"At least he's alive. What about the other guy?" asked Rat.

"Don't think so," said Andre as he shielded his face from the intense heat. In the distance, fire truck sirens filled the hollows of the night. "Let's pull him out of here. I'll roll him onto your jacket, and we'll slide him," shouted Andre over the din of the fire.

Rat laid his jacket on the ground, gently rolling the man atop. He groaned. Then each grabbed a sleeve, and they pulled him to the alley. Misty rain drizzled as Rat shined a flashlight into the man's face. He blinked. "A good sign. Maybe he'll talk."

Out of the night, the two hunched-over beat cops approached cautiously. Recognizing no threat, they moved into the circle of Rat's flashlight, looked down at the man, and then back to the agents. A cop, built like a meat packer, spoke, "Ambulance on the way. Think he'll make it?"

"Looks like it. I hope so."

"You're an optimist," said the other. "What happened to the other guy?"

Rat pointed to the building.

"Toast."

"What set it off?"

"Lightning,' he pointed to the smoking transformer above, "ran down the wire right into the building. One big gas bomb."

The burned man, now sedated, was slid into a fire department ambulance six minutes later. The driver weaved her way through the gathered crowd of bystanders. Rat, Andre, and the two beat cops watched the firemen strike the fire discussing the events of the evening. Later they talked with a fire captain and evidence techs who had arrived on the scene. Eventually, the two Squad 7 men departed, leaving it to the cops to make a report. Grabbing coffee at a local diner, they placed another call to Tron. Then they relaxed for a few minutes before heading for the hospital.

CHAPTER THIRTY-NINE

"No, we don't know if they were members of the White Tiger. We don't have any I.D. on them. The guy we brought in was clean. Checking the truck plates now." Rat's shrill voice bounced off the tiled walls of the hospital emergency room. "You can forget a visual, Tron. The one guy's a barbecued chicken in the morgue, and Claude Rains in here is wrapped like the Invisible Man."

"Burned pretty badly?" asked Tron.

"Doctor says sixty-five percent," answered Andre.

"Can we talk to him?"

Rat nodded. "You can for a few minutes. That's all the doctor will give us. We didn't want to waste our time. It's your show. You better read him his rights in English and Vietnamese. Doctor says he won't be able to talk. You'll have to figure something else out."

Tron rolled his eyes. "I'm not Jesus," he said grimly, "but I'll give it a try. We go for the Tien connection right away?" Tron looked at the two men for confirmation.

"Makes sense to me," answered Andre.

"Let's go," said Rat as the trio passed the uniformed Chicago cop who guarded the private intensive care room. Surrounded by state-of-the-art electronic monitoring devices, a drip bag connected, and his upper body and head bandaged except for viewports, the would-be arsonist reclined, seemingly comatose. They stared at him. The quiet singing of a heartbeat monitor provided the only sound besides the man's heavy breathing. Rat motioned to Tron to take the lead position next to the head. Andre stood adjacent to the monitor on one side of the bed. Rat stood at the foot of the bed, ready to operate the portable video camera he had secured from the tech van. "You're on, Tron," said Rat as he triggered the tape.

Tron spoke in Vietnamese. "Wake up, friend. Wake up." The man stirred, and his eyelids flickered. "My name is Do Tron. I am with the Federal Bureau of Investigation. I am a policeman. These are two of my coworkers. Do you understand me?" The man's black eyes looked out past the mass of bandages, searching for focus. "If you hear my words, blink your eyes. Do you understand?" They waited. About five seconds later, the eyes blinked slowly. "Good. Now, I will inform you of your rights as a citizen." Tron pulled a small plastic-coated sheet from his chest pocket and fulfilled his legal obligation in a slow, halting fashion, stopping after each sentence and requesting the man acknowledge his understanding of them at the end by blinking again, twice. He did so. Then Tron reread the rights in English.

"Do you think he understood his rights?" asked Andre. Tron nodded affirmatively.

"He's got the 'remain silent' part down cold," said Rat. "Go ahead. Ask him."

Tron leaned close, placing his face into the man's line of vision. "Can you see me?" The man blinked. "I would like to help you in your next life. You have made a mess of this one. Your friend is dead, and, to some degree, you must accept responsibility. You have an opportunity now to change the direction of your life. We need to know who told you to set the fire tonight. Will you help yourself by helping us?"

The man's eyes studied Tron's face. For his part, Tron never wavered. He stared at the man with a face full of sympathy and concern. Seconds passed. Then a minute. Out of the black depth of the eyes of the young arsonist, tears filled the corners. Tron grabbed a nearby tissue and dabbed them away. The eyes blinked.

"Good for you," said Tron. "Now, I will ask the question once, very slowly. I want you to blink three times if the answer is yes. Were you directed to torch the building by Pham Van Tien?"

The eyes remained still, then blinked once, twice, and again. "Good. Do you understand English?" He blinked. In English now, he asked, "Were you directed to torch the building by Pham Van Tien, the Special Assistant to the Mayor? If this is true, blink three times." Rat and Andre watched the man's face intently. The eyes blinked again. "Very good. We will leave you now. We know you will get better, and we look forward to your cooperation in the future. We leave you with our blessings. Goodbye."

Tron turned toward the other agents and motioned them to leave the room. They left quietly and spoke to the doctor on duty on the way out. He confirmed that the young man would likely survive to face trial, but not soon. He had a long period of recovery ahead. They left the doctor and moved on, heading to the coffee shop. "Not much," said Rat as they stopped mid-way down the long corridor. "A blinking arsonist. You think it's enough to haul in Tien's butt?"

Andre nodded. "That, the tape recording and the real estate and city contract records. I think we can get his attention. After all, one man died tonight, and Mr. Wong died in another fire in one of Tien's buildings. I say go for it."

"Let's run it by Buck and Elliot," suggested Tron smiling. "I think it's time to light a fire of our own." Then they headed down the hall for a long day's last cup of coffee.

—CHAPTER FORTY—

"Thank you for coming in, Mr. Tien," said Buck, seated at the head of the conference table in the elegant, large meeting room in the executive area of the Chicago Bureau office. It was very unusual to interview in this room, but the Mayor's Special Assistant was given this courtesy at Elliot's suggestion. Pham Van Tien and his attorney sat to Buck's right, while Do Tron and Pete Hansen sat to his left.

Mai Van Ba, Tien's attorney, quickly brought forth his agenda. "Mr. Tien is here because he wishes to be a cooperative citizen...and no other reason. If there are matters for which he might be helpful to your investigation of the death of Mr. Wong, he will, of course, offer his complete cooperation. You have been informed of the level of interest on behalf of the leaders of the Vietnamese community to help solve this case and their very generous offer of a reward."

"Yes, the Bureau is aware of those efforts, and they are appreciated."

The attorney smiled and looked toward his client, who sat peacefully, elbows resting on the chair with his hands loosely intertwined. Ba spoke, his words flowing, connected one to the next in a mellifluous singsong, "Of course, given the voluntary nature of this meeting, we would request that no recording is necessary." He studied the reel-to-reel tape recorder at the end of the table with mild concern.

"That machine will not be used for recording. You will note we do not have a reporter present. You are correct, Mr. Ba. We are here to discuss matters that may relate to the Wong matter. May we begin?" Buck asked the question as if Ba's answer mattered.

"Yes, Agent Buck," said Tien, looking Buck directly eye-to-eye. "Please, let us begin. I have a busy day ahead, including a meeting with the Mayor about two hours from now." As Tien spoke, he straightened his chair, separating his hands and turning to face Buck. He placed his right hand flat on the table, and while he didn't tap his fingers, they appeared to be ready to dance.

Buck read the body language. "We will take no more than an hour of your time, sir." He opened the manila file, read from it, and then looked at the Mayor's Special Assistant. "I'm sure you know the apartment building in the fifty-two hundred block of Broadway suffered a fire last night," said Buck.

"Yes," replied Tien, his eyes narrowing.

"And you are the owner of that building."

"Not really." Tien looked away from Buck momentarily, preparing as if contemplating how to explain something to a child. "Much of our land is owned in real estate trusts. The holdings in trusts are owned by limited partnerships and operated by a general partner that is a corporation. I am the president of that corporation. The real estate firm in which I share ownership manages the real estate in these trusts. However, my firm was only under contract to manage the specific building that burned last night. It is owned by others also in trust, I believe. Our management firm, as managers, would probably be listed as a contact on the trust document."

Buck looked over to Hansen for assistance. Hansen offered none. "Fine, who are the others?"

"The owners?"

"Yes."

Tien looked at his attorney, who nodded. "They are two local businessmen. They intended to remodel this building and rent it. Of course, now, it is a total loss. My inspectors indicate it must be demolished."

Hansen cleared his throat. "I have a question. Mr. Tien, isn't it true that you...let's say the owners have assembled a rather large

247

piece of land surrounding the burned building by purchasing many small buildings and then demolishing them to get a large cleared site?"

Tien looked at Hansen and smiled. "Ah, Agent Hansen, I see you have been reading our local Vietnamese newspaper. That was a story for which I was interviewed last month. In fact, the zoning of this property is before the Zoning Committee of the City Council. It is in for rezoning from mostly residential uses to commercial." Tien moved his gaze off of Hansen and focused on Buck. "You are correct. I am, of course, a proponent of the new shopping center which will be built on the site. This project will be a wonderful addition to the neighborhood. Something for everyone. Like Westminster, California. It will be good for the Vietnamese and everyone else in Chicago."

"What about the burned building? Is that part of the site?" asked Hansen.

"No." Tien smiled. "Although it sits at the edge, our architects have been able to design around it."

"Insurance?" asked Buck.

"You mean on the burned building?"

"Right."

Tien shrugged his shoulders. "I would hope so. Almost all of the buildings are insured. It's required by the lenders."

Hansen leaned in. "Would the land under the burned building be a useful addition to the shopping center site?

"Useful, yes," said Tien, "essential, no. As I said, the current plan works well without it."

"Agent Buck," interrupted Mai Van Ba, holding the soft fist of one hand cradled in the other, "if I may ask, what does all of this have to do with the death of Mr. Wong? Regrettably, Mr. Wong died in a fire in a building owned by my client. But there have been no allegations of arson. I can understand your concern with last night's fire."

"We're interested in connections." Buck looked at Tien. "Did you know the two men involved in the arson?"

For the first time in the interview, Tien appeared somewhat uncomfortable. He twisted slightly in his chair. His words seemed forced. "In the interest of the community." He looked at his attorney. "After I heard about the fire, I asked Mr. Ba to check with some friends. I don't know the two men involved. But I believe they may have helped to provide security for some of our meetings."

"You mean the National Freedom Union?" asked Buck.

"Yes."

"Are they part of the White Tigers?"

"I am not certain," said Tien. "It is often the case with our young men. The gang seems to serve a function for them. I wish it were not the case, but I am a realist, and I...we...must work with them in our community."

"But you never spoke with them?" asked Buck.

Tien hesitated. "I don't think so, but I am not in charge of security. That is the General's assignment."

"Mr. Tien. We would like to play a tape recording for you."

Tien looked at Buck, then at the tape recorder atop the table, then at Do Tron, who activated it on Buck's nod. The machine played the ten-second sound bite captured by Rat and Andre the night before. Tien listened but said nothing.

"Play it again, Tron," directed Buck. The Vietnamese voice repeated the apparent coded message. "Is that your voice, Mr. Tien?"

Tien was about to answer when his attorney interrupted. "Excuse me, Agent Buck. But what are we listening to?"

"This is a tape of a phone conversation between a pay phone in the Uptown area and Mr. Tien's cell phone. It was made last night just before the building fire."

Tien's face turned red. "You mean you have been listening to and taping my private phone conversations? This is

249

preposterous." His voice became loud and animated. "I am appalled. I came here to be of help, but..." Tien stopped in mid-stream, seemingly to regain control.

Ba picked up the conversational slack. "I assume you had the authority to make this recording?"

"Yes, we have a court order." Buck looked at Tien. "Well, sir, do you agree that is your voice speaking?"

Tien had settled down somewhat, wearing only a pink face now. "I don't know whose voice that is. It goes so fast and makes no sense."

Hansen spoke. "Did you get a call last night on your cell phone about eight-thirty?"

"I was at home last night. I remember a call. I couldn't understand. Wrong number. I hung up. I get many wrong numbers on my cell phone."

"Then you admit it is your voice?"

"I..." said Tien before Ba interjected.

"Is Mr. Tien on trial here?"

Buck leaned back in his chair. "No. No, not at all. But we would like to clear this up."

"Let me talk," said Tien. "I can't tell if it is my voice. If you were spying on me, you should know. It could be anyone's voice. The words. They mean nothing." He sounded exasperated.

Buck looked at Tron. For the first time, the Vietnamese detective spoke. "We think it could be a coded message authorizing the arson last night."

Pham Van Tien looked at Tron in mock amazement. "Is that what you think? You should write mystery stories, Detective Tron. You have a fertile imagination." Tien sipped from his glass of water. The glass shook in his hand. He chuckled nervously. "It's gibberish, Tron. A wrong number and gibberish." He looked to his attorney, then down to his watch.

Ba got the message. "We do have to be moving along. Is there anything else, Agent Buck?"

Buck rechecked his notes. "You have collected fire insurance proceeds on some of your buildings?"

"Yes. Of course. We have many buildings to manage. Some have had fires."

"What were the causes?" asked Buck.

Tien shrugged his shoulders. "Any number of things. Some like Wong's building We don't know."

"Arson?" asked Buck.

Tien didn't hesitate. "Some...maybe. Maybe vagrants. Some were vacant buildings. We try to keep them locked up, but..." he shook his head. "Could have been arsonists. But the insurance companies paid. If you're inferring something, Agent Buck. They don't pay unless they are satisfied."

Buck raised the stakes. "Did you know that one of the men involved in last night's fire died in the blaze?"

"Yes, that made the *Tribune* this morning. It is sad." Tien lowered his eyes. "And the other?"

"He's in the hospital. Burned pretty badly. But we were able to talk to him." Buck paused, looking at Tron and the tape recorder, then at Tien. "He indicated you may have been involved."

Tien said nothing. He glanced at Ba.

"Indicated. How is that Agent Buck?" asked the attorney. "Did he say something about my client?"

"According to Detective Tron, the remaining arsonist identified Mr. Tien as the one who ordered the fire."

"He told you that?" Ba looked at Tron.

Tron leaned into the table, squaring himself with the two men sitting across, who now edged forward. "He couldn't speak. His mouth is burned. I asked him the question. He blinked his eyes affirmatively in response to my question."

Tien pushed his chair back and turned his body to face Buck. "Agent Buck. I came here in good faith to help you with the Wong

251

matter. First, I answer a wrong number. Then Mr. Tron gets blinked at. Then I am some kind of suspect?"

Buck lowered his eyes. "A man died last night in the course of a felony. His death falls under the felony murder rule. Anyone directly associated with the arson crime could be convicted of murder even if they were not at the crime scene."

"Murder!" Tien almost shouted the word. "Mr. Buck, you amaze me."

Attorney Ba stayed cool. He spoke again in clear, modulated tones. "Isn't it true Agent Buck, such a felony murder case would be challenging to prosecute? Don't you agree without entertaining your finger-pointing that you are stretching even the remote possibilities here?"

"I don't think..." said Buck, interrupted by Tien.

"No, you don't. I would like to speak to Agent Marsden right now, please."

Buck looked at Tien. His neck was a crimson collar containing a face full of rage. "Certainly," said Buck, grabbing the nearby desk phone and placing it atop the table before the Mayor's man. "It's 3484. Do you want us to leave?"

"No," said Tien, "I want to straighten this matter out now." He tapped the extension number on the phone. Everyone remained still as he waited for a response. The air was charged with the odor of activated adrenals. Then Marsden's muffled voice escaped from the earpiece. "Hello. Agent Marsden. This is Pham Van Tien. I am in the building in a conference room with Agent Buck and others. I have my attorney here, Mr. Ba. I came here voluntarily to offer more assistance to your Bureau concerning Mr. Wong's death. However, it appears that Agent Buck is intent upon accusing me of murder. I would hope your organization would have a greater appreciation of my position within the community. I am personally offended by this inquisition and..." Tien stopped speaking. "Yes, he's here." He paused. "Thank you." Tien passed the receiver to Buck. He smiled. "He wants to talk to you."

Buck acknowledged his presence on the line and listened for two minutes before speaking. "All right." He listened again. "Agreed. I'll call you." With that, he deliberately placed the receiver in the phone cradle. He looked at Pram first, then at the attorney. "Gentlemen. I thank you for coming in today. Mr. Tien, I will be speaking later to Agent Marsden about your situation. He will contact you."

Tien summoned up a half-smile and looked at his attorney. Ba spoke. "I would hope we have completed our discussion of this matter."

"For the moment, Mr. Ba. Agent Marsden will talk later. Thank you both." With that, Buck stood. Hansen and Tron looked a bit perplexed but followed suit. Tien and Ba shook hands with the trio, then left the room with Buck showing them the way out of the office. He returned shortly and shut the door of the conference room behind him. Standing at the head of the table, he faced Hansen and Tron. "Let's talk."

Hansen and Buck took their suit coats off and tossed them on chairs. Tron maintained his formality. They sat, and Hansen spoke first. "I'm sorry, Mike. We messed up on that landholding. But you must realize Tien's intentionally created a crazy quilt of ownership. Concealed land trusts. Legal smoke screens. The man's a master at this. Maybe that burned-out building isn't formally owned by him and his partners, but the shopping center site certainly is, and we can tie that back to that South Side paving contractor."

Buck smiled. "Forget it, Pete," his voice expressed genuine empathy. "We're all going to have to do a lot more homework to catch this fish. Anyway, I talked to Marsden, and for once, I agree with him. He's aware of what we have on Tien. Elliot briefed him. From what I can tell, he's protective of his asset, but he sees the bigger picture."

Tron scratched his forehead and looked at Buck. "I don't get it."

"You mean Marsden?"

"Yes."

"Elliot showed him everything we have. I wouldn't have done it, but I'm not the boss," he said, opening his palms like an interdepartmental Pontius Pilate. "Anyway, I think it's for the best. We're running out of time. We need a break on Wong. Marsden's going to push Tien's button hard. If he's got anything, Marsden says he'll get it."

"You trust him?" asked Tron.

"He's an agent with an asset who's starting to smell. Marsden's no fool. He's not going to take the heat for anyone. Even Pham Van Tien. Look at it this way, guys. We've been stirring the pot around here. Well, things are finally floating up to the surface. Marsden just wants to get our spoon out of his pot. That's fine with me. Let's see what he can come up with. OK?"

Hansen spoke. "OK with me, Mike."

"Good," said Buck, obviously somewhat relieved. "Incidentally, Marsden assures me Tien is not our guy on the Wong case. I think he believes we're on to something real with this latest arson and the Political Corruption case. He'll work on Tien. For the moment, he'll look like his savior. Get some cooperation. After that, if he's dirty...he'll give him up."

"Fair enough. I'm going to make this corruption case as airtight as possible. Tien doesn't know we're crawling up his ass. He's focused on those fires and Wong. Let's keep it that way. The corruption case is for real. The rest is pretty muddy. Marsden's not going to queer my case, is he?"

"If nothing else, he was quite succinct on the phone. We have a coordinated effort now with FCI. On Tien. Wong. Everything. And we've got a meeting here with Elliot and Marsden in..." he checked his watch, "twenty-three minutes. I'm going to take a leak. Have a coffee, and we'll see what happens." With that, Buck headed for the washroom, crossing paths in the bullpen with the Professor.

"Hey, Professor. Any news?" asked Buck.

"Maybe, I'm running down our first dead man out in LA. Tron's aunt, Mrs. Hang, called me this morning with the name of a San Francisco dentist. You remember the guy that died in the car crash had a full mouth of bridges and caps. Kind of unusual for a boat person. I'm following that angle. I'm also tracking down a co-worker of our man. A guy who worked with him at a restaurant in LA. This looks pretty promising. I might have something today."

Buck leaned away. "Sorry, I need to see a man about a dog. I'll check back with you."

—CHAPTER FORTY-ONE—

The morning coordination meeting with Elliot and Marsden was cool but on point. Buck was satisfied that the FCI Squad and Squad 7 were on the same page. Around three o'clock, Buck got a call from Marsden. He wanted to meet. He said Tien had uncovered a person who witnessed the fire that killed Wong. The woman, a cleaning lady, was in Marsden's office at that moment, as was Tien's attorney, Mai Van Ba. Buck requested Do Tron also attend. Marsden agreed. He hung up and walked toward Marsden's office, contemplating this new event and mentally framed his approach to Marsden. Even though he disliked him, Marsden knew what it took to make things work. Buck was determined to be professional without any trace of an edge. He met Tron at his desk, and after a few words, the two proceeded to the FCI offices.

They entered a conference room with shielded overhead lighting over the large oak conference table. Three people sat at one end of a place for twenty. A diminutive, aged Vietnamese woman with grey-black hair, wire-rim glasses, her face full of wrinkles, and wearing a multi-colored duster sat between Marsden, at the table's head, and the attorney, Mai Van Ba. They sat, and Marsden introduced the woman. Mrs. Nuong cautiously viewed them, pausing longer on Tron.

"She speaks very little English," said the attorney. "I will have to translate. I would like to say also that this woman is here today because of the efforts of the NFU and particularly Mr. Pham Van Tien. She was unaware of the reward. However, her son, a Mr. Phong, had seen one of the flyers placed about the community. He recognized the connection to his mother's story and advised Mr. Tien. She is here of her own free will."

"Great," said Buck. He looked over to Marsden. "Jeff," the familiarity almost caught in his throat, "you're handling this one. Why don't you ask the questions."

Marsden looked pleased. "Thanks. I think you'll be interested in this woman's story." He turned to face the elderly woman. "Mr. Ba, you will translate, please." Ba nodded. "Mrs. Nuong, tell us, were you in the vicinity of the Viet Valley Restaurant at the moment of the fire?"

Ba translated, and the woman's black eyes watched his lips as he spoke. She began to whisper. Ba said something to her, and she started again, this time louder. Ba interpreted. "I am a cleaning lady. I was walking in the alley behind the restaurant. Coming from Mrs. Ha's house."

"Was this near the time of the fire?"

"Oh. Yes. I was only a few stores down when the explosions happened. I am a slow walker now. I was lucky. I passed the restaurant. I walked a little more, and then 'boom.'"

"Did you see anyone in the alley before the fire?"

Ba translated, and the woman's eyes begged to be elsewhere, but she responded slowly and deliberately. "Yes. I saw a gang boy. A boy named Tommy Mac."

Buck tensed at the mention of the boy's name; no doubt this was the same brash kid who worked and lived at Le An's father's house.

"What was he doing in the alley?" asked Marsden.

She shrugged. "I think he was looking into the building at the back door. I was not thinking much about him at the time."

"Are you certain it was him?"

She answered quickly. "Yes, it was him. He ran right by me. I saw his face. It was all red. He ran very fast."

"How long was it between the time he passed you and when the fire started?"

"I walk slow. Maybe three or four minutes."

"Did he have anything in his hands as he ran by you?"

257

She shrugged her shoulders. "I do not know. I only saw his face. When I first look, he is at the back door. When I look up again, he is running by me."

"Did you see anyone else in the alley?"

"No."

"What did you do after the explosions?"

"I ran. Well, I walked fast. Away. I was scared."

"Do you know this man, Tommy?"

"Yes. I see him sometimes at Dr. Le's house. I clean his house too. But I do not clean there again."

"Have you seen Tommy Mac since that day?"

"No."

"Why did you wait until today to come forward with this information?"

She swallowed, tried to speak, cleared her throat, and coughed violently for about fifteen seconds. Ba offered her a glass of water. She sipped from it and was able to control the outburst. "I was afraid. This boy Tommy is a White Tiger. They are dangerous. He saw me."

"Anything else?"

"I am not always making a business report to the government."

"Report. You mean an income tax filing?"

"Yes. And..."

"What?" Marsden's voice was taut.

"And...I am not yet a citizen." Again, she lowered her eyes and dropped her head as if awaiting a blade to fall upon her neck.

Ba spoke. "Gentlemen. This woman is here at the request of Mr. Tien. She wants none of the reward money. Mr. Tien assured her she would not have to fear any retribution from the government regarding her tax situation and her alien status. I hope we agree on that."

Marsden spoke. "We have no interest in those matters, Mr. Ba. However, if such does come to light officially, I suggest you take some of that reward money and provide some of your very effective legal services and assist her as required. Agreed?"

"Yes...and Mr. Tien?"

Marsden looked at Buck before returning to Tien's legal counsel. "We will be taking all of Mr. Tien's helpful services to the Bureau into account as we review all the matters at hand, including the matter of last night's fire."

Ba looked toward Buck. Buck said nothing, but they would know if they could read his mind; he was less concerned now about Tien and more concerned with Le An and her father's helper, Tommy.

"I'm sure we are all in agreement. Right, Mike?"

Buck couldn't tell if Marsden's question only related to Tien. It was the first time Marsden had ever called him by his first name. He offered no objection.

Ba smiled. The woman looked confused. Ba helped her with her coat, and Tron agreed to walk them to the elevators. Marsden and Buck were alone in the cavernous conference room. Buck spoke first.

"I know this, Tommy. He works for Dr. Le. Do Tron also knows him."

"Bad boy?" asked Marsden.

"He's a banger. But he's got his supporters. Tron thinks he's OK., and Dr. Le's daughter put in a good word. She says he is just a kid looking to find his way in life."

Marsden's eyebrow raised with the mention of Le An, but he said nothing about her. "Well, I doubt he has anything to do with Tien. He's in enough trouble with fires. He wouldn't bring this witness in if he thought Tommy would tie back to him."

"Tron says this Tommy is sort of a wannabe banger if there is such a thing."

"Well, what should we do?"

Without hesitation, Buck answered, "Let's bring him in."

Marsden puckered his lips and nodded before speaking as if to bless the occasion, "He's all yours, Buck. Keep me apprised."

Buck nodded, and they parted without further words. Feeling a little dirty and uneasy about the Tommy revelation, Buck headed back to the friendly confines of the Squad 7 offices, determined to break the case.

—CHAPTER FORTY-TWO—

Nelson O. Watson engaged in a lively discussion about the future of artificial intelligence as a crime-stopping tool. Watson argued the merits of a thinking-computerized agent, suggesting that such a machine might even replace successful, high-thinkers like the Professor. He diagramed his scheme on a legal pad as he spoke, "All we have to do is devise a program which follows the same logical sequence you do in your typical case analysis, and we can repeat your efforts. Each time the program runs, it will learn a little more. You simply load in the facts, highlight the gaps, and wait for it to point to the perp."

"Good luck," said the Professor. "I don't know if you could detect any logical thinking process in my daily activities. I'm everywhere and nowhere all at once. Thinking is an art. Not a science. I admit I line my ducks up every once and a while. I make my little matrices and mind maps. But the real work is done in here." He tapped the top of his bald head with his index finger. Not by me. Half the time, I have no idea how I get my answers. One moment I'm permanently stuck in the mud, and the next moment the waters part. You could film me day and night and not make sense of it."

"But that's just it, Professor. We can get a computer to analyze every..."

Clark's phone rang. Anticipating the call, he picked it up on the first ring. "Agent Clark."

"This is Bao," said the telephone voice wearing a crisp Vietnamese accent. "I'm returning your call. How may I help you?"

"I spoke with the people at the *Maison Vietnam*. I am interested in a man named Trung Xuan Truc. They said you worked in the restaurant at the same time he did. About 1978. Do you remember him?"

The voice on the other end laughed. "Remember him? How could I forget him? He was the first gay Vietnamese guy I ever saw. Sharp dresser. A real swinger."

"How do you know he was gay?"

"Hey, I wasn't born yesterday. This guy made a living waiting tables and hitting on guys."

The Professor was puzzled. "Mr. Bao..."

"Just Bao...like *ciao*. No 'Mister.'"

"Right. Listen, the man I'm talking about was a boat person who arrived here in 1977. A refugee."

It was Bao's turn to stumble. "Doesn't sound like Truc. The man was cosmopolitan. Great language skills. Spoke English with only a hint of an accent. Covered French nicely too. Truc was no refugee."

Clark paused for a moment to absorb the new information. "Maybe you're right. Maybe he wasn't a refugee. Maybe he was an actor."

"That I could believe."

"What did this fellow Truc look like?" The Professor motioned to Watson to hand him the legal pad.

"Dark hair, good complexion, good looks, athletic body, five-nine, five-ten. Carried himself like he owned the world."

"How old?"

"Um. Maybe mid-to-late twenties."

"What about his teeth?"

There was a pause. "Teeth? Nice. Good set of choppers. Nice, white, straight teeth."

"What happened to Truc?"

"You mean after he quit? I don't know. I never saw him again. We were pretty close, but..."

"Do you know why he quit?" There was a pause as Clark could hear Bao chuckling on the other end.

"I think he took off for greener pastures."

"What do you mean?"

"Well, as I said, he was always hitting on guys. But only Vietnamese guys. One of his customers became a regular. I think they were an item. I spoke with this guy one night before Truc arrived. He said they were going to take off. Start a new life. Not too long after that, Truc just quit. No notice. Just didn't show. I never saw him or his friend after that."

"Do you know his friend's name?"

"Um. No. Sorry."

"Where he lived?"

"Let's see..." Bao paused. "Maybe Seal Beach. I'm not sure. Maybe Seal Beach."

"OK. How about his job. Do you know what he did for a living?"

"I think he worked in a clinic or something. Maybe some kind of technician. He always came in late at night."

"After work?"

"Maybe. It was always after midnight. Real sharp-looking guy."

"Think he had money?"

"I'd say so."

"Educated?"

"Absolutely."

"What did he look like?"

"Good looking. Always smiling. Maybe in his late twenties. Fairly tall. Pretty good build."

"Sounds like a description of Truc."

"Hmm. You're right. Maybe that's why they liked each other. They say opposites attract, but I don't believe it. I think people love to love themselves. Right?"

"Could be. What about his teeth?"

"Hey, you're really into teeth, aren't you?"

The Professor waited.

"I think his teeth matched his looks. Very nice. As I said, he smiled a lot. People with nice teeth do that. Bad teeth. No smile. Good teeth. Always on camera. You know what I mean."

"I do. One more thing. Was there anything special about this friend of Truc's jewelry? Rings? Eyeglasses? Car? Tattoos? Anything?"

"Let me think...no...wait a minute. He wore a cross. You know, like a gold crucifix on a gold chain around his neck. Kind of gauche. Pushing the religious envelope. It wasn't just a cross. It had a little, tiny Christ figure on it. Weirdest thing. I remember because he used to finger it all the time. Like a good luck charm or something."

"Anything else?"

"No, that's it. Say, what happened to Truc?"

"The records show he died in a car crash."

"Oh," Bao's otherwise cheerful voice dropped off. "That's too bad. You should really find his boyfriend. He could fill you in. I'll bet he was really sad. He was nuts over Truc."

The Professor thanked the man, ended the call, and turned to his protégé.

"Let's use those fancy computers of yours," he said.

Watson smiled.

"We're looking for the fellow who actually died in that flaming auto crash in California in 1978."

"Wasn't the spy guy?"

"Nope. Get this. Vietnamese male, 5'-10", weight 165, black hair, significant well-done dental work. A bridge and two caps. Possibly worked in a medical facility in the Los Angeles area in 1978. Might have lived in the Seal Beach area. About 28 to 30 at that time. Liked fine food. Worked out. Had a decent job. Probably worked a late shift. And he wore a gold cross on a gold chain around his neck with a miniature Christ figure on it."

"On the cross?" asked Watson, his pen flying across the page, writing in large bold strokes as the Professor spoke.

"Right. What else? Oh yeah. Probably gay. Smiled a lot. Check a Dr. Johnny Viem in LA. Orthodontist. He handled a lot of Vietnamese dental work. Also, our man most likely left the Los Angeles area in the fall of 1978, never to be seen again."

Watson brushed the hair out of his eyes. "That's it? How about family? Schooling? Make of car?"

"That's it."

"Did he drive?"

The Professor smiled. "He was from LA. Everybody drives in Los Angeles."

"Got it, boss. Don't worry. It won't take long. A walk in the park. Of course, a name would help."

"If we had a name. We would be out of a job." Clark said, smiling. "Get me the name of our Lazarus spy, and we'll make Buck's day."

—CHAPTER FORTY-THREE—

Buck wasted no time. He covered his bases with Elliot, then organized a team to invite Tommy Mac to join them for a talk downtown. Rat, Andre, and Tron were briefed. About a half-hour before sunset, search warrant in hand, they arrived in two cars at Dr. Le's residence. Andre and Tron would take him in for questioning. His apartment would be searched. They parked the cars in front of the concrete driveway between the two brick piers, effectively blocking it as an exit from the garage. The four men moved quickly. Buck and Tron walked around the large house, looking for ways in and out of the basement apartment.

Rat went to the front door entrance to speak with Dr. Le. Andre stood his ground at the front of the house. Buck found three steps leading to a short concrete walk and the portico sheltering the side entrance door for Tommy's English basement apartment. They could take positions on both sides of the door. Tron rang the bell. Buck wondered if they would be lucky and catch Tommy Mac at home. If not, they would have two men maintain surveillance until he arrived. He got his answer when the young Vietnamese gangbanger wannabe opened the door. The kid wore a look of disgust, said nothing, and fidgeted. Buck watched his hands.

Tron spoke. "Hello, Tommy. How are you doing?"

"OK."

"Agent Buck and I are here to ask you a few questions. Please step outside." Tron swung open the screen door, and Buck stepped aside to make room. Tommy emerged slowly as Tron held the door open, rubbing the back of his bleached-blonde prison cut as if somewhat dazed or sleepy. He gave Buck a look. For his part, Buck studied his demeanor and carefully surveyed his clothes, looking for weapons. He didn't see anything to make him nervous. Tron closed the door. Tommy eyed him. "Sorry, Tommy, but put your hands up against the wall."

"What?"

"Face the wall. Hands up and spread," said Buck.

Tommy was slow to react, and Buck helped him assume the position. He frisked him, then nodded to Tron, indicating he was clean. He pulled out his handcuffs. Tron shook his head, and Buck, understanding, returned them to his belt pouch. "Can I turn around now?"

"Yes, you're fine, Tommy," said Tron.

He faced his accusers. "No. What's this shit? What's your problem?"

Tron moved closer to Tommy and stood in front of him. "You'll have to come downtown for questioning regarding the death of Mr. Wong. Also, we have this search warrant." Tron held the paper in front of him. "Do you want to read it?"

Sullen and red-faced, he spat out his answer. "This is bullshit."

"Do you need anything from inside?" asked Tron.

"How long is this going to take?"

"Hard to say, Tommy. Why don't we just do it? I'll take you downtown and bring you back. Let's go." Buck grabbed Mac's arm lightly, but Mac pulled away violently.

"I can walk by myself."

They made their way toward the front. Rat appeared at the corner of the house, followed by Dr. Le, who moved ahead quickly and faced Tommy. Buck and Tron stood to either side. "Wait a minute. Agent Buck, what is the meaning of this? Why are you arresting this young man?"

Buck looked at Dr. Le. "I'm sorry. We're not arresting him. We're taking him downtown for questioning. We're also going to search his apartment. The Wong case."

"Wong? Tommy has nothing to do with Wong." His voice became more animated.

Buck motioned to Andre, who moved onto the scene with a few fast-paced steps. "Go ahead," said Buck to Tron and Andre. Tron led Tommy ahead, now escorted by Andre. Dr. Le stared at the scene with apparent disbelief. Buck returned his attention to Dr. Le. "I'm sorry, but this is official business. We have a search warrant." He handed it to Dr. Le. "The door to the basement apartment is open. We will let ourselves in. We'll call you if we need any help. Thank you, Dr. Le. Now please return to your place."

Le stood his ground. "I'll watch," said Le, his voice betraying perturbation.

"I'm sorry," said Buck. "You'll have to stay outside. It's getting late and cold. Why don't you just go in? I'll stop by on our way out. OK?" Dr. Le seemed to accept the idea. He turned away without comment and headed for the front door.

The inside of Tommy's apartment looked like any other teenager's room. The walls were covered with posters of young people whom Buck assumed were current rock stars. CDs and video games were strewn about the floor in front of the TV. A half-eaten apple lay atop the beat-up wooden coffee table, and a small ashtray overflowing with cigarette butts and several partially filled glasses nearby revealed Tommy's housekeeping deficiencies. Given the green and orange color scheme, Buck thought Dr. Le must have let Tommy decorate. Rat sniffed around the living room of the three-room apartment, touching nothing. "What a shit hole," he pronounced.

"Hey, you were young once, Rat. This is typical," said Buck reflecting on his own son's bedroom.

"My old man would have beat my ass if I kept a place like this."

"Times change. Let's do it. You take the bedroom, and I'll search in here."

"Right." Rat disappeared into the adjacent bedroom while Buck systematically searched the living room and kitchen. He found nothing interesting in the kitchen. He checked drawers and worked his flashlight over the interiors of the base cabinets. The usual cleaners were lined up. A one-pint green glass bottle with a large yellow warning label: *For Animal Use Only* caught Buck's attention. Its chemical name meant nothing to Buck, but he carefully placed it in the evidence bag. The bathroom offered fewer hiding spots, nothing in and under the toilet tank, and the medicine cabinet was clean except for some prescription items. Buck noted the quantity and type and tossed them in the evidence bag. The bathtub was empty, as was the back of the door. The linen closet held one clean towel and one bar of soap.

He moved to the living room and checked the sofa. There was no desk or files.

"Bingo." Rat's voice bounced into the living room from beyond the bedroom door.

"You a winner?" asked Buck.

"Come on in."

Buck stepped into the bedroom, finding Rat kneeling before a dresser. "Check it out. This was under the dresser." He lifted a shoebox, top open, and exposed its contents to Buck. Inside was a hypodermic syringe with a small bottle cork stuck on the end of the needle. A brown glass bottle was capped and filled with a liquid, and a canning jar was half-filled with a crystalline substance. "What's this?"

"It's a hypo," said Buck. "Take it. We'll have it run through at the lab. Is that it?"

"Yeah. Except for these ping pong balls." He held up a three-pack of balls. "They were in the box too. Should I take them along?"

"Take them. And don't drop that box. I've got a hunch you're carrying the makings of a firebomb."

"What?" Rat seemed to jump as he popped the question.

"That bottle may be filled with acid, and the stuff in the jar might be potassium chloride. Toss some plain old sugar in a paper bag. Mix it with the potassium. Drop in a ping pong ball injected with acid. And you've got yourself a halfway decent time fuse."

"You mean to set off a bomb?"

"More likely to start a fire. The bag bomb could set off an accelerant. Doesn't leave much evidence of arson. Everything's consumed. You can vary the time delay by the strength of the acid. A little more dilution, a little longer fuse. Stronger acid, shorter fuse. I never saw one used, but we covered them in demolitions class. Careful with that shit."

"Hey, don't worry." Rat slid the box into the evidence bag with great respect. "OK, I'm done. You?"

"Done."

"Find anything?"

"Not much. Some prescription bottles and a lot of dirt."

"Let's get out of here." They flipped off the lights and exited, ensuring the door was locked. Outside, they walked along the side of the house.

"I've got to stop and see Le. Take this back," Buck said as he handed Rat the evidence bag. "Be back in a minute." Buck climbed the stairs leading to Dr. Le's front door. He got halfway up the stairs, and the porch light lit. The door opened, and Dr. Le appeared. Buck stopped at the top of the steps.

"We're leaving now. The door's locked. Sorry to bother you."

"Did you find anything? Asked Le."

Buck looked away. "I can't tell you until we have a closer look at the office."

"He's a good kid, Agent Buck. He's been hanging around the wrong people, but Le An and I think he's OK. She's the one who got me to take him in as a caretaker. I'm sure he's all right. Right?"

"We'll see. But remember, Tommy's a gang-banger. Please, Dr. Le. Don't forget that. Good night." He turned to face the stairs.

Dr. Le asked one more question. "It's OK to tell Le An, isn't it?"

Buck looked back.

"About Tommy. She'll be concerned."

Buck frowned. "Tell her what you want. I'm just doing my job. Good night, Dr. Le."

Le nodded and slowly closed the door. Buck drifted down the stairs and back to the car. "You look lost. Something wrong?" said Rat.

Buck looked back to the house, then back to his partner. "Nothing. Let's go."

—CHAPTER FORTY-FOUR—

Buck stared out the passenger-side window, feeling uneasy as if he had just opened a wound. A buzzing in his body told him something was wrong; soldiers don't deny intuition, hunches, and gut feelings. He remembered the same edginess in Nam. Several times it saved his life. A tripwire across a booby-trapped trail caught his eye one step from blowing his foot off. Another time he set up a stay-behind after breaking camp. He had the feeling that Charlie was near. He and two others took a concealed position and destroyed sixteen VC as they approached the camp Buck's platoon had vacated a half-hour earlier. He knew his feeling wouldn't disappear until he found the source.

Rat drove, and Buck looked beyond his partner's head at Lake Michigan's foamy and eternal blackness, which offered no clue about his mental itch. At Belmont Avenue, Rat exited the Drive. They headed west toward the City of Chicago Police Headquarters, Area 3.

"Rat got your tongue?"

"Huh?"

"You haven't said dick since we left Le's place."

"Oh. Sorry. I've just been thinking about this whole Wong business."

"It's a bitch. Isn't it?"

"That it is. I don't know what it is. I had the same shit in Nam. It must be a Vietnamese thing. Nothing ever made sense. This Wong thing is starting to smell like Nam."

Rat glanced at Buck, then snapped back to view the traffic ahead. "Don't give up the ship, Mike. I think we're getting near the end. Things are happening now. Tien's talking. Tommy's talking. We got reward money witnesses popping up. We've got ping-pong ball time-delay fuses. We got eight dead spies. We're moving along, my friend. Just go with the flow. Old Rat-a-reno knows. Trust me."

Buck stared straight ahead, looking unconvinced. "I hope you're right. I would like to wrap this thing up and move on."

Rat said he wasn't feeling well. He was going home to bed.

"You do look a little pale. Get some sleep," suggested Buck.

Exiting the car, he faced the nondescript brown brick and glass building which looked more like a suburban office than a traditional jailhouse. Once inside, Buck found Tron standing outside an interview room in one of the corridors. He peered through the small window in the door. Tommy Mac appeared to have lost much of his swagger. Andre and Tron had questioned him for over an hour. He sat head down now, alone in the room. "What did he say about the old woman's story?"

Tron's face was placid. "He admitted he had been in the alley shortly before the fire started. Also, being at the rear door. He says he doesn't remember running past the old woman. According to him, he heard noises inside and saw smoke leaking around the metal door. Too hot to the touch. He says he ran away to call the fire department."

"Did he call?"

"He says he did. A pay phone at a service station at the end of the block. It's there. I've been there. We're checking records now."

"What the hell was he doing in the alley?"

Tron rubbed his chin and smiled. "Won't say. He said he just happened to be there."

"I see. I smell some bullshit here."

Tron nodded. "You want to talk to him?"

"Right. We found the makings of an arson fuse along with a hypodermic needle. Maybe he used the needle on the old man and the fuse to torch the place?"

"Seems kind of neat. Got a motive?"

"No, but we do have means and opportunity. Let's shake him up a little. Did he lawyer-up?"

"Says he doesn't need one."

"Fine. Let's go." Buck opened the door, and the two men entered. Tommy Mac turned around in his chair to see who had arrived. One look at Buck and his head turned back abruptly. Tron and Buck stood at either side of the table before Mac. "Detective Tron told me you admitted being in the alley behind Mr. Wong's restaurant before the place went up in flames."

Tommy flipped his palms up into the air. "Just being a good citizen. Reporting the fire."

Buck leaned into the kid's pockmarked face. "You know, Mac, you seem to have an attitude. But what you really have is a problem."

Tommy looked down at the table.

"We've been through your apartment. The place is dirty in more ways than one. We found your arson kit. Is that how you torched Wong's place? You weren't in that alley by accident. You knocked Wong out and left a paper bag fuse ready to pop. Maybe it went off too soon. While you were locking the old man in his death chamber."

"I don't know what you are talking about," he said, stammering.

"I'm sure you don't. You just like to play table tennis?"

Tommy looked up, his face wearing a look of exasperation. "I don't know anything about any fuse bullshit."

"Well, you can deny it, but we've got it. A box full of bomb makings was found under your dresser. It's off to the lab now for analysis and fingerprints."

"Fuck you," he said, half-standing and facing Buck nose-to-nose with hate in his eyes. Buck shoved him back in his chair. He gripped his shoulder with a firm hand.

"You...you're trying to frame me. I don't know anything about any bomb. I want a lawyer."

Tron looked at Buck and down at his hand, still on Mac's shoulder. Buck slowly released and withdrew it. Tron spoke softly. "Tommy. Maybe you're right. We don't have any lab results yet. But it doesn't look good. Why don't you tell us what you were doing in that alley? Did someone in the Tiger order you to go there?"

Sullen-faced, he didn't respond.

Tron stepped back and smiled at him while Buck took a neutral position, leaning into the room's far corner. "What do you say?" Tron smiled.

He looked up at Tron. "Lawyer. I want a lawyer."

Tron looked back at Buck, and they decided to pack it in. On the way out, Buck commented. "Maybe you'll be spending the night here. It might sharpen your memory."

Mac smirked.

A few minutes later, Buck sipped a cup of coffee alone at a table in the employee lounge. Little could be done now. Tommy Mac was waiting for a public defender in the cooler, and the evidence was on its way to a local testing lab for analysis. After Tron left for the night, Buck called to check on his son. As he got up to go, an Area 3 Detective approached him. "Someone at the front desk in the lobby who wants to see you."

"Who?"

"A lady. Very pretty. Asian." The big cop had a twinkle in his eye.

"Oh. Right. Thanks. Front desk. OK." Buck reacted, somewhat stunned at this news. He had not expected Le An to arrive at the station house, and he braced himself for the encounter. She paced across the hard tiles, her high heels clicking like a metronome. She spotted him and walked briskly to face him.

"Mike. Where is Tommy?"

Not much of a greeting—he followed suit. "In the lock-up."

"Why?"

"He might be an arsonist."

"What?" Le An's face crinkled in disbelief.

"They found bomb fuse parts in his place."

"They? My father said you brought him in." Her face reddened.

"I...we did. Anyway, what are you doing here?"

"I was going to give him a ride home. But I guess that's out of the question. Does he need an attorney?"

"He'll get a public defender if we charge him with felony arson."

"No. I'll get him a real attorney. He hasn't done anything. He's not a bad person, Mike. Believe me. I don't know why you did this."

Buck said nothing.

"Can I see him?"

"No," said Buck. "Tomorrow, if you want." He looked at his watch. It was close to eleven. "Can you drive me home? I don't have my car here."

She looked at him without attachment, her face cold under the fluorescent lights. "I have to run. Sorry. Goodnight." The dark-haired beauty turned and headed for the door leaving Buck wondering about everything but too tired to think.

"Screw it," he said under his breath. He waited for Le An to pull out of the parking lot before grabbing a cab. He ignored the driver's chatter on the way home, his body on autopilot, his mind running on empty.

Upon entering his place, he received a call from Tron. "We've got a new lead. Your buddy, the *Thay Phap*, found Wong's busboy."

—CHAPTER FORTY-FIVE—

Buck pulled back the sleeve of his leather jacket and looked at his watch. 7:30. A steady, cold, early morning wind whipped off Lake Michigan, hitting him full face as he made his way to the end of the pier. Waves crashed into the north side of the concrete structure, every seventh one large enough to slide a sheet of icy water in his path. He walked carefully, avoiding a freezing footbath. Tron stood at the end of the pier and waved to him as he approached.

"Hell of a morning. I hope this is worth it."

"Me too." They turned their backs to the wind and looked down the length of the pier. Unconsciously, they positioned themselves atop a slab of concrete an inch higher than others, offering higher ground from the occasional washed-over waves. Above them, a steel cable flapped incessantly in the wind, beating the metal framework of the warning light tower.

"I would have brought my boots if I'd known," said Tron, looking down at his shiny black shoes as the wave water made its way onto the pier, voiding into the cracks and crevices. "I hope they're on time. Damn cold."

"Your Voodoo Man said 7:30, right?"

"Look," his head motioned to the two people making their way down the barrier stones lining the shore, "here's our boy." As they approached, Buck could make out the details of their faces. Duc, the *Tray Phap*, took the lead, looking dignified, wearing a tailored black overcoat and red beret. Trailing behind, a short man dressed in a windbreaker, sweatshirt, and jeans jumped whenever a wave hit. Duc approached, wearing a broad smile.

"This is Mr. Hu." He turned and grabbed the young man by the sleeve to bring him into the conversation.

Buck remembered the acne-covered face and the prominent ears and teeth. Wong's busboy shielded his face from the wind, tightened his jacket collar, and tucked in his head. The kid had fear in his eyes; they would have to be gentle.

"Thank you for coming, Mr. Duc. And you, also, Mr. Hu."

"I apologize for the venue Agent Buck, but Mr. Hu is very concerned about his well-being. Since the fire at Mr. Wong's restaurant, he has been hiding, fearing for his life. He did call his mother, though, and she called me. I felt the most appropriate action would be to bring him to you. He told me his story, and I believe what he knows may be of use to you in your search for the person responsible for Mr. Wong's death." Duc smiled. "He is aware of the reward offered by the National Freedom Union, and I hope his coming directly to you will not decrease the possibility of reward for him."

"That's not in our hands. But whatever we can do, we'll do. Let's hear what he has to say."

Duc turned to the boy. "Go ahead, son, tell them what you told me."

The boy looked up, and the wind caught his face. Tiny tears oozed from the corners of his black eyes. He wiped them with the back of his index finger knuckle and then looked to Duc, who nodded for him to proceed. He spoke slowly with a difficult accent. "I work for Mr. Wong. I am a busboy. I remember you," he said, looking at Buck. "You came into the restaurant the day Mr. Wong died. With another man. Mr. Wong upset after you go. Very upset. Then he received a telephone call."

"When was that? Asked Tron.

"About five minutes after you gone," he answered, looking again at Buck.

"Then what?"

"Then Mr. Wong told me to leave for the day. He told me to go out front and close the gate."

Buck moved in closer. "You mean the security grille?"

The boy nodded. "And to lock it."

"The padlock on the outside."

"Yes. I did this and left. Later, I heard about Mr. Wong."

"Did Mr. Wong appear afraid after he received the call?"

The boy nodded and looked down.

Tron looked at the Voodoo Man. "You told me the boy was threatened."

"I didn't say that. He said he was aware of rumors in the community. Rumors that someone was looking for him. That's why he is still in hiding."

"OK." Tron turned his attention back to the boy. He looked into his eyes. "You need not be afraid. We will not cause you harm. Do you understand?"

The boy nodded.

"Good. Just relax and think. After taking the phone call, did Mr. Wong appear to be expecting someone?"

"Yes. I think so. This happened before. Mr. Wong get call. Then he asks me to leave. Lock up. Happen two times before. But I never see the person who called. Never see anyone."

"Did you place the lock on the back door?"

The boy thought and then shook his head. "Front door only. No back door."

"Then the back door was unlocked."

"The back door not locked.."

"Did you ever answer the phone for Mr. Wong?" asked Buck.

The boy shook his head. "Mr. Wong only answer."

"Did anyone else work at the restaurant?"

"No. Only me and Mr. Wong. Not much business. We open only for lunch. No dinner."

"Do you think the White Tiger is threatening you?"

The boy's eyes widened. "I do not know."

279

"We can give you protection."

The boy looked at Duc as if he did not understand. Duc spoke to him in Vietnamese, and the boy appeared to respond. Duc looked to Buck. "He is not interested. He is not going to stay here in Chicago. He is leaving town soon. He wants to go now, if we may."

Buck and Tron glanced at each other. "No problem. Thank you very much, Mr. Duc."

"It was my pleasure to be of assistance. And, please, do stop by when you can, Agent Buck. We could talk."

"Maybe I will," said Buck.

The boy had already turned away and made a few steps toward freedom. Duc smiled at the two. "I guess he has no faith in law enforcement."

"Fortunately, he had faith in you," said Tron. "Let me ask you. What do you think about the boy's story?"

The Voodoo Man rubbed his fingers together, warming them. As Duc mulled over the question, the wind caught his beret. He used both hands to snug it into place, and he didn't smile this time. He looked with concern, first at Tron, then at Buck. "I feel the man who called that day is powerful. I would be careful, my friends." With that said, he backed away slightly. "Thank you again for listening. I hope we have been of some help."

Tron shook his hand. "Yes, thank you very much." He shook hands with Buck and then joined his charge. Tron and Buck watched them walk away rapidly, ignoring the waves washing across their feet.

"The kid's in a hurry," said Buck.

"The kid is afraid."

"Well, it was something. Not much. But now I think we can say the fire was probably not accidental. Someone was in the restaurant just before the fire."

"Tommy Mac?"

"Well, we know he was at the back door. Two and two might put him in the building with Wong."

"Maybe, but I don't think he was operating on his own. The only motive Tommy might have would be tied to the Tiger or somebody else. Tommy's just a kid. Kid crimes are pretty straightforward. Money, drugs, fights. Wong was poor, clean, and too old to fight. Someone had to put him up to it."

"Let's go. Those two are clear. I'm freezing my ass."

Avoiding the splashing water, they made their way back to land. On the way, Buck replied to Tron's proposition about Tommy's motive, "You may be right about someone putting him up to it. But who?" As Buck and Tron split for their cars and headed for the office, that question remained unanswered.

—CHAPTER FORTY-SIX—

Vince Gorski sounded exasperated. "Shit. I don't know, Mike. Maybe he didn't drug him. Maybe Tommy strong-armed the old man, and he couldn't take it. He died on the spot, and Tommy tried to cover himself by starting a fire. Whatever. I'll call you back after I meet with Dr. Washburn. OK?"

"Right. Good luck. Call me on my cell."

Buck hung up and called Pete Hansen. He informed him about the incendiary fuse without mentioning the speculation. Hansen agreed they had no case against Pham Van Tien concerning Wong's death. He told Buck the case against Pham in the apartment arson was weak. The recorded telephone conversations were ambiguous. It would be Tien's word against the blinking eyes of an incompetent arsonist. Tien was the Mayor's man and, therefore, no contest. But the Political Corruption team would advance the influence and bribery charges. Setting the phone down, Buck looked for Tron. Instead, he found Rat sneezing at his desk.

"Have you seen Tron?"

The little man sneezed again and then blew his nose noisily. His face was flushed, and he looked tired.

"You don't look good," said Buck. "Why don't you go home?"

"I think I've got the flu. But shit, I'm not bailing out now. We're near the end here, Mike. Tron's in with Elliot. Got anything new?"

Buck nodded. "Tommy's incendiary fuse was for real. Vince got the lab report."

"Son of a bitch. Anything else?"

"Vince is checking out that bottle I found under the sink. It was an animal tranquilizer. He thinks it could have been the same stuff they found traces of in Wong's body. But that's just a guess now."

Rat got out of his chair, pushed it back, and did a little dance. "I told you, Mike. It's coming together."

Buck made a face and left Rat dancing by himself. As he headed for Elliot's office, he heard Rat sneeze again. Buck looked back. His dance over, Rat dumped into his chair. "Go home, Rat. You're making me sick".

Buck found Tron in Elliot's office. As they explained the situation, Elliot confirmed it was time to talk again with Tommy Mac. Buck knew that Le An would have found him an attorney by now. They grabbed their coats and hustled to the parking garage. Tron called ahead to Area 3 headquarters. He was told that Tommy Mac was meeting with his attorney. He asked the desk sergeant to inform the attorney they were coming for an interview. Twenty minutes later, they arrived at Area 3. As they walked through the parking lot, they passed several groups of pedestrians heading to their cars, each squawking stories about people going to jail, in jail, getting out of jail, or the injustice of the criminal system. Tron and Buck plodded on, replaying their notes to each other about how they wanted to do the interview.

She seemed to come out of nowhere. Buck swung the door open into the lobby, and Le An was directly in front of him. "Oh. Hi," he got that out, but nothing followed. She picked up the slack.

"Hi," she turned to Tron and smiled. "Hello, Detective Tron. Good to see you. May I have a moment with your partner?"

Tron nodded and excused himself, heading for the interrogation area. Then Le An herded Buck out of the traffic into a quiet part of the lobby. He didn't want to sit on the bench, but at her insistence, he sat. She placed her body down next to his, their thighs barely touching. It was as close as they had been for quite a while. She looked into his eyes. "I'm sorry."

"It's…"

"No, I was upset. Too upset. I'm sorry I left you. Did you get home OK?"

In her repentance, she looked angelic to Buck. "No problem. Took a cab. I probably got home before you."

"Good." She moved nearer to him, her face just inches from his. "I am very fond of you, Agent Buck. I want you to know that. I also want you to know that sometimes a woman can get excited. Overwhelmed by circumstances. I was that way last night. I know you were only doing your job. Forgive me."

Buck looked around the lobby, then kissed her on her forehead. He pulled back, and she smiled. "You're forgiven. I wasn't very friendly last night, either. A long day. And last night was the one time our paths should not have crossed."

"I know. Are you seeing Tommy today?"

"Yes," he said as he stood. "You know I've got nothing against him. I've got to go now."

"Call me later. OK.?" She said in the quiet voice of a little girl.

"I will." He said, smiling.

"Don't be too hard on Tommy. He's just a boy. He's very loyal to my father and me. I've done what I can. He has the best attorney I could find." She waved him off with a playful back of her hand-gesture. "Go ahead, Agent Buck. Do your job. I'll see you later, I hope."

Buck smiled. "I'll call you. Bye." He walked away feeling better. Tron was waiting at the end of the corridor. "Sorry. Thanks for waiting."

"No problem," said Tron. "I've got Tommy in there," he pointed to the door, "with his attorney."

"OK, let's go." Buck moved to enter, but his ringing cell phone stopped him. He glanced at the telephone I.D. and answered. "Hello, Vince. What's up?"

"Got it all," replied Vince, his voice smiling. "Washburn says we have a match. He's 99% certain that the animal tranquilizer you found in Mac's place matches the unknown chemical he found in Wong's body. The tranquilizer might freeze the old man. But it wouldn't kill him. Wong was injected with the tranquilizer. Then left to die in the fire. He probably died of a heart attack. Fear killed him. Doc says it's a weird one, but a homicide."

"All right. Thanks. We're interviewing Mac and his attorney now." Buck killed the call and relayed Vince's news to Tron.

"Are we going to charge him with Wong's murder?" asked Tron.

"Not yet. Let's see if we can get anything out of him. He might break."

CHAPTER FORTY-SEVEN

They entered the interview room, knowing more than their suspect. Tommy Mac sat in a far chair. His attorney, Mr. Tesco, a small round man with designer-framed glasses, was seated to his right, wearing an expensive but ill-fitting suit. Buck knew him as one of the top criminal defense attorneys in town. Le An didn't screw around. Tesco informed the two that since Mac had not been charged, he would cooperate as much as possible to clear himself. After starting a tape recorder, Tron began the interrogation of Mac by asking him to review his whereabouts for the entire day of the fire. The review process was tedious. Mac remembered working at the Le residence all morning, planting some evergreens in the backyard. He remembered the type and size of each tree he planted, the lunch he ate in his apartment, and that lunch consisted of a microwaved burger and chips. Then he walked into Wong's neighborhood, a distance of about five blocks. He didn't recall why he happened to walk in that direction. He now remembered the old woman in the alley when he ran to call the fire department. Tesco suggested they check the 911 records, and Tron told him it had been done, and a call was made.

Buck played a recording of the call, and they asked Tommy Mac why the voice of the man making the 911 call didn't sound like him. Mac, looking somewhat sheepish, said he had disguised his voice. Fearing the appearance of a connection to the White Tiger, he didn't want it known that he was involved, even if only as a bystander. The Tiger was not very forgiving of mistakes. After making the call, he watched the fire trucks arrive and wandered for the next hour before returning to his apartment.

Under questioning from Buck, he denied seeing anyone other than the old woman near the restaurant at that time. According to him, he was alone. Buck pushed for an answer regarding the incendiary fuse. The attorney told Mac not to answer, but he answered anyway. Tommy had no idea the box was under the dresser. He had never seen the box before. Buck told him Wong had been injected with an animal tranquilizer exactly like the substance found in the green glass bottle under Tommy Mac's sink, suggesting the match proved that Mac injected the man and then created the fire with one of the ping-pong ball fuses. Tesco objected again, and this time Mac didn't answer.

Over the next hour, Tron and Buck covered the same ground again, hoping to break Mac down, but his attorney would have no part of it. He declared his client would have nothing else to say. There was no physical evidence bearing a trace of his client's fingerprints. He reminded the two men that Mac, disguised voice or not, had called the fire department an act without reason if he was guilty of murder. According to Tesco, the police were only speculating, and the evidence wasn't convincing, only tantalizing. The boy should be allowed to go home. He was cooperating and would continue to do so. Keeping him in jail was unjustified, and if he wasn't released shortly, he would seek a court order demanding his release.

Tron looked at Buck for direction. Buck wore a stone face. They would continue to hold Mac. The interview ended, and Tommy Mac was escorted back to his cell. Tesco exited the room, leaving no doubt he would seek a hearing for Tommy's release. After securing the tape from the recorder and briefly discussing their next move, Tron and Buck headed for the employee lounge.

"I thought I was going to die in there. Next time a forty-five-minute limit," said Tron as he walked next to Buck.

"It's an environment that's supposed to break the perp. Not us, Tron," said Buck with a smile.

"Tell that to my bladder."

They used the washroom facilities and joined a half-dozen other cops in the lounge. A television located above a vending machine provided the potential for entertainment. The newscaster droned on, a sonic wallpaper cladding the environment. Tron poured a couple of cups of coffee and laid them on the table Buck had selected. Buck stared into the steaming cup. "What are you thinking, Mike? Asked Tron.

Buck looked up expressionless. "I think Mr. Tommy Mac is hiding something. He was in that alley for a reason." "Tiger spying?" asked Tron as he sipped his coffee. "No. I don't think so. From what I know, Wong was on a most favored list."

"Maybe, but not if he was identified as a Communist spy. Then he would be a target."

Buck looked at Tron. "Tell me. If you wanted to kill old man Wong, would you send Tommy Mac? Especially when you have people like Ky available."

Tron rubbed his narrow chin. "I see your point. Maybe Tommy was only on the edge of the deal. A lookout, not knowing what was going down. Then he figured it out and called for help."

"Whoever called Wong had done it before. Wong knew his killer and trusted him enough to let him in."

"Maybe," said Tron. "Maybe. And I think Tommy's OK, but things happen. We know somebody was coming over. Maybe Tommy or maybe someone else. But we know Tommy was there when the fire occurred. And we've got the physical evidence."

"Right. But no prints. And the ping-pong ball fuse from an evidence standpoint, assuming it is Tommy's, is like a box of matches. Just potential but no connection to the crime scene. Fact is, this kind of device doesn't leave a trace in a fire. So we're left with the animal tranquilizer and the hypo."

"The tranquilizer is good. We need to find out where Mac purchased it and when. If we can show that he bought it, we don't need fingerprints. It's his."

"So you're sure he did it?" asked Buck.

"If he purchased it, he's going to have to have one hell of an excuse to explain it away. If he plays the dummy, then he's our guy," said Tron. At that moment, one of the cops turned up the volume on the television. All heads looked up. The screen indicated a special broadcast would follow. A reporter said: "We are live in a conference room at City Hall. Reporters have gathered to hear an announcement at this impromptu press conference called by the Mayor's Special Assistant for Minority Affairs, Pram Van Tien. While we have not been told the topic of this special press conference by the Mayor's Office, we have it on reliable sources that Mr. Tien is being investigated for improper activities by the U.S. Attorney's office. Wait. I see Mr. Tien now. It looks like we are about to begin."

The camera focused on Pham Van Tien and Mai Van Ba entering the large conference room. The harsh camera lights washed Tien's face. He appeared stressed and ill at ease as he stepped before the lectern. After clearing his throat rather loudly, he began. "Thank you for being here. I offer my apologies to the Mayor for interrupting the activities of the day here at City Hall. However, I have taken this action, unprecedented for me, to call this press conference because of unwarranted and undisciplined actions of the Attorney General's office. I have been advised that a Grand Jury has been called to investigate me concerning my role as Special Assistant and my private business activities. While I do not know what specific allegations have been made about my conduct, I have been told they may include bribery and corruption."

"As you know..." his voice went up an octave, and he stopped and sipped from a glass of water. "As you know, I have faithfully and diligently worked as the Special Assistant for Minority Affairs for the past three years. And if I might say I am proud of my record for helping the citizens of Chicago, whatever race, creed, religious background, or color, to receive the benefits and blessings of America. With the support of the Mayor, the people

289

of this great city, and my family, I will continue to do my job as I have always done. Even in the face of the activities of this bureaucratic mistake on the part of the Attorney General, I am looking forward to clearing my name and reputation as soon as possible. But..." he lightly pounded his fist on the lectern, "in the meantime, I will not be driven or diverted from my responsibilities to the people. We have work to do, and we must move on. Thank you."

The camera followed Tien as he left the room with Mai Van Ba in tow, dogged by reporters' shouts of unanswered questions. The cop turned the sound down, and the room buzzed with conversation.

"Looks like Hansen moved faster than we thought," said Tron.

"Yeah." Buck nodded. "Hansen doesn't screw around. My guess is they closed in this morning with a million subpoenas. Tien must have freaked out."

"Couldn't happen to a nicer firebug," said Tron smiling.

—CHAPTER FORTY-EIGHT—

Watson sat before the Professor like a prize pupil polishing an apple for his teacher. "You're going to love this. I got it all worked out."

Randolph Clark chewed aggressively on his empty pipe. "The mysterious Mr. Truc?"

"Yep. Truc might have died, but he didn't die in that car crash." Watson paused, enjoying every moment.

"Go ahead."

"Well, I checked out both sides of this puzzle. The car crash. And your 1978 mystery man who dated Truc." He looked at his notes. "First, the man in the car crash. I checked with LA, and I got someone to dig out the file. No person ever identified Trung Xuan Truc as the guy who burned in that auto accident. Not surprising since his face looked like a barbecued Italian sausage. I checked the reports filed by the cops. They brought the burned-out car into the police auto pound. Based on the file dates, it sat there for a week before someone decided to search it. Maybe the Coroner's Office asked them. The record says they found a wallet in the locked glove compartment of the car. Between the accident and the fire, not much of the car remained. But the glove compartment stayed intact."

"The wallet contained Truc's ID?"

"Right."

"So Truc stole the car. Locked his wallet in the glove compartment and then killed himself in the accident. Very convenient."

"That's official. It doesn't mean it's right. But that's the story. Anyway, you saw the autopsy photo of the dead man."

The Professor nodded. "Burned head to toe."

"Right. But there was something noted on the autopsy doctor's report that wasn't visible in the photo." Watson reviewed his notes and read from them. He flipped the page. "There are burn-pattern indications in the skin at the base of the neck. The subject may have been wearing a chain necklace at the time of his death."

The Professor's eyebrows raised. "A gold chain?"

Watson smiled. "Better yet. They found the damn gold cross on the floor of the burned-out car. Ain't that something."

"Nice setup. That rivals finding Oswald's wallet in a pool of Officer Tippet's blood in Dallas. I like this. It fits. Truc hooks up with Mr. X. and kills him. He places his own wallet and ID in the glove compartment. Then rigs a car crash, burning Mr. X beyond recognition. That's the kind of behavior I'd expect from a spy. Buck was right. This guy was slick. What else do you have?"

"I saved the best for last." He smiled. "You know what you gave me on this Mr. X. Height, weight, sexual preference. Bridgework. Seal Beach area. Late worker. Liked food." Watson pushed his glasses back with a thumb and then brushed his tousled hair out of his eyes. "Good stuff. Well. I made lemonade out of those lemons. First, we figured this guy drove a car. Driver's license, right? Need a name, right? Here's what I did. I found the phone directory for the LA area, and then I locked onto Westminster, California. Two hundred thousand Vietnamese-Americans. I ran it through a pattern language program looking for commonalities found in Vietnamese names. Then I contacted the Division of Motor Vehicles in California. They have records of driver licenses issued back to the 70s. I got access to an electronic file of all names and addresses of people with driver's licenses. I started with 1978. Do you know how many people drive in that state?"

"Quite a few, I'd imagine."

"You bet. Millions. But it's all on a computer in Sacramento. Believe it or not, they let me hack directly into it. 'Read-only,' of course. But I was able to run my program on their system. I got a list of drivers with Vietnamese names, addresses, telephone numbers, age, height, weight, and hair color. No social security numbers, but I grabbed the list and left their system. Our equipment could handle this. Thousands of names. Not millions. Anyway. Then I ran our boy's description. I cut down the list to the hundreds. Then I cross-checked zip codes with the addresses and honed in on the Seal Beach area. And I struck pay dirt. I found three drivers who fit the description and lived in that area." Watson paused for applause.

"Go ahead," said the Professor.

"Maybe he worked at a medical facility. Remember? So I checked the state records to see if these guys matched with doctors, nurses, and veterinarians' registration. My next step would have been private medical association records. But I didn't need to. I think I've got him." Watson looked in his notes and read. "'Le Van Luy.' This fellow was a doctor who worked at a clinic in LA. I get the impression it was one of those "doc-in-the-box" places. I checked with the clinic. Nobody there remembers him, but he's in their files. He left their employment after working only nine months. Left in August 1978. No forwarding address."

"Any family or friends?"

"No, but..." He smiled. "Better." He chuckled. "Just for fun, I checked again with the State of Illinois. Guess what? Wait for it. Somehow the dead doctor is still practicing. His records were transferred to Springfield in 1979."

"Illinois?" The Professor scratched his head.

"That's right. Dr. Le Van Luy set up shop in Illinois. Right here in Chicago. Under the name of Luy Van Le..."

"Our Dr. Le?"

"None other."

"Damn good work, Watson."

Watson stretched out his long frame, leaned back in his chair, and beamed.

"Set up a meeting with Elliot and Marsden," said the Professor.

Tom Elliot looked up at the head of the FCI Squad, who stood, arms folded in front of him.

"We'll work with you," said Elliot to Marsden, "but it's an FCI case."

"Thanks," returned Marsden, wearing a rare smile as he uncrossed his arms, "we appreciate your cooperation."

"What about Buck?" asked the Professor.

"Right," said Elliot. "Why don't you give him the news." He looked at Marsden and then dialed his speakerphone.

Three rings later, Buck answered. "Mike, this is Marsden. I'm here in a meeting with Elliot and the Professor. We got a break. Agent Watson did some fancy detective work and determined our man Dr. Le is a spy."

Buck went quiet.

"Got that, Mike? Dr. Le Van Luy. He's a Communist agent who grabbed another guy's identity decades ago. A true sleeper."

"Then I was right about that auto accident."

"Right as rain, Mike," said the Professor. He jumped in and quickly summarized Watson's findings.

"So. That's it, Mike," said Marsden.

"I hate to say it. But, I didn't have a clue about Dr. Le," said Buck. "Tron's with me now. I'll bring him up to date. Do you need my help? Do you want me to bring Dr. Le in?"

"No, thanks. Elliot's handing him over to us. We'll take care of him." Marsden stumbled and seemed to search for the words. "Thanks for your help. You hung in there."

"That's me." A long pause followed. "Like a dog with a bone."

—CHAPTER FORTY-NINE—

Over coffee in the Area 3 lounge, Buck and Tron shared ideas. Buck shook his head. "You know. I knew Dr. Le spent time in California. He interned in Los Angeles. I saw his sheepskin on the wall at his office. I should have suspected something."

Tron smiled. "That would have been a leap, Mike. We needed Watson and his computers to wring this out of a million miles of data. Intuition only goes so far."

"You may be right. Or maybe I had a blind spot. I missed it."

"Forget it, Mike," said Tron. "I just wonder how this will unravel. "If right-wing anti-Communists were responsible for all the deaths, Dr. Le might be the final target of the spy-killers. They have their sources too. Dr. Le's charade is over. It's a good time for him to come in from the cold. So we bust a spy, and we've got Tommy Mac for the murder."

Buck reflected. "You know, Tommy Mac may look like a wrong-way kid, but he is at the center of this deal. He's at Wong's place. He's got arson fuses. He's got that animal tranquilizer. He somehow manages to live in the same building as the last remaining NVA spy in America."

"Well, we're going to have to decide on charging him pretty soon," said Tron, "that attorney Le An bought won't waste any time springing him.

Buck nodded.

"And what about Dr. Le? He should be taken into protective custody. He's a good candidate for a hit."

"Yes," said Buck solemnly. "Elliot's working on that with Marsden. I'm afraid he's coming in for good. If he's a spy, he'll be deported, at least." Buck's voice betrayed his thinking.

"Are you thinking about Le An?"

Buck looked up. "Yep. I've brought a lot of trouble into her life."

"Not you, Mike. The trouble was always there. You just got in the middle of it."

"You're right. But that won't make any difference. In the end, it's guilt by association."

"Well, you can't do anything about it. The wheels are in motion. Fate has dealt you a bad hand, my friend."

Buck lowered his head and stared at the table. Le An replayed in an endless earworm. Tron spoke. Buck half-listened. He was anxious.

"Are you all right?" asked Tron.

In a daze, Buck looked up. "I'll be right back." He stood. "Back in five minutes."

"OK. I'll check with Elliot while you're gone."

Buck hoped to clear his head. The crisp, late morning air and bright sun helped refresh him. He was upset with himself for allowing his work and his relationship with Le An to coalesce. He called her. "Le An, this is Mike."

"Hi. What a pleasant surprise. What's the occasion?"

He should tell her about Dr. Le's deception, that her father was in danger, and that he might be jailed or deported. He wanted to tell her he would book Tommy Mac for the murder of Mr. Wong. He wanted to let her know he cared about her. He didn't want her to find out from the newspaper or a reporter's call. But he knew he couldn't tell her. He had to do his job without allowance for personal complications. Everything was done by the book. And the book didn't have a chapter on Le An and Buck. "I'm still at the station house. I just wanted you to know I'm thinking about you."

There was silence at the other end. "I've been thinking of you too. Can I see you tonight? I need to talk to you."

"About what?"

She paused. "It's important. But not now. I have to meet my father for lunch now."

"You're seeing your father for lunch?"

"Yes. Why?" She sounded concerned.

"Nothing," He would talk to Elliot soon. Maybe he would let him break the news to Le An. "Tonight's fine. I'll pick you up at your place at seven. OK?"

"No. I'll make something for us. Just stop by." There was a pause. "Mike…"

"Yes?"

"I wish I could see you right now."

"Me too. We'll have to settle for tonight. I'll give you a big hug."

"That would help. Later then."

"Goodbye," he said with unintentional finality.

—CHAPTER FIFTY—

Le An met her father in the lobby of a fashionable old hotel overlooking Lake Michigan. Halfway between their places of employment, it was their favorite dining spot. Le An gazed out the window at Oak Street Beach and the lake beyond. Passive waves, the distant concrete breakwater having tamed their power, rolled gracefully into the shore. But at the breakwater, wild waves in open waters attacked the barriers spraying misty rainbows into the air.

"Le An," said Dr. Le.

She turned to face him. "Sorry. The waves way out there are quite beautiful."

"You are too, my child, but you've always been a daydreamer."

She nodded as the waiter arrived to take their order. Officious in his manner, Le ordered for both, then dismissed the waiter. His attention returned to Le An, and he opened a conversation about Buck and her relationship with him. She was less than candid, not admitting to her true feelings. However, he was unequivocal. Buck's interference was hurting his family and their community. "You know, he may only be doing his job, but things have not gone well since he appeared in our lives."

Le An interjected defensively, "It's only because of *Bac* Wong's death."

Dr. Le's look became severe. "Obviously. But my good friend Pham Van Tien is now under indictment, Tommy Mac is in jail, and my daughter is involved in police matters."

She dropped her head.

"I know you want to help Tommy, and I admire your concern. But I am disappointed you brought in an attorney without consulting me."

"I'm sorry," she said. "I know I should have spoken with you. I just wanted Tommy to have someone there to protect him. He's very vulnerable and very young. I guess I acted impetuously."

Dr. Le wore a forgiving mask. "I can understand, but you can imagine how this would look in the community. It wasn't right. A father should be consulted by his daughter." The words weighed on Le An. "I know you understand. Of course," he said, lowering his voice, "it was necessary for me to replace the attorney you hired for Tommy. Mr. Ba will be more suitable. He will make the transition today. So, you said you visited with Tommy. Is he all right?"

She didn't respond but instead looked out the window. Dr. Le stared at her, not pleased with her silence. The waiter arrived with their lunch, and they ate, only exchanging a few words. "Le An. You never answered me about Tommy. What is bothering you? I realize this matter is complicated for you, but I am sure it will end well. Is there something else?"

She dabbed her face with a napkin, returning it to her lap while carefully studying her father's face. After a moment, she gathered her courage. "I spoke with him in jail. In confidence and alone. He told me something disturbing. About you. I don't want to believe him, but..." She held back tears and took a drink of water. Her father waited. His eyes betrayed more fear than concern. "He told me he had followed you to the restaurant on the day of the fire. That you were there. Tommy says he never entered the restaurant, but *you* did. Is it true?"

He looked at her, then stared out the window. She lowered her head and began to cry softly into her napkin. He looked back at her and reached over, lifting her chin gently with his hand. They looked at each other eye-to-eye. "Yes. Tommy is telling the truth. I was with my friend Wong Suu that day."

She swallowed. "Why?" she asked.

He looked up with a fierce look that she had never seen before. He cleared his throat as the waiter arrived to check on their progress. With a wave of the back of his hand, he dismissed him and returned to her. "I will tell you a tale you will not like, but it is true. First, has Tommy talked to anyone else about me?"

"No. I mean, I don't think so. He wants to believe you didn't have anything to do with *Bac* Wong's death. He wants to be loyal to you. I'm sure he will protect your secret."

"That is good. Because it is not just my secret, we all have secrets, Le An. Wong had his secret, and I found out about it. You know I have many contacts here and in Vietnam. People who know the truth. Wong was a Communist. The Union had identified him as a spy. You know that there are people in the Union who would not stop to eliminate a Communist spy."

She stiffened, eyes wide and listening intently.

"I didn't want that to happen. Whatever the facts. I was Wong's friend. I didn't want him dead. I called him that day and told him I was coming to talk to him. He was very agitated. I guess Agent Buck and another cop had just left him. I went to the restaurant." He shook his head. "I didn't know Tommy was following me. That was unfortunate. I believed I was alone. Wong was upset. Very upset. And I didn't help his attitude. I didn't know what to do, so I confronted him with what I had heard. I told him that they knew he was a Communist spy. I told him they might kill him." Le's voice rose in intensity and pitch as he spoke. "He didn't deny the charge. But he didn't admit it. I told him I was there to help him. I could get him out of the country. Risky, but I would have done this. But it wasn't to be. He became crazed. He grabbed a butcher knife and came at me. I tried to block the blow. He cut my arm. I knocked him down on the floor. He must have hit his head." Le brushed his hair back with one hand. "I didn't mean it, Le An. I just pushed him down. But he hit his head." He whispered, leaning into her across the table, "When I

300

looked at him, I knew he was dead. I checked his pulse. I'm sorry, Le An. The past came back to haunt him. You have to believe I didn't mean to kill him, but I had to stop him."

She turned away and sobbed into her napkin.

"I don't know how the fire started. I had nothing to do with that. I didn't want anyone to see me, so I left by the back door and returned home."

She looked up and spoke with some defiance in her voice. "Michael Buck told me he heard screams. Mr. Wong wasn't dead then. Why did you start the fire? The fire killed him. He had a heart attack. He was locked in a burning building."

The allegation stunned Le. He stammered. "I didn't know. He was dead. I don't know why I put the padlock on. I didn't think. I just reacted. I was afraid."

"You started the fire, didn't you?"

Le sipped from his water glass and then declared. "I did. I did it to conceal my act. I panicked. If for a moment I knew he was still alive." He paused. "I would not have started the fire."

"You're a doctor." her voice was flat.

Le nodded. "Even doctors make mistakes, Le An. Can't you accept that?"

"I don't know what I believe now."

Dr. Le reached over, grasping her hands in his. Again he looked into her eyes. "Le An. I am your father. You must help me. Wong is dead, and that cannot change. But there would be no point in revealing my part." His lips held a tight smile. "I'm sure Mai Van Ba will convince Tommy to forget he ever saw me. He will be rewarded handsomely. I will pay all the legal bills. He has done nothing, and therefore he has nothing to fear. Agreed?" She didn't respond. "You trust me, don't you?"

She looked carefully into his dark eyes, searching for an answer. His eyes were without emotion, black and uncompromising as usual. She had always wondered about his eyes. She gazed into them as a child hoping for love and understanding, but she never found it. He was always distant. She had always obeyed him, but she never loved him. That disturbed her. It was a burden she carried her entire life. Throughout her childhood, *Bac* Wong was the one who gave her emotional support, hugs, kisses, and a soft shoulder to lean on. He had stories of her mother's beauty, understanding, and skill as an artist, her devotion to Le An, and her love for her daughter. All her life, she held Wong's vision in her heart. It was a tiny hot coal of meaning, warming her otherwise cold and emotionally empty childhood. *Bac* Wong never talked about her father, which only increased her suspicions. Again she searched her father's black eyes for a glimmer of love but found none, and then uncontrollably, she leaped over the edge. "You're not my father are you?"

The color drained from Dr. Le's face, and he swallowed hard. He didn't say anything. Le An cried softly into her chest. Then she dabbed her eyes to dry them and looked around the restaurant in a daze, seeing nothing but a blur of color and light, lost in the endless silence following her question. She stared into space while his voice, distant and hollow, echoed.

"I'm sorry. Very sorry, Le An," said her father in a firm voice without emotion. "I knew this day would come eventually, but now that it is here, I can only say I am sorry. Did Wong tell you?"

She looked at him. At that moment, he was a stranger, no longer her father, mentor, or authority. She shook her head quickly as if to rid herself of the pain. "He never told me. I just knew." She wiped her nose and looked into his eyes. "Why?" she asked through her tears.

He folded his hands in his lap. "That is the only fair question to ask Le An. I respect you, and I hope you still respect me. Do you?"

"I do, but you must respect me. I am lost. I don't know who I am. I must know."

He pursed his lips before answering. "You are Mr. Wong's granddaughter. He brought you to this country when you were a small child, and he settled in Chicago, where I met him. We had little in common except for our background as refugees, but we became friends nevertheless. Wong knew that I was in a position to succeed. That I would have more youth, more money, and power than he could ever hope to have. He was older, unable to speak English, and living in poverty in a strange country with a small child he loved. And to tell you the truth, he was concerned about his past. He committed a sensible but illegal act while in Vietnam. He stole money to pay for passage out of the country. From a Communist at that." He looked at her as if waiting for a reaction. She gave none. He continued. "He was a wanted man even before he left the country. Deportation was possible. He was very anxious. He had promised your mother on her deathbed that he would always take care of you. So, he looked to me for help. He had no one to turn to, so he asked me to take you. And I did. An act I have never regretted," he said, smiling.

"Why?" she asked.

"Why did I take you as my daughter? Is that what you want to know?"

She nodded.

"Because I wanted to help, and I knew it would be good for me. Good for my position in society. A single father with a beautiful daughter would provide exactly the image I wanted to create. I am ashamed to admit it, but this was my plan. Le An, you know I am a pragmatist. I knew I would never marry, but with you, I would be accepted. And I was. It was a great help to my career and my relationship with the community. But it became more. For me, I did become your father. Maybe not the father you wished for, but I did try. I wanted you to have a good life in America, and you have. You know. I am very proud of you." He looked to her for affirmation.

She sat silent, thinking, absorbing, and trying to understand her life. "I want to go," she said with clarity.

"Yes. We should leave. You are upset, Le An. I understand that, but please let me drive you to my house. I don't want to leave you alone. Please."

"Why? Why do you care?"

Dr. Le looked offended. "Please, Le An. I know you were hurt. But I have only deceived you once, and I did it for you. Here..." he said, reaching into his pocket to retrieve a small silvered case. He opened the pillbox and offered her two capsules. "Take these. They will calm your nerves."

She hesitated but then accepted them.

"Go ahead," he said, handing her a glass of water. She swallowed the pills. Dr. Le summoned the waiter and paid the bill. As he helped her to her feet, he whispered in her ear. "Let me have your car keys. I'll drive us home."

The medicine hit her. Relaxed, almost dazed, she reached into her purse for her car keys and handed them to him. He placed her jacket over her shoulders, and they left the restaurant, her arm in his for guidance. She was drifting, letting the medicine take her to a place of comfort. She felt like a child again. For the moment, this illusion of childhood was comforting.

He looked back at her and proclaimed, "Don't worry, I'll take care of you, dear."

She wasn't worried. At that moment, she wasn't anything or anybody. She had drifted into a pleasant mental fog bank.

—CHAPTER FIFTY-ONE—

Vince Gorski had checked with the desk clerk at Area 3. He returned to the lounge and stood before Tron and Buck like a fleshy oak tree, his full girth stretching the limits of his buttoned sportcoat lapels. "They say the kid wants to see you, Tron."

Tron looked up from his coffee at Vince and smiled. "You weren't listening at the door, were you?"

"No, but the kid seems to have two attorneys now. Tesco and Mai Van Ba. This guy's doing all right for a gangbanger-nobody. He's got eight hundred dollars an hour worth of legal talent entertaining him. They're gone now. And Mac's sitting alone in the interview room. Wants to see you. Only you."

"This is an honor," said Tron. "Sit down, Vince. Mike will buy you a coffee. I'll see what our boy wants. Maybe this is a break."

"Pass the word if you need our help," said Buck.

Tron headed for the interview room. He asked the uniformed cop to step outside. Closing the door, Tron turned and smiled at Mac, who sat alone, confined by the grey concrete block walls. Under the glare of fluorescent lighting, his face was pale. "Hey, Tommy. I understand you want to see me." He sat across from his captive.

"Yes." He spoke as if his mind was elsewhere. The word was soft and distant.

"You know you have the right to have your attorney present. Do you want to waive that, right?"

"Yes." His mouth sagged. "I want to talk about my attorney."

"Go ahead."

Tommy Mac made a face. "You know Mr. Tesco was my attorney."

"Was?"

"Well, I don't know. Le An hired him for me. But now her father has hired Mr. Ba to replace him."

"Is this what you want?"

He shrugged his shoulders. "I don't know. I don't get it."

"What don't you get?"

"I just wonder how Dr. Le got involved. Le An said she would help me. Now Tesco says he's being pulled off my case. He says he got a call from Dr. Le saying Ba will be my attorney. They seem to have worked some kind of deal between them. What about me?"

Tron looked Tommy in the eyes. "What about you, Tommy?"

"I don't trust him."

"Who, Ba?"

"Tesco...Ba...Le...I'm being set up. I'm out of the loop. These guys are cutting deals, and I'm sitting on the sidelines."

"Who do you trust?"

He looked down at his hands, which rested flat on the table. "Le An."

"Do you trust me?"

"I don't know. You're a cop. Why should I trust you?"

Tron spoke slowly, and Tommy seemed to hang onto each word, hoping for the correct answer. "Unfortunately, you're a decent young man who selected your friends poorly. I'm not talking about Le An. She must be a real friend. But your Tiger friends are not here to help you are they?" Tron waited. "And you are in some trouble this time. Arson. Murder. These are serious charges. You could screw up your whole life if you make the wrong decision now. Look, I don't believe you had anything to do with Wong's death. But the evidence is against you: the incendiary fuse, the tranquilizer, the old woman who saw you at the scene. No matter. You might be clean, but you're not telling us everything. Are you afraid of somebody? Did somebody get you into this?"

"I'm not afraid of anyone. Not even you. Or the FBI."

306

Tron leaned back. "Well then, what's holding you back from telling the truth here, Tommy?"

The kid turned to look into space before returning his gaze to the tabletop. "Forget it." He said under his breath. "Forget it. Get me another attorney. A public defender or something."

"Look. You called me in here. You said you wanted to talk without your attorney present. Can we keep talking? It can't hurt to talk. Neither of us has anywhere to go, do we?" Tron smiled. "I'd like to bring Mike Buck in here. I know you two are not exactly buddies, but you have one thing in common, you both have Le An as a friend. OK?"

"I don't want any bullshit from him."

Tron waited for an answer.

"OK."

"Want a can of soda or something?" Tron said as he opened the door. Tommy nodded. Tron poked his head out the door and asked the uniformed cop to summon Buck and Gorski and bring something to drink. He left the door open. Tommy Mac could hear every word. Then he returned to his chair.

"Relax. I've got a good feeling about this," said Tron, his voice calm and smooth.

A couple of minutes passed with neither speaking before Buck and Gorski arrived. Tron introduced Vince and took the can of soda, handing it to Tommy. The kid popped it open and took a long swig. To Tron, he appeared more relaxed. "Mike, Vince. Tommy's agreed to meet with us without his attorney for now. That's OK with you, right, Tommy?"

"Yes."

"He's debating his choice of attorney at this moment. Be that as it may," he said, looking at Buck, "since you and he have the same mutual friend, Le An. Maybe there might be some common ground to start from."

Buck recognized the cue. "Right," said Buck with a hint of a smile on an otherwise neutral visage. "Well, I suppose there is,

Tommy. You've ended up in a bad spot. If Le An were here, she'd tell me to go easy on you. She thinks you have a future. What do you think?" His tone was conversational. At that moment, Tommy looked stunned. He seemed to lose his ever-present harsh edge. Buck noticed it. Maybe nobody in authority had ever asked his opinion of his future before.

"I think she's right. I think I have a future."

"Good. I don't think your future includes going to jail for a crime you say you didn't commit. Is that true?"

"Yeah. Does that mean I can walk?" He said this with more humor than aggression. He took a quick sip of his drink and set it on the table, focusing on the red can.

Buck looked him in the eyes. "Tommy." He waited until their eyes met, "You can walk out of here today if you tell the truth. And that would be the best thing you could do if you want a future. Somehow the facts make you look guilty, but if you're not involved, get out of the way. We have work to do. Tell us something before someone else gets hurt."

Vince slid some photos in front of Tommy. The young gangbanger looked down. Three autopsy photos of Mr. Wong flashed before him. Wong looked old, naked, wrinkled, and dead. "Take a good look," said Vince. "Did you kill him? Somebody drugged him and left him to burn to death. Was that you? Did the Tiger order you to kill him? You play ball with us, Tommy-boy, and we can do somethin' for you. Just tell us what you were doing at Wong's place that day."

Tommy stared at the color shots without touching them. Seconds passed. The room was empty of sounds but for the constant hum of the fluorescent light above. He looked up at Vince. "I didn't kill anybody. Old man Wong was a friend of Le An. And the Tiger could give two shits about him. He didn't have a nickel."

"So no Tiger. Then explain why you were there?" asked Vince. "Because if you can't come up with a good one…."

Tommy tightened his lips and leaned back, regaining some of his toughness.

Buck moved to maintain control with a lighter approach, "Look, Tommy, you have friends. Le An, her father. These people could help you have a future if you can clear yourself. No jail time. No White Tiger. A future with some meaning. You don't want to end up like Ky. You're too smart for that. The train's leaving the station. Why don't you make Le An right? She'd like that."

"I don't think so."

"Why not?"

"Because," he looked up, "because I can only make things worse."

"The truth will eventually arrive, Tommy. Whether you give it life now or it oozes out over time with you sitting in a jail cell waiting for it to appear. Last chance. And I wouldn't worry about things getting worse. You're facing a life sentence."

He scratched the top of his chopped, bleached blond hair. "It's not me."

"What?"

"It's not me. It's Le An," he almost swallowed his words.

Buck's back tingled, and his question that followed was personal, "What about her?"

The kid didn't speak. He just looked at Buck, maybe for the first time squaring up with him. Finally, the words came out, "You care about her, don't you?"

"Yes," said Buck unabashedly, as if he and the kid were the only people in the room.

"Then I'll give my problem to you. Do you want it?"

"What?"

"Le An. She's your responsibility. Are you goin' to take it on?"

Buck's look narrowed. "What are you saying? What does Le An have to do with this?"

"She knows."

"What?"

"I told her I saw her father at Wong's place that day. He was in with Wong. Then I saw him leave. He locked the door and took off. He never saw me. But I knew something was going down. By the time I got to the door, smoke was coming out. I ran to call it in. That's it."

"You followed Le to Wong's place?" asked Vince.

"Not exactly. I was in my apartment. I heard Dr. Le talking to someone on the phone. His phone was right above me. He was arguing. Blowing off steam. He yelled out Wong's name. He told him to keep his mouth shut. Then he hung up. I heard him stomping around upstairs. Then he slammed the door and left. I knew where he was going. After he left, I ran over to Wong's."

"Why did you care about Wong?"

He looked at Buck. "I didn't. Le An did. She loved the old Wong. He was like an uncle to her. She told me so. Anyway, I know Dr. Le. He looks like a cool customer, but I've seen him pop his top. He can be fuckin' nuts. I didn't know what he was up to. Maybe I could do something."

"Did you think he might hurt the old man?"

"Sounded that way to me. I guess it worked out that way too. I'm sorry for Le An."

"How do you think that stuff got into your apartment?"

Tommy smiled. "Give you three guesses."

"You mean Dr. Le."

He nodded.

"When did you tell Le An?"

"This morning."

"What did she say?"

"She was upset. She defended him. It might have been an accident. But I could tell she was worried. I don't think she figured out that he was trying to frame me. She was happy I tried to help Wong. She said she was going to talk to her old man."

"You should have told us this earlier."

"I didn't want to rat on Le An's father. I don't know what happened."

Buck turned to his partners. They left Mac wondering and reassembled in the corridor. "Le An was having lunch with her father today," said Buck. "I'm going to track her down. Le's will get grabbed by FCI or us. I don't want her anywhere near him when that happens. You understand?"

"Right, Mike," said Tron. "Need any help?"

"No. Just take over here. Most likely, Wong knew who Dr. Le really was. It makes sense. Dead men don't talk." He grabbed his jacket. "I'm gone. Keep him under wraps until I call you." Without waiting for a response, he stopped briefly in the lobby to call the university. She hadn't returned from lunch. He tried a call to Le An. After four rings, she answered.

"Hel..."

"Le An."

"Mike." It sounded like the speakerphone to him.

"Where are you?"

There was no answer.

"Le An."

"Father's..."

"Are you at your father's place?"

"Yes." Her voice was distant. "Mike. Love you."

"Le An. Go home. Right now. Can you hear me?"

"Mike...help." Her last word was very weak, almost inaudible.

He shoved the phone into his pocket, turned quickly, and almost bumped into Tron, who had followed him into the lobby.

"What's up?"

"Le An is in trouble. I've got to get to her."

"Where is she?"

"At her father's house." Buck turned away from Tron.

"I'll go with you, Mike. Don't go alone. You need backup to deal with this guy."

"There's no time." Buck ran out the door.

"Mike. Wait!"

—CHAPTER FIFTY-TWO—

As Buck wheeled ahead, he worried about Le An and drove at high speed without caution into the late-afternoon traffic. His hand groped around for the cell phone in an attempt again to talk to her. He made the call. No answer now. He glanced ahead. A pickup truck pulled out from a drive-in restaurant directly into his path. He dropped the phone, braked hard, and swerved into the oncoming lane. The truck driver spotted him. The man must have panicked and hit the accelerator instead of the brake. The truck rammed its front bumper into Buck's car's rear quarter, spinning it around and back to the right side of the street. Buck bore down on the concrete curb. His choice was to cut the wheel back or go straight ahead. In microseconds, he decided to drive straight forward into the curb. His eyes closed as the wheels hit. The car leaped high into the air screaming, its rear wheels clearing the curb, but the rear bumper caught the concrete, ripping off the muffler.

Buck opened his eyes. His car had crossed the sidewalk, entered a debris-riddled empty lot between two buildings, and bounced off a wall knocking the steering wheel out of Buck's hands. Chips of brick shot through his open window, slicing his cheek. The other building rushed toward him. The car hit the wall at an oblique angle. It scraped along until it came to a complete stop. Buck reset himself physically and mentally, then revved the engine. Unmuffled, it roared. He twisted the wheel, slapped the accelerator pedal, and ripped across the wet ground, kicking up mud behind him. The alley lay ahead. He slowed the car enough to make the turn.

Ahead standing near the edge of the alley, a small boy held a puppy in his arms. His face frozen with fear and disbelief, the boy gripped the animal tighter as the car approached. The car shot past and picked up speed as it crossed the first five side streets. It shot down the alley like a dragster, gaining momentum at each intersection. Garages and fences blurred in his peripheral vision at fifty miles an hour. Ashland Avenue was ahead. Buck slowed slightly and hoped for the best as he exploded into the bright sunlight through the slot between the buildings lining either side of the narrow way. Fortunately, there was a gap in traffic.

He went north on Ashland, spinning wheels and fishtailing for a block before straightening as he blew through the stoplight at Irving. Other cars approaching the intersection slammed on their brakes to avoid a collision. Oblivious to the others, Buck jammed the accelerator down, the vehicle rolling at about eighty now. Thirty-five seconds later, he braked hard, turned right, and headed east to Dr. Le's place. The car bounced along the one-way side street, engine throbbing with Buck sweating at the wheel, not slowing for intersections, unconcerned about others, focused only on his destination. He gritted his teeth. Finally, the familiar brick piers of Le's driveway appeared ahead on his right. Braking, he slid the last twenty feet to a stop halfway past the concrete driveway entrance and directly in front of Dr. Le's house.

He killed the engine and readied himself in a few seconds. A solemn calm enveloped him. He popped out of the car, all senses wide open, eyes searching and ears listening. As he ran up the drive, a cold lake breeze cut into his face. Holding his cell phone, his only connection to Le An, he stopped running and called her again. There was no response. He slipped the phone into his jacket pocket and reached under his lapel to touch his holstered gun. Its predictable presence helped ease the tension. He looked behind him, almost hoping Tron had followed him from Area 3. But he was alone.

Fifteen paces brought him to the front steps of Dr. Le's house. He rushed up the stairs, looked inside through the front window, rang the bell, waited, and watched. Across the street, a neighbor's dog barked at him. A few seconds later, he slammed his jacketed elbow through a pane of glass in the door, reached in, freed the lock, and entered. Pieces of glass crunched between his shoes and the hardwood floor. He paused and listened as he pulled out his gun and moved deliberately toward the back of the house. The living room, study, dining room, and butler pantry were empty. He stopped in the middle of the kitchen and took a moment. She said she was at her father's place. She was here. But where? He rested his hand on the kitchen counter and looked outside through the breakfast nook window. Although he saw nothing unusual, he sensed something.

He focused and detected minute vibrations. Then he sensed a low rumbling, distant, not loud, but continuous, like a prop-plane high overhead. The two-car brick garage had two overhead doors, no windows, and one side door visible, and everything looked tight. His gut told him where Le An was. He raced out of the kitchen, down the short flight of steps, and out the back door. The sound was louder now. A car inside the garage was running. Fumes seeped out. The odor of carbon monoxide filled the air. He shouted for her.

He pulled on the door handles, but they were all locked. Facing the man-door, he backed up a few feet and ran into it. His shoulder hit it at full force. The jamb split, the door flew open, and Buck stumbled deep into the darkened garage. The interior was a choking poison-gas nightmare. His eyes burned. He slipped off his jacket, rolled it into a ball, and held it over his nose and mouth as he pushed forward in the dim light. He found himself at the driver's side window of the SUV. "Le An," he shouted."

Her lips were bright red, her face pink, and the steering wheel was her pillow. There was no response. She looked dead.

Again he shouted her name.

He ran around the car and broke open the passenger side window with the butt of his gun. After he popped open the door, he dove across the seat and grasped the petite woman's arm to

315

drag her out. Her body was belted in and wouldn't budge. He was weakening now. Then he heard a noise behind him. A sharp pain shot through his right shoulder. Someone had stabbed him. He looked away from Le An, catching a vision of Dr. Le with a hypodermic needle in his hand.

Buck could hardly breathe. His lungs screamed. He turned and reached out for Dr. Le, grabbing him by the lapels of his jacket and pulling him into his space. The hypo fell to the floor. Le's face was inches from his. In the confined gaseous environment, he extracted his left hand, bundled his fist, and brought it up quickly, catching Le with a glancing blow across the temple. Dr. Le took it, and with a sweeping upward movement of both his arms, he instantly broke Buck's grip on his coat. Then, his hands raised high above his head, Le expertly and violently brought them down, chopping them into the base of Buck's neck, stunning him into submission. The injection and the beating took Buck down. He couldn't focus, and his mind drifted away before a reserve of adrenaline awakened him. Dr. Le grabbed his legs. He wanted to kick but couldn't fight the man's powerful grip. Le stuffed Buck's legs into the car and shoved Buck toward Le An. The door slammed shut.

All was quiet, dark, and tomb-like. Buck and Le An were dying. His muscles were rubbery, but his mind had life. The side door of the garage slammed shut as Dr. Le ran out. A lucid thought floated in the misty air. Could he move the car? He slid down the seat, his head falling onto Le An's right thigh. He focused on the gear shift lever. At his limit, he reached out for the lever. His fingers edged toward the center console and found it.

He willed his hand to climb the rod to the top. It found the handle in time; how long he couldn't judge. He pulled, but it resisted. The button...the damn button. Slowly repositioning his hand, he squeezed the button and pushed the handle. Jesus, I'm going to die too. His mind did backflips to generate solutions, but the fumes and Dr. Le's tranquilizer had done their deed. He was dying, and he knew it. Some reservoir of strength left in a tiny corner of his consciousness let him see the brake pedal. He let his head slide down Le An's leg until his back straddled the center console, head into the floor under the steering wheel. He raised his left hand blindly, searching for the brake pedal. His fingers touched it and then bounced away. Once more, fingers moved up, inch by inch, finally reaching the hard rubber. He gripped the brake pedal, pushed it in, and held it down. He looked at his other hand, which appeared to belong to someone else. It remained on the gearshift lever. He willed the thumb to push the black button to allow the lever to move. Slowly it swung into place, and it depressed the button. Somehow the hand, seemingly on its own, slid the lever into reverse. Buck's left hand still leaned on the brake pedal. It was locked in that position, frozen. The car moved a few inches. He remembered the brake and eased his left hand a few inches to the right. It slipped off the brake pedal and onto the gas pedal. He leaned in and pushed. The engine ran wild, and the car leaped ahead.

—CHAPTER FIFTY-THREE—

The garage door flew off its rollers. In one movement, the three-hundred-pound door pancaked Dr. Le to the ground, slamming his head into the concrete slab and cracking his skull. The SUV followed. It raced backward at full throttle over the door and Dr. Le's body underneath, killing him a second time. The car rammed into the kitchen wall of the house. Immediately a ruptured pipe spouted water. The rear hatch popped open. Clouds of carbon monoxide drifted out into the spray of falling water. The engine stalled. Gasoline poured out of the damaged fuel tank and mixed with the water billowing from the broken pipe. A river of gas and water flowed back under the fallen garage door, past the body of Dr. Le, and into the garage.

Le An and Buck didn't move. With the gift of clear air, Buck's head began to function. He extracted it from its contorted position. He pulled himself up. With his right hand, he felt above his left eye. His hand slid off, dropping into his lap, covered with blood. He was weak. He momentarily leaned against Le An's warm body, then regained his senses. He was able to right himself and face her. What he saw in the afternoon light was not pleasant. Her face had taken on the look of a china doll, lips bright red and clown-like. Mucous drooled from the corners of her mouth. Blood, probably his own, streaked her perspiration-soaked starched white blouse. He placed his two fingers on her neck. Maybe he detected a pulse. He had to get her to a hospital. He peered through the windshield toward the garage and could now witness the destructive power of his violent exodus. He also spotted a hand protruding out from under the wreckage of the door. Still dazed, he stared at it and wondered.

Then another smell gripped him in fear, the unmistakable odor of gasoline from the ruptured tank. He had to free Le An from her seat belt. He opened his door, leaned out, and fell onto the concrete into a puddle of gasoline. Gas dripped from his hair into his eyes as he righted himself, painfully reducing his vision. His attempt to clean his eyes with his shirtsleeve, now soaked in blood and gasoline, only aggravated the condition.

He was practically blind, unstable, dripping with flammable fluid, and fighting for balance on rubber legs. Finally, grabbing his kneecaps with both hands, he steadied himself. He squinted, sensed the danger, and moved haltingly around the car, using it for support as he dragged himself toward Le An. Her door had popped open when the car hit the wall. She sat dumbly behind the wheel, oblivious to the danger. It could go any second. Flinging open the door, he put his arms under her legs and around her back. Bloody sweat dripped from his brow onto her chest. As he turned, she slipped out of his grasp. He lifted her again. He limped a few feet from the car, dropped her onto the grass, and fell upon her, exhausted.

Buck couldn't move. But he heard the sound of another car entering the drive. Moments later, Tron stood over him. His partner helped him to his feet. Buck muttered. "Le An."

"Can you walk? Get out of here," said Tron. "I've got her. Get going. This thing may blow." He watched Tron gather up Le An's body. Together they moved away. Buck followed his partner. "Get down behind my car," said Tron.

They took refuge. Buck sat with his back leaning against the rear bumper. Tron laid Le An's body on the ground with her head resting on Buck's leg. Buck looked at her and stroked her forehead and hair gently.

Fumes now filled the garage. The broken water pipe had activated a gas water heater inside. Fumes turned to flames and blasted out, creating an inferno. Just before the SUV exploded, Tron dropped to the ground. A rush of flaming hot air, smoke, and debris enveloped them. Then everything went quiet. Buck's head drifted over toward Tron. He offered a weak smile, reached out, found Tron's wrist, and with his hand shaking violently, he hung onto his partner. His other hand still rested lightly on Le An's forehead. Drained of blood, drugged into a stupor, and gassed into oblivion, Buck passed out.

In the distance, sirens screamed.

—CHAPTER FIFTY-FOUR—

The psychic movie set in ancient Egypt found Dr. Le in a starring role. Le stood somewhere in a stone-carved temple, dressed in the high priest's vestments, before a small group of soldiers. He held a long wooden hooked staff in his hand. Entwined around its top was a giant black snake. One by one, Dr. Le touched its point to the soldier's chests; the snake belched fire, and they burst into flames and died. Rat, seated in front-row-center, was unable to move a muscle, his subconscious fascinated by the plot's simplicity and the scene's surrealistic splendor. But some part of him understood the meaning of his vision. That part dragged itself out of the feverous, heavy-cream coma of flu-driven sleep and fought to reconcile the obligations of ordinary reality with the freedom of a dream. Even sleeping, Rat, ever the movie buff, awoke alone in his bedroom, smothered in a sweaty sheet. He sat up, eyes wide, shaking off delta, then sidetracked in alpha before reaching beta consciousness. He had taken off work, and upon arriving home, he fell into bed and slept for a full day.

"Hot shit. That's it." He reached for the phone on the nightstand and called Buck, but it went to voicemail. Frustrated, he left a message with Buck's disembodied voice. Brimming over with the news, he called Elliot. His boss answered on the first ring.

"Squad 7. Agent Elliot speaking."

"Tom. Rat here."

"Rat. I thought you were dead."

"Not yet. I'm feeling great. I just solved the puzzle."

"What?"

"The spies. I know the killer. It was Dr. Le. He was the Pharaoh. He killed the guardians of the tomb. Just like in *The Mummy*."

"Mummy? What are you talking about?"

"The old movie with Boris Karloff. You know? Anyway, Dr. Le was the head spy. And he killed all the other spies. He killed them to silence them forever."

"How do you know that?"

"I had a dream. Just now, Tom. I'm telling you. This is it. I know it."

"Why did he kill them, Rat?"

"Why? Because it was time to terminate the secret mission. Time to shut down the organization. The economic climate changed. The spies were obsolete. You know what's going on now with Vietnam. It's a goddamned vacation hotspot, and the Commies don't need no stinking spies. They need tour guides. All those spies were a liability. A ring of spies would be a little embarrassing to the nicey-nice diplomacy between Vietnam, and the U.S. Dr. Le's last official act was to ice the spies. He did it. He killed all of them. It wasn't some hard-liner conspiracy. It was just like in *The Mummy*. A 'strictly need to know' situation. And Dr. Le was the only person the Commies could trust to bury the spies and keep the secret. Get it?"

Rat's phone was silent for a few moments, then Elliot spoke. "You're on to something, Rat. He was the one guy who knew everything and everybody. He was in a position to set it up to look like a right-wing vendetta. We had Le figured wrong. He didn't need protection. He was the killer."

"I tried to get Buck, but his line is busy. Got it, boss?. You got to admit. I am fuckin' brilliant. I'll be in tomorrow to accept my award."

"Right. You're brilliant. Only one problem."

Rat sneezed, then blew his nose. "You mean arresting Dr. Le?"

"No, not that. You're a day late and a couple of dollars short, Rat. Dr. Le is dead. Buck and Tron broke the case yesterday while you were dreaming."

"What?"

Elliot explained everything to Rat. After he escaped Dr. Le's trap, Buck survived. He made a quick trip back to the living, reviving in pain after a few minutes of bottled oxygen. Dr. Le injected Buck only to temporarily incapacitate him. The carbon monoxide was supposed to kill him. Le An's hospitalization was a more serious matter, full-oxygen ventilation in a hyperbaric chamber and a blood transfusion. "But she'll be OK. And Buck will be out tomorrow. Stop by if you're up to it. We'll have a party."

"Son of a gun," said Rat. "Good for Buck. I'll be there." He sneezed and recovered. "That *Mummy* thing is still a good story. The Team will love it. Anyway, no matter. I figured it out. Right?"

"I'll buy you a drink. Get well, Sherlock."

—CHAPTER FIFTY-FIVE—

The late and murderous North Vietnamese spy, Dr. Le Van Luy, cooled his heels in the giant refrigerator. Le An sat next to Buck in the waiting room of the Medical Examiner's building, shuffling magazines, making small talk, and mentally preparing to identify the body of the man she had known as her father almost her entire life. Dr. Washburn entered. He smiled at the two as they stood to greet him.

"I understand you had quite a rough week. Everything all right now?" He moved close to Buck and studied his face. "You look like you've been through a war, and you," he said, turning to Le An, "look beautiful."

She smiled. "Thanks. I'm happy to be back with the living."

"You ready?" Buck looked down at the woman who stood at his side.

She nodded. "Yes. Let's get it over with."

She grasped Buck's hand, and together they walked to the viewing room. Le's body lay under a sheet on a gurney. Bright lights overhead illuminated every detail of the cloth and etched the outline of the man beneath. Washburn took a position at the head and slowly pulled back the sheet, exposing the upper torso.

Buck surveyed the body. Dr. Le looked pretty good for a guy who had been knocked down by a garage door and crushed by a three thousand-pound vehicle. After viewing his black-eyed face in the mirror earlier that morning, he was sure Dr. Le would be declared the winner of a beauty contest between them.

"Is this Le Van Luy, my dear?" asked Washburn.

"Yes."

Buck was filled with pained recognition as his eyes drifted to the man's chest. Above the left nipple of the hairless chest was a nasty old scar, hooked in shape, looking almost like a branding. The last time Buck saw this scar was as a soldier thirty-two years ago in a jungle in Vietnam. Buck never saw the face of the man who killed and tortured his Vietnamese guide Van Chuong. But he never forgot that scar. Somehow in a twist of fate, he had unknowingly found retribution. "Son of a bitch," he muttered.

Dr. Washburn looked at him. "Are you all right, Mike?"

Buck's mind was lost in memories of Vietnam, reliving that awful combat mission and the death of his warrior friend. He didn't answer. He didn't want to explain the sadness, relief, and sense of closure that overwhelmed him. He ached to yell out and tell the world. But the story was his and his alone. He quieted himself and offered up another bit of truth.

"Mike…"

"Yeah. I'm fine, Doc." Buck regrouped. "I'm just thinking it's ironic."

"What's that?"

Buck cocked his head to the side with a smirk on his face. "Just thinking. This guy was a fraud. A spy who became a respected doctor and the pretend father of the most beautiful and loving woman I have ever known." Buck squeezed the hand of his fiancée. She drew closer to him. "Decades ago, he stole the identity of an innocent man. Murdered him in a flaming auto crash made to look like an accident. Then he tries to kill Le An and me. But ends up dead in a flaming car crash." He shook his head and rolled his eyes.

Washburn chuckled. "Some delayed justice there…an eye for an eye and a tooth for a tooth." He pursed his lips and nodded.

"I guess…" Buck tightened his grip on Le An's hand. Then in a low voice for no one to hear, he mumbled, "…the war has ended." He took a deep breath. "Let's go, Le An."

* * *

In a private ceremony at the Reunification Palace in Ho Chi Minh City, Vietnam, Ngo Hai Tuan (AKA Le Van Luy) was posthumously recognized for his service to the Fatherland. The citation reads:

By decree of the President of the Socialist Republic of Vietnam on 12 April 2003, Ngo Hai Tuan was awarded Hero of the People's Armed Force medal for exceptionally outstanding achievements in combat and work in Vietnam and foreign locations, representing revolutionary heroism in the cause of national liberation, national defense, and the protection of the people.

—END—

ABOUT THE AUTHORS

Tom Smith, FBI Ret., attended the University of Illinois on a football scholarship and became an FBI Special Agent in the Chicago Division of the FBI after graduation. As a Special Agent with the FBI, he worked on reactive-investigations (bank robberies, fugitives, kidnappings) and International and Domestic Terrorism. Smith also served as a managing agent for special events like the 1994 World Cup Chicago venue and the 1996 Democratic National Convention. He retired from the FBI in 1995 to become the Chicago Police Department (CPD) Chief Investigator for the Office of Professional Standards, supervising and investigating excessive force investigations of CPD officers.

Bill Green has degrees from the University of Illinois in architecture and Loyola University of Chicago in Law. He is a retired architect and a writer living in Sarasota, Florida. His novels include the five-novel alternate-history series of Time Travel Twins books and Becoming Irrelevant.

—

Thank you for reading **Dead Wong.** We hope you will kindly create an Online Review of this book.

Tom Smith and W. Green